PRAISE FOR EUGENE LINDEN AND HIS BOOKS

THE PARROT'S LAMENT

"Wonderful, humane, touching. You cannot read it and remain unmoved."

—JEFFREY MOUSSAIEFF MASSON, AUTHOR OF *WHEN ELEPHANTS WEEP*

THE WINDS OF CHANGE

"A lucidly written guide to the near future and a provocative manual of public policy."

—EDWARD O. WILSON

"*The Winds of Change* is fascinating—a tour de force. Linden has accumulated a greater comprehension of paleo-climatic and oceanographic issues than all but a very few scientists. I have nothing but admiration for this book, which is just what we need right now."

—GEORGE WOODWELL, FOUNDER OF THE WOODS HOLE RESEARCH CENTER AND FORMER PRESIDENT OF THE ECOLOGICAL SOCIETY OF AMERICA

THE FUTURE IN PLAIN SIGHT

"May well be the most important book of the decade."

—*ROCKY MOUNTAIN NEWS*

SILENT PARTNERS

"Mr. Linden knows the minefield well and guides us through it with intelligence and unfailing good humor . . . A great display of science as snake pit, and those who liked *The Double Helix* can get the same evil glee from it."

—URSULA K. LE GUIN IN *THE NEW YORK TIMES BOOK REVIEW*

"The ultimate fate of a group of primate research animals in *Silent Partners* poses deeply disturbing questions about science and society. Eugene Linden's handling of this important material is poised, compassionate, and insightful."

—BARRY LOPEZ,
AUTHOR OF *OF WOLVES AND MEN* AND *ARCTIC DREAMS*

THE RAGGED EDGE OF THE WORLD

"*The Ragged Edge of the World* is a call to arms—albeit one that may already be too late, given humankind's astonishing ability to destroy the environment. It underlines the need for those organisations most concerned with understanding the natural world and its fragile complexities to do much more to reverse the tide."

—*FINANCIAL TIMES*

"Thoughtful and compelling."

—*NATIONAL GEOGRAPHIC*

"*The Ragged Edge of the World* offers a fascinating tour of vanishing places. Eugene Linden is a keen observer who never loses sight of the bigger picture."

—ELIZABETH KOLBERT, AUTHOR OF *FIELD NOTES FROM A CATASTROPHE*

"In days of yore, our explorers had vast tracts of wild and often very little in the way of self-awareness. Our world has shrunk, but Eugene Linden goes to its farthest corners with a great deal of hard-earned wisdom, not to mention constant good humor."

—BILL MCKIBBEN, AUTHOR OF *EAARTH*

DEEP PAST

EUGENE LINDEN

RosettaBooks®

New York 2019

First edition published 2019 by RosettaBooks

Cover design by Mimi Bark
Interior design by Janet Evans-Scanlon
Illustrations by Diana Wege

Library of Congress Control Number: 2018960907
ISBN-13 (print): 978-1-9481-2237-5

www.RosettaBooks.com
Printed in Canada

I dedicate this book to all those researchers who have gone to live in the far corners of the planet in order to understand nature and, once there, discovered a deeper mission in protecting earth's last remaining wildlands.

" . . . if consciousness is important to us, and it exists in other animals it is probably important to them."

—DONALD REDFIELD GRIFFIN
(1915–2003)

TRANSTEPPE

INTRODUCTION

THERE ARE PLACES ON THE PLANET WHOSE SCALE REMINDS US that we are but a crushed bug on the windshield of time. The great Kazakh Steppe is one such place, bounded by the endless grasslands of Mongolia to the east, the formidable mountain ranges of Russia to the north, the arid deserts to the south, and the Caspian Sea and Europe's forests to the west. It stretches over one thousand miles, and travelers making their way across this landscape encounter interminable empty vistas to remind them of their insignificance.

There are also places on the planet where the weather serves as a constant reminder of just how tenuous is our hold on life, places that serve notice that the clement circumstances that permit us to grow crops and prosper is not a right, but a lucky break. In the Sahara, it's the heat and aridity that provide this useful lesson; in Antarctica, the cold; while on the Kazakh Plain, it's all of the above—and the constant wind. The scale of the place, its uninterrupted expanses, its position between the cold north and the hot south, and the very turning of the planet combine to channel and augment the winds into an implacable force.

And when these winds hit, say, the Quonsets erected for the camp of an archaeological expedition, they give voice in protest, rising intermittently from a moan to a shriek and then fading, but never dying. The sound is desolation itself.

The wind also shapes and scours. Carrying dust over thousands of miles, it buries the present and, very rarely, uncovers the past. Most often it's the near past that's revealed, scrap from Soviet-era military maneuvers, a fire pit from a nomadic encampment. Rarer still, the wind might uncover the long-buried detritus of the ancient cultures that transited the plain: a weathered sword sheath worn by one of Genghis Khan's warriors, an ornament from the Botai culture, the first nomads to leave any trace of their presence.

Rare is a term that has no meaning when the wind has had eternity to remold the plain. In this context contradictions collapse, and the impossible becomes the inevitable. And so, amid an epic storm, the wind blew the last bits of dirt off a mound lying where scrubland gave way to desert, and something that by any probability should never have seen the light of day lay exposed to the sunlight; something impossible, but also—it would later come to be understood—inevitable.

1

BY EXPEDITION STANDARDS, THE QUONSET WAS RELATIVELY snug, albeit stiflingly hot. The wind from the steppes howled outside as it had for three days, confining the archaeological team to their huts. It was late May, a time of year when temperatures were soaring and dust storms frequent as the winds picked up dirt and sand from the desert.

Still, only stray bits of grit blew in on those occasions when Claire had ventured out to the mess during the storm. The hot air in Claire's hut was dry enough to mummify the plum she had left sitting in a bowl. She had pretty much stripped down as she sat at her plywood desk. She thought back on the whirlwind of events that in a few short weeks had brought her from a well-established life doing research in Florida to the searing heat of the Kazakh Steppes. It had all begun with a site visit from her funders, a visit that had gone well—too well, as it turned out. She thought back to the day.

One of the sweetest moments was the shower demonstration. Claire smiled as she thought of baby Teddy.

"No, no, sweetie, you're doing it all wrong." Claire had walked over and pushed the lever. "See," she said, looking into the soft brown eyes of the toddler, "you push the lever and the water comes out." Claire had extended her arm to push a long handle so that she didn't get doused by the shower. The baby cocked his head and looked at Claire expectantly but didn't reach for the lever.

Claire sighed and turned behind her. "Come here, Mona. Why don't you try."

At the mention of her name, Mona, who had been standing placidly by, perked up and began lumbering forward.

Claire turned back to the baby. "OK, Teddy, Mommy's going to show you how." Then she nimbly and quickly stepped back to make way for the massive elephant.

Mona walked under the twelve-foot-high showerhead in the enclosure and pushed the lever with her trunk. She gave a soft rumble of pleasure as the cool water offered relief from the hot Floridian sun. Then she stepped back and, with her trunk, gently nudged baby Teddy forward. Teddy looked at Mona, glanced over at Claire, and then turned to the lever. Mona emitted another soft sound and put her trunk on the lever. Teddy tentatively extended his trunk and put it on the lever, too. Then Mona pushed the lever and water gushed down on the five-hundred-pound baby. Teddy jumped and gave an alarm call.

Claire laughed. She turned to two men and a woman standing behind protective mesh and said, "I know I shouldn't say this, but I'd guess Mona was laughing, too." That produced chuckles in the group, who were sweltering in business attire and mopping their brows with handkerchiefs. Claire took pity. "OK, let's get out of the sun, and we can talk about the real work going on here."

Later, as she waved goodbye, Claire had skeptically replayed the site visit. Not knowing what it was really about, she'd thought it had gone well. On surprisingly short notice, the Delamain Foundation, which funded her work, had sent a group of two trustees and the executive director to visit. Claire knew where her bread was buttered, and she'd made sure to mix the hard science—experiments to determine what information elephants conveyed through ultrasonic communication, and how they perceived it—with the fun stuff.

They'd loved the fun stuff.

Apart from the shower demonstration, Claire had set up a pitching contest between one of the elephants, Flo, and one of the volunteers at the park who had previously played baseball in high school. Delamain was headquartered in Chicago, and so Claire had put a Chicago Cubs blanket on Flo's back. The first two times she tried to put the blanket on, Flo shook it off. When Flo finally seemed to accept that Claire was determined to keep the blanket on her back, Claire patted Flo behind her huge ears before climbing down, saying, "You could have told me earlier that you're really a Mets fan."

Separated by a wire mesh, the elephant and a somewhat nervous volunteer had taken turns trying to throw softballs through a tire about forty feet away. Flo was rewarded with a treat for every successful throw, as well as lusty cheers from the Delamain delegation. While the delegation was delighted and dumbfounded when Flo won, Claire was not surprised. She knew that Flo's favorite game was throwing things. Indeed, the reason Flo had ended up at the park—which had been set up to serve as a refuge for superannuated elephants—was that one of her games in her former life at an Ohio zoo had been to throw rocks at the monorail that brought tourists through the elephant enclosure. Her accuracy had properly unnerved the administrators. Once Flo had arrived, Claire had set up the tire as a way of redirecting Flo's interest in throwing things in less destructive ways.

Following the Delamain group's departure, Claire stopped by the trailer where the postdocs and grad students were collecting and analyzing data. She thanked them for taking the time to explain their work. "Should I be polishing my résumé?" asked Thelma, an acoustic specialist from Arizona State.

Claire smiled. She had really promoted the team, telling the delegation that the project basically ran itself. She'd noticed that when she made that point, one of the trustees had caught the eye of the other and arched an eyebrow. What was that about? With the vantage of hindsight, Claire now realized that this should have put her on full alert. At the time, though, she had simply thought that the trustee was signaling that he'd been impressed. That's what she told the staff.

"I think we're good for the duration. Fingers crossed, anyway."

"Hope so," said Pete, a statistician and pattern recognition expert, "and if it's so, I'd bet it was Flo, not us, who sealed the deal."

Claire shrugged amiably. He was right. "Could be, but they're not funding Flo's baseball career. They're funding us—you. This is good, solid work, and you all should be proud."

She then took her leave and stopped by to thank Flo and Mona, but mostly to spend a few moments with Teddy. She couldn't get enough of Teddy, who was, without success, chasing a flock of squawking geese. Teddy's earnest clumsiness had endeared him to every elephant and human he encountered.

The park was situated on land donated by an elephant-loving farmer, and a converted bunkhouse served as Claire's lodging. That evening, with a warm breeze rustling the palmettos, Claire sat on her tiny porch, sipped a glass of wine, and took stock of her situation.

Sitting in the Quonset, Claire shook her head at her naïveté of just a few weeks earlier. Back then, she'd thought she was set on a solid career path. She had settled in to the work and her experiments. The team was producing pioneering research on ultrasonic communication. Byron Gwynne, who was writing a comprehensive and highly anticipated monograph on elephant evolution, had written that he would be citing one of her papers. And the head of the Center for the Study of Evolution at Rushmere University, where she was attached as an adjunct professor, had told her that if she continued producing solid research, she was up for a tenure-track associate professorship.

She had made compromises. She'd had to put aside the study of animal intelligence—her true passion—but she felt well situated for a productive career in academia.

A slight frown had wrinkled her features as she considered her romantic life, which might best have been described as idling on care and maintenance. It consisted of an on-again, off-again, long-distance relationship with an utterly unreliable writer (they'd met when he interviewed her for an article on elephant communication—he called her for what he termed "follow-up" two weeks after the article was published).

It was something of a wonder that the relationship continued at all. True, John was *very* funny, which ranked him high in the attributes Claire considered important, and he was anathema to her mother, which also gave him a certain cachet. Her mother would regularly send her clippings about how writers earned less than baristas at Starbucks—hell, Claire thought, many *were* baristas at Starbucks—while reminding her that she was thirty-two and not getting any younger. Or, as her mother, with her inexhaustible store of mixed metaphors, had phrased it, "You don't want to be rushing for the train after the ship has left port."

With regard to the prospect of children, her mother had a point, though Claire would have happily co-parented with Mona and devoted her maternal feelings to raising Teddy to be a successful young elephant. She smiled at the thought of her mother's expression if she presented *that* idea. John would probably start looking pretty good in her mother's eyes.

Human factors notwithstanding, Claire had thought she was in a good place. In a world where talented scientists scrambled for any work, she had a good position and it involved meaningful research. If she played it right, a tenured professorship could be hers. She decided that she would put her all into that prospect. Then she might turn her attention to upgrading her love life. In truth, her mother needn't worry about her marrying John. She smiled at the thought of how John, who had a very lofty opinion of his place in the universe, would react if he knew that he was serving as a placeholder. "Don't screw things up," she murmured to herself as she took her last sip of wine.

2

IT WAS THREE WEEKS AFTER THAT DAY THAT CLAIRE GOT THE news. It came in the form of a phone call while she was with the research staff.

Pete had looked with alarm at Claire's stricken face after she put down the phone. "What? We didn't get the funding?"

Claire shook her head. "Oh, we got the funding, all right. All we wanted."

Pete sighed with relief. "If you don't mind me saying, you've got a strange way of conveying joy."

Claire was distracted. "Oh, sorry, Pete. That was just something that has come up at Rushmere that I've got to deal with. I'll be back in a bit." As she left, she patted Pete's hand. "Don't worry, funding's secure."

Claire went back to her cabin to think about the call. She shook her head at the irony. Things with Delamain had gone well—too well.

The call had come not from Delamain, but from William Friedl, the chairman of her department at Rushmere. Like Flo, a baseball fan, Friedl had begun the conversation jovially, saying, "Well, Claire, you hit a four-bagger with Delamain."

Claire was instantly on her guard. Friedl, a legendary sourpuss, did not do jovial without some ulterior motive. "Thanks, Bill. I'm glad. But why did they call you, not me?"

Friedl had cleared his throat. "Well, turns out that they have a problem, and it's actually a problem for Rushmere as well." He paused, as though gathering his thoughts, and then said brightly, "And they were so impressed with you that they think you're the solution."

At this point, Claire thought back with bitter irony to her taking-stock moment of a few weeks ago when she had thought that she had a predictable and satisfying glide path to her career. "That's flattering,

Bill, but what can I do for Delamain from Florida that I'm not already doing?"

There was a long pause. "You're right, Claire. You can't solve our problem from Florida." He let that sink in.

Claire could barely get out the words. "So where would I have to be to solve their and your problem?"

Again Friedl cleared his throat. "Maybe I should give you a bit of context."

Claire was alarmed, "Where are we talking about, Bill?"

"Hold your horses." Friedl laughed for reasons that soon became apparent. "I think you know that yours is not the only project affiliated with Rushmere that Delamain is funding."

Friedl went on to explain that the lead investigator of a project investigating the domestication of horses, Russell Clausner, had become gravely ill. He'd been picked up by medevac and flown back to the US, and it was unclear when he would be able to return to the field.

"Just where is this field site?" Claire interrupted with a bit more edge in her voice. She'd been out of touch and the sprawling Center for the Study of Evolution, which housed anthropology, sponsored many field projects.

"I'll get to that, but hear me out. This study is a big ticket for both Delamain and us. As you know, the mandate of Delamain is to promote the understanding of the relationship between humans and animals"—Claire knew that the Delamain spinster whose money funded the foundation had died without heirs, but for seventeen cats—"The project has to do with a new theory about the domestication of horses. It's a big deal for them, and with the field season just beginning, they don't want it to be leaderless."

"But I'm needed here," Claire said, only partially succeeding in keeping a plaintive note out of her voice.

"Actually, the trustees said that you'd so effectively set things up that—and I think I'm quoting you—'The project could run itself.'"

Fuck, thought Claire, as the tumblers fell into place on the surprise visit and the arched eyebrow.

Sensing that he had the advantage, Friedl had plowed on. "I think it would be a good thing to do this, Claire. I know you did some work on domestication as a grad student, and if you're going to get that full professorship in the anthropology department, don't you think it would help if you *actually* did some research that directly related to humans?"

The message was loud and clear: "Don't rock the boat."

Claire wanted to say that her work was related to humans, but she knew she was trapped.

"So, where?"

There was silence.

"Where, William? If I'm going to go there, you're going to have to tell me at some point."

"Kazakhstan."

THE KAZAKH
STEPPES

3

IN THE QUONSET, CLAIRE FRETTED WITH HER DIRTY-BLOND hair and stared at her laptop as she turned her attention to the email that she had been dreading, a report to her funders that would—without laying blame—give them a sense of her first impressions of where the project stood.

Claire was settling in. She'd been at the site for three weeks now. The research team had been standoffish and nervous at first. Claire had explained that the project had to be a high priority for both Rushmere and Delamain, as they had requested that she put aside her own work to make sure the research continued here. She'd also said that she had no ambitions to bigfoot onto their territory, take credit for their work, or change the direction of the project. She told them that she was just there as an administrator until Russell could return.

The trouble was, Russell's three years of exploration really hadn't turned up much. Which was too bad, because she had been pleasantly surprised when she dug into the proposal and initial field reports. Russell had proposed to explore the origins of horse domestication in the Botai culture of northern Kazakhstan. The Botai and horses had been bound together sometime around fifty-five hundred years ago, when the relationship shifted from predator-prey to partnership. It would have helped, however, if, over the past three seasons, the researchers had subsequently found *one* horse bone dated more than fifty-five hundred years old to submit for DNA sampling, or any archaeological evidence at all that might have supported Russell's thesis that domestication did not occur in Kazakhstan, but Mongolia, and had traveled West with nomads.

Russell had been intrigued by new evidence that cats had domesticated humans—DNA evidence showed that domestic cats from the Middle East traveled into Asia, suggesting that rather than different peoples domesticating their local cats, the cats themselves had chosen to follow nomads and invaders eastward—he had wondered whether other animals, horses for instance, also had undergone a more complicated history of domestication.

Claire now had plenty of time to bone up on the project, since she was confined by the weather to quarters on the harsh verge of the Kazakh Desert. A particularly sharp gust of wind rattled the Quonset and brought her thoughts back to her initial status report. Claire was about to take another stab at writing when she heard a knock at her door.

She started to get up to answer when she remembered that she wasn't really dressed. "Just a sec," she called as she threw on a khaki shirt and pulled on a pair of shorts, wondering who in the world would be out in this storm. Most likely it was one of her research assistants. She prayed it wasn't Tamerlan, the creepy minder from the government she had taken an instant dislike to when she had made the initial round of introductions.

It wasn't. She opened the door a crack to see a tall, rangy man she didn't recognize, covered in dust and shielding his face from the stinging wind. "Dr. Knowland," he said from behind his shielding arm, "I'm Rob Rebolet, head of security for Transteppe—you know, the mining company."

Mystified, Claire didn't know what to say. "Uh-oh. Has one of the team taken a bulldozer for a joy ride? I promise I'll make them return it," she stammered.

The man offered a small smile and said, "Maybe I could step in?"

"Uh, sure." Claire cracked the door so he could slip through along with a few pounds of windblown sand.

Once inside, he remained standing. There was no place to sit except for Claire's chair.

"OK," said Claire, all business. "What's up? Something must have happened to cause the chief of security to trek forty miles in this weather."

The big man looked at his hands. "Well, that's the thing . . ." He paused and changed directions. "I heard that the team here is researching horses, ancient horses, right?"

Claire relaxed and nodded cautiously. She knew this drill. On any dig, someone, usually a tribesman, would show up with samples of what they were looking for, usually concocted in the previous few weeks. "You should know that I'm brand-new here. Russell, the project leader, got sick and had to be taken home."

"I'd heard about that. I think we supplied the medevac helicopter. I hope he's OK."

Claire nodded her head. Nobody was hoping for Russell's speedy recovery more than her. "We all do. Thanks. So what's up?"

"Anyway, in the lower quarter of the concession, which is basically desert, the wind uncovered something—bones." Rob, sensing her skepticism, looked embarrassed. "The thing is, the bones were arrayed, they were big, but I don't think they were horse bones."

Claire made an effort to sound interested. "Have you seen many horse bones?"

"Some—my family works a ranch outside Prescott."

Claire realized that she was sounding like a jerk and changed her tone. "If they aren't horse, what do you think they are?"

"Don't know. But they're big."

"Big?" said Claire, distracted. "How big?"

"Bigger 'n any horse bone I ever saw."

Claire was disappointed. The ancient horses she was looking for were much smaller than the present-day animals.

Knowing now that he came from a ranching background, she said, "Cow?"

Rob shook his head, "Seemed thicker, longer—would be a cow for the ages."

Claire pulled out the chair for her desk. "Please sit down."

4

NOT WILLING TO SIT WHILE CLAIRE STOOD, HE LAUNCHED INTO his tale.

As Rob described the array the wind had uncovered, Claire tried to remember what other animals had inhabited the area during its prehistory. She came up blank. Then she remembered something he had said earlier.

"You said they were arrayed. What do you mean by that?"

"We thought that they looked like someone had laid them out on purpose."

The word *we* brought another thought to mind. "Have you reported this find to your boss?" She knew little about Kazakhstan, but she knew that mining companies never liked to interrupt operations or exploration for a dig.

Once again Rob looked embarrassed. "Dr. Knowland, you're putting me on the spot . . ." He trailed off. He looked directly at her. "You're new here, but I'll bet you know how things work in places like this?" She nodded. He looked at her. "Do you have a minder?"

She nodded and grimaced as she thought of Tamerlan. "He wouldn't call himself that, but yes."

Rob was expecting her answer. "We've got more. We're a mining company. This country *lives* off oil and mining payments. Our concession is a multibillion-dollar project for chromium, lead, and manganese. The law requires a complete review if exploration uncovers a site of historical significance, and a complete review could slow down a project for a year or more—and also exposes the company to a whole new group of bureaucrats who could speed up the process for a price.

"Then think about the larger context. The president made a huge bet that an oil concession in the Caspian would produce enough money that he could buy off the masses who've been promised a piece of the supposed riches. That oil is eight years overdue, and there's no knowing when it will begin flowing. There have already been riots in the capital. So, knowing all that, what do you think the government *mining* ministry would do if they heard that a windstorm uncovered some bones that might be of historical significance?"

Claire knew exactly what they'd do—either bury those bones so deep they would never be found, or, equally likely, some corrupt official would use them as leverage to extract more money from either the concession, the government, or both. What would *not* happen was a professional archaeological dig. "Won't someone else see them?"

"For sure, but maybe not for a while. The geologists have to finish their assessment before they decide whether, how, and when to enter this quadrant. That'll take a few months." Rob assumed an innocent look. "The bones have nothing to do with our work, and if someone took them, who'd know that they were gone?"

Claire caught his drift. "What kind of strata were they buried in?

Rob smiled. "That's a question for a geologist, not me. There's one you might want to meet—the guy who discovered the bones. He's a Russian, Sergei Anachev. I can vouch for him, though he's only been with us a year—he's a good guy. He knew what would happen if our minders got wind of this, and he couldn't come to you without drawing attention. That's why he asked me to make contact—as head of security, I'm always on the go. Anyway, Sergei will help. He's dying of curiosity. Frankly, so am I."

Claire was confused and conflicted. She was here for ancient horses, not to pursue the paleohistory of the Kazakh Plain. She remembered

Friedl's subtle warning to not rock the boat. But she was intrigued. "Tell me again what made Sergei think these bones were worth asking you to trek up here."

"Well, as I mentioned, they seemed too big to be horse. Sergei couldn't think of any really big mammal that lived on the plain in historical times, so maybe they're *really* old, but, the other thing was the fact that they seem to have been arranged. And the question occurred to Sergei—and to me, too, though I'm not qualified—that if they were *really* old, who would have been around to arrange them?"

Good question! Claire decided then and there that she could hold off submitting her status report for a few weeks. She was excited and worried at the same time. She had told the team that she was not going to make any big changes, and she remembered her admonition to herself—"Don't screw up!" Still, it would be dereliction of scientific duty not to follow up. Claire felt a fire stirring in her that had been absent in her solid but conventional research. If Rob and the Russian had found something really significant, she would kick herself the rest of her life if she let it go just to be safe. She was going to see where this went.

She shook hands with the tall man standing by her desk. "Well, Mr. Rebolet, you've got me hooked."

After she let Rob out, Claire sat down in her chair and looked down. "OK, Lawrence, give it to me straight. Is he on the level?"

The object of this question hopped up onto her makeshift desk and pushed his forehead into her shoulder. He was covered in dust, and Claire coughed as she tried to brush him off. She scratched him affectionately behind his ears. He'd come in as Rob had exited, and now the tomcat made himself comfortable on top of Claire's papers, scattering a few to the floor.

Claire looked at the animal affectionately. He was an orphaned sand cat, an endangered desert hunter of small mammals and birds, who had been found and brought to the camp as a kitten by one of the cooks. The cat had the run of the camp, but in the past few weeks he had taken a shine to Claire, who often sought his advice. "I agree," she said to the cat after a moment, "he looks like he'd be a reliable supplier of cat food."

At the mention of food, Lawrence's ears seemed to perk up (though she never could be sure). He looked her directly in the eye. "OK, OK," said Claire, getting up. "Stop exercising mind control." She picked up a can of cat food and popped the top. "I think you'll like my new recipe," she said, plopping the food into a dish. "I worked on it *all* day."

5

BY THE FIFTH DAY OF THE WINDSTORM, CLAIRE WAS GOING stir-crazy. Her frustration was supercharged by her hunger to see the bones. She had some geologic maps of the region, but they did not cover the areas Rob had described. To keep from completely losing it, she took to spending more time at the mess Quonset. Other members of the team lingered as well, either catching up on paperwork or playing cards. She demurred when a couple of graduate students asked her if she wanted to join a game of Pictionary. The background chatter from the game—"Duck!" "Pterodactyl!" "Dracula!"—was enough to drive out the chill of isolation. Put aside the mummifying dryness and the heat and it was almost cozy. There was only one human voice she did not want to hear.

And there it was.

"Hello, Claire, what a nice surprise," said the square-faced Kazakh with unreadable eyes, as though Claire might have been doing any number of things on this fine day in the middle of nowhere with the wind driving sand hard enough to strip the paint off a car. Unbidden, he sat down on the opposite side of the long mess table.

"Tamerlan," she said, looking up briefly from her reading, hoping that he would take the hint. Hints, however, were not something that the Kazakh official ever took. He sat there smiling, a little insolently, and waited as though he had all the time in the world. Sighing, Claire finally looked up. "Can I help you?"

"Terrible about this weather, isn't it? I hear it's going to break, though."

At this Claire looked up, trying to mask the hope in her eyes.

When she didn't say anything, Tamerlan continued. "So what have you been doing to keep yourself occupied?"

"Not very much . . . Paperwork."

"Ah, paperwork . . ." He was content to leave the sentence hanging.

Claire shrugged. Tamerlan couldn't know about Rob's visit, could he? Yet Tamerlan never said or did anything casually. The last thing she wanted was to arouse suspicion. She stood up and gathered her papers. "Speaking of paperwork, I'd better get back to it." She gave Tamerlan a bright smile. "I really hope you're right that the weather's going to break."

She'd almost escaped when she heard Tamerlan's voice behind her. "Before you go back to your *paperwork*," he said, "please indulge a request."

Claire stopped and turned around, almost succeeding in keeping a neutral smile on her face. "Of course."

"My nephew Sauat is a university student in Astana. He has gotten, how you say—the bug—for archaeology, and asked if he could spend some time on the dig. I promise he won't get in the way."

At this point, the last thing Claire wanted was another set of eyes in the camp, but she noted that his second sentence indicated that her decision was a foregone conclusion. "I'm sure we can find him something to do."

As she left, Tamerlan's smile faded.

6

TWO DAYS LATER, THE WIND HAD ABATED TO THE POINT WHERE Claire could begin to execute the plan she and Rob had cooked up. She kept a running diary of the dig on her website, and they'd agreed that when the weather cleared, she would post an innocuous item about getting back to work. This would be a signal for a prearranged rendezvous the following day.

They decided to use this means of communicating given the very real chance that they were both being monitored. Rob suggested they meet at a junction where an old caravan trail crossed a dried-up stream and then proceed into the desert quadrant of the mining concession. She figured that no one would miss her if she kept her absence to a few hours.

She looked at her watch. Six a.m.—just before dawn. It was time. She quickly donned lightweight khaki pants and a shirt. She actually preferred US Army-issue desert khakis, but she didn't want to look military in the unlikely event she encountered Kazakhs in the field. A scarf that could serve as a dust screen and a broad-brimmed hat completed the ensemble.

After making sure the coast was clear, she scribbled a note saying that she would be back in the afternoon and stuck it on her door before she dashed out with her field pack of tools and day pack filled with water bottles. She quickly hopped in the beaten-up Land Cruiser and headed out, thankful that no one seemed to have seen her. Once clear of the camp, she headed south. The sun rose, and, as it peeked over the horizon, shooting lava-orange beams into the lapis-blue sky, a breeze immediately followed. The steppe could summon a wind from nothing.

Twenty kilometers along the road, she started looking for the cairn and thornbush that marked the turnoff Rob had described, which would put her on the old caravan path that led to the stream crossing. The air was mercifully still here, and cool pockets of air, relics of the night, quickly disappeared as the sun rose. Dust billowed up behind the Land Cruiser, telling anyone for miles where she was. She reassured herself that there was no one near except for Rob and the geologist, Sergei, presumably waiting at the stream crossing. Still, she worried about the telltale dust.

After bumping along the caravan route for fifteen kilometers, she arrived at the crossing, a somewhat misleading description since there was neither a crossing nor a stream, only a declivity where water once might have flowed. She knew she was at the right spot, however, because Rob and a wiry, compact, thirty-something man (whom she assumed was Sergei) were waiting for her, along with three saddled horses tied to a trailer. She hopped out of her truck, nodded to Rob, and turned to introduce herself to the Russian, who was leaning against a boulder. She started when she saw Sergei. Instead of the classic Russian with lank blond hair, he was an intellectual-looking young man with wavy brown hair, a sensual mouth, and quick, intense brown eyes that missed nothing, including the fact that Claire had done a double take.

"Not what you were expecting?" he asked with an ironic smile as he shrugged himself away from the boulder and extended a hand. His English was good.

A *thin-skinned rock hound?* thought Claire. Sergei finished the thought. "Kazakhstan collects misfits, and being a misfit is an ancient and honorable profession."

Not knowing where he was going with this, Claire said, "Amen!" and shook his hand. "I'm Claire."

Rob had been watching the scene with slight amusement. He nodded toward the horses. "Let's get going. It's going to be a scorcher." He looked at Claire, "You OK with—how shall I put it—*living* horses?"

She was mildly annoyed, "Oh, please!"

"Sorry," said Rob, holding up his hands in surrender.

She slid her field pack into one of the panniers on the chestnut Rob had pointed to and then lightly mounted the saddle. Sergei looked more resigned than enthusiastic about the prospect of a long ride, but he hopped on his horse and they headed off into the desert. Rob turned toward a mesa-like formation in the distance, the one bump in the endless horizon. At first the ride was monotonous. Rob seemed content to ride in silence, while Sergei rode up beside Claire and started up a conversation. He asked her about her project, and she described her theory about domestication and horses as well as her frustrations with the lack of results. Sergei was clearly intelligent and a good listener, and she found him easy to talk to.

They stopped to stretch their legs and take a drink. Claire turned to Rob and in a bratty voice whined, "Are we there yet?"

Rob laughed, "We've got at least another hour."

After they remounted, Sergei turned to her again. "Forgive me if I'm being too personal, but often when I've encountered an interesting person in a remote place—even if it's their job to be there—there's an even more interesting story that they are trying to get as far away from as possible."

Claire didn't answer. For a guy who didn't want to pry, Sergei was remarkably insouciant about boundaries. She glanced at Rob, who was riding ahead, and noticed that he seemed to have cocked an ear. On the one hand, this was a remarkably provocative question, since they had known each other for just a couple of hours. On the other hand, she didn't want to be rude and reminded herself that things moved fast when expatriates met in remote places. She briefly thought of concocting an amusing story—running from the authorities, relationship with a camel driver—but ultimately decided just to tell the truth. As a scientist, Claire didn't truck much with guile.

"I'm here by accident. To my misfortune, I've turned out to be a too-good utility infielder."

Sergei looked confused. "You work on telephone lines in fields?"

Claire and Rob both laughed.

"Sorry—your English is so good, I assumed you knew about baseball." Claire went on to explain how she was called on to fill in for Russell.

Claire stole a look at Sergei. She couldn't help but smile. He really was very good-looking, and she liked that he was funny. She decided to turn the tables. "And you?"

She could see the hurt flash across Sergei's face and instantly regretted asking. "Oh, I'm a cliché," he said softly. "Relationship gone bad. But I was not so much running away as being strapped to a Soyuz against my will and launched, with her family cheering for the rocket to crash."

Claire had only just met Sergei, but the bitter tone surprised her. She also noted that Rob seemed particularly interested in hearing what Sergei would say. Without looking at either of them, Sergei said, "It's a long story, and not a good one."

Claire wanted to know more, but Sergei suddenly brightened and deftly shifted the conversation. "I'm curious. Back at the base we watch American TV a lot. Most shows are about couples, and in the comedies and dramas, everybody is fighting all the time. Is this the way Americans relate to each other—through fights?"

Claire had never thought about it this way, but, reviewing the scarred landscape of her relationship with the utterly unreliable John, she could see how even that on-again, off-again thing met the pattern. "Absolutely," she said, nodding, "and American couples can fight about anything!"

Sergei lit up, delighted. "Please, give me an example."

Claire thought a minute. "OK, here's a doozy."

Again, Sergei looked confused.

"Doozy," interjected Rob, riding just ahead of them but clearly listening, "means great example."

"OK, I get it." Sergei nodded vigorously. "Please . . ."

"One of my biggest fights with a boyfriend was about energy conservation."

At this Rob turned around in his saddle. "Energy conservation? Really?"

Claire nodded. "Yup."

"Why?"

"Exactly!" said Claire. Now enjoying herself, she turned to Sergei. "Didn't you and your girlfriend—wife?—fight about energy conservation?"

Sergei shrugged. "Not exactly," he said with a straight face, "but it was always there, just beneath the surface."

At this both Rob and Claire laughed.

Claire wanted to keep the conversation going. "What about you, Rob?"

"Me?" Rob clearly wasn't eager to open up. "Not much to tell except that every time I've gotten lucky, I've gotten extremely unlucky shortly thereafter." Claire and Sergei both chuckled.

As they rode on in silence, she savored this easy camaraderie. It was worth the trip, even if the bones turned out to be from a camel that died last year.

After a few miles, the terrain got rougher, and Rob began consulting his GPS as they negotiated a jumble of boulders and outcroppings. Most were dun colored, but here and there strata were visible where formations erupted from the earth in twists and curves, as though they were trying to escape some torment underground. It was an altogether alien landscape, both beautiful and strange. Claire could easily imagine why a geologist might want to investigate the area. Claire looked away from the rocks and shot a quick glance at Sergei. She was curious about his story, but any thought of pursuing the conversation ended when Rob stopped his horse and turned to Claire. "It's just up ahead. Uh, how do you want to go about this?"

"Carefully," said Claire. "If it turns out to be something—whatever it is—there may be more bones not yet exposed. Let's shift to foot, let me get my first impression, and then maybe Sergei could explain the geologic context. OK?"

"Sounds good to me," said Rob. Sergei smiled at Claire as Rob found a suitable shrub to which he could tie the horses. As they walked through a narrow passage toward an outcropping, Claire took in the desolate landscape, which consisted of a jumble of reddish and dun-colored rock protrusions.

After a few minutes, Rob clambered up one that angled up from the desert and began walking up its back. Claire and Sergei scrambled after him. The mesa was about as long as a football field and sloped upward to about fifty feet above the plain with an apron of scree at the bottom of the bluff, on top of which was a jumble of boulders. As they approached the highest point, Rob stopped.

"We're here," he said, gesturing for Claire to go forward. "The edge might be crumbly, so don't get too close. If you look down, you can see that big pieces have been falling off."

Claire shrugged off her day pack, picked up her camera, and slowly walked toward the edge. Though she was facing away from them, Rob and Sergei could see the exact moment that she first saw their find. She first stiffened as though she had hit an invisible wall and then walked forward very slowly. What they couldn't see was the amazement, confusion, and shock that flashed across her face.

Protruding from the hard-packed ground were the ends of five very large bones arrayed in parallel. The bones extended into the earth, but she instantly recognized the large hook-like ends as the trochlear notches of an ulna, the bone that forms the forearm and elbow of mammals. Such bones were quite suitable as clubs, and her first thought was that she was looking at long-buried weapons. But, staring at the size of the ulnae, she also knew that no human, present-day or past, would have been strong enough to use these bones as a weapon. She felt a flash of anger and whirled to face Rob and Sergei. "OK, guys, if this is some practical joke, now is the time to come clean."

Both men looked as though they had been slapped. "Do you honestly think I'd risk my job to stage a practical joke?" Rob snapped.

Claire's anger vanished instantly, replaced by embarrassment. "Of course not," she said, chastened. "Sorry. It's just that this"—she pointed to the bones—"doesn't make sense."

"Agreed," said Rob mildly. "That's why we contacted you."

Claire continued, "I know an elephant ulna when I see one—that's my real field—and I also know that there haven't been any elephants here in recorded history."

Rob was dumbstruck. "Elephant?"

Sergei was dumbstruck, too, Claire noted with satisfaction. "Elephant?" But then he regained his poise. "Ah, elephant," he said, as though this was another answer that had been on the tip of his tongue.

"Yup, elephant."

"Could a Neanderthal have used that bone as a weapon?" Rob asked.

That gave Claire pause, but Sergei was shaking his head. "Look around you."

Claire dutifully looked around but had no idea what Sergei was talking about. She shrugged.

Sergei pointed to the face of an outcropping a few hundred yards away. It looked similar to the one they were standing on, except that its side showed bands of different-colored rock folded almost perfectly into a giant letter C. "Since I first saw the bones, I've taken—what is the phrase?—ah yes, a deeper dive into the geology of the area. See that letter C? That's what we call a recumbent fold. The bottom of the C shows the geology of the area as it was deposited over time, yes?"

Claire nodded, and Sergei continued, "So you see the lowest band is lighter colored than the dark rock that forms the next band, and you also see that as a result of the fold, the lowest band ends up on top?"

Again Claire nodded. Sergei was obviously enjoying himself. "So, the last shall be first, as they say in the Bible. Now, if you studied the stratigraphy of the formation we're standing on now, you'd see that we are on that same lighter-colored band of sedimentary rock as we're looking at over there, but while we might think that this was the newest layer to be deposited, it is actually the oldest."

By this point Claire was so disoriented that she put off asking the obvious question—"How do you know so much about this area?"

But Sergei continued as if she had. "Oh, this is a special place. It's where the past erupts from the earth and blabs its secrets," he said, gesturing to the folds and faults in the strata exposed on the sides of the outcrops and mesas around them. "It's a good place for a geologist to orient himself to the composition and history of the area. That's why we found these bones, actually. I was up here happily studying the various strata, and I kicked what I thought was a rock. My kick knocked the last bit of soil off what turned out to be that bone," he said, pointing to one of the ulnae.

The mention of the bones brought her back to the question she'd been dreading. "How old is that strata?"

"I only just completed the dating," Sergei said brightly. "Five and a half million years!" Now he beamed at the look of utter disbelief that came over Claire's face.

"Five million years?" said Rob numbly, fulfilling the role of Greek chorus. "Okaaaay, I guess that rules out Neanderthal."

Claire thought furiously. "It would rule out any hominin—that we know of . . . Our ancestors were pipsqueaks back then, and probably not smart enough to use a bone weapon anyway, much less arrange the bones in some ritual. Besides, five and a half million years ago was over four million years before any of our ancestors left Africa." She turned to Sergei. "But what if these bones were buried purposefully rather than deposited? Someone could have dug into that layer?"

"Yes, exactly!" said Sergei with a pleased look that annoyed Claire.

"But . . . ," she said impatiently.

It dawned on Sergei that she was tired of playing the foil. He sighed and then said simply, "OK, OK, take a closer look at that bone. Do you have a magnifier?"

Claire was confused. "Yeah, sure," she said, digging a pocket microscope out of her field kit. She knelt down and peered through the lens at the bone. One look and she became completely disoriented. She looked up at Sergei. "Petrified?"

Sergei nodded. "I don't know that much about mineralization, but it usually takes millions of years, doesn't it? I do know that sedimentary rocks—like this particular strata—are suited for fossilization. Anyway, it's a brain twister." He paused a moment. "That's why I contacted you."

Claire was speechless. Elephant bones where elephants didn't exist, arrayed by some creature at a time when humans probably didn't use weapons and wouldn't have been able to wield these enormous bones if they did. Possible alternative explanations raced through her mind— were they the treasured artifacts of some ancient trader that were subsequently discarded by a raiding party going for a caravan's gold? That was more likely than what was staring her in the face.

There was always the possibility that there was some prosaic explanation for the array, but if the simple story that someone—some creature?—purposefully arranged those bones five million years ago held up, the possible explanations were nothing short of surreal, overturning basic postulates of paleontology and the evolution of thought and civilization as well.

She photographed the array from every angle, while Sergei documented the geology of the area. She debated how best to pursue this find systematically. Ideally, she would have left them in place until they could devise a plan for the excavation of the area, but she knew that was a nonstarter. The implications of the find were so explosive that the confirmation of the age of the array, once known, would unleash forces far, far beyond her ability to control. Claire was well aware of the bizarre tug-of-war that resulted from the discovery of the so-called hobbits, a mysterious miniature group of people given the scientific name *Homo floresiensis*, because Indonesian and Australian researchers found their bones in a cave on the Indonesian island of Flores. The discovery of the three-foot-tall skeletons with *Homo erectus* features produced a furor because the bones dated to fifty thousand years ago—more than fifty thousand years past the official expiration date of *Homo erectus*. At one point an Indonesian scientist absconded with the hobbit bones and held them for many months while the Australian researchers were denied access to their own find.

The age of Sergei's discovery made the implications so much more revolutionary than the hobbits that Claire couldn't begin to find the words to describe the scale of the scientific upheaval that would result. And Kazakhstan made Indonesia look like a Trappist monastery in terms of corruption. Claire knew that the Kazakhs had a right to share in the discovery and the exploration of the site. But she had to find a way to pursue the find to the point where it was sufficiently documented and confirmed that it could not be swept under the rug. She also knew that if there was no simple explanation for the bones, her life was going to change forever. And, finally, she knew that she couldn't do this alone, even if Rob and Sergei gave her the bones as Rob had earlier intimated. She needed to find a partner or partners with the scientific expertise to study the bones, but first off she needed to put together a team to dig. She needed people she could trust and who, at least for the time being, would be willing to do the work in secret. She couldn't begin to envision the reaction of her team when Claire, an interim leader who had promised not to rock the boat, told them that the dig was going to go in a completely different direction and that it was also going to proceed in secrecy.

That thought brought her back to the two men who had actually found the array: Rob, with a background in security and the military, and Sergei with his scientific chops. She had an idea.

"So, guys," she said, standing up and stretching, "all I can say is thank you for bringing me in on this."

"Glad it's not a wild goose chase," said Rob. Sergei gave a brief "you're welcome" nod.

"Well," said Claire, "it's *probably* not a wild goose chase. But we've got to be sure . . ." She was struggling to get out the words. When she could resume speaking, her voice was wheezy. "Because," she said softly, "if these bones were actually *arrayed* five million years ago, this will rank as the greatest paleontological find of all time."

In the silence that followed, Sergei just stared at Claire, stunned. After a moment, Claire continued, "There, I've said it, and don't even try to imagine what's going to come down on us once this gets out." She paused. "Now, we don't want to get ahead of ourselves, but if this turns out to be what it looks like, I promise you that I will make sure that you two are credited with the discovery."

"And you, too," blurted Rob. Sergei seemed distracted but finally nodded.

"I was hoping you'd say that," Claire said with obvious relief. That was a question that had been hanging in the air from the very second she realized what Sergei had stumbled on. She added, "So now that you know what we're dealing with, I think you'd agree that we've got to be extremely careful about what we do next. Here's the problem: if we simply took the bones, spirited them out of the country and did an analysis, no reputable foundation would support the work and no reputable scientific journal would publish the findings. We'd have the discovery—whatever it turned out to be—but no credibility. Credibility is everything in science. You could find the cure for cancer, but if there's a taint of scandal or weirdness about it, it will just sit on a shelf. It's not what you know in science, it's who believes that it is actually worthwhile. We've gotta go about this the right way."

Sergei thought about this. Being Russian, the idea of doing something by the book was a novel idea that generally surfaced only when an official was trying to extract a bribe.

"But," Claire continued, "as we all know, given the circumstances, simply following protocol is a nonstarter. So, somehow, we've got to bring in the right Kazakh official without revealing where the bones are and without revealing the bones' significance . . ."

Sergei's eyes lit up with understanding. "I get it. You said the significance was in the array, yes?" Claire nodded and took a silent vow never to play chess with Sergei. "So," said Sergei, "if *one* petrified bone found its way to you—in a manner that proved you didn't know where or whom it came from—then you could innocently solicit Kazakh help because a petrified elephant ulna of what may be an entirely new species would be enough to get anyone excited. Am I close?"

"Christ"—she shook her head—"you Russians! Not just close, but on the money."

Sergei looked confused, but Rob, now acting as official translator of American expressions, jumped in. "On the money means that you hit it on the head."

Sergei still looked a little confused, so Claire added, "Hit it on the head means exactly."

"Ah," said Sergei, "I get it, the money is what you give the utility infielder after he hits the nail on the head." Both Claire and Rob gave Sergei an exasperated look.

Rob turned back to the array. "But if you took one of the bones, wouldn't the site then be disturbed in an obvious way, and wouldn't the question of who took the bone come back to bite you when you went public?"

He was right. Claire deflated.

Sergei got up and peered over the edge of the bluff. He turned back to Rob and Claire. "We're standing on a lip," he said. The other two looked at him expectantly. "We're standing on a lip, and I'm a geologist." Rob's eyes widened. Now he got it. Claire was still in the dark.

"What he's saying," said Rob, once again assuming the role of translator, this time for the geologist, "is that we have machines—like that

Bucyrus RH400 that can hold ninety-five tons of rock in its shovel—that could break off this entire lip . . ."

Claire shook her head and interrupted, "We need to study this thing in place. Who knows what else is in there?"

" . . . in one piece," Rob finished his sentence.

"In one piece?"

"Yes, one piece," seconded Sergei, "*if* we do it carefully."

Sergei nodded his approval. "So that I could study the strata back at the warehouse," he continued, "where I keep many samples. We could document the removal of the lip. Back at the warehouse, I could 'discover' the array and bring it to your attention. You could do some preliminary work—you'll have a head start, yes?—and then bring it to the attention of the authorities *at the same time* you bring it to the attention of relevant experts and the press. If the bones are in the warehouse, they aren't going to interfere with the dig. Do you see where this is going?"

Claire nodded slowly. "I get it—go big or go home."

Rob started to translate when Sergei said, "I get it—I got the other sayings, too."

Claire looked at Rob, then they both turned to Sergei. "We know," they said in unison.

"It's a huge risk," she said. "Lemme think about this a sec." She walked away and looked out toward the other mesas. As she walked, she glanced at Sergei's back. He was rangy, his back and shoulders roped with muscles—which she wanted to touch, she thought with surprise.

"There may be other bones scattered beyond what you could transport. There's the issue of getting other people involved . . ."

"That's actually not a risk, but a plus," said Rob, interrupting. "The more it looks like Sergei's ordinary work, the less suspicion there will be. We just have to make sure that the bones remain covered."

"Every option is a risk," said Sergei, "but the biggest one is doing it by the book—as you Americans might say. Besides," he continued, "once the significance of this find is known, it is much more likely that we can cordon off that bluff to expand the dig."

"How long do you think it will take to get that piece of equipment out here and the lip back to the warehouse?" asked Claire.

"Given the priority of this mining concession," said Rob, "Sergei can get what he wants when he wants it, but I'd think he'd want to collect a couple of samples from other spots so as not to call attention to this bluff . . ." Rob paused for a moment, doing some calculations in his head. "The actual cutting of the rock and transporting it back would take a couple of days—the Bucyrus runs on huge tractor treads that can bulldoze through anything—so figure twenty days or so."

Claire sighed. "I don't have a better idea. How will you get in touch with me?"

Rob thought. "Best to do this as low-key as possible. We'll send a messenger with a picture of a single bone and an invitation to come inspect them for yourself."

"Do you have dating equipment?"

Sergei answered, "We do. I've got everything. We can use stratigraphy on the surrounding rock—already did that—and maybe paleomagnetism or thermo-luminescence on the bones to show that their age matches the surrounding rock."

"Good, then we don't have to take the bones out of the country to do a lot of the work."

"You're going to have to work very fast and send out your data in real time, because all bets are off once word gets out," said Rob.

Claire nodded with trepidation. Science could do a lot of things, but the one thing it couldn't do was do something fast.

———

For the next hour, the three finished measuring, filming, and photographing the bones, the site, and the surroundings. Sergei pointed out that doing so was producing evidence that would directly contradict their story, but Claire insisted that when and if they needed to produce this documentation, they could explain why they had needed to keep things under wraps. They used both a GoPro and a digital camera, and they photographed Sergei and then his hand next to the bones to give a sense of scale. Under Claire's instruction, Rob cautiously dug a small trench near the bones to reveal the strata and also prove that the sedimentary rock in which the bones were embedded was undisturbed. Then they carefully covered the exposed bones with dirt and small rocks. Once satisfied that the landscape looked natural, the three headed back to the rendezvous point. The ride was quiet. But as Claire relaxed to the rhythm of the horse, she felt a thrill of anticipation that she hadn't enjoyed in many years.

Once they were back at the vehicles, Claire went over their plan one last time stressing that it was vital that there be no way to connect the three of them. Then she drove off.

At camp, to Claire's relief, no one seemed particularly curious about her absence. Waylon, her slow-moving dogsbody, came by to complain that the cook staff was siphoning off the best cuts of meat for themselves, and to gossip about a blossoming romance between two of the graduate students. One of the Kazakhs came by to ask for the following day off because of "car trouble." Claire knew he didn't have a car but played along—the last thing she needed right now was a Kazakh with a chip on his shoulder.

Then she settled in for the wait. Rob had said about two and a half weeks. If it was much longer than that, she was going to be desperate, given the impatience of the Delamain Foundation. As it was, she had a lot to do while she waited. First, she had to figure out how to convince the foundation that the discovery of a new five-million-year-old species in the elephant ancestral tree was a perfectly natural segue from investigating the domestication of horses. She knew that if she presented the full story she could write her own ticket, but she also knew that it was by no means certain that she would be able to present the full story—whatever that was.

7

SERGEI HAD GONE QUIET AFTER RETURNING TO TRANSTEPPE. His office in an enormous hangar-like structure was empty when he returned, and he plunked wearily into his swivel chair and thought. His joking reference to the breakup with his fiancée brought back memories of the real story of the chain of events that had brought him to Kazakhstan. He shook his head. What he'd told Rob and Claire was true as far as it went, but it did not go very far. He hadn't been kidding when he said that it was not a good story. It began with his greatest triumph, which he very quickly came to realize would curse him forever.

Sergei had been good at chess—very good. After he graduated from the Technical Institute in St. Petersburg, Sergei had spent some months competing in chess. At university, he had been good enough to earn a master rating, with a couple of brilliant wins that attracted enough notice that he was encouraged to try to get to the level of international competition.

During a regional tournament in the Russian Far East, he was paired against a young up-and-comer in finance and politics. As they sat down, the man gave a perfunctory handshake and introduced himself as Andrei. He was gaunt, with deep circles under his eyes. The closest he came to smiling was when they shook hands, and that slight wrinkling of the corner of one side of his mouth had all the warmth of a flickering fluorescent light in an unheated KGB interrogation room in January. Standing behind him was an auburn-haired and very beautiful young woman—Sergei had seen her floating around the room, and one of the other players had told him that her name was Ludmilla, and that her grandfather had been a famous general. She would have stood out in any context, but amid the eccentrics that disproportionately populate the chess demographic, she was in a different world. Sergei made the mistake of trying to show off.

Playing the black pieces, he had responded to white's opening of moving the pawn in the D file to the four position, by moving his E pawn to the sixth spot. White responded by moving his knight to F-3, and after Sergei's response, he was certain that his opponent recognized that he was offering a replay of a famous 1912 match between Edward Lasker, a player, like Sergei, a step short of grandmaster, and George Alan Thomas. In the twelfth move of that game, Lasker moved his queen to H-7, fatally tempting Thomas to take the queen with his king. By forcing continual checks, Lasker forced Thomas to embark on what came to be called "the Immortal King Walk," in which the king was moved ever farther from his protective army on the other side of the board until a mate became inevitable. Sergei's opponent glanced up at Sergei as if to determine whether he was sane, and then shrugged. Both knew every move of this famous match, and Sergei's opponent, supremely confident, seemed curious to see whether Sergei had better ideas than the unfortunate George Thomas.

A murmur went through the onlookers as they realized what was happening. One of Thomas's moves, the one that had set up the fateful sacrifice, had been to castle. When the game progressed to that point, Sergei instead took one of white's knights with his bishop, which was then sacrificed to white's pawn. On paper the exchange looked somewhat even, but it left white's pawn in a weak position. That was all the advantage Sergei needed, and ten moves later, white resigned.

There was a swell of applause as Andrei stood up and took his leave. Sergei didn't notice the malevolent glare that accompanied the terse handshake, because he was searching the crowd for the lovely Ludmilla. Sergei's pulse quickened when he noticed that she was discreetly applauding as well. Sergei detached himself from the well-wishers to introduce himself. Would she like a drink? She would. She allowed that she was nominally attached to Andrei. By the end of the evening, she wasn't.

There began a two-year romance. Ludmilla had a quiet confidence that suggested depths in even the simplest things she said. She had the Russian sense of the ironic and liked to shock—when Sergei first spoke to her, she had remarked, "Maybe it's because we're in a room full of chess players, but I find your muscles exciting"—as well as a sophistication that utterly awed Sergei. He dropped out of competitive chess shortly after the match. He recognized that for the best, chess was an obsession, and one needed the hyperfocus of autism or Asperger's syndrome to allow chess to become your entire world. Faced with a choice of a blossoming romance or the austere demands of chess, Sergei made his choice. For a time he was happy.

Turning away from chess, Sergei also threw himself back into his studies, choosing to specialize in exploration geophysics. He became known as something of a wizard at profiling the subsurface of the earth through remote sensing, developing ingenious algorithms for sorting through overwhelming masses of data. The combination of geological and remote sensing expertise put Sergei in the crosshairs of recruiters from multinational resource companies. Then it all came apart.

Sergei winced as he remembered the brutal end. As was his custom, he called Ludmilla's cell phone on his way back from work to talk about dinner plans. There was no answer, only a message that the number was no longer in operation. Alarmed, he sped home. Ludmilla had cleared out. She had left a note: "I'm sorry. It's impossible. Don't try to contact me."

He did try to contact her, by phone, email, and by showing up at her parents' compound in St. Petersburg. All he could show for these efforts were some bruises earned through a humiliating scuffle with security. Eventually, he pieced together that someone had poisoned the family against him through a series of slickly packaged slanders linking him, using faked photographs and faked notes, with a notorious antigovernment radical who used sex to seal alliances (Sergei actually admired the woman, though he didn't know her). The story sold to the family suggested that Sergei had used Ludmilla to insinuate himself in order to facilitate a kidnapping/extortion plot to fund the radical movement. Her father was prepared to believe the lies. Like most thinking people in Russia who didn't have a place at the trough, Sergei *was* antigovernment and had made his opinions known during heated dinner-table conversations. A sympathetic cousin later told Sergei that Ludmilla's father had threatened to cut her off completely if she ever spoke with Sergei again.

Ultimately, Sergei came to realize that it was for the best: Ludmilla clearly felt that access to the family cash was more important than their relationship, regardless of the truth of allegations.

But who had dropped the dime? Even though it was two years after the match, Sergei had an idea. Andrei's career in business had skyrocketed in the intervening years, and so it was not hard to track him down.

Sergei reached Andrei by phone. After Sergei accused him of launching the smear campaign, Andrei cut him off dismissively. "I've got better things to do than worry about nobodies."

Frustrated, Sergei was about to hang up, when Andrei spoke again. "Life is not like chess, is it? Someone who looks like a pawn might be a king, while a queen can be turned into a pawn . . ." He paused again, as though in mid-thought.

Sergei said nothing, wondering where this was going.

"Yes, chess is so clean and strictly demarcated with an inviolable set of rules. In life there are rules, too, but, most often, they aren't official rules. They have to be learned, yes?"

Sergei still said nothing.

"And if you want the skills of chess to apply to life, you have to know how to make a pawn behave like a pawn."

Involuntarily, Sergei held his breath.

"And the first step in that process is to make sure the pawn knows that he is but a pawn . . ." Andrei let that sink in. "Sometimes that takes more than one lesson, but once it has sunk in, pawns can be very useful in life. They can be moved around, and, if needed, they can be sacrificed. Don't you agree?"

Andrei abruptly ended the connection.

The message was clear: Andrei was not done with Sergei.

8

OVER THE NEXT FEW DAYS, CLAIRE SPENT LONG HOURS PORING over the evolution of elephants as well as the climate history of the plain. She realized that she was supposed to be surprised when contacted by Sergei, and anyone looking at her computer would see that she had been investigating elephants before the surprise delivery of the bone. On the other hand, it was well-known that her primary research involved elephants. She thought about this. Operating clandestinely involved skills she had never developed. She cleared her search history, which left her feeling as though she'd done something illicit.

There was always a beginning to the slippery slope of corruption, and the first step would be easy to justify—e.g., a corrupt official in the Cultural Ministry sells artifacts on the black market because he needs to pay for the wedding of a destitute cousin. The next time would be easier.

Claire knew the "proper" way to pursue this discovery would have been to notify the Kazakh government and then start negotiating the bureaucratic maze to get permission to dig in the mining concession. She would then need to inform the Delamain Foundation and Rushmere University, to which she still was nominally attached.

The mere recitation of the proper protocol reassured her a bit, as she knew no sane gambler would bet that she would get past stage one, given that the Kazakh president had made an all-in bet on the mining concession. Nor did the governments of the region have a spotless record in terms of preserving the past. She thought of the Taliban's use of artillery to destroy the enormous seventeen-hundred-year-old Bamiyan Buddhas. The more than 150-foot-tall statues carved into cliffs were blown up, notwithstanding a concerted campaign by the United Nations to convince the government otherwise, and all because the religious fanatics who guided the Taliban considered them an affront to Allah. International opinion offered little protection when governments decided to act.

She knew that she had to get the find announced following strict scientific protocol or the bones would be marginalized to fringe science, no matter how revolutionary the implications. She didn't want to change the course of her career only to find her work lumped with studies of Atlantis, Bigfoot, and the Loch Ness Monster.

So, she went back to work. She had always liked puzzles. Claire used a variant of an approach described by Norbert Wiener, a pioneer of artificial intelligence who once remarked that solving a problem consisted of framing it in such a way that the answer became obvious. Then she would take one piece of the problem and work back to what it might imply. Pondering the array of bones, she assumed that it was unlikely that they ended up parallel by accident. Then the question became, why might someone or something arrange them like that? One obvious possibility (leaving aside the question of their extreme age) was that the ulnae were in fact weapons, and that the array was part of some ritual. But if they were weapons, who—what?—might have used them?

Not our ancestors, she thought. She knew that chimps had been observed using weapons—sticks in this case—in the Impenetrable Forest of Uganda, and that Savannah chimps in Senegal fashioned sticks into spears to hunt small primates, so it was conceivable, though unlikely, that some hominin might have done the same. Still, she reminded herself, absence of evidence is not evidence of absence. But, again, there was no evidence of human ancestors making ritualistic arrangements of any artifacts for another few million years. Was it possible that something other than a hominin arrayed the bones? To reorient herself, she went back to her earlier ruminations about the global frenzy that the discovery of the hobbits had precipitated.

Earlier, she had focused on the story because it illustrated how distinguished scientists could be driven to near-criminal behavior by the treasure fever of an important find. But there was another, more intriguing side story to this find.

Claire wondered whether the hobbits were an example of a phenomenon called "the Island Rule." This so-called rule came from the observations by a Canadian biogeographer named J. Bristol Foster. He showed that on islands, small animals tend to get bigger and large animals tend to get smaller. This is because islands are hard to get to and typically have fewer species. On the mainland, the greater diversity means that for any given ecological niche, something is there to fill it. On an island, this is not the case, and it opens the door for the existing animals to adapt and move into otherwise vacant ecological niches, particularly since there are fewer predators to pick them off.

Mice might get bigger, for example. Claire remembered reading that Anguilla, the tiny island in the Caribbean, once supported a three-hundred-pound rodent. And with fewer predators, big animals could get smaller without losing the protection that size confers. In the extreme case, Crete sported a mammoth the size of a Great Dane. That was the magic of the Island Rule: a natural sorcery that could create a rodent larger than an elephant.

Despite the publication of many studies of the Hobbit bones, they remained a mystery. They stood about three feet tall and had heads the size of a grapefruit. They lived until about fifty thousand years ago, but what energized the paleontological community was that their features suggested that they were a relic form of *Homo erectus*. While some speculated that the Hobbits were simply human dwarfs, Hobbit features like long, flat feet were characteristic of early bipedal hominins, and not modern humans whose feet evolved to be better suited for long-distance running.

What caught Claire's attention was that the diminutive Hobbits cohabited an island with an abundance of bizarre creatures, including a pony-size elephant. Claire looked off into the distance. Did it mean something that elephants kept turning up in unexpected places? Her thoughts kept wandering in new directions. Why shouldn't the Island Rule apply to human ancestors as well as elephants and rodents? Could she connect this thought experiment to the matter at hand? If ecological isolation let the Hobbits get smaller, mightn't it permit another, yet undiscovered hominin, to get larger?

But the enormous Kazakh Steppe was about as far from an island as any geographic feature could get. That didn't mean that in the sweep of history some Lost World might not have been isolated by eruptions or other events, but it didn't make some application of the Island Rule the obvious choice. Then there was the showstopper: that 5.5 million years ago all known hominins were still bottled up in Africa.

Claire decided this train of thought was one of her typical false starts. Trouble was, she had no alternative theory.

9

TAMERLAN WAS JUST ONE OF CLAIRE'S PROBLEMS. SHE WAS getting increasingly insistent emails from the Delamain Foundation asking for that overdue progress report. She could hardly tell them that she was on the verge of something momentous, but she could not put them off much longer. This made the agony of waiting that much harder. A line from a Colin Hay song floated through her mind: "Suddenly, nothing happened."

The first visitors, who arrived two weeks later, were not the ones for whom Claire had been hoping. Sauat, her newly acquired intern, appeared without prior notice in a three-car caravan, led by his uncle, the slippery Tamerlan, along with an impressive entourage from the Aliyev clan. The group included Sauat's father, his weeping mother, who was apparently traumatized at the thought of her son leaving for a few weeks, Sauat's pretty but sullen teenaged sister, and a few other relatives. No wife, Claire noted. She wished he'd brought one—even a girlfriend would have been welcome. The older men were wearing jackets and ties, the wrinkled old woman wore traditional dress, and the girl wore tight-fitting jeans and a revealing, almost peekaboo, T-shirt with the phrase "I Have Issues" stenciled on the back. When she saw Claire, disappointment registered in the girl's expression. Apparently Claire's desert chic didn't pass muster even in the boonies of Kazakhstan. Since everyone was sizing everybody else up, Claire decided to take a closer look at Sauat.

He was a nice-looking young man with bright eyes and the high cheekbones characteristic of the steppes. He was wearing outdoor gear, but it didn't quite work. It was, Claire thought, the type of outfit a Martian might buy if he landed in Maine and visited an LL Bean outlet in an effort to fit in with the earthlings. The bright-blue work shirt and plaid golf trousers just didn't go together. He seemed eager and shy, and Claire felt a momentary relief, if not tenderness. If he was to be Tamerlan's eyes on the ground, he was the least likely spy Claire could imagine. Or maybe that was the point, she thought.

Spy or nice young kid, this was a potential disaster given the scenario that she, Rob, and Sergei had worked out. They felt it best that she didn't know when the bones would appear so that she could be as surprised as the rest of the camp when the truck showed up. If someone showed up now, she would have no trouble at all feigning surprise, if not outright panic.

Controlling her frustration, she tried to think of a way to get rid of Sauat's relatives as quickly as possible. They had come a long way, and hospitality was a big deal among the Kazakhs. Fortunately, most of the research team was out with remote sensing gear looking for evidence of ancient settlements, so Claire could beg off after a decent interval for introductions. She could offer them the tent set up for outside meals if they wanted a picnic before taking off. Even better, she could insist on taking Sauat with her so that he could see how things worked in the field.

It was not to be. With his unerring instincts, Tamerlan homed in on the worst-case scenario. He asked in a way that left her no choice but to give them a tour of the camp, and then insisted that she join them for lunch, which the women unpacked and set up on the table under the tent. Sauat's sister helped out sullenly but dutifully.

They had brought a veritable feast. Using pantomime, Claire showed them where to find pans for heating the food. Once seated, the Kazakh equivalent of a smorgasbord lay before them with mutton, samosa-like stuffed pastries called *kausyrma*, drinks of fermented mare's milk, and *kurt*, salted cheese balls. Claire briefly welcomed the group and then nodded to Tamerlan, who spoke in Kazakh, pausing to translate for Claire, about how wonderful it was that Sauat had developed an interest in Kazakhstan's rich history.

Claire sat next to Sauat's father. Tegev Aliyev spoke broken but serviceable English and turned out to be everything his brother, Tamerlan, was not. A rough-looking man with a direct gaze, he was clearly steeped in Kazakh hospitality, offering her a piece of the traditional *besbarmak*, a meat taken from the pelvic bone and meant to be eaten by hand. He also turned out to be Claire's salvation when she turned to him and asked where his family was from.

"Oh," he said with a wry smile, "we come from a small village, but near a famous place."

Tamerlan shot him a warning glance, which he ignored as Claire asked, "Where's that?"

"Perhaps you've heard of it, Semipalatinsk? Our village was just to the west."

"Was?"

He nodded. "Yes, was. Our parents decided to leave in 1982 after the Russian usurpers exploded three hundred nuclear bombs in Semipalatinsk. After we left, they exploded another 150."

Tamerlan interrupted, "Tegev! As well you know, people working there had the highest pay of any workers in the country."

"Of course," agreed his brother, again with a smile. "And there were many other benefits. For instance, there was no need to pay for electricity, because the village glowed in the dark."

"The Russians put food on our family's table for many years. We should be respectful," warned Tamerlan.

"Oh yes, they were very nice. The Russians were like a beautiful blue butterfly we have in Kazakhstan."

"What's that?" asked Claire.

Sauat took this opportunity to say his first words since arrival. His English was excellent. "We learned about it in entomology," he said diffidently, not noticing that Tamerlan was seething. "It's a very beautiful large blue butterfly that lives near the desert. But it has an evil secret. It lives by fooling a particular type of ant into thinking that the butterfly's larvae are the ants' larvae. The ants take the caterpillar larvae into their nest, and then the butterfly larva feeds on the ants' larvae until it's ready to emerge. Taking advantage of hospitality in a big way," he concluded with a shy smile. He then noticed his uncle's expression, and the color drained from his face. Tegev, however, was smiling, proud of his son.

Claire decided she liked the father, all the more because he didn't seem to be the least bit afraid of his brother. She couldn't resist the opportunity to say, "It sounds like the family did well after you moved. Tamerlan is an important man in the Ministry of Culture."

"Oh yes," Tegev agreed, "Tamerlan is a big man by Astana's standards." He delicately left hanging the question of whether the standards of a dictatorship would be what an honorable man would choose to live by.

Claire could see that Tamerlan was now smoldering, so she threw a few more logs on the fire. "Tell me what he was like as a little boy," she asked innocently.

At this, Tamerlan had had enough. "We've got a long drive back," he said before his brother could reply, "and we have taken up too much of Dr. Knowland's valuable time. Claire, if you would be so kind, could you show us where we should put Sauat's bags?"

At this, the women went in to a frenzy of cleaning up, tailed by Claire waving her arms and pantomiming that they needn't bother. The clan was packed up and gone not thirty minutes later. Before they left, Tegev gave Claire his phone number to keep in case there was an emergency. Sauat waved sadly as they pulled out in a cloud of dust, his grief-stricken mother peering out for a last look. Claire looked at Sauat, whose only words had been his disquisition on the blue butterfly. He looked vulnerable. Her fear that he would be an agent in place was giving way to concern that she would be assuming the duties of a babysitter for the next two weeks.

10

CLAIRE NEEDN'T HAVE WORRIED ABOUT THE EMISSARY ARRIVING while Tamerlan's clan was visiting. She had two more days to test her patience. She also had bigger worries. First an email from Delamain said that while they appreciated her willingness to step in and help with the project, they still needed a progress report in order to set funding priorities for the coming year.

Then there were increasingly worrisome signs of defeatism among her research team as every probe turned up empty. She worried that their restiveness would make it even more difficult for her to announce the discovery of the elephant bones to the team. She had been proud of the esprit de corps of her research team in Florida and felt responsible for the morale of the project.

One bright spot turned out to be Sauat. He was bright, inquisitive, and with an eagerness to learn about fieldwork that was endearing, if not a little exhausting. He seemed far more his father's son than his uncle's minion. Having tea with him one day, she asked him who was his favorite professor in archaeology. Sauat's eyes lit up. "Oh, no question, Dr. Timur Tabiliev. He . . ." Sauat searched for a word " . . . he becomes giant when he talks about the Botai. He becomes illuminated?"

"Lights up?" Claire offered.

"Yes, that's it, lights up! He just loves to teach. And he is very brave—he once stood up to the president's son-in-law when a favorite project was to be built near an important dig in Kyzylorda."

"Really?" said Claire with genuine interest. It dawned on her that Sauat might actually be helpful as events unfolded.

And unfold they did. A grizzled man driving a Transteppe pickup truck showed up late that day asking for her. He handed her a large manila envelope, bowed, and took his leave. Everybody was curious, but she waved off the staff and took the envelope to a corner table. In it was a photo of one of the ulnae, as well as a picture of the lip Sergei had cut from the mesa, and which was now sitting in his warehouse. The picture had been taken from an angle that did not show the array. There was also a letter from Sergei, signed with his full name and title—chief geologist, Transteppe. The letter described Sergei's "discovery" of the bone, gave its dimensions, where it was found in the strata, and its likely age. It went on to say that if it was five million years old, it might be a significant find, and Claire was hereby invited to oversee the testing and exploration of the artifact to make sure that they proceeded in a proper fashion. There it was. She had to act fast.

She looked up into a sea of staring eyes. "OK, everybody, there may be something here for us," she said, "but I need to check a few things out. I'm going to have to leave, but I'll be back for dinner. I'll explain then." As she walked to the door of the mess, she was peppered with questions. Turning just before she left, she said to the group, "I promise you, if it's good news, you'll be the first to know." That seemed to satisfy the group. She headed for her Quonset. She had a few urgent emails to send before heading for Transteppe.

11

THE OLIGARCH MET WITH HIS GOVERNMENT COUNTERPART IN a room impervious to electronic snooping deep in the interior of his yacht *Iridium*, then anchored off the French Riviera. In contrast to the elegance of the rest of the boat, this room was spare, furnished with a coffee table and a couple of chairs. There was no computer or any electronics whatsoever. Those who knew about what was referred to as "the Project" only spoke in person for fear of surveillance and never communicated by email or text. Andrei's visitor was an up-and-comer in the Foreign Service, but also a cousin of Andrei's wife, so anyone monitoring the comings and goings on the boat would simply assume that Andrei had extended an invitation to his in-laws.

Arkady Surkov had come to deliver a timetable, and Andrei was not happy. "I know there are a lot of moving parts, but I need more information, information that will confirm the strategic aspects of the plan. And I need it before things start, because I won't be getting any afterward—at least for a while. I need to know what I'm getting, and it has to look clean."

"Andrei, everybody knows that yours is a critical piece, but there are geopolitical considerations that impact the timetable as well."

Andrei steepled his fingers and frowned. "Understood. I've got someone in place. As I'm sure you'll understand, I need to know things that management doesn't know . . ."

"Is this man loyal?"

Andrei laughed harshly. "He hates me."

Arkady cocked an eyebrow. "And you trust him?"

"Of course," Andrei said smoothly. "He hates me because I control him. He knows what will happen if he betrays me." Andrei took a sip of tea. "And he has exactly the skills we need."

Surkov took a sip of vodka. "Probably best that *I* don't know the details."

"Agreed, let's rejoin the others before people start to wonder. Stay for dinner. You're not a vegetarian, are you?"

"Nope, I'm old-school, meat and potatoes."

Arkady raised his vodka. "To success!"

Andrei raised his glass of Russian tea, and they clinked glasses. "To success."

12

CLAIRE DROVE THE CAMP'S PICKUP TO TRANSTEPPE. IT TOOK HER well over an hour to make the forty-mile trip over the deeply potholed road. The security office was a formidable structure. A hard-looking man came out and waved her car to a stop with a gesture that brooked no argument. She rolled down her window and told the guard that Dr. Anachev had invited her. Without a word, the guard returned to his booth and picked up a phone. He spoke briefly and then handed her a visitor badge and a hard hat. "Wear both at all times. You can leave the pickup over there," he said, pointing to a lot just inside the gates. "Dr. Anachev is coming out to escort you in."

After parking the truck, she took the opportunity to look at the mine complex's layout. It was impressive, with truly enormous, windowless structures for processing various types of ore, massive conveyors, and a network of rail tracks both in the concession and connecting to the outside world. Much of the infrastructure seemed to be under construction as hundreds of hard-hatted workers welded, hammered, ferried, and hoisted. The sheer scale of the vista made it easy for Claire to imagine how a mining project could swallow billions of dollars before the first ounce of ore was processed. It was also easy to imagine how such a project might simply squash anything that got in its path.

Sergei arrived a few minutes later, halting his pickup inside the gate. "That's Dr. Anachev," said the guard, nodding in the direction of the pickup.

Sergei walked up to Claire, extending a hand. "Sergei Anachev. Please call me Sergei."

Maintaining a neutral expression, Claire simply said, "Claire." Sergei opened the passenger door, and they drove off.

"Think we got through that OK?"

"We don't have much time before others get curious," said Sergei.

"So who's going to be in the warehouse when we arrive?"

"There shouldn't be anyone. I sent my team out to do some prospecting about twenty kilometers from here. They'll be checking in by radio, so I'll know if they're coming back. I'm exercising a routine courtesy, and as chief of geology I have some latitude. But, again, if you make multiple trips out here, people are going to start getting curious.

And once word gets out, you're at the mercy of the Transteppe bureaucracy and the Kazakh minders."

"I've already emailed the picture and a scan of the letter you sent me to people I trust asking them to keep the information confidential until I follow up. Can we get the paleomagnetometry done today on a bone sample?"

"Probably not—we'll be lucky to get the array cut out for examination."

"Once it's out, where should we keep it?"

"Probably best that it's in the hands of archaeologists. And if we're going to get it out of here at all, we'd better do it today. So take the array with you and tomorrow you can start looking at the rest of the lip."

Claire knew that this was not the way things were done. "Jesus, Sergei, I don't know . . ."

"It's your decision, but you know the risks of leaving it here."

Claire was miserable. "How would I take it?"

Sergei thought a second. "Hmm, the block holding the bones will weigh a lot, but maybe we can chisel some of the excess away so that we can move it on a trolley. I'll have to figure where we go from there."

As they got out of the car, Sergei put a finger to his lips. "We've got to be careful what we say inside, even if we don't see anyone around. If I want to discuss something privately, I'll go outside for a smoke."

"You smoke?"

"No, but I'm Russian—all Russians smoke . . ."

The warehouse was a giant green shed that looked like it could hold a few 747s. Sergei placed his ID card on the reader by the door to buzz them in. They walked through the first section, where some of the giant machines were stored. Men were working and moving equipment. A couple of men gave them a glance and then went back to work. Passing through a door in a floor-to-ceiling partition, they entered another huge space, part of which was filled with rock samples taken from various parts of the concession, while the back was given over to a glassed-off laboratory filled with high-tech equipment.

Sergei was surprised to see a Kazakh janitor in a red Transteppe jumpsuit sweeping the area. He went over to the man and had a quick conversation in Russian. The janitor looked meekly at the ground and nodded as Sergei spoke. Then he left and Sergei walked back to Claire, taking one more puzzled look at the janitor as he exited.

While they were talking, Claire looked around the warehouse, fascinated. Everywhere there were samples, cuttings from outcroppings, cores from boreholes, and extractions from trenches, all neatly cordoned off and marked. She immediately spied the cut-off lip of the bluff. It was set on a series of rectangular metal supports, the lowest of which was about three feet high to allow access to the underside of the big piece of sedimentary rock. As they walked over, Sergei gave her a quick run-down of all the testing equipment they used on samples. They were able to do chemical, metallurgical, X-ray, spectrographic, and radiometric analyses right there in the lab.

Sergei had made sure that the sample was deposited upside down and tilted so that the bones were not visible except if someone lay on the ground, crawled under, and looked up.

They got right to work.

The good news was that the bones were in sedimentary rock. The stratigraphy itself gave them natural points at which to split off a layer of the lip. The bad news was that the fossils were in highly friable sedimentary rock. If the array fell when they split it off, the rock in which it was embedded might simply crumble. Sergei arranged a thick layer of foam on a low trolley, which he then slid under the rock to help protect against that possibility, and then briefly discussed his plan. It was not the way any archaeologist would go about it, but speed was of the essence. After he finished, Claire gave a quick nod of agreement.

He placed two jacks on either side of the trolley and winched them up until the large plates at the top of each jack were touching the rock on either side of the array. There were a few inches between each of the ulnae, so that the entire array was about thirty inches wide. He then took out a portable rock saw and made two vertical cuts about eighteen inches deep into the strata fault lines. On the bluff, he and Claire had estimated the bone to be about forty inches long. He told Claire that he had calculated from the angle of the visible part of the bone that eighteen inches should be sufficient depth.

Then Sergei took a deep breath, sighed, and said, "OK, here's where I put my life on the line for science." Claire's eyes widened as she realized what he meant. He had to slide under the rock between the jacks to make the cut parallel to the lip. Fortunately, the bones were arrayed parallel to the lip so that he did not need to slide in that far, but if, after the three cuts, the sample cracked at the strata line, there were only the two jacks preventing him from being crushed.

"Hold it," Claire said urgently. "It's not worth it—there's got to be another way."

Sergei smiled. "Why, Claire, I didn't know you cared! Thank you!" Without waiting for a reply, he put on a dust mask, lay down on the trolley, and, holding the saw, slid under the lip. As he did, he said in a muffled voice, "Don't worry, I've done this before. A little drama, yes?"

Claire didn't believe it but held her tongue as well as her breath.

The cut took just a couple of minutes, and Sergei scooted out as soon as he was done. He got off the trolley, slid it back under, and raised it until one edge of the foam was in contact with the rock. Now came the most delicate part of the operation. Sergei briefly explained how the two of them would slowly and simultaneously hammer in wedges along the horizontal strata line, about ten inches in from the vertical cuts. After each tap, Sergei would tap in a third wedge midway between the other two. After the first couple of taps, Claire stepped back and took a picture of the operation with her phone.

With several wedges in place, Sergei was tapping in yet another when the block broke off and settled on the foam. Intact. When the dust settled, Sergei tried to pull out the trolley. It didn't budge. He looked at Claire. "OK, forty inches by forty-eight by eighteen . . ." He scribbled a minute on a pad. ". . . 34,460 cubic inches, divided by 1,728 equals twenty cubic feet, times 150 pounds per cubic foot equals three thousand pounds. I'll get a tug to get it out of here, but then we've got to get the weight down before moving it to your truck—and fast."

The archaeologist in Claire was horrified by what she was doing. Still, she nodded, resigned. Moving quickly, Sergei wheeled over a small electric tug, which he controlled by a remote, attached it to the trolley and slowly pulled the block out from under the lip. At the speed of a slow walk, the tug pulled the trolley across the hangar floor and through a door into a shed adjacent to the building. There was a jumble of rocks on the floor. Sergei turned to Claire. "Nobody goes in here; it's where we put samples. Still, we've got to hustle." Sergei had taken along the portable saw, wedges, and mallets. "Tell me what to do." Seeing Claire's miserable expression, he added, "Look, at least it's sedimentary. It should come off in layers, and we can be precise."

Claire did a quick calculation and then decided that at the points farthest away from the array, they could start chipping away three-inch-wide blocks. They got right at it, and after an hour they had chipped away a few hundred pounds of surrounding rock. Not enough, but Claire was beginning to worry about the depositional context for the array—archaeologists and paleontologists would want more than photos to get a picture of how the bones were embedded in the strata. Then there was the question of structural integrity. Take away too much rock and the whole array might fall apart.

A squawk from Sergei's radio interrupted her thoughts. Sergei listened, said, "See you then," and signed off. "They're on their way back." He looked at the somewhat reduced block. Then he looked around the shed and signaled that they should go outside.

He took out a cigarette and looked at it distastefully. "How much can your truck hold?"

Claire thought a bit. "It's got reinforced suspension, but I wouldn't want to carry more than a ton on these roads."

"Well, you've got to decide," said Sergei. "Either we leave it on the trolley overnight or get it on your truck—now!"

Claire fidgeted. Sergei's tone changed. "Claire? Decide!"

"OK, let's do it. How do I get it out?"

Sergei thought for a minute. "I'll call Rob and tell him you are taking a rock sample and borrowing a trolley. He'll clear it with the gate. There's a lift and loading platform on the other side of the building, where we can push the trolley onto the pickup. The bones are on the underside now, so no one is going to see them until you unload. We don't have much time, so let's get going."

Claire looked miserable.

Sergei smiled sympathetically. "Claire, you're obviously an honest scientist, but sometimes we have to adapt, and it's for a good cause, yes?"

Claire flushed in spite of herself. "It's not just that, Sergei. The grad students are getting demoralized by the failure of the project, and I'm worried about how they will react when I tell them to forget about horses and think about elephants . . . or Delamain, for that matter."

Sergei nodded and thought about that as they rolled the trolley to the pickup and loaded the bones. Sergei hopped in on the passenger side to make sure she didn't have any trouble at the gate. He could see that she was still worried. "Don't worry about your team, Claire." He gave her a sly smile. "If they've been spinning their wheels, this discovery will be a shot in the arm, and I'm sure they'll see the forest for the trees."

Claire couldn't help but laugh—Sergei did know American idioms! But he was also exactly right. As she started the pickup, she was smiling.

13

THE TRIP WENT SMOOTHLY—AT FIRST. THE BLOCK WAS COVERED with a tarp, and there were random rocks and tools scattered in the bed of the pickup. With Sergei in attendance and Rob's authorization, Claire got out of Transteppe with a minimum of fuss. The guard didn't even look under the tarp, not that he would have seen anything suspicious. She drove carefully, as the truck felt unstable with its big load. Worse, the rock was on a trolley, which even at its lowest setting made the load top-heavy. They had jerry-rigged cartons on either side to keep it from rolling, but the buffer would provide little protection in a crash or serious lurch.

Claire drove slowly. The combination of shadow and glare made it difficult to see potholes. She barely missed a couple of craters and felt a stabbing pain in the pit of her stomach as she heard the cargo bang in the back of the truck.

Most of the time the only hazards in driving the steppe were potholes and monotony, as it was possible to see approaching vehicles miles before they passed by. But late afternoon turned to dusk before Claire had traveled twenty kilometers. Very few drivers plied the roads in this part of the steppe, but a good number of those who did put off turning on their headlamps until the last vestiges of light disappeared, under the belief that doing so would extend the life of the lamp. Thus it was that with almost no warning Claire was suddenly confronted by an ancient, overloaded truck bearing down on her as it hewed to the center of the road. Reacting on instinct, she veered violently to the right, putting the truck in a near spin that was aggravated when her left front tire hit a pothole. She was going relatively slowly, so the truck didn't tip over, but the lurch caused the trolley to crush the carton buffer on the left, and the block of rock to slide off, hitting the inside panel.

When she heard the impact, Claire felt a stab in the pit of her stomach that had nothing to do with physical injury. The truck she had avoided continued on, unmindful of or uninterested in the near collision. Claire halted the Land Cruiser and jumped out. She was nearly hyperventilating when she looked in the back. What she saw was a jumble of the fragile rock and the five bones. Three had separated, and one of those three had broken in half. Two bones were still encased in rock.

It didn't take but a second for her to realize how enmeshed she was in the trap she had built for herself. Unbidden, a vision of various éminences grises staring at her, asking questions for which she had no answer. "Why did you feel it was so important to reduce the mass, which made the block vulnerable to cracking . . . why didn't you take the time to find a sturdier vehicle in which to move the block . . . what evidence do you have of this so-called array? Why did you take it upon yourself to do this alone?"

She let out an anguished cry and began to sob. All thoughts of a glorious reset to her career vanished, replaced by images of the bleakest possible future. As she tried to rearrange the pieces to limit any further damage, she kept thinking, *You knew it! You knew it! You knew it!*

Filled with self-recrimination, she started the truck and headed back on the road to camp. After a half hour of beating herself up, her self-pity began to ebb. She had to pull herself together.

The bones were an extraordinary find in and of themselves, and she did have two of them still arrayed as well as copious visual documentation of the original find. Then she started lobbing mortars into her plan. Her basic problem was that she couldn't explain why she had done what she had. If she had brought back the array intact, amazement over the discovery would probably have glossed over her transgressions, particularly since she would have simultaneously revealed the find to the Kazakh authorities. Instead she had cast an arc light on the stupidity of trying to be Indiana Jones, in the process turning herself into a case study of how to ruin a career. It was easy to imagine how her team would react, how excitement would give way to confusion, anger, and self-righteousness.

In an exercise of black humor, she tried to guess how her team would react. Abigail and Tony, the two young graduate students who had started a romance, would probably filter everything through what it meant for them continuing the dig/affair (Tony was married, but, apparently, not fanatical about it). She expected self-righteous disapproval from Samantha, who had studied feminism and Marxism at Bennington before turning to archaeology—she would probably see what Claire had done as a betrayal of women and some sort of patriarchal or imperialist slight to the noble Kazakhs. Samantha was capable of connecting mayonnaise to patriarchy and/or imperialism. Waylon would have difficulty processing why she was bringing back fossilized elephant bones when they were looking for horses. Katie, who had been an animal rights activist before returning to school, and had been around the block, would probably snort with derision at Claire's fecklessness—if you're going to launch a caper, at least do it right! Francisco, from the University of Florence, would get it, but would also be vastly amused by the web Claire had caught herself in. *Well*, she thought to herself, *at least Lawrence will remain my friend.*

She tried not to think about Tamerlan. He was going to find out pretty soon and would find himself in the catbird seat. Claire was sure that he would not be shy in using any leverage he could. She shuddered.

And then there was Sauat; Sauat with his worship of Timur Tabiliev from the museum. She realized that she really needed Sauat.

14

AN INNOCUOUS MESSAGE—"REMEMBER YOUR LOVED ONES WITH flowers"—popped up in Sergei's email, though the Russian's response was to grit his teeth. The email was a coded signal that he was to report in on a secure line. Following protocol, Sergei retrieved an encrypted phone and dialed a number.

Without preamble, the voice on the other end launched in. "You've been busy. What's with the odd trips, the huge rocks? And who's the woman?"

Sergei's blood went cold. He knew that they probably had eyes on him, though he'd yet to figure out just whose were those eyes. Thinking quickly, he wondered whether to spin some tale, but, just as quickly, he put that aside. He didn't want to think about the consequences of being caught in a lie, and besides, the archaeological moonlighting was no threat to any plans his controllers might have, whatever they were. So he told the caller the partial truth; he said that Claire was an archaeologist and that they'd found some bones on the concession that she was interested in. He did not say that they were over five million years old.

The caller took this in. "Archaeology could be the perfect cover for industrial espionage."

"All the more reason for me to stay involved," said Sergei smoothly.

Andrei Bezanov grunted. "Remember, when I put you in at Transteppe, I said I needed a geologist I could trust."

Sergei kept his voice calm, although he was quivering with rage. "Message received."

"Excellent. Now is the time to be a good pawn!"

After he hung up, he took several deep breaths. He thought back to the call that brought him to Transteppe.

A recruiter had contacted him about Transteppe's search for a chief geologist. With his growing reputation in the field, Sergei was used to these approaches and had demurred, saying that he was happy in his role doing research at Lomonosov Moscow State University. Not long after this conversation, he found a small package in his mailbox. It had no return address. He opened it, and there was a note and a few pictures. He felt near panic. Shortly thereafter his phone rang. After seeing the contents of the package, he expected the call.

"You should take the job at Transteppe."

"Why?"

"Pawns don't get to ask questions."

"I won't do anything illegal."

Andrei gave a short laugh. "We'll see what you will or will not do, but, for the moment, I just need reports."

"Why me?"

"Isn't that obvious? I need a geologist I can trust, someone who can give me details of subsurface profiling that may or may not be given to management. It's a bit of luck—for me at least—that you have just the skills I need."

15

SITTING IN HIS TEMPORARY OFFICE AT THE PAGE MUSEUM IN Hancock Park in Los Angeles, Byron Gwynne absently tapped his finger as he read the email for the third time. A coiled, dark-haired man in his mid-forties, Gwynne radiated energy. If he always looked on the verge of anger, it was because he always *was* on the verge of anger. He swiveled his chair to face a stack of papers and monographs on the shelf behind him. He riffled through a few until he found the illustration he was looking for. Grabbing it, he swiveled back to his computer screen and, holding the drawing alongside, stared intently as he compared the images. After a few moments, he hit reply and began writing a message. Then, abruptly, he stopped. He got up from his chair. "I'm going for a walk," he said to the administrative secretary as he passed her without stopping. "If anyone calls, I'll be back in about half an hour."

Outside, it was beastly hot. It was May, a time of year when Southern California ordinarily would be lush and green, but the beautiful lawn that surrounded the Page Museum was already scorched brown. He pondered the dilemma that prompted the walk. What the fuck was that creature doing in Kazakhstan? Worse, whatever that ulna came from, it was not his discovery, and Byron Gwynne did not like the idea of someone waltzing in and stealing the spotlight. He tried to remember where he had met Claire. He certainly remembered what she looked like. He'd even tried to humor her absurd ideas about elephant consciousness in the hopes that he might get lucky.

On his return to his office, the receptionist handed him a padded book mailer. *Great!* He thought with some bitterness. A week earlier he would have been overjoyed to receive the package. He snatched the envelope, went back to his office, and tore the mailer open.

There it was, the result of fifteen years' work. He looked at the title of the copyedited manuscript: *The Evolutionary History of Elephantidae.* He let out a groan. The last thing he needed was an eleventh-hour discovery of some previously unknown branch of the family, particularly if it was contemporaneous to *Primelephas,* the ancestor of both modern elephants and mammoths. He looked again at the image of the ulna. Suddenly, he was glad Claire Knowland had reached out to him. He knew what he had to do.

16

WHEN CLAIRE ARRIVED BACK AT THE CAMP, THE TEAM, WHICH had been speculating among themselves about what their leader was up to, drifted out of the mess to greet her, forming a rough line in front of her. If the situation wasn't so fraught, she would have laughed, as they looked like birds perched on a wire. Naturally, Abigail and Tony were standing together, furtively pressing into each other at the hip as if their hookup wasn't known to, and hadn't been exhaustively discussed by, every other member of the team. As the silence stretched to awkward lengths, Claire finally sighed. "OK, I don't know where to begin, so maybe I'll just show you." She started walking to the back of the truck, and the team, even Francisco, who made a point of never hurrying anywhere, dropped all pretense of cool and rushed to the back of the pickup.

Everybody crowded up to look at the jumble of rock and bone. Naturally, it was Waylon who stated the obvious. "These aren't horse bones."

"That's right, Waylon," she said in a voice she might use to address a not-particularly-bright third grader, "these aren't horse bones."

Katie, smart as a whip, was the first to get it. She looked at Claire. "Elephant?"

Claire nodded.

At this, the whole group closed in, jostling each other and peppering her with so many questions that Claire couldn't begin to answer until Sauat interrupted.

He had been staring at the bones and took out a pocket magnifier and studied the one closest to him. He then tapped it with his finger. He looked up at Claire and said, "Petrified?" At that the group went silent.

Claire nodded. "Let me tell you the bare bones—so to speak." When no one smiled, she hurried on. She took them through Sergei's discovery of the array, the dating of the strata to over five million years old, and her near accident that broke the array on the way back. She didn't lie, but she did not give them the whole story.

It didn't matter, as the team absorbed the sheer irresponsibility of her ad hoc transport of such a monumental discovery. Samantha looked daggers at Claire and muttered loud enough for all to hear, "This bitch needs help." Katie shook her head. Abigail shrank back as though Claire's blunder might be contagious. Francisco spoke for the group when he said, "Delamain's not going to like this." Claire took it all in numbly.

Sauat, however, got it. He had, after all, grown up in Kazakhstan. "Sergei wanted to help, yes? He wanted the bones out of there because they were in the mining concession?"

Claire looked at him gratefully though she knew that she still had to tread carefully. "Something like that. He just felt that they weren't safe there and needed to be examined by professionals. We were the nearest around." Maybe her makeshift plan could work.

She looked at the rest of the team. "Francisco's right. Delamain is going to freak—at least at first." After an uncomfortable silence, she added, "You're probably thinking that I screwed up. You're right." Nobody protested. Abigail looked at the ground and traced the outline of a horse in the dust with the tip of her sneaker.

Claire forged on. "You're going to have to make your own decisions about whether you want to continue, but I know what I'm going to do. The most probable explanation, even though it's hard to believe, is that somehow these bones were arrayed five million years ago. I'm going to do everything I can to find out who or what did it and why . . . with or without the support of the Delamain Foundation . . . with or without this team," she added. She looked directly at Sauat. "And I'm going to do it working with the Kazakh antiquity authorities." His intelligent eyes widened. He suddenly realized what she was saying and why she was saying it to him. Claire's mind lingered briefly on the irony that her career and a momentous discovery depended on the insight and integrity of an overeager teenager.

She thought of what Sergei had said before she left and turned back to the group. "Look. When I came here to fill in, you'd had two years of spinning your wheels. I can't comment on whether you—we—might ultimately find something of interest, but clearly, there was—is—a strong likelihood or Delamain wouldn't have invested its money and you wouldn't have invested your time." She paused for a second. "But this"—she pointed to the pickup—"is real, and it's here now."

Claire let that sink in before continuing. "Things are going to have to happen fast, so let me know tomorrow whether you want to continue with me. I completely understand if any of you don't, and for those who do, right now I've got no idea of how I'm going to get the money for it. In the meantime, I'd appreciate some help."

Katie, Tony, Abigail, and Waylon struggled with the trolley to get the bones into the storage Quonset. After locking it, Waylon started to put away the key, but Claire held out her hand. "I'd better take the keys until we figure out what's going on."

Back at her desk, Claire spent two hours composing an email to the Delamain Foundation. It was perhaps the most persuasive thing she had ever written. She began by pointing out that many of the greatest discoveries in paleontology came from looking for one thing and finding another or from accidental discoveries, particularly, she stressed, in mining concessions. She cited workers finding a hominid at the Broken Hill Mine in Zambia, the first Australopithecus remains in a quarry in Taung, South Africa, and the discoveries of Neanderthal and Cro-Magnon fossils by workers in limestone quarries. She also cited a number of major scientific discoveries that resulted from scientists making finds they hadn't been looking for.

With that introduction, she moved on to the invitation from Sergei to examine the bones, focusing on their age and the fact that they seemed arrayed, which raised the most profound questions about the origins and nature of intelligence. If the bones were not arrayed by some ancient human ancestor, could they represent the rise of intelligence in some other mammalian line, which became extinct many millions of years ago? Given the long sweep of life on earth, if evolution could produce intelligence once, could it have produced it more than once?

One million years from now, how much evidence would there be that intelligent humans once dominated the planet? How much in five million years? She didn't put all these thoughts into the email, but she stressed that the mission of the Delamain Foundation was to explore the linkages between animals and humans, and what could be more central to that mission than evidence that intelligent creatures inhabited the planet many millions of years before modern humans took the stage?

Claire wrote a straightforward account of the lurch that splintered the array but downplayed the circumstances that caused her to be transporting the fossils in the first place. She noted that she was planning to contact Timor Tabiliev from the National Museum to determine the best way to proceed, and she attached some photos of the array before the block had been extracted as well as a picture of the array of two bones after the accident. In her last sentence, she humbly requested that the foundation consider supporting this change in direction in the research considering the profound implications of the find.

After she finished the email, she reread it several times and then spent a few long moments with her finger hovering over the send button before finally hitting it. Before going to bed, Claire sent several more emails, including one to Sergei. After thinking a bit, she wrote one more email that she didn't send but kept in her drafts folder.

17

SHE AWAKENED IN THE MORNING TO FIND A REPLY FROM DELA-
main. As she opened it, she remembered someone once saying that bad
news travels at the speed of light, while good news arrives in a horse
cart. This was fast!

"Dear Dr. Knowland," it began, and she steeled herself for what
would follow.

*As you noted in your email, the Delamain Foundation supports basic
research on the relationship between animals and humans in scores of
projects spread across the globe. Our ability to work in many different jurisdictions has always been facilitated by our reputation for scrupulously
abiding by the negotiated contracts that specify the responsibilities of the
researcher, the governing local regulations, and the involvement of local
counterparts. Maintaining that relationship supersedes the requirements
of any one project—no matter how important that research may be. The
Delamain Foundation cannot be associated with any scientist who puts
at risk that reputation. Counsel has reviewed your account of the "discovery" of ancient bones that appear to be elephant, and reviewed your
actions against the agreed-upon protocols specified in the work permit
that governs the dig in Kazakhstan. In counsel's opinion, your actions
subsequent to the discovery contained no less than eight serious instances
of improper procedures and failure to follow protocol . . .*

The email went on to detail each of the infractions. The final blow
came in the concluding paragraph:

*While the "discovery" may well constitute a significant find, it is the
decision of the board, following the advice of counsel, that you are directed
to immediately cease work and secure all objects and related papers while
the foundation assesses the proper way to notify and involve Kazakh*

authorities without further damage to our relationship. The foundation has already commenced a search for a qualified research scientist who might continue this project in a way that does not blight the reputation that the foundation has taken such pains to develop over many years.

The remainder of the message recited the various relevant clauses from her grant from Delamain that gave the foundation the right to take over the project.

Claire reeled. Then came a punch of unbearable shame. This was immediately followed by a flood of deep rage. "Pompous assholes," she muttered. She looked at her watch. It was seven a.m., six p.m. in Chicago. She had maybe the rest of the day to decide what to do. She wrote a brief message to Sergei. "Want to update your team on what we've found. Exciting stuff! Is there a good time to meet?" She hoped that he would realize that she wanted Rob to meet as well, and, even in her misery, she was happy to have an excuse to see Sergei. A minute later, she dashed out of the Quonset to rouse Sauat.

She'd installed the boy in a spare room on the rear of the storage Quonset. He was already up and looked bright-eyed as he answered her knock. "Dr. Knowland."

"Hi, Sauat. Have you got a moment?" He nodded mutely, a bit awed that the leader of the dig had sought him out. "Good." She jerked her head toward the picnic tables. "We can talk over there."

Once they were seated, she got right to the point. "I appreciate that you seem to understand that this is a very delicate situation."

Sauat dropped his eyes, embarrassed. "Yes," he said softly, "I know I'm young, but I've seen how things work in my country."

"Then you will understand that it is urgent that I speak with Timor Tabiliev. For reasons that I think you understand, I can't now go through ordinary channels."

Sauat nodded slowly, but he looked troubled. What he understood completely was that Dr. Knowland did not want to go through his uncle Tamerlan.

"Can you arrange that—this morning if possible?"

Sauat looked worried. "Maybe. As you know, I am just a student, and he is a great man." Claire waited while Sauat thought it over. Then something clicked. "Yes, maybe he will take my call. It was Dr. Tabiliev who encouraged me to do some fieldwork."

"OK, let's give it a try. And don't worry—all you are doing is helping me to get in touch with one of Kazakhstan's most distinguished scientists."

"My uncle Tamerlan . . ."

Claire didn't let him finish. "Sauat, look at me." The young man looked up reluctantly. "Be assured that I'm trying to make sure that a truly significant find gets studied in the proper way and with Kazakh involvement."

This time Sauat did not drop his eyes.

"All you need to say is that an American scientist would like to talk to Professor Tabiliev about a potentially very significant find. And you might add that she says that it is potentially more significant than Kyzylorda."

Sauat's eyes widened as he grasped the full significance of what she was saying. He nodded with determination.

Claire took a look at her watch. It was seven thirty. Everybody would be at breakfast. She took a deep breath and headed over to the mess. She wanted to know who was staying and who was going, and she owed it to the group to provide clarity, but she needed to know a bit more before she could address them. She poked her head in to the mess. As she expected, everybody was locked in animated conversation. The din immediately died down when they saw her. She did not want to get trapped into an extended conversation, not yet anyway, so she hesitated at the door. "I know everybody's got a lot of questions, and I'm sure some of you have already made up your minds about what you want to do. I'd like to talk to each of you individually this afternoon. Waylon?" She saw him standing in the back. "Will you set up a schedule, starting at two thirty? Say, fifteen minutes apiece? We'll talk at the mess." Waylon nodded.

"Why not now?" someone, she didn't see who, yelled aggressively.

Claire had never been in the military, but she knew enough to know that tolerating insubordination could allow a situation to spiral out of control. "Quiet!" she said in a voice that—she hoped—brooked no rejoinder. "Things are moving fast," she said evenly. "I'll know a lot more by this afternoon." With that she ducked out and went back to her Quonset.

She immediately checked her email. She was gratified to see that everyone had responded—they were taking her seriously—but she put off reading all but one until after she had spoken to the staff. The one she did respond to was from Sergei and consisted of one word: "When?" She typed in, "Does nine a.m. work at the picnic spot? I'll bring sandwiches for three," hoping that he would understand the reference to the creek crossing and that she hoped Rob would come.

She got up, quickly threw together a day pack, and started to leave. At the door, she stopped and looked at her laptop on her desk. After a second, she put that in her pack as well.

18

THE DAY WAS SETTING UP TO BE ANOTHER SCORCHER. THE AIR shimmered on the horizon. A kettle of white-headed griffon vultures drew lazy circles as they rode the rising air. For a moment she enjoyed the elemental simplicity of the parched land and brilliant blue sky. Yes, she thought, this elemental landscape of dust, rock, and scrub against a cloudless sky could hold secrets for millions of years.

Rob and Sergei were both at the crossing when she arrived, standing in the shade of a jumble of boulders not far from the arroyo. Sergei was wearing shorts and a soccer jersey with the name Capablanca on the back. Rob looked like he was dressed for fishing, with a shirt that had lots of pockets and a Velcro strip across the chest, which was amusing since they were standing near a creek bed that looked like it hadn't seen water in a hundred years. Sergei took one look at Claire's expression and said, "*Blyad*, I was really hoping that you really meant 'exciting' when you wrote 'exciting' . . ."

Claire shook her head. "Worst-case scenario." She took them through events since she left with the bones, ending with a simple, "I blew it."

She let Rob and Sergei absorb what had happened. "OK," Rob said, "so your team's falling apart, the array is broken, your reputation has been ruined, and your funding has been cut off."

Claire nodded. "Yup, that sums it up nicely!"

Rob paused. "So what's the bad news?"

Sergei snorted, and even Claire gave a wan smile.

Sergei held up a finger. "I'm thinking." He nodded to himself in some internal dialogue. "There's really only one solution, and it's obvious. We—Transteppe—take the bones back."

A brief flash of paranoia swept over Claire. Then she realized what Sergei was saying. Her eyes widened.

Sergei nodded. "You understand? We sent the bones to you for analysis. It's only natural that we take them back . . ." Sergei paused, just enough to convince Claire that there was a little bit of a sadist in this otherwise nice man, before continuing, "and that we hire you as a consultant to analyze the bones at our laboratory."

It made sense. Now that word of the bones was getting out, their existence couldn't be buried and she could still pursue her work. On the other hand, Sergei was Russian. She looked at Sergei. "Can you do that?"

Sergei looked at Rob. "Can we do that?"

Rob looked at both of them. "I don't know. Lemme think . . ." He wandered off.

Sergei and Claire stood there in silence. After a couple of minutes, Claire asked, "What team does Capablanca play for?"

Sergei smiled. "Cuba, but he died over one hundred years ago."

Claire looked more confused.

"And he played chess, not football."

Claire laughed. "Of course!"

Rob came back. He looked at Claire. He did not look comfortable. "As for taking the bones back—yes. It makes sense, particularly since a lot of people now know they exist." He paused. "As for the consultancy, I'm not sure . . . we're getting close to things that might impact Transteppe's relationship with the host country." He looked at Sergei. "Do you have discretion to spend money on something like this without approval?"

Sergei, a veteran of negotiating bureaucracies, albeit not a particularly successful one, nodded confidently. "Absolutely!" And then he added, trailing off, "On an interim basis . . ."

Both Claire and Rob noticed the hedge.

"Also"—Sergei looked at Claire—"remember that you were going to come over today to look at the rest of the lip."

Rob was confused, "What?"

Claire got it instantly. "We haven't investigated the rest of the lip. He's saying that there might be other stuff in the piece you cut off from the escarpment, right?"

Sergei nodded. "Exactly!" Then, almost mumbling, he added, "Longer term, I probably *should* notify senior management and probably *should* get something worked out on paper."

Claire liked to think of herself as willing to push the envelope, but she was still a scientist, and scientists were used to working in controlled situations where they could focus on minutiae without distractions.

While she understood the logic of shifting her work to Transteppe, she wished that she had more time to think through the implications such a radical move would entail. One occurred to her immediately.

"What about those minders who caused you to come to me in the first place?" she asked, directing her question to both Rob and Sergei.

"Good question," said Rob. "Sergei?"

"I agree," said Sergei. "Good question!" He thought a second. "Now that the bones are public, it will be far harder to make the whole thing disappear . . . but if they think this is a big deal, they can still cause quite a bit of trouble . . . it would help if you had already established communication with some official . . ." Sergei trailed off.

This was one place where Claire had a ready answer. "I was thinking about how best to bring in the Kazakhstan antiquity authorities—the right antiquity authorities—you know, in a way that would make sure that the project got the proper attention from the right people." Rob and Sergei were both listening—life would be much easier if Kazakh experts were involved. "And so I thought about getting Dr. Timor Tabiliev out to see the bones—fast, before all our minders gum up the works . . ."

"Who's this Tabiliev?" Rob and Sergei spoke in unison.

"A supposedly incorruptible academic at the National Museum. I'm hoping to give him the two bones that are still connected so that Kazakhstan shares in the discovery and analysis."

"An incorruptible bureaucrat? Really? In Kazakhstan? I'd like to meet this man," Sergei said slowly with the tone he might have used if Claire had said she was going to introduce him to a tap-dancing unicorn.

Rob brought the conversation back to the questions at hand. "OK, interim'll work, but I think I'm going to send a note to one of our board members."

Claire looked apprehensive, but she was in no position to argue. "OK, but is that wise?"

Sergei looked uncomfortable. "I agree with Claire, it might slow things down."

Rob gave Sergei a hard look but addressed his answer to Claire. "Part of my job is to anticipate trouble, and this is beginning to look like it could really blow up."

Claire could not argue with that. Sergei said nothing but looked uncomfortable, even sad.

"What are you thinking, Sergei?" she asked.

Sergei had been thinking about the vise he was in, but he wasn't going to talk about that. "Nothing, except that an intelligent Russian's instinctive reaction on hearing that the top guys are involved is to head for the hills."

Rob laughed. "This guy is different," he said. "The board came through here last year for a visit. One member—guy named Fletcher Hayden, Canadian—used to run a gold-mining company. Turns out he's an amateur archaeologist. I took him out on horseback through the concession last year—right to the spot where we found the bones, come to think of it—and he told me that he spends most of his vacations volunteering on digs. I think he's a widower. Anyway, I'll send him a friendly note, using his interest in archaeology as an excuse, and let him know that something turned up on the concession that might be a big deal, but stressing that it won't interfere with development. That way, when it comes time that we have to inform senior management why Claire's in the lab, we might have a friend in our court. It'll also help big-time if the minders see that Transteppe is totally behind us."

For Rob that was a long speech. She knew he was going out on a limb for her, and she felt bad about what was going to come next.

"Actually, there are a couple more things . . ."

Rob gave her a look. "Yes?"

"First is that I would like to bring along some of my team . . ." Both Sergei and Rob gave her doubtful looks . . . "OK, OK, here's a thought . . . you pay me whatever you think fair as a consultant, and I'll split it with whoever I bring along—doesn't cost you anything extra."

Sergei opened his hands in surrender and nodded. "That works."

"You said there were a couple more things?" Rob said warily.

"Yup," Claire said enthusiastically. "When I came to collect the bones, I couldn't help noticing a helicopter sitting on a pad," she said as cheerfully as she could. "Just sitting there . . ." Rob looked wary. "It looked lonely and underused?"

Rob wasn't giving her any help. "And . . . ?"

"OK," she sighed and then went on quickly, "think about it. Best-case scenario: legitimate involvement from distinguished Kazakh authority, yes? That's Tabiliev. Best case for the best case: get him here as quickly as possible so that there is a relationship established before various interests start trying to take control. Therefore . . . helicopter!" She brought an imaginary drumstick down on an imaginary snare drum in a pantomime of a rimshot.

Sergei smiled.

"I'll think about that helicopter," said Rob, interrupting before she could go on. "In the meantime, we'll get a truck out to pick up the bones. This afternoon good?"

Claire thought about her scheduled meetings with the staff. She gave Rob a thumbs-up. "Any time after four o'clock is perfect." As she turned toward her truck, she felt a wave of gratitude. She kissed them both on their cheeks. "You two are my heroes!"

Rob, embarrassed, made a Gary Cooper anyone-would-have-done-the-same-thing-ma'am wave of his hand. Sergei blushed despite himself and then recovered and bowed, "At your service . . . besides, if things go wrong, where could they exile me?" He furrowed his brow. "Wait a minute, I've got it! Kazakhstan!"

As Claire drove back to the camp, she smiled again at the memory of Sergei wearing a soccer jersey with a famous chess champion's name on the back. He came across as extremely intelligent, funny, and straightforward, but he was also Russian, had come to Kazakhstan with baggage, and played chess. There was no way he was as straightforward as he seemed. Then she remembered how Rob had vouched for him. The one thing she was certain of was that Rob carried no hidden agenda.

19

CLAIRE WAS ALMOST FEELING GOOD WHEN SHE ARRIVED BACK at her Quonset. Lawrence was waiting outside her door. She scratched behind his ears, and then he jumped ahead of her when she opened the door and immediately began looking around for his food bowl. She assumed he'd already been fed (she knew the desert cat scored about five meals a day, and besides, he was supposed to be in training to get back to the desert, not to become a house cat) so she went directly to her computer to check the emails she'd put off reading earlier. The first she opened was from Adam Constantine of the *New York Times*.

She had met Constantine at a scientific conference—he had seemed interested in her and chatted her up—and he had been one of the people she had emailed when she received the photo of the bone from Sergei. In that email, she had mentioned a potentially momentous find in the steppes of Kazakhstan. Getting no reply, she had again emailed him the previous night saying that events had taken an unexpected turn and urged him to contact her in the event that he wanted to know more about the find. Constantine was the *Times*'s go-to reporter on all things paleontological, and her logic had been that the best protection against any attacks would be early disclosure in a credible and widely read publication.

Constantine's email started off breezily. *Sorry for not responding sooner. As you can imagine, I get deluged with solicitations, and with deadlines, etc.,—you get the picture. That said, I remember meeting you very well and you certainly got my attention with the stuff about five-*

million-year-old bones that seemed to be arrayed. On the other hand
I was troubled by some of the uncertainties surrounding this situation.
I did my due diligence, and when I contacted Delamain, they said that
you were no longer affiliated with this dig and suggested that I speak with
them again when your replacement was on-site? What's up with that?

Constantine then went on to say that before he asked the *Times* to
commit to funding a trip to Kazakhstan, he needed to know a lot more
about the circumstances that led to her replacement. He ended by saying that he would be back in touch at some point, and in the meantime,
whom would she suggest that he contact in the Kazakh officialdom?

Claire could have dealt with a smug dismissal, or pretentious
put-down, but this was far more devastating because it was entirely
reasonable. Hell, it was what she would have written had she been in
Constantine's position and received Claire's email.

She looked at the list of other unread emails. There was a new one
from Delamain. This could not possibly be good news.

It was a formal notification that Delamain had named a replacement. Her heart pounded when she saw the name. At least now she
knew why he had not answered the email she had sent the day she first
received the manila envelope from Sergei containing the photo of one
of the ulnae. Even as she fumed, she silently patted herself on the back
for the idea of sending a photo of only one of the bones.

Her Judas was Benoit Richard, a newly minted PhD paleontologist
and a bona fide hotshot at the University of Montana. She had met him
at a conference on early mammalian evolution. He had done some pioneering work on environmental stress and brain size, confirming a
theory that in periods of environmental stress, the more specialized
mammals tended to die out, while the generalists survived. She had
thought that he would be the perfect credible scientist to recognize the
significance of the find. Ruefully she realized that she had been right,
but Delamain apparently recognized that, too, and Benoit, obviously,
had had better things to do when his peers were learning about ethics.

While he was too busy to reply to her email notifying him of the find, he'd apparently had the time to make a deal with Delamain to take it over. One of her mother's favorite phrases drifted through her mind—"The wheels can come off pretty quickly once you're in the rapids"—and she smiled in spite of herself at the memory of her mother's bottomless store of mixed metaphors, most of which actually made perfect sense once you got past their literal impossibility.

Her thoughts returned to the ways in which Benoit's arrival changed things. She tried to imagine his rage when he discovered that the bones were back at Transteppe. That would be satisfying, but, she thought, it might still be possible to get him on her side. To do that, she realized, she might literally have to toss him a bone.

She returned to the email, which went on to say that he would be arriving to assume control of the repurposed dig as soon as Delamain could arrange the necessary clearances, which might take a few days. In the interim Benoit hoped that she would behave professionally in reassuring the staff during the transition. Once again Claire's blood boiled; they were asking her to do the scientific equivalent of tipping her own executioner! She read on. Delamain said that they were holding off notifying the staff to give her time to frame her resignation in a way she preferred. The email ended with a boilerplate statement that Delamain regretted that their relationship had been forced to come to an end, but that they hoped she understood that the foundation had to protect its reputation for straightforward dealings with host governments. There was one more slightly mollifying statement at the end, which said that Delamain would continue to honor its commitments to the project in Florida.

Claire looked at her watch. It was 2:15. She just had time to check with Sauat to see whether he had contacted Tabiliev before she had the dreaded series of conversations with her staff. As she started to leave her Quonset, another thought came to her. She hadn't heard from Byron Gwynne. Given what had happened with Benoit, she didn't have a good feeling about that.

20

IT WAS TWO A.M. IN LOS ANGELES, AND BYRON GWYNNE FI-
nally got up from his desk. He walked stiffly toward the door. "OK,
Byron," he said to himself, thinking of the classic divide among taxon-
omists, "so, after three decades as a splitter, you're now a lumper." He
shook his head, "God help me if I'm wrong."

He'd spent several hours going over the galleys of his book, many
of those hours being devoted to his chapter on *Primelephas*, the ancestor of modern elephants who trudged the African plains just before
the great radiation of species 5.5 million years ago that saw the genus
splitting into three separate lines. Gwynne looked over the very long
endnote that he had added to the chapter. The publisher was not going
to be happy because it would necessitate a good deal of resetting and
repagination, but, thought Gwynne, it was better than ripping up the
script altogether.

"*As this book went to press,*" it began, he had received a communication from a field researcher describing the find in Kazakhstan of
the petrified ulna of some species of *Proboscidea*, whose surrounding
rock was 5.5 million years old. Gwynne noted that the dimensions were
indeed different than any other known relative of *Primelephas* at the
time. Then he explored at length the long history of misidentification of
fossil remains as researchers were thrown off by the impacts of disease,
dwarfism, or other syndromes that malformed bones and led to the
unwarranted identification of new species. He ticked off other warning signals: the bone was found in Kazakhstan, not previously known
as the habitat of any proboscides; the area where the bone was found
was quite near ancient caravan routes; the discovery came from a researcher with no credentials in proboscid phylogeny; and there were
questions about the circumstances of the find and chain of custody.

By the end of this recitation, any academic would be ready to convict Claire of a hate crime.

Gwynne was careful to hedge his endnote seven ways from Sunday, leaving open the possibility that further exploration might indeed reveal more about what creature this bone came from, as well as where and when it lived. At this point, however, Gwynne's note concluded, there was no reason to tear open the phylogenetic tree of Elephantidae, which was the product of decades of meticulous work by researchers around the world. No one reading this endnote would give Claire's find a second thought. And, thought Gwynne, as he closed his computer, this was only his first act.

21

ON HER WAY TO THE MESS, CLAIRE STOPPED TO SEE SAUAT, WHO said that he had in fact contacted Dr. Tabiliev. "He was surprised to hear from me," said Sauat, "and I could tell that his email was . . . carefully written? But he did say that he was always open to meeting a visiting scientist."

Claire sighed with relief. "Thanks so much, Sauat! I'll follow up with my own email and set up a meeting."

Sauat looked relieved. "Yes, I think that would be best."

Claire went to the mess, where she found Waylon waiting for her outside. It was blast-furnace hot, and there was no wind. The only sound was a fly buzzing around and the scraping of Waylon's chair as he rose to meet her. She briefed Waylon, who looked both relieved and confused, as usual. She told him to start sending her team in, and to knock after each staff member had fifteen minutes—she wanted to limit opportunities for this to turn into a two-hour clusterfuck of Monday morning quarterbacking.

First in was Katie. For Claire this was a no-brainer. Katie had gone off the reservation many times in her earlier life as an animal activist and probably understood why Claire had felt compelled to take the path she did. She wanted Katie to come with her to Transteppe, so she laid out—most of—the situation.

With high cheekbones, a wide smile, and wavy auburn hair, Katie was very pretty. Claire thought that if an anthropologist were to describe a woman's face that had universal appeal, Katie's would be a good place to start. There was an unselfconscious confidence about her that Claire envied a bit. Claire gestured toward the bench opposite her.

First she told Katie that the dig would go on under new management and that Benoit was a big name in paleontology. She also said that she would try to continue her own investigation into the bones and that she would want Katie to work with her if she felt she could. Claire did not mention that Transteppe was coming to pick up the bones this afternoon.

Katie looked at her levelly. The thing you noticed most about her were her eyes—at least if you were a woman—wide set, light blue, and penetrating. Men might notice other things about her, also appealing. Claire had never seen her lose her cool. If Claire was going to need someone to watch her back with an ability to improvise, Katie would be a good choice.

Katie wasn't about to lose her cool now. After Claire finished laying out the situation, Katie remained silent. Finally, she said, "I get what you're doing. But I'm sure you can also appreciate that because of my earlier . . . adventures"—the flicker of an amused smile crossed her face—"I've got to be a goody two-shoes if I'm going to continue my studies." Claire nodded. Katie continued, "A whole lotta people would love to see me fuck up." That last bit Katie seemed to say to herself, so Claire did not reply.

Katie looked up. "So what's your take on those bones?"

Claire sat back. "It's early, but here's what I think: high probability the bones are five million years old and were arranged back then."

Katie seemed to be thinking. "Really? Five million years?"

Claire nodded, trying not to punch the air. She had her. "Five million years from now do you think that there will be any evidence that an intelligent species—us—was ever on the planet?"

Katie thought about that a minute. "We're basically an invasive species that has terraformed the entire planet. *Some* part of our footprint will be around for someone or something to find."

"Right," said Claire, "but say we had died out ten thousand years ago."

Katie's eyes widened.

"Exactly," said Claire. "Ten thousand years ago humans were just as intelligent as we are today, but our material culture was almost nonexistent. Evolution produced human intelligence in the blink of an eye; our material culture has developed in a nanosecond, geologically speaking." Katie was listening intensely. "So I'm thinking that if evolution produced intelligence in us," Claire continued, "it might have done so before, perhaps several times. Over tens of millions of years, a lot of things can come and go and leave no trace." It was the first time Claire had said this out loud. "So," she finished, "I think whether we've come upon evidence of a much earlier intelligent being is a question that I could devote my life to pursuing."

Now there was fire in Katie's eyes, too. "I'm in!"

"That makes me very happy. I'm going to need all the help I can get. Let's talk again after the rest of these meetings." She shook Katie's hand and watched as the young woman got up and walked out the door. There was artless sexuality, an animal languor to Katie. Claire wondered why she was only noticing that now. With a pang Claire thought that Sergei was going to be very happy to have Katie joining the team. Claire sighed and then went to the door and signaled Waylon to send in the next team member.

That turned out to be Samantha, who, after her crack the previous evening, was in a tie with Benoit for the person Claire would most like to attack with a chain saw. She decided from the outset that she wasn't going to give any quarter. Once the young woman had taken a seat, Claire folded her arms and leaned forward. Instinctively, Samantha leaned back. "This can be short and sweet," Claire said, "I'm leaving the project. You can either stay on with the new leader or go home. You won't be working with me, whatever I end up doing. You can make your decision after he arrives." Claire leaned back. "Any questions?" Whatever bravado Samantha might have brought into this meeting vanished. She awkwardly got up from the bench and stumbled for the door without saying a word. Claire let out a long breath and counted to ten.

Next came Tony. Claire had half expected that he and Abigail would come in together. Tony was a graduate student at the University of California, Davis. Claire liked him. She told him the situation and, without mentioning Abigail, said that he might find it best to stay on at least long enough to see whether Benoit would continue the project. Tony gave the briefest nod of appreciation for Claire's tact and delicately coded message. As he got up to leave, Claire said that she'd enjoyed working with him and hoped that they could stay in touch.

Claire repeated the performance with Abigail. There hadn't been enough time between the two meetings for Abigail and Tony to confer, and Claire noted with amusement that she seemed to be in a hurry to wind things up once she got the drift of what Claire was saying.

Finally, Francisco sauntered in. As with Katie, Francisco had skills that went beyond the academic, in his case a cosmopolitan knowledge of how the world worked, which might come in useful. A scion of a wealthy family from Florence, he had started out as an investment banker. When his father died suddenly, leaving Francisco some money—how much being the subject of active conjecture around the camp—he promptly quit his job and applied to study mammalian anatomy at the University of Florence, mammal evolution having been a passion of his since his parents had shipped him off on *National Geographic* student expeditions when he was a teenager. Claire had been impressed by the seriousness and intelligence that lurked behind his louche facade.

She decided to take a no-nonsense approach. She briefed him on the situation and likely change of direction of the project and then made her pitch. "I've no definite prospects for funding and may become a pariah with both academia and the Kazakh authorities, but I think you know why I'm willing to take these risks."

Francisco tapped his fingers on the table. "You make it sound irresistible." Then he got down to business. "I get a crack at the morphology? Whether it's a new species, etc., yes?"

Claire relaxed. They were negotiating. "Of course," said Claire. "That's why I want to work with you."

Francisco thought a minute. "One question: Where are we going to live, where are we going to work?"

"That's two questions," said Claire with a smile. "And I don't know."

Now it was Francisco's turn to smile. "I didn't think so. So, to sum up: No funding, no living situation, no sponsoring academic institution, and no plan? Anything I'm leaving out?"

"Well, there's the fact that you'd be working with a pariah . . ."

Francisco smiled. "Well, when you put it that way, who could possibly say no?"

Once again Claire breathed a sigh of relief. "OK, let's keep in close touch. I'll know more soon."

Claire looked at her watch. It was close to four o'clock. She was getting nervous about the plan for Transteppe to take back the bones. They had a right, particularly since the dig was in chaos. But would the project members see it that way? She had a plan to defuse tension but had no idea whether it would work. She sat for a moment wondering whether she should have told Francisco and Katie what was about to happen. Too late now. Besides, they weren't going to be the only ones surprised this afternoon.

22

IT WAS THE HEAT OF THE DAY, AND THE DIG MEMBERS WERE scattered around the grounds in what shade there was. The only sounds were murmured conversations. Samantha was talking urgently with Tony and Abigail. Claire assumed she was trying to put together an alliance for a coup.

At 4:45 Rob and Sergei showed up in a big Mercedes van with *Transteppe* emblazoned on the sides. As the vehicle slowed to a stop in a cloud of dust, various dig members stopped and gawked. Claire pocketed the key to the storage room and emerged from her Quonset. "Give me a few minutes with these men," Claire said and led them over to the mess. Samantha looked to be on high alert, but she kept her mouth shut.

When they got inside, Claire said, "I think you've got to do this fast."

"No problem with that," replied Rob.

"And I hope that you will agree to leave one of the ulnae here."

Sergei didn't get it. "What? Why?"

"Because the team will freak out if you don't, because it will give Benoit something to play with—and he may yet prove useful—and also it might buy us time with the Kazakh authorities who otherwise might mount a full-court press on Transteppe . . ."

Sergei nodded. "And because the real game is the array, not any one bone, and the key to the array might still be in the lip. OK, makes sense to me."

Claire once again looked at Sergei in wonder. No way was he as straightforward as he seemed.

Rob wasn't convinced. "If Transteppe had all the bones, your foundation and this guy Benoit would have to deal with us. You're letting them pursue a parallel track. Why?"

Claire took a breath. "This is science, maybe hugely important science, and science is collaborative. I gave you practical reasons for why we should leave a bone, but another reason is that I want to show good faith. If this turns out to be as important as I think, I don't want to undermine its significance by doing things that could be interpreted as an attempt to hog all the glory."

Rob still looked dubious, so Claire continued. "Look, if I leave Benoit a bone, he will realize that this is the real deal and will have every motivation to want to coordinate with Transteppe. If we take them all, he'll try to undermine the importance of the find." She paused a second to collect her thoughts. "Remember what I said when you first took me to see the bones? In science, much as we'd like to think otherwise, it's not so much what you know or discover, it's who believes you. You can make a fundamental discovery and you and your discovery can be written off because you didn't show proper deference to tradition. I've already got people pissed off—so let me toss Benoit a bone."

Rob and Sergei laughed. Rob relented. "OK, since Sergei seems to be on board. How do you want to do this?"

Claire looked at Sergei. "I'll introduce you and let you tell them why you are repossessing the bones." Sergei looked uncomfortable, but nodded. "And then," Claire continued, "while they're getting ready to kill you, I'll tell them that you've decided to leave one bone here so that the team can continue its analysis." She handed the key to the storage locker to Rob. "Then you two should get out of Dodge as fast as possible."

"What is meaning of this 'Get out of Dodge?'" asked Sergei in a thick, movie-Russian accent, but when Claire shot him a glance, he put up his hands in mock surrender.

Claire didn't have any trouble mustering the troops once they exited the mess tent. She pointed to Sergei. "Group, I'd like you to meet Dr. Sergei Anachev, chief geologist for Transteppe. It was Sergei who originally contacted me about the bones *he* discovered on the Transteppe concession. Sergei?"

Sergei looked at the assembled scientists and students. "OK, as Dr. Knowland said, I'm chief geologist at Transteppe. We contacted Dr. Knowland and arranged for her to take temporary possession of the bones to see whether they had any significance. Based on very preliminary examination and our documentation of the discovery, she assures me that there is cause to pursue this discovery. She has also informed me that she is leaving this project. As a matter of prudence, we have decided to take the bones back to Transteppe while we consider how best to proceed in coordination with the Kazakh authorities. And—"

He was interrupted by angry voices, the loudest of which was Samantha's saying, "Are you fucking kidding me!"

Once again Claire took charge. "Quiet! Dr. Anachev has agreed to leave one ulna temporarily with the project so that Dr. Benoit Richard and those who remain can continue to study this find. I'm sure you will appreciate this generous gesture, as Transteppe and the Kazakh authorities have the right to determine how this project will proceed."

That somewhat mollified the group. Claire saw Francisco in the back. When he caught her eye, he mimed clapping his hands. Sergei left to help Rob transfer the bones to the van.

Claire followed to help with the transfer. The heat was so dry that she didn't even sweat as she put the bones in the padded box. She could see that Sergei had put enough foam and restraints in the carrying cases that the bones would probably survive an asteroid strike.

Rob swung into the driver's seat. As Sergei closed the sliding door and slid into the passenger seat, Rob rolled down the window and handed back the key to the storage area. "One last thing I should mention," he said. "Fletcher Hayden is coming over to see for himself, and I got him to authorize a helicopter trip for Dr. Tabiliev." He looked at Claire. "He'll be here tomorrow night, and you should be at Transteppe to meet him. If ever there was the time for you to sparkle, that is going to be it."

Everything was moving too fast, but Claire managed to nod. "I'm going to try to reach Tabiliev now. If everything works, I'll go in with the helicopter tomorrow and convince the doctor to accompany me back." Then something occurred to her. "Do the authorities monitor your helicopter trips?"

Rob nodded. "They sure do. We've got a pad on top of our offices in Astana. See if you can meet somewhere close to the building? Let me know as soon as you know." With that Rob and Sergei took off.

Claire looked after the van as it disappeared, trailing a plume of dust. Was it her imagination or had Rob been a bit more formal, a bit less friendly? She didn't have time to worry as she had to try to reach Dr. Tabiliev. She found Sauat talking to Lawrence by the picnic area.

Sauat looked up when he saw her. "This is desert cat, but he is like house cat."

Claire smiled and sat down. "He came here with one of the staff as a kitten," she said. "We're trying to get him big enough so that he can go back to the desert. I'm not sure he agrees with the plan. I think he has aspirations to join the middle class." She reached down to pet the cat, who promptly jumped onto her lap and started purring loudly. She turned back to Sauat. "Thanks for making that introduction. I'm going to email him now. Where do you think would be the best place for us to talk?" Claire raised an eyebrow so he got the import of her question.

Sauat thought a minute. "Office is probably not so good. I do know that he likes to have coffee with his students at a café near the museum. Astana is new city. Dr. Tabiliev was brought up from Almaty to help start the National Museum. He is old-fashioned, and the bazaar is a little like old Kazakhstan."

Claire snapped her fingers and pointed at Sauat, "Perfect! You're a rock star!" While Sauat pondered what exactly she meant, Claire headed for her Quonset.

There she quickly emailed Dr. Tabiliev, thanking him for agreeing to see her. She mentioned that she had an opportunity to come in to Astana the very next morning. Did he have time to meet for coffee at the usual spot? Tabiliev replied almost immediately and seemed to understand the subtext of the message. He simply said that he looked forward to it, and would 10:45 be convenient? She dashed off her acceptance and then immediately emailed Rob that the trip was on.

23

CLAIRE PREVIOUSLY HAD GOTTEN ONLY BRIEF GLIMPSES OF Astana when coming and going to the project site. Now riding in Transteppe's comfortable AgustaWestland AW139 helicopter, she had the leisure to survey what billions of dollars and the megalomania of an absolute ruler could do to create an instant capital. As was the case when Brazil's government built a new capital, Brasilia, the Kazakh government had hired some of the world's most celebrated architects and top engineering firms to create a showcase. The British architect Norman Foster had designed the Baiterek Monument, a gleaming tower that was the centerpiece of an imperial-scale district, which included the Palace of Independence, the Presidential Palace, Nazarbayev University, and now the National Museum, all gigantic buildings surrounded by expansive parks and promenades. The place screamed "oil billions," which was ironic since the impetus that forced Claire, Rob, and Sergei to improvise was the president's desperation to find income to replace the next phase of oil money that had not yet started flowing.

Gazing over Astana's gleaming center, Claire couldn't help but wonder how long this monument to vanity would last. Lines from Shelley's wonderful paean to the transitory nature of worldly glory, "Ozymandias," came to mind:

". . . My name is Ozymandias, King of Kings;
Look on my Works, ye Mighty, and despair!
Nothing beside remains. Round the decay
Of that colossal Wreck, boundless and bare
The lone and level sands stretch far away."

Claire had visited Brasilia, and she wondered whether Astana would suffer the same fate in fifty years: cracked concrete, fading paint, and squalor. It didn't bode well that Norman Foster had in the past spoken rapturously about Oscar Niemeyer's visionary work in that other instant capital.

The copter landed on the roof of Transteppe's office building, and Claire got out, accompanied by Rob, who had come along to make sure she had what she needed to meet with Dr. Tabiliev and to oversee logistics for Fletcher Hayden's transport from the airport to the concession. If Claire convinced Tabiliev to come out to Transteppe, the helicopter could bring him back and drop him off before picking up Hayden.

Claire had asked for a nondescript car, and the dented beater Rob had waiting for her certainly fit the bill. There were many good reasons to fly under the radar until she had lined up Tabiliev or some other honest Kazakh counterpart. The driver looked scruffy, but Rob had assured Claire that he was one of his men and he was used to assignments that required discretion.

The man, who said his name was Igor, dropped her off near a coffee shop and pulled around the corner. It was 10:35. She ordered an ultrasweet Turkish coffee and was about to take her first sip when a young Kazakh man appeared. He was wearing a sports jacket made out of some synthetic material that had seen better days.

"Hello, beautiful!" he said with boundless confidence. "May I sit with you and practice my English?" He sat down without waiting for an answer and was about to begin speaking. Claire knew English was a big deal in Kazakhstan; indeed, the entire curriculum of the brand-new

National University was to be conducted in English. But she doubted that the young man simply wanted to practice his language skills.

"I'm meeting someone and have to prepare, so if you will excuse me . . . ," she said in a friendly but firm voice.

"Oh, who are you meeting? I will translate for you." He spoke jauntily enough, but there was something more than boyish enthusiasm in the young man's cold eyes.

Claire sighed. She picked up her coffee and day pack and got up to move to another table. The young man started to follow, but he was immediately intercepted by Igor, who spat out rapid-fire Kazakh. The young man sneered and shook his coat when Igor let go of his arm but didn't attempt to follow her. As he left the café, he turned to Claire and said, "Bitch! I had plans for you. Make you porn star."

Claire sat down again, a bit ruffled. "Bitch." She was hearing that word a lot. Maybe she could introduce the young man to Samantha. He could "make her porn star"—which Samantha would then somehow rationalize as the apex of female empowerment.

The encounter crystallized her unease about Astana. Many of the new buildings were stunning, but there was something sinister in the air. She signaled the waiter for another Turkish coffee. The waiter, glancing around nervously for Igor, hustled to bring it over.

Claire spotted Tabiliev when he showed up ten minutes later. She had looked up his picture on the web. She waved to him and rose when he came over. The waiter recognized the professor and greeted him warmly. This was good; the waiter would conclude that Claire was just another student.

The academic introduced himself. "Welcome to the ancient capital of Kazakhstan with its storied past dating back almost sixteen years," he said with a sad smile as he made a dismissive gesture at the brand-new buildings around them. When he sat down, however, he adopted a no-nonsense expression that suggested that he wasn't sure what she was selling but that he would listen to what she had to say. Understanding his reticence, she decided to be as brief and straightforward as possible. After he had settled and been brought coffee, she reached into her bag and brought out a photo of the array as she first saw it on the lip of the escarpment. She placed it in front of him on the table.

Tabiliev stared at it for a long time. "What kind of bones are these?"

"Ulnae, probably from some unknown species of ancient elephant."

Tabiliev snorted. "Elephants in Kazakhstan? Who knew? How old?"

"Five million years, thereabouts."

At this Tabiliev's head snapped. "Was there any evidence that the ground around this arrangement had been disturbed?"

"None, and the bones are petrified."

"How did they come to be arranged this way?"

"Good question! That's what I'm hoping to find out—with your help."

Tabiliev thought about this for a long time. "Tell me everything."

Very quickly, Claire walked him through events exactly as they had unfolded, including the changing of the guard at the dig and her interim consultancy with Transteppe.

"So, in the middle of the Transteppe concession . . ." Tabiliev whistled softly. "I can see why you felt the need to be so cloak-and-dagger . . ." He tapped his fingers on the small table and took another sip of coffee. "Five million years old and arranged . . . ," he muttered to himself. After a few more minutes, he looked at Claire. "What do you want from me?"

"I'm hoping that you will come out with me to Transteppe—their helicopter can bring us both out there and have you back this afternoon—and while there you will be informed by Transteppe of the discovery and asked by them to guide them in the proper coordination with the appropriate Kazakh authorities."

Tabiliev leaned forward, listening. "If I do this, we must proceed, or," he said with a wry smile, "let me rephrase—try to proceed—in an impeccably proper fashion, yes?" He raised an eyebrow.

Claire couldn't help it. Her eyes welled up. "That's all I've ever wanted from the very beginning; that's why I reached out to you."

Another long silence ensued. Finally he sighed. "As they say in your movies, 'What could possibly go wrong?'"

As they were getting up, she turned to Tabiliev. "There's one other thing that I hope you will consider." She explained how Sauat's praise and admiration had first brought Dr. Tabiliev to her attention, and how the boy's position at the dig was now untenable. She said that she hoped that he would consider taking on Sauat as an intern.

As they walked to the car, Tabiliev nodded. "I'll think about it. I can see how he might be useful." Then he stopped and turned to Claire. "You do realize, though, that doing things in an impeccably proper fashion entails some risk in my native land. Are you sure you want to bring more attention on this young man?" He let that thought linger.

24

CLAIRE INTRODUCED DR. TABILIEV TO ROB AT THE TRANSTEPPE office in Astana, and the group quickly boarded the helicopter for the trip back. Claire encouraged Dr. Tabiliev to sit next to Rob so that the two could get to know each other, while she took a seat in the back.

Sergei met them when they landed, and Claire introduced him to Tabiliev. The Kazakh scientist looked at Sergei curiously. "You're Russian?" he said mildly.

"Don't worry," Sergei replied, "I'm even less popular in Russia than Russians are here."

Dr. Tabiliev smiled, not warmly, but still a smile. Claire wondered if what Sergei had said was true.

Once introductions were complete, Sergei told them that while Claire had been meeting with Tabiliev, he had briefed Transteppe's senior officials by email and had taken a quick meeting with the project manager, a man named Ripley, on the discovery and his proposed plan going forward. Sergei said that he had stressed that the investigation would in no way impede the work of the concession. "At first he got red in the face," Sergei told Rob and Claire with a smile, "then the penny dropped. He said, 'Fuck's sake! So that's why Hayden's coming with almost no notice.'" That's when Ripley decided to reserve judgment and also to skip the meeting with the Kazakh liaison. "God bless bureaucrats," said Sergei. "They have a sixth sense to know when to stay away."

At the warehouse, Sergei showed Tabiliev the bones and the lip and confirmed the account of events that Claire had given the professor earlier. Sergei stressed that with the lip now in the warehouse, announcement of the find need not interfere with mining operations, at least for the foreseeable future, as the part of the escarpment from which the lip had been taken was not on any immediate schedule for exploration. They then discussed the details of formal notification of the Kazakh authorities and the sensitive matter of bringing the minders into the loop. They agreed that it was best to do that while Dr. Tabiliev was there, as he had sufficient stature within the Cultural Ministry to limit opportunities for mischief.

While Sergei dispatched a clerk to invite his Kazakh counterpart to the warehouse, Rob went over the logistical details of Claire, Katie, and Francisco's transfer to Transteppe. He'd arranged lodging at visitors' quarters as well as a vehicle. He said that he would come over later that afternoon to fetch all three of them. Claire asked Sergei if she could use the company Wi-Fi network to send emails (she had brought her laptop) and he installed her in his office. Claire quickly dashed off notes to Katie and Francisco saying that they should be packed and ready and added Sergei and Rob's contact info. After sending, she remained online for a few minutes in the hope that one of them would acknowledge. Nothing appeared, and she logged off and rejoined the group.

The representative of the mining ministry had arrived. Sergei, Dr. Tabiliev, and a middle-aged Kazakh in a business suit were sitting at a worktable talking.

They all rose when Claire arrived, and Sergei made the introductions. "Dr. Knowland, I'd like you to meet Azamat Suleimenov, our liaison to the mining ministry. Azamat," he said, turning to the Kazakh, "Dr. Knowland did the first analysis of the find, and Transteppe has hired her as the company's principal scientific consultant on the find." The man gave Claire a quick look and an absentminded handshake.

After the introduction, Sergei said, "I was just telling Azamat that since we're dealing with objects five million years old, they fall into the category of a discovery of scientific—paleontological—interest rather than something that is culturally important. This is a significant distinction, because its further study will not invoke all the regulations pertaining to matters of cultural sensitivity—unless, of course," he joked, "it becomes evident that there were very, very large Kazakhs here five million years ago." Sergei's attempt at humor was either lost on or ignored by Suleimenov, whose expression never changed.

Once again, Claire was struck by Sergei's ability to find room to maneuver where none was apparent. Moreover, she liked the distinction he was making—it might prove useful in her inevitable confrontation with Tamerlan. "That said," Sergei continued, "Dr. Tabiliev, who has broad discretion over all studies of Kazakhstan's past, has graciously offered to intermediate so that Kazakh scientists can offer their expertise in the study of this remarkable find."

Suleimenov looked cornered and angry. He addressed his remarks to Sergei. "This is a matter that must be brought to the attention of the relevant authorities," he said, stressing the plural and thereby implying that the suffocating regulations of the Cultural Ministry—and all its attendant opportunities for bribery and extortion—were not off the table despite Sergei's finely drawn distinction.

With that, the meeting broke up. Claire sought out Sergei while Tabiliev talked with Rob about logistics. "I thought you were brilliant! Don't know why I hadn't thought of stressing that the find predated any conceivable Kazakh culture."

Sergei looked at her, smiling. "Brilliant, no. I simply have a gift for seeing the obvious." Sergei paused, and then added, "And it's obvious to me that we should get a drink later and talk about elephants."

Caught off guard, Claire stammered, "Oh, look, Tabiliev's leaving. I've got to thank him." And she rushed off. As she was walking, she glanced back and saw that Sergei was still smiling. As she turned back, she smiled as well. What the hell—she held up an imaginary glass and mouthed, "Later."

When she caught up to Tabiliev, he waved off her thanks. "I'm never going to be rich," he said, "but there are better satisfactions to be had in doing the right thing, yes? Besides," he continued a bit wistfully, "Five million years? Arrayed? How could I not?"

After confirming when Rob would arrive at the Delamain camp, Claire started for the Land Cruiser. After two steps she stopped and called after Rob. "Might be better if you held on to this," she said, handing him her laptop. "Who knows what's going on back at camp."

25

AS CLAIRE DROVE INTO THE ENCAMPMENT AT ABOUT THREE p.m., Katie intercepted her, mouthing the word, "Tamerlan!" Katie then made fake bug eyes. Claire rolled her eyes. "Oh," Katie added, "and we're packed!"

Claire steeled herself as she entered her Quonset. Tamerlan was sitting in the one chair. He looked up when she came in. He was seething but composed. "Anything new I should know about?" he asked.

"Much," Claire said, "but we're not talking here. I'm heading over to the mess. We can talk there, or you can continue to go through my stuff." With that she left.

She had calmed herself down by the time she seated herself at a table. Waylon was the only one there when she arrived. "I need this to talk to Tamerlan," she said. Waylon got the message and beat a hasty retreat. Tamerlan arrived shortly thereafter.

He sat down and launched right in. "Failure to follow procedure, failure to notify the ministry, stealing artifacts, moving artifacts without following proper procedure, damaging artifacts because of your irresponsible actions, failure to notify your counterpart that you have been removed from this project—shall I go on? Do you know what I—Tamerlan—can do to you on any one of these violations?"

Claire was shaken by the sheer venom of Tamerlan's recitation. She took a breath. "You know as well as I do that not one bit of that is true."

Tamerlan leaped up and slammed the table. "What?"

Claire flinched but held her ground. "They aren't artifacts, Tamerlan, they're bones. I didn't find them—Transteppe did. We didn't know what they were at first, and when the age came back—five million years plus—Transteppe did not know which ministry to notify, since they clearly predated anything that could be called Kazakh, and now Transteppe is coordinating with one of the most eminent scientists in Kazakhstan. Nothing was stolen. Transteppe reclaimed them while they are deciding what to do, leaving one here for further analysis."

The mention of Transteppe and an eminent Kazakh scientist paused Tamerlan's rage. "No matter," he said, "I will have your visa revoked on the basis of the change in leadership." He leaned back with an evil smile. "I want you out of Kazakhstan in twenty-four hours." He paused a second, measuring his words. "If this gets to the president," he said in a voice laden with menace, "I doubt you'd want to stay anyway." He stood up and leaned over her. "And I'm going to get those bones!"

It was boiling in the Quonset, but Claire felt a chill with those words.

"Of course, you could decide to help me out . . ." He left that hanging but didn't need to draw her a picture since he was staring at the open button on her blouse.

Claire got up and left. Let him think she was considering it. As she was leaving, Tamerlan followed her with his eyes but said nothing.

Outside, Claire shuddered. She knew Tamerlan was bluffing about kicking her out in twenty-four hours, but the bit about the president opened up unpleasant possibilities. He wasn't bluffing about getting the bones, either. She thought a bit more. He had not asked Claire which eminent scientist Transteppe had contacted. Either he already knew— unlikely—or he was just trying to take advantage of the situation. He might be a tin-pot tyrant, but Tamerlan was not going to take unilateral action without first investigating how strong her ties might be to Transteppe and which scientist they had contacted.

Still, she was faced with a dilemma. Now that she was vulnerable, Tamerlan might not wait for a yes before deciding to have Claire "help him out." The sooner she got out of there, the better. On the other hand, she owed it to the others on the dig to wait until Benoit arrived to hand over control, and she also needed to get back to Transteppe for the meeting with Fletcher Hayden. If she was going to talk anything other than gibberish, she also desperately needed some rest before that.

On her way to her Quonset, she waved down Waylon, who was reading in the picnic area. "Isn't Benoit supposed to arrive today?" she asked. Waylon nodded.

"OK, here's the deal. I'm going to go over to Transteppe to consult with them on the bones." Waylon's eyes widened; he was clearly curious. "I'll have cleared out my Quonset so that he can take it over. Please have the mess attendant clean it and make it ready. I'll stay at Transteppe tonight, but I'll come back tomorrow morning to brief him and formally pass the torch. That sound OK?" Waylon clearly had a thousand questions but held himself to another nod. "Katie and Francisco are coming, too," she added. Claire was about to walk to her Quonset when she had another thought. "By the way, Tamerlan seemed to have a complete but distorted picture of what's been happening. Any idea how?"

Waylon shook his head vigorously. "No idea, probably Delamain."

"Probably," said Claire in a tone dripping with doubt.

Once in her Quonset, she spent a few minutes stuffing her belongings into large duffel bags. It didn't take long, as she traveled light. There was a scratch at the door. It was Lawrence. He sniffed the duffels and then looked up at her. "OK, today you get a feast," she said as she opened two cans of food.

She looked at her watch. She had maybe forty-five minutes before Rob arrived to pick the three of them up. She lay down on her cot. Lawrence hopped up, too, and snuggled in beside her, purring loudly. She looked at him. "Maybe you can come, too. You could guard the site!"

Her thoughts were swirling again. She reviewed the litany of disasters. Was she missing anything? Actually, she was, but she was understandably preoccupied with the many missteps and betrayals in her own world of science and academia.

She tried to think of anything good. There was Tabiliev. And there was Sergei's sweet approach. She thought about that for a second. She wondered what he might be like in bed. She liked his wiry strength and wondered where he got it. Rock climbing? Windsurfing? The thought of the brainy Russian on a windsurfer brought a laugh. Her thoughts returned to sex. Oddly, she felt that it would be familiar. Thinking about his intelligence and perceptiveness, she decided that he was one of those men who could read a woman's thoughts and anticipate what they wanted. Maybe it would happen, she thought—if Katie didn't get there first.

Claire dozed off. She found herself in an airy room in a magic land filled with brilliantly colored flowers, puffy white clouds against a deep-blue sky, and the song of many birds, a perfect dream marred only by the booming explosions from a howitzer that was lobbing shells into the meadow. After a minute she realized the howitzer was someone knocking on the door. Sitting up, she said, "Hello?"

"It's Rob."

She went to the door. She could have slept for eight more hours, but the half hour left her refreshed. She was smiling when she let Rob in. "Ready," she said. "Ready for my real life to begin."

He gave her a quizzical look.

"It's from a song about my life, written by someone who doesn't know who I am."

"Got it," he said, although he clearly didn't. "Let's collect the others and get going."

Claire looked at Lawrence and then at Rob, arching an eyebrow.

Rob rolled his eyes. "Maybe. Later. Maybe. I'm a dog person." But he petted Lawrence on the back when the cat rubbed up against his leg.

Claire put the cat outside. As Lawrence ran off after a dragonfly, Claire said, "He's a wild desert cat. Orphan. We're training him . . ." She saw Rob's glance fall on the dishes of cat food. "Sort of—to take care of himself in the wild. He wouldn't be much trouble."

Rob smiled. "We'll see."

He loaded up Katie's and Francisco's bags. Claire could not resist stealing a glance at Rob to see his reaction upon meeting Katie. It might have been Marc Antony meeting Cleopatra for all the scrutiny Claire gave that introduction. Rob was cool as a cucumber, but was there a message in Katie's brief second glance? She turned to the rest of the team to say goodbye.

"I'm coming back tomorrow to brief Benoit. I understand that Delamain has its rules, but I really do hope that he realizes that we should find a way to work together on this. It couldn't be more important." She trailed off, choking up, and hurried to the big SUV.

While the door of the SUV was open, Lawrence appeared, put his paws on the step below the door, and looked in, sniffing. Claire smiled and turned to Rob. "It looks like he's made up his mind if you haven't." With that, Rob rolled his eyes again in mock exasperation and made a quick "bring him in" gesture with his hand.

26

AT TRANSTEPPE, CLAIRE INTRODUCED KATIE AND FRANCISCO to Sergei, watching Sergei's reaction to his new female colleague. Was there a tell—straightening up? Pulling in his stomach? Running a hand through his hair? But, like Rob, Sergei could have been meeting a Mother Superior. She wondered where these guys had learned their tradecraft—certainly not at the mining concession. Sergei offered to give Katie and Francisco a tour while Claire got ready to meet Fletcher Hayden. *Humph*, Claire thought.

She went to her room to freshen up and maybe steal a quick nap in the two hours she had before dinner. Compared to the austere furnishings of the camp, her room at Transteppe was the Mandarin Oriental. Each room had its own bathroom, its own refrigerator (stocked with juices and even a bottle of vodka), desks, even a couch. She had two hours. After a shower Claire lay down, setting an alarm for one hour. She hoped her subconscious got the message that she was ready to re-enter the land of enchantment.

No such luck. She fell into such a deep sleep, however, that she woke up disoriented, not knowing where she was or what time it was. After she figured that out, Claire faced the daunting task of deciding what to wear for this high-stakes meeting. She was sure Rob had meant the word *sparkle* in the intellectual sense, but she couldn't be certain. As she rummaged around, she remembered her mother scolding her as a teenager as she headed off to the first day of school in cutoffs: "First impressions are like wild cards in poker—they can be anything you want but can't be changed after you've chosen."

Color choices seemed to be limited to various shades of khaki, and she decided it prudent to choose her ensemble using cleanliness (in these circumstances a relative term) as a gating criteria rather than style. She began digging through another duffel. She found a folded blouse that had apparently escaped usage and then, lo and behold, a skirt! Holding it up and giving it an appraising eye, she remembered that she had brought it on the off chance that she would be required to attend some official function. If this meeting didn't work out, she mused, most likely the outfit she would need for her next official function would be something with stripes.

As Rob had explained it, the plan was to meet Hayden and Sergei at the warehouse at 6:30, which would give Hayden time to meet with Ripley, the project manager, first. Sergei and Claire would then show Hayden the bones and the rock lip, while Rob would take Katie and Francisco to the mess hall. Claire and Hayden would then have dinner alone in the VIP dining room, and then Rob and Sergei would join them for after-dinner drinks.

On the way to the warehouse, she passed Rob, who did a double take when he saw her. "Why, Dr. Knowland," he said with a gallant bow, "you look beautiful."

Claire blushed deeply. "Too much?"

"Absolutely not, it's just that I haven't seen you wear anything but desert gear." He pointed to the warehouse. "Hayden's already there, chatting with Sergei. By the way, he was charmed by Lawrence, who we've installed at the provisions warehouse—apparently they were looking for a mouser, and he can get outdoors."

Claire nodded, thinking to herself that Lawrence was more likely to throw a birthday party than hunt any mouse he encountered. She took a deep breath. "Wish me luck."

Rob smiled broadly. "You don't need it, you've got the one thing he—and I, for that matter—can't resist."

Claire did a quick check of her outfit, blushing again despite herself. "What's that?"

"A five-million-year-old mystery."

———

Fletcher Hayden was leaning against the worktable talking with Sergei when Claire arrived. What she saw was a man either in his late fifties or early sixties who looked remarkably fresh for someone who had just traveled sixteen hours. Then she reminded herself that he had probably come by private plane and slept for most of the trip. He was wearing khaki trousers, a crisp blue shirt, and a casual black jacket. He looked fit, probably one of those men who was within five pounds of his college weight, but not physically imposing. His hair, going to gray, was short and combed straight back. He had fine features, startlingly bright brown eyes, and a mouth that suggested a state of permanent amusement. He had the relaxed, confident posture of someone who had for a long time been used to giving, rather than taking, orders.

Hayden looked at Claire and then stepped forward before Sergei could make the introduction. "Fletcher Hayden," he said. "You must be Dr. Knowland."

"Please call me Claire," she said demurely, "and thank you for disrupting your schedule to come here."

"Call me Fletcher," he said with the slightest trace of warmth. "Sergei's been telling me some of the history, but he wanted to wait for you to arrive before showing me anything. So, now that you're here . . ." He left the rest of the sentence hanging.

"Right," said Sergei, "let's have a look."

He led them over to a sealed workroom with a newly installed lock. As they walked, Sergei sidled up to Claire and whispered, "You look *very* nice!"

Inside the workroom, laid out on the table were the bones they had brought back from Claire's camp. Sergei had tried to arrange them as they had found them on the escarpment, with a cutout photo taking the place of the bone they had left for Benoit. Sergei had pinned to a portable bulletin board a number of photos of the array as it was in place in the escarpment as well as pictures of their operation to separate the array from the rest of the lip. Hayden looked intently at the two bones that were still arrayed in the sedimentary rock. He tapped one bone with his finger. His expression changed to one of rapt awe. No one said a word. Sergei handed him a magnifying loupe, and Hayden looked not at the bone but the sedimentary rock in which the bones were encased. After another ten minutes, which seemed like an eternity, Hayden finally spoke. "Let's take a look at the lip you told me about."

As they headed over to that part of the warehouse, Sergei grabbed some photos from a desk. Hayden gave the lip a close inspection. Sergei told him that it came from the area where Rob had taken him on an earlier trip. Hayden peppered Sergei and Claire with questions—whether the bones could have moved through the sedimentary rock over time, tectonic movements in the area, volcanic activity between then and now. They answered what they could but didn't try to guess when they didn't know.

Hayden looked again at the ninety-ton lip and then at the picture of the lip in situ. He turned to Sergei and Claire. "So, if I have this straight, you mounted an expensive rogue operation on your own authority in my mining concession." Sergei went pale, and Claire felt the blood drain from her face. Hayden laughed when he saw their stricken looks. "Don't worry, given what I'm seeing, I would have done the same." Claire felt a surge of relief. Hayden turned to Sergei. "I think your instinct was spot-on. Our counterparts would have seen this as nothing but trouble—the best way to make sure this discovery got proper attention was to get it to the point where it couldn't be deep-sixed by some bureaucrat."

Sergei looked at Claire and mouthed, "Deep-sixed?" with a quizzical look. She smiled, trying to suppress a laugh.

Hayden looked at his watch. He turned to Claire. "We've got a lot to talk about. I'll meet you at the VIP dining room in twenty minutes." With that he was gone.

Claire and Sergei looked at each other. "Hard to read," said Claire, "but he didn't say no."

"Here's an American phrase I know," said Sergei. "He has all the cards, and he wants us, particularly you, to know that he does."

So, wondered Claire, as she walked over to the VIP dining room, *how do you win when one player has all the cards and you have none?*

27

THE DINING ROOM WAS A WORLD APART FROM THE REST OF THE mining concession. The walls were of blond wood, the floors covered with lush rugs made by Kazakh artisans. The room was dominated by a long cherrywood dining table, and there were comfortable armchairs and sofas scattered in corners, presumably so whatever group was using the room could break into private conversations. A bar was at the far end of the room. Hayden was standing by it holding a heavy crystal glass that the uniformed bartender was in the process of filling with Bunnahabhain single-malt scotch. He waved Claire over. Seeing her wide-eyed expression, he said, "Surprised? When we built this, we were advised that life would be much better if we had a room like this in case the president got it in his head to visit. What's your fancy?" he said, glancing at an array of spirits that would have made the bartenders at Claridge's envious. Claire ordered an amontillado neat, and Hayden pointed to two facing armchairs in the corner, saying, "I understand that you've been very much on the go. We can slow down a bit and enjoy our drinks before dinner."

"We're just talking here," he said amiably once they were seated, "so don't be afraid of saying the wrong thing." He took a sip of his scotch. "And I understand it's far too early to draw any conclusions." Another sip. "But when you first realized that those bones might have been arrayed over five million years ago, how did you make sense of that?"

He could have taken any tack in opening the conversation, but, from Claire's point of view, this was the best: he wanted to jump right in. She gathered her thoughts. "Well, I couldn't make sense of it at first," she admitted. "I don't think anyone who knows anything about human evolution could." Hayden nodded. "But then I stepped back and thought that if the *facts* before me were what they seemed to be, then something intentionally arranged those bones, and if it was intentional, then whatever arranged those bones was probably intelligent."

"Let's think about that a bit," said Hayden. "What is intelligence?"

"That one is easy," said Claire, smiling. "No one knows." Hayden looked at her with slight annoyance. "Well, it might be better put to say that no one agrees on what it is," she continued hastily. "Various ideas have been put forward, but there is no standard theory as, say, there is in physics."

"So what do you think it is?"

"Well, I tend to think that there are various kinds of intelligence—social intelligence or emotional intelligence, to name a couple—but I'm assuming that most people focus on quantitative intelligence, the ability to symbolically construct a model of the world and then manipulate that model through rules and laws in order to be able to predict or influence events."

"That's certainly how I think about it," said Hayden a bit more warmly. "There's more?"

"Yes," Claire affirmed, nodding. "So I think about intelligence in evolutionary terms—what it does, rather than what it is." She paused to let this sink in. "I'm not being modest when I say that I don't think I'm going to be the one to define what philosophers and scientists have failed to do for four thousand years."

"So what does intelligence do?" Hayden leaned forward. "By the way, I'm liking this," he said, gesturing vaguely to the space between them so that she understood he was talking about the conversation and not his drink.

"When you think about it, the ability to build those models reduces the risk to actually trying out different strategies or what have you in the world. Instead of trial and error—which can be fatal in the real world—you can test or discard a lot of more different approaches to a problem if you're doing it in the safe confines of a symbolic world, than you ever might in the real world."

"That sounds reasonable. So why isn't every animal intelligent?"

Claire paused before answering this one. She knew this was entering dangerous territory, and she didn't want him to write her off as a nut. "That's the heart of it, and I'm going to try to answer it as one of the great zoologists of our time did." She took a breath. "I'm in Donald Griffin's camp; I think almost every animal has *some* degree of intelligence—the stress here is on the word *some*." She tried to read Hayden's expression but couldn't. "Let me explain, because this context is crucial to what I think is going on with those bones."

"I'm listening," said Hayden noncommittally.

"Griffin argued that nature could not hard wire every creature for every eventuality, that it was evolutionarily efficient to endow any creature with some degree of consciousness that might enable midcourse corrections as circumstances changed. There's a whole literature on examples of this, ranging down to scientists at Princeton showing that honeybees exercise some degree of judgment when interpreting the dance that scout bees perform to show the hive the location and richness of sources of honey." Claire thought a minute. "Want to hear how? It's a bit of a digression, but it's almost comical."

"Sure, why not?"

"OK, bees send out scouts to locate sources of pollen. The scouts then return and, by what's called a 'waggle' dance, tell the other bees how much and where the pollen is. Then they fly back along with a posse of other bees. Still with me?"

Hayden nodded.

"So, some evil scientists at Princeton brought some pollen and some bees out to the middle of Lake Carnegie in a rowboat and then released them. When these bees returned to the hive and did their waggle dance, almost no bees followed them. In effect, the bees were saying, 'You can't be serious. Pollen in the middle of a lake!'"

Hayden laughed.

"If, by their actions, bees indicated that they were weighing the credibility of information brought by other bees, Griffin argued that this implied that something more than a genetically wired response was at work."

"So how does nature sort out which animals need more and which less of this magic ability?"

"Again, exactly the right question!" Claire knew she was laying it on—she was doing everything but batting her eyes—but it *was* the right question. "Diverting energy to build and run a bigger brain inevitably involves a trade-off with an animal's strength and speed. I think the principle of 'if it ain't broke, don't fix it' comes into play here."

"So, in evolutionary terms, when the world changes for whatever reason," said Hayden, "those with slightly more ability to assess tend to have an advantage over the dumber of their species. So the specialists die out and the generalists survive and breed."

Claire looked at Hayden with genuine surprise. It had taken her years to develop her perspective on intelligence. "Do you by chance happen to have an advanced degree in evolutionary biology?"

Hayden laughed. "That's just common sense—and I suspect it isn't as simple as that."

"Nothing ever is. Because change begets change, and changes that are derivative can have their own impacts that eventually become primary."

"Better put that in plain English. I'm a simple geologist."

"I don't believe that for a second!" Claire said, "But here goes: let's say change happens, maybe it's the climate, maybe something else. And one species of animal discovers that those better equipped to form groups and work together have an advantage over those that go it alone. Well, as the group gets larger, those in the group better equipped to understand social dynamics tend to have an advantage. Maybe the clever ones discover that forming alliances neutralizes advantages in strength others might have; maybe they figure out that by coordinating they can kill bigger game than an individual can; maybe some figure out that they can fool others in the group for their own purposes. The point is that being in the group itself sets in motion a set of selective pressures for bigger brains that speed the evolution of intelligence more than simply reacting to the external change in the first place."

She looked at Hayden. "Are you with me?" He nodded. "OK, good," she continued. "So at some point the real selective pressure *can*—key word—shift from being the smartest at adapting to the outside world to being the smartest in the group. And, because the group is now big enough and robust enough to deal with the challenges of getting food, on the one hand, the risks of shifting blood from the muscles to the brain become less onerous, and, on the other hand, the selective pressures to be the best and brightest within the group accelerate. So, ta-da!" She gestured triumphantly to some imaginary brain with her left hand. "You get runaway brain growth. That happened with us in spades, but I'd argue that it has happened to varying degrees with other animals as well."

Hayden spent a long time digesting what Claire had just said. "So, when you look at intelligence in terms of what it does rather than what it is, you see it as an adaptive strategy that nature might produce in varying degrees depending on the circumstances?" Claire nodded excitedly. "And," he went on, "that would be why the highly social creatures would be more intelligent. I can see that with dolphins and humans and what I've read about chimps. What else?"

"Think big," said Claire.

"Whales?"

"Sure. What else?"

"Elephants?"

Claire didn't say anything. She simply nodded.

"And we're sure those are elephant bones?"

Claire got more cautious. "We can't say anything with certainty at this point, but the strong odds are that they are some form of elephant ancestor. We'll find out—that's a huge deal in and of itself, by the way."

Again there was a long pause before Hayden said, "So this might be evidence of some ancient intelligent elephant?"

"Anything's possible at this point, but everything points to some intelligence at work."

"Say it turns out to be an intelligent ancient elephant; how could we know if its intelligence was similar to ours?"

"If this does point to some ancient intelligence, elephant or otherwise, it might well be very different, but there is one strong theme in evolution that would suggest that it would be familiar to us in some way."

"What's that?"

"It's called convergent evolution. Here's an example: anteaters and pangolins have entirely different evolutionary histories, but they are shaped almost exactly alike. That's because, over millions of years, nature optimized their snouts and strong forearms to digging for their prey underground. If there is an optimum physical shape for various physical tasks, it's likely that nature will also converge on the optimum design for mental tasks. That's not to say there wouldn't be different strokes for different folks, but there likely would be basic elements of consciousness that smarter creatures would converge on."

"So a dolphin dealing with managing his relationships in a group might think to some degree like a chimp?"

"That's what *I* think. Because while their worlds are utterly different, there are some big similarities in the social pressures of thriving in a large group—who's Mr. Big, who can you trust, who can you not trust, who can you *fool*? What you find is that they resort to a lot of the strategies we use in competing and negotiating with their peers, and that makes it possible that they might think in similar ways as well."

"Then, according to the world you describe, it's got different . . . very different animals, but similar social pressures supercharging brain growth. In some respects, a chimp, a dolphin, an elephant, and a human would have a mix of the various types of intelligence people have identified—social, emotional, quantitative, etc." Claire nodded. "So, help me visualize this." Hayden thought a minute about how best to frame his question. "What's one game that all these different creatures might play if this convergent evolution was at work?"

It was an interesting question worthy of a serious answer. After a couple of minutes, Claire looked at Hayden. "Poker."

"Poker? Not chess?"

"Yes. You can't win at poker if you just have quantitative skills. Proof of that is that many online poker stars crash and burn when they play face-to-face. In order to win at poker, you need quantitative skills and memory, but you also need what's called metacognition—the ability to understand and manipulate another's beliefs—and you need emotional intelligence, social intelligence, and the ability to modify your own reactions to stress and excitement. Yes, poker."

"Why not chess?"

Claire had thought about this many times. "Chess requires a type of pure intelligence, but it requires no social intelligence. You can mislead in chess, but you cannot bluff."

Hayden thought about that. "Poker," he said again. "I like that!"

As Hayden reflected on what they had just discussed, Claire looked around the room. It was truly bizarre to be having this conversation with someone she didn't know in a room that might have been in a tony club in London. She cautioned herself that the audition was not over. Hayden might be the intellectual soul mate she had been looking for and still not protect her research because the needs of the concession trumped his hobby. Still, he seemed genuinely engaged.

"What you've said has got me thinking in about a dozen different directions," Hayden said with a smile. He glanced at his watch. "But we've been talking for an hour. Maybe we should continue over dinner?"

Once they were seated in the dining room, a waiter presented Claire with a menu. Naturally there was a steak—this was a mining concession, after all—but another choice was vegetable curry over rice, with the notation that the vegetables were from the concessions hydroponic greenhouse. She chose the curry, as did Hayden, and when the waiter appeared with both red and white wines, she chose the red, mainly because the blue-and-red coat of arms on the label of the Mascarello Barolo made it look expensive. The waiter brought salads of baby lettuce. "Grown here, hydroponic, using waste heat," Hayden said, waving toward the west. Then he changed the topic. "Tell me a little about how you got to Kazakhstan."

For the next few minutes, Claire gave him a candid recounting of her career, about abandoning an earlier interest in animal intelligence for work on more easily provable abilities, and how her success in this more mundane avenue of research led Delamain to ask her to take over the Kazakh project. She then told him how Delamain had promptly fired her and told her never to darken their door again after her adventure with the bones. She knew that she was supposed to be selling herself, but in this day of web data immortality, even the most cursory due diligence on his part would turn up anything she tried to hide.

Hayden chuckled. "I've been pitched by a lot of people over the years." He laughed more and took a sip of wine. "But that may be the worst job of selling yourself that I've ever encountered. Seriously, though, you were willing to jeopardize your career over this?"

Claire flushed and forced herself to count to ten. "Actually," she said in what she hoped was a conversational voice, "I think the fact that the scientific disciplines are too hidebound and tribal to acknowledge that the study of the evolution and nature of intelligence has to be interdisciplinary doesn't mean that I have to wait for the world to catch up."

"Attagirl!" Hayden said and clapped his hands. "Only people with that kind of confidence and conviction ever get anything done." He held up a glass to toast her. Claire somewhat shyly brought up her own glass to clink. "I was just pulling your chain."

"Well, to tell the truth, a few days ago, when things hit rock bottom, I did briefly fantasize about becoming a real estate agent."

Hayden laughed again. "Glad you didn't act on that impulse." He smiled. "For one thing, you'd be terrible at it. I can just see you saying that the roof leaked, and the basement floods, and pointing out the termites marching across the floor."

Claire clapped her hands in delight. "And then when they still wanted to close, I'd say, 'And then there's the toxic mold!'"

They ate in silence for a couple of minutes. Then Hayden said, "You know, I've been thinking about a lot of the same things you're studying, but from an entirely different angle."

Claire looked up, curious.

"Yeah, entirely different," Hayden went on. "It's along the lines of your 'intelligence is as intelligence does' theme. What intrigues me—a lot—is how capricious the march of civilization has been. For instance, at least some of the ancient Greek thinkers realized that the earth was round, but then civilization forgot that for eighteen hundred years. Why did it take several thousand years to invent the rolling suitcase?"

Claire laughed.

"Yeah," Hayden continued, "so much was determined by accident. It seems inevitable in retrospect, but it was really set in motion by some insignificant event. Maybe intelligence is the ultimate complex, non-linear system."

"If that was the case, I'd give up right now," said Claire, "but I think that studying intelligence in an evolutionary context could tell us a lot about who we are, where we came from, and whether there are other intelligences out there. I think that's worth pursuing."

"I agree," said Hayden, "but getting back to that idea of the accidental nature of progress, here's another aspect that intrigues me—and actually ties into your present predicament."

Claire had no idea where he was going, but this change of direction made her nervous.

"Turn it around. Another aspect of the haphazard course of progress is when the collective intelligence of a group is ignored. In other words, what gets in the way of intelligence being deployed?"

Claire got it. "Well, I mentioned that in science there's a kind of tribal mentality that rejects anything that comes from the outside," she said. "But what were you thinking?"

"This may surprise you, coming from a mining guy, but one example is the way in which your country—I'm Canadian, as you may know—has for three decades ignored a huge body of science on climate change. Going back to what I was saying about the capricious nature of progress, do you think five hundred years from now, historians—if there are any—are going to look at the present era and say, 'Oh, their scientists predicted that humanity was causing climate catastrophe and society took steps to avert it,' or will they say, 'What a bunch of dolts?'"

Claire nodded, though she still couldn't see the connection. "So, what do you think interferes with a group acting on its collective brainpower?"

"That's what I'm getting to. It's very hard for a geologist to believe that there are educated people who still believe the earth is only five thousand years old, but there are. Ideology, really religion in another form, can also gum up the works. Plenty of conservatives, for instance, who might otherwise understand the threat of climate change, can't get past the idea that the threat is exaggerated to pave the way for world government. Then there's self-interest, which is the reason that many of my colleagues in the extractive industries aren't going to admit that anything is a problem that might impede their livelihood."

Claire still didn't get the connection. "You said this connected to my predicament, how?" she asked.

"Right," he said, "sorry. Several ways. In a perfect world, what would have happened is that Transteppe and the Kazakh government should have fast-tracked approval for you to study the lip in place. Had they done that, you would never have been driving that Land Cruiser off the road and cracked the array, right?"

"Right!"

"But that was never going to happen. So you ran afoul of the self-interest of several different parties, Transteppe—I've gotta admit that had Rob and Sergei gone through channels, management here would have ixnayed the project in anticipation of the Kazakh authorities, whose self-interest was also to ignore or bury this find. Then there was Delamain, whose self-interest caused them to throw you under the bus."

Claire marveled at the ever-growing population of people who seemed to be very good at summing up why she was screwed. "And then," she said, picking up the thread, "there's the fact that without Delamain I've become some sort of ronin researcher without affiliation, so that even if this is the greatest find in history, I face a wall of skepticism."

Hayden looked amused again. "I was getting to that. I've got to say, you've got a genius for helping others find cracks in your armor."

Claire froze, realizing what she had just said. In a quiet voice she asked, "Are you thinking of replacing me?"

Hayden smiled with genuine warmth and put a hand on her arm. "Not for a minute! For one thing, Rob and Sergei wouldn't stand for it, particularly Sergei."

The tensions of the past few weeks flooded through her. She couldn't help it; she started sobbing quietly. Hayden tentatively started to put a comforting arm around her, but she shook her head. "I'm sorry. I'm *such* a girl. Just give me a minute." She dabbed her eyes and smiled. "It's been a tough few days." She was mortified, and the thought entered her mind that this was probably the first time anyone had ever cried in Transteppe's VIP dining room.

"I can well imagine." Hayden again looked at his watch. "We've got to join the others, but I'm going to tell you a few things. First off, I admire that you're willing to take a lonely path to pursue what's important. I am serious about archaeology, but while you might have problems with credibility because your work doesn't neatly fit in some discipline, I've got the opposite problem."

"I don't understand."

"It's not revealing any great secret to admit that I've made some money. That opens doors, because everyone is hoping for support in one way or another. Hell, I could make a big donation and buy ten tables at a gala and be made Man of the Year by organizations that hate mining. But that's meaningless. Having money—and I'm not complaining, mind you—means I'm never really certain how to gauge the significance of my archaeology, for instance."

"At this point, I wish I had that problem."

Hayden chuckled. "Here's the bottom line: whichever way things turn out, this discovery is truly exciting. I'm going to support it." Claire's heart leaped. "I've got to figure out the best way, and you've got to work on finding an affiliation with a credible institution, but I think I can make sure that you can pursue the analysis with fewer distractions for the next few weeks." He scraped his chair back and started to get up. "Now, let's go find Rob and Sergei."

For Claire, the rest of the evening was a blur. She barely noticed that Rob pulled Hayden aside for a conversation. Rob said a few short sentences. Then they both subtly glanced at Sergei. As the Russian approached, she put it out of her head.

"I heard things went well," said Sergei. He put a warm hand on her shoulder. "I'm so glad."

"Yes, they went well," said Claire. Holding his gaze she said, "Thank you."

Later, before she fell asleep, she realized there was something nagging at the back of her mind. Something wasn't right back at the camp. She reviewed what had happened since she had gone back to collect her stuff. Then it came to her. Sauat. Where was Sauat? Exhausted, she reassured herself that he was around somewhere and fell asleep thinking of Sergei. She had discovered that imagining him as a windsurfer always could put a smile on her face.

28

BEZANOV LISTENED TO THE LATEST REPORT FROM TRANSTEPPE. It was not from Sergei, but from his other, more lethal, set of eyes on the ground. The Project, of which Bezanov was just a part, though an important one, was approaching a sensitive stage, and he decided that it was better not to ask the geologist questions that might give some hint of what was up. He also thought it useful to get some ground truthing of what he had been hearing from Sergei.

By the end of the call, the oligarch was thoroughly alarmed. The woman had gone to Astana with the head of security and returned with some Kazakh whom everyone treated with great deference. Worse, a major Transteppe board member, one who represented the big Canadian interests, had shown up unexpectedly. Ostensibly, this had something to do with the archaeological find. This led to some interesting thought trains: a find that enticed a board member halfway around the world was a lot more significant than what Sergei had described—a black mark for Sergei. But, if he was being straightforward, then the find was a cover for something bigger. But what?

Bezanov was pleased that he had had the foresight to implant someone besides Sergei at Transteppe. Until now, he had used the man to keep an eye on Sergei. Now, however, he might have use for some of the contact's darker skills, which were considerable.

He realized the man was waiting for further instructions. "I might need you to go active," he said. "I'll let you know soon."

After he put down the phone, Bezanov thought a bit more about the mystery woman and whatever it was that allowed her to have the highest officials at Transteppe at her beck and call. "I think I have to meet this woman," he said to himself.

29

THE NEXT MORNING, CLAIRE DROVE A TRANSTEPPE PICKUP TO what had been her camp. She owed it to her former team to help make the transition to Benoit as smooth as possible, but she needed to make the point that it would be best for science if they continued to work together—though separately—and, most of all, she needed to let Benoit know that she was willing to collaborate. She could handle numbers one and two, she thought as she pulled into the camp. Number three was going to be a tall order.

Once she arrived, it was clear that Benoit was not going to make it any easier. Not that he was hostile—far from it. It was his breezy sense of entitlement that put her off. He was sitting at a table in the picnic area when she drove in and gave her a laconic, friendly wave, as though it was the most natural thing in the world that he should be taking over her project. Claire pulled over and tried to get command of her temper. As she walked up the hill, she imagined Benoit wearing a polka-dot clown suit and a cap with a propeller on it, and that helped.

The real Benoit, as opposed to the clown in her imagination, was a handsome, trim, dark-haired man in his mid-thirties. He was wearing jeans and a loose-fitting gray shirt that was probably better suited for the streets of Soho than the steppes of central Asia. Claire had to admit, paleontology's newest superstar wore his confidence well.

"No hard feelings?" Benoit asked as he took her hand.

"This find is too important for hard feelings," said Claire truthfully.

Benoit breathed a sigh of relief. "Amen to that!"

The two sat down. Claire let the silence build. Finally Benoit spread his hands. "Now what?"

"You've met the team?"

"Sure, all good . . . ," said Benoit, drumming his fingers on the picnic table as though he was playing something on the piano. "All good," he repeated absently. "We've already started on the analysis on that petrified bone you so kindly left for us." There definitely was something lurking behind that statement.

"That's what I was hoping to hear," she said. "I can't think of anyone better to help describe this find and place it in an ecological context," she went on, hoping that he took notice of the word *help*.

"Thank you . . . yeah, once we get a better date, we can focus on what was going on with climate at that time and whether it was a period of rapid speciation for other mammals . . ." He trailed off. "And what are you going to be doing?"

Claire could tell that he hated having to ask that question. It was dawning on him that he didn't hold all the cards.

"Oh, we've just begun looking at the rest of the lip—might be much more in there."

Hearing this, Benoit looked down at the table. Clearly, he wanted in on this.

The remaining team started trickling out of the mess tent. When Tony saw that Benoit was talking with Claire, he started heading over. Claire waved him off.

"One other thing," Claire said to Benoit.

She paused, about to step into a minefield. "I've established contact with a distinguished Kazakh archaeologist, Timur Tabiliev, who's agreed to work with us." She looked at Benoit to see whether he realized the import of what she was saying. "It would be terrific if you could arrange to work with him as well . . . it would simplify things . . ." She trailed off.

Benoit stared. She realized that he had met Tamerlan. He looked anguished. After a couple of awkward moments, he said, "That sounds logical, and I hope that comes to pass. Delamain was adamant that I work through established channels. I'm sure you understand."

What Claire understood was that her troubles were not over—and that Benoit's had only just begun.

"OK, that's that," she said, starting to get up. "By the way, analyzing the bones is truly important, but I'm going to be focusing on the array and what it means." She let that sentence hang.

"Ah yes, the array." Benoit knew that finding a new species of ancient elephant was a big deal, but that the array was the biggest deal ever. Benoit reached over and grabbed his laptop. "Just a sec before you leave . . ." Claire sat back down.

He opened the computer, fired it up, and hit a few rapid keystrokes. He looked intently at something running on the screen and then nodded, satisfied. "I've been doing some noodling. Take a look at this." He slid the computer over so that Claire could see the screen and then hit a button.

Claire nearly snorted. She had come upon things like this all the time when working on animal intelligence. What Benoit had done was program a series of simulations. Using crude caricatures of elephant skeletons, the simulation showed a series of elephants falling and dying in some elephant graveyard. As the simulation progressed, a timeline at the bottom marked the passage of years. Bones fell and settled in random ways. One ulna settled into the muck, then some years later, another, then another, until there were five ulnae side by side, looking as if they had been purposefully arrayed. When the series finished, she gave Benoit a withering look. "Seriously?"

Benoit held up his hands. "I'm not saying this is what happened. I'm just showing you what a reductionist might use. You know, Occam's razor, Morgan's canon, and all that."

She wasn't sure whether Benoit was trying to give her an honest warning or subtly suggest that he would make a formidable opponent. She chose to look on the bright side. "I agree, Benoit," she said with a smile, "a reductionist would use that, but do you really think that's the most likely explanation?" She got up again. "I've got a couple of things to do before I head back."

Before leaving the Quonset, she turned back to him. "Let's keep in touch." Claire took a couple of steps. "Really? Benoit, what are the odds? Even over thousands of years, there wouldn't be that many elephants, and for the ulnae to fall just so . . . ?" She turned, shaking her head.

As she walked into the heat, Benoit, who had followed her out of the Quonset, called after her, "I'm just trying to give you a picture of what you're likely to be up against."

She had to admit he was right about that.

"Thanks, Benoit." She turned around. "You know, it would actually be good news if we were attacked in the way you modeled"—Claire waved her hand at his computer—"because if I'm attacked in the way you describe, it means I've won the battle over whether there were elephants in Kazakhstan five million years ago, and that's a pretty big deal in itself."

Not waiting for a reply, she turned to find Tony and Waylon. She had only taken a few steps when she remembered her last thought from the previous night. Sauat? She stopped by his room and knocked. No answer. Ordinarily this would be no cause for concern, but given the events of the past week, Claire was worried. She did a quick reconnoiter of the camp. He wasn't there; nobody had seen him. Claire sat down in the picnic area, fished around in her purse and pulled out the scrap of paper Tegev had given to her before departing. She hesitated a minute. What if he was just out jogging? But Sauat didn't strike her as the jogging type. She dialed the number. The call went to voice mail, and she recognized Tegev's voice as he said what she assumed was the equivalent of "Please leave a message" in Kazakh. Claire left her number and asked him to call her back.

Claire tracked down Tony and Waylon. Her original intent had been to talk to them about the logistics, but her concerns about Sauat caused her to put that aside and urge them to contact her if they heard any news of his whereabouts. She left a note for Sauat in his room. Still worried, she headed back to Transteppe.

30

CLAIRE BEGAN HER NEW JOB BY GETTING UP AT DAWN AND heading over to the warehouse. She wanted to spend some time alone with the lip. The huge warehouse was still, quiet, and cool when she arrived. The lights had been turned down overnight, and in the pale dawn light, the lip looked like something alien hovering above the floor. Claire walked around it slowly.

Close inspection of its surfaces revealed nothing that might suggest more bones or other objects. The rough monolith had kept its secrets for five million years, and those to discover its secrets were going to have to work hard. Claire's reverie was broken as she heard a door open. Sergei arrived with two cups of coffee. He hadn't seen her, and she was about to walk over when he picked up his phone and made a call. He had a brief conversation in Russian. In stark contrast to his usual animated style, his voice was flat, even harsh. As he hung up, he noticed Claire.

"What was that about?" She tried to keep her voice as neutral as possible.

If Sergei was startled, he didn't show it. "Oh, every now and then, I check in with Primorskichem, a company that is a partner in Transteppe. Mostly, I try to discourage them from visiting."

Claire laughed. It sounded plausible. She hadn't known about the Russian partner, but Sergei had never really said how he got to Transteppe.

"Did you tell them about the bones?"

"No, I tell them as little as possible."

Sergei looked over at the lip as he handed Claire a cup of coffee.

"I thought you might be here," said Sergei. "Like a kid getting up early for Christmas, yes?" As she sipped, she looked around the room. Once again, her pulse quickened as she scanned the cornucopia of remote sensing equipment in the warehouse. After some discussion, they decided to first have a go with X-ray computed tomography, familiar to most people from medical CAT scans. For objects as thick as the lip, the machine had to have a very high-energy source to penetrate the rock without signal distortion. Sergei had written the computer algorithms that would differentiate the materials scanned according to density and their atomic properties. A contraption directed beams from both the top and bottom, which sat on a trolley that could be run along a flexible track. By bombarding the lip with X-rays from different angles, the device could create thousands of slices that could be processed into a composite view. It wouldn't be as precise as a medical CT scan, but it could show them where, if anywhere, something might be located in the rock.

"Right now, I'm assuming you just want to see whether there's any more fossilized bone in there. So, we're not going to do the most precise imaging. OK?"

Claire nodded, and they got to work. It took the rest of the morning and assistance from a couple of workers Sergei press-ganged into helping to get the equipment set up.

Sergei looked at his handiwork with approval. "We'll do some passes, and while you're interpreting the results, I'll do some work for my day job." Sergei compiled the results and then cleared a workspace for Claire.

As Sergei worked, Claire looked at the Russian scientist with approval, and not just for his facility with the analytical equipment. She was attracted to his mind, and, she had to admit, his body, but there were quintessentially Russian paradoxes about the man. He came with baggage—he'd admitted as much—but she trusted him. There was an endearing quality to his energy and enthusiasm that spoke to simplicity even though she knew he was anything but simple. There was no denying that she was beginning to feel an easy intimacy around Sergei, which was the biggest paradox of all, since that feeling was something she would treasure with a boyfriend, and her relationship with Sergei was purely professional. *That's going to change*, she thought, turning her attention back to work.

Sergei set her up with a computer with her own log-in and strong security. He then transferred his results to a flash drive and handed it to her. Once it was loaded on her computer, he showed her how to massage the data so that different substances would show up as different colors. Among the files he had transferred was one where he had analyzed the fossilized bone from one of the ulnae. He assigned the color red to its mineral profile so that she could easily identify other fossils if more were concealed within the rock. "I'm going to put in a few other tags—there might be interesting minerals in the area." He looked at Claire with an eyebrow raised.

She could hardly say no. "Sure."

"OK, and I'm going to assign the color purple for anything other than the dominant rock and the tags we've specified." That done, he then set up a secure link to Transteppe's processors. Compiling the data required massive computing power.

He walked her through how to use the program. Then he erased the data from his own computer. "That's it. You can go to village!" Seeing her roll her eyes, he sighed. "OK, no more Russian movie villain bad guy act. Go to town!"

Claire smiled. "That would be most kind."

Claire was itching to go to "village" on the imaging. It seemed like months since she'd last focused on the prehistoric ulnae, but it had really only been a couple of weeks since Rob had showed up at her Quonset. What was the significance of ulnae? She had no idea what to expect, but the prospect of peering inside the lip without blindly digging was thrilling. Claire tried to keep her hopes from skyrocketing. Wind, rain, even the movement of the great tectonic plates had had millions of years to move things around.

Her computer estimated the amount of time remaining for Transteppe's processors to finish compiling the three-dimensional profile at one and a half hours. She couldn't sit still. She decided to use the time to set up a work plan with Katie and Francisco.

First, she decided to see how Lawrence was doing. She wandered over to the provisions warehouse. There was a Kazakh worker sitting outside smoking. Claire smiled and tried to remember the Kazakh word for cat. The man stood up. First she tried English. "Is there a new cat around here?" The man looked at her blankly. OK, so a game of charades. Claire reached down and pretended to pet an imaginary cat. Now the man got it.

"Mu-sick," he said, and then went on in what for Claire was an unintelligible string of phrases. She gathered from his enthusiasm that Lawrence had hit it off with the staff.

She put her hands up, palms extended out in the universal gesture for "where."

He pointed inside the storehouse.

She found Lawrence snoozing happily beside an empty food bowl. He seemed very pleased to see her and let her pick him up. He might have put on an ounce or two. He purred loudly while she petted him and asked him how his new job as mouser was going. If the empty food bowl could be taken as evidence, she suspected that motivational problems might already have surfaced.

Claire looked at her watch and realized that there wasn't much time left before the compilation was finished. Giving Lawrence a final pat on the head, she hustled off in search of Katie and Francisco.

She found them in the cafeteria. They were both dressed in lightweight cotton outfits. Claire couldn't help noticing that even the simple outfit looked sexy on Katie. Sergei might have noticed, too. *Why am I acting like I'm fourteen?* she thought as she grabbed a coffee and the three of them walked back over to the warehouse. She explained how Sergei had set things up. When they got there, Francisco whistled at the technological arsenal. "They must have huge computing power. Wonder what they use it for?"

Claire shrugged. It was an interesting question.

While they were going over details, Claire heard a ping and looked over at her computer. The imaging was completed.

Claire sat down and waved Francisco and Katie over. Sergei's program allowed the user to move the mouse along the object being imaged. If Claire clicked on any particular location, she could zoom in and study it in more detail. Claire took a deep breath and called up the image. They were looking at the whole lip, which necessitated the lowest possible resolution, but all could see that there were a number of objects that showed up as red. No one said a word.

Claire moved the mouse over to one splotch. It looked like a rack of jumbo-size baby back ribs. She tried to zoom in on the object, but Sergei had sacrificed resolution for speed in this preliminary run, and they couldn't quite make out what the object was or indeed whether it was composed of several objects arranged in parallel. She couldn't say it was another array, but it didn't matter; it was fossilized bone.

Claire looked at her hands. They were trembling. Claire turned to Katie. "Let's write down this precise location, just in case."

Katie nodded, wide-eyed. Francisco murmured softly, "Absolution."

Claire turned back to the image. "We'll come back to that." She moved the mouse to another red splotch. Could it be a very large cranium? They couldn't be sure.

Katie was staring at another object on the screen. "Can we take a closer look at that?" she asked, pointing to a round object. It was purple, the catch-all tag assigned to anomalous materials that were different than the surrounding stone.

Claire tried to zoom in. It was definitely round. "Maybe it's just a stone."

"Sure looks like an elephant foot." Katie peered at the screen. "But the soft tissue of an elephant foot wouldn't be fossilized, and this is different than the bones according to your color scheme." She shrugged. "OK, thanks, just thought it was worth a look."

Claire looked at it more closely. "Mark it down anyway—insurance against regrets later." Her voice had returned to normal.

They all stared at the screen a bit more.

Claire picked up a radio. She decided that this was a good excuse to call Sergei.

She could hear heavy machinery and wind in the background when he picked up. "Something tells me this is a case where good news travels faster than bad news, yes?"

"Oh yes! Can you get back here?"

"On my way."

She turned to Katie and Francisco. "I think Hayden would want to see this." Claire started to walk away. Then she stopped. A wave of pure happiness washed over her.

31

SHE FOUND HAYDEN IN THE BOARDROOM. HE WAS TALKING with Ripley, the site manager. Was she imagining things, or did she hear one of them mention Sergei?

"I can come back later." She started to leave.

"Hold it." Hayden turned to Ripley and added, "OK if we finish this in a bit?"

If Ripley was irritated, he didn't show it. "No worries, I've got to deal with a foreman—someone hurt his feelings." He arched an eyebrow. "Who knew that foremen had feelings?"

Hayden laughed and got up to greet Claire. "There's news?"

Claire simply held up her hands and said, "Eureka!" Then she did a quick vaudevillian two-step, tipping an imaginary hat.

Hayden was already heading for the door. When they got to the warehouse, Sergei was already there, staring at the screen. He looked up and, seeing Hayden and Claire, stepped back so they could see the image.

"Sergei used the atomic signal and density of the fossilized bone as a search criterion for the scan. The matching areas are tagged in red."

Hayden peered intently. "Is that what I think it is?" he asked, moving the cursor over to the rectangular splotch.

"That's what I'm hopin'," said Claire, nodding vigorously.

Hayden continued exploring the image, pausing over the other red splotch. Something seemed to catch his attention. He moved the cursor over to a green tag. "What's this?"

Claire shrugged. "Dunno." She turned to the Russian. "Sergei?"

Claire was surprised to see Sergei give the slightest start. "Let me see," he said, moving toward the screen. Sergei's reaction had been fleeting, but Claire thought that he had to know every marker instantaneously—after all, he had set them up.

Sergei took the mouse and clicked on the green tag in a box below the screen. "Phospherite," he said, moving back.

Hayden looked straight at Sergei. "Phospherite?"

Now Sergei looked flustered. "Yeah, sedimentary rock, millions of years of deposition, perfect conditions to find phospherite. Seemed like it was worth marking."

What was going on? Claire looked at both men.

If the explanation didn't satisfy Hayden, he wasn't letting on—or he wasn't going to get into it here. He gave Sergei a quick look and returned to the screen.

After a few more seconds looking at the red splotches, Hayden swiveled to face the group.

"Well, it looks like things are going to get very exciting." He turned to Claire. "What are your plans?"

"We know where to dig, so I'd like to get right to it. I'd also like to invite Dr. Tabiliev to come out to observe." Hayden nodded his agreement, and Claire went on. "If in fact these are more fossil remains, I think we write up a systematic description of the find—fast—and send it as a letter to a refereed journal, basically to put a stake in the ground. Then we can try to figure out exactly what is going on."

Again Hayden nodded. "Sounds good. I'll OK the helicopter once Tabiliev agrees to come." He got up and looked at Claire. "Let's chat a sec. Can you walk me to the other building?" Before they left, he turned to the group. "It looks like we're on the verge of something extraordinary and wonderful. Let's make sure we do it right."

They walked out in to the sunlight. The superheated air shimmered off the hoods of passing vehicles. Hayden waited until they were out of earshot and then said to Claire, "I know you want to see what's in the rock, but I think we have to make sure that you have a credible institutional affiliation."

It was said in a friendly way, but clearly this was very important to Hayden. Claire nodded; she'd been thinking the same thing. "Agreed."

"So," Hayden continued, "is there some sort of kabuki dance to getting that done?"

Claire thought of the department chairman at Rushmere and laughed. "At most universities, it's more like a lap dance—money greases a lot of wheels."

"I'm not surprised. So let's get your university guy on Skype. Once you've made your pitch, I can ask him what hoops I have to jump through to get this funded."

Claire wasn't used to things going so well. "Thanks so much! If we try later tonight, it'll be morning in New Hampshire."

Hayden nodded. "Anything else you need?"

Claire thought of the one email she had not sent that first day. If ever there was a time to ask, this was it. "There is . . . assuming this is a new species, it is one more of a bunch of species of elephant-like animals that began to appear at the same time. One big missing piece in this puzzle is what was going on five and a half million years ago. We need the input of a credible, big-thinking polymath with an open mind, someone with the chops in geophysics, physical chemistry, and evolutionary biology who can help fit these bones into a context of what else was happening at that time."

Hayden was amused. "Such a person actually exists?"

"Oh yes."

"Why haven't you contacted him—or is it a her?"

Claire smiled. "I actually wrote him—it's a he—an email a few weeks ago but didn't send it."

"I see—he bites?"

Claire nodded. "You could say so. He doesn't suffer fools—or anyone, for that matter—gladly. But now, with the new stuff, I think I've got enough ammunition to tempt him."

"Is it a funding question?"

Claire shook her head. "I think he can do pretty much what he wants at this point."

"What's the problem, then?"

Claire squirmed. She looked at Hayden and spread her hands. "I'm scared of him."

Hayden laughed heartily. "Well, I'll be . . ." He laughed again. "I didn't think you were scared of anyone. I suppose I should be insulted. Well, get him out here. This is someone I want to meet. Does he have a name?"

"Willem Keerbrock."

"Oh, the MacArthur award winner, then Nobel in chemistry, too, right."

"And many other awards, too, most of which he doesn't show up to receive. He doesn't care about awards. What he does care about is a well-defended big idea. Hopefully this qualifies."

Claire thought about her own—traumatic—encounter with Keerbrock a decade earlier. It still left her feeling queasy. They walked in silence until they got to the office complex.

Before disappearing, he turned to her. "Get in touch when you get close to pulling something out of the rock. I want to be there." He turned to go in. Then he glanced at her face. "Something else?"

Claire wasn't sure if she should go ahead, but she was going to be working with Sergei, so it seemed OK to ask. She took a deep breath. "If this is confidential mining business, please tell me . . ." She paused to see his reaction, but his face gave away nothing.

"Ask. I'll tell you if it is."

Claire fidgeted. "OK, here goes: What's the significance of phospherite?"

"Let's talk inside." Hayden led her up to the boardroom, which he had commandeered as an office. He gestured for her to take a seat. He drummed his fingers on the table and then cleared his throat. He looked weary, and Claire thought that his interest in archaeology must also be a respite from a far more complicated world.

"If you're asking the significance of phospherite, that's easy. Phosphorous comes from phosphate rock, which is sometimes called phospherite. It's an essential building block for all living things." He looked directly at Claire. "But I think you're asking something else?"

Claire gave a quick, nervous nod.

Hayden paused a minute. He seemed to be making a decision. "OK, here are the bullet points: Only a few countries on the planet have significant deposits of phosphorous—the US, China, Morocco . . . and Kazakhstan. So phosphorous can be regarded as a strategic mineral. Russia, to the north, has very little. Russia is also increasingly isolated and could vastly improve its geopolitical position to the degree that it has access and control over strategic resources. You've probably followed how it keeps Europe in line through its control of natural gas pipelines. Now that game is ending, as Europe is rapidly developing alternative supplies, and they're looking for new leverage. You with me?" Claire nodded. "OK, here's a few more points: Kazakhstan was once part of the Soviet Union, but Kazakhstan's phosphorous deposits are hundreds of miles to the south; the Russia petrochemical giant Primorskichem is a twenty percent owner of Transteppe . . ." He paused again. "And Sergei is Russian . . . so I had to wonder why he was looking for phospherite way up here . . . so close to the border."

Claire's heart pounded. "Sergei's . . ." She shook her head. "Sergei's been nothing but helpful to me . . . I've got to give him the benefit of the doubt . . ." She trailed off.

"I agree, and I like Sergei very much." Hayden offered a tired smile. "Here's a question of my own: Have you ever met an uncomplicated Russian?" He wasn't looking for an answer. Almost as an afterthought, he added, "And it was Primorskichem that put him up for the job. And more than once he's been overheard speaking Russian on the phone—that's what Rob was telling me when we met for a drink."

By this point Claire did not want to hear any more. She had also heard Sergei speaking Russian on the phone. "I've got to believe in him."

"So do I." Hayden tapped a finger as though pondering whether he should say more. "But what if he's being squeezed . . . what if they have something on him and they're forcing him to do something? And if that's the case, why would they be doing that—what's the agenda?"

He paused again. "I trust Sergei, but not for a New York minute do I trust our Russian partners, and by that I don't just mean the chemical company, but its unofficial ties to the Russian government. I knew this from the get-go, and, if I did anything good during the negotiations that set up the partnership, it was insisting on strong fraudulent conveyances language that could be used to unwind a transaction should Primorskichem try to strong-arm a takeover." He gave a short laugh. "*That* should stop them in their tracks! Right," he added bitterly.

As Claire walked back to the giant shed, she thought about Hayden's candor. He worked in an entirely different context, one that trumped and trivialized the academic and scientific hurdles she was dealing with. It was inspiring that he devoted so much attention to the discovery. True, the scientific issues she was pursuing were momentous, and ultimately could impact the world, but the flashpoint Hayden was concerned with had the potential for great power conflict and might impact the world in a much more immediate way.

Her thoughts turned back to Sergei, and a question popped into her head, one that she should have posed to Hayden. When Sergei marked various minerals with tags, he knew that Hayden would see them, and he also knew that he would probably ask about them. If he did have a hidden agenda involving phosphates, and if Sergei was as brilliant as she thought he was, why would he do something so obvious?

The answer was also obvious. He was trying to tell them something. A conversation she had had with Sergei a few weeks back came back to her. They had been talking about what it was like, growing up in Russia.

It started off light enough. "It's an upside world," he had said.

"Upside down?"

"Yes, upside down. In the West you have laws to make society function better. In my country we have many more laws. In theory we should be the best-functioning society on earth! Instead Russia is one of the least functional societies in the world. A functioning society is not the purpose of our laws. They only exist to give those in control leverage. And they always get it because it is not possible to get through a day in Russia without breaking some law. And then, if you rise to the attention of those in power—in my case expressing an opinion at a rally protesting the murder of a journalist—they always have something."

"They?"

Sergei waved a hand. "Oligarchs, organs of state, affiliates of what we used to call the *nomenklatura*."

"Do they have something on you?"

He grew guarded. "Even if they don't, they find a way to get leverage."

Claire had been alarmed. "What do they have? What do they want?"

Sergei had cut the conversation off. "Listen to me!" he'd said back then. "I would never do anything to hurt Rob, Mr. Hayden, and most of all, you."

32

BY THE TIME CLAIRE RETURNED, SERGEI AND THE TEAM HAD already run a more detailed scan of the lip that promised to hold more fossilized bone.

Katie looked at Claire. "Something wrong?"

Claire realized that she had been staring absently at Sergei. She blushed in spite of herself. "Nope, not a thing. Let's go in."

After two hours of careful cutting with a handheld trim saw, they were at the edge of the intriguing red rectangle. They cut it out as a block with enough margin that they were sure they were not damaging anything inside. With the help of a technician, Katie and Francisco did some more detailed imaging of the block, while Sergei and Claire started cutting toward the other red splotch. By five o'clock they had placed both blocks on stands so that they could begin the delicate task of uncovering what was within.

What had been a rectangular blotch in the first low-resolution scan was now revealed to be a near duplicate of the first array. That there were two identical arrays mooted the issue raised by Benoit about co-incidence. Someone—something—had arranged those bones. Under higher-resolution scrutiny, the second blotch turned out to look very much like a cranium. They decided to expose it first, as it would tell them a lot about what sort of animal this was, if, in fact, the ulnae came from the same species. It would take some time to chip away the rock surrounding the cranium, but Claire had printed some of the high-resolution images and she was feeling fairly well armed for her conversation with William Friedl, the head of the psych department at Rushmere.

Sergei was starting to put away the saws when Katie spoke up. "Uh, boss? While we've got the saws out, can we cut out the elephant foot–like thingy?"

Claire, focused on the bones, had forgotten about that purple blotch. "Good idea."

Another two hours of cutting and a third block was sitting on a stand. "This one's your baby," said Claire to Katie as she got ready to leave and prepare for her scheduled conversation with the department chair at Rushmere.

She had decided to divulge the discovery of the cranium but not yet mention the second array. Years of butting her head against the behavioral science establishment convinced her that it would be an easier sell to pitch a new species and hold the second array in reserve as a trump card. The rat runners were not going to greet the news of an ancient intelligence with open arms.

She was not wrong. "Let me get this straight," said Friedl after Claire had laid out her pitch for Rushmere's sponsorship of her work. "You go rogue on Delamain and the Kazakh government, and then you come to the chair of the psych department for sponsorship of a paleontology project and ask me to put the prestige of Rushmere behind a project studying evidence of intelligence millions of years before intelligence was invented? How am I doing so far?"

This was not really far from what Claire expected, though this time, she wasn't coming to Friedl hat in hand. "Well, Bill," she began, "if you put it *that* way, it doesn't sound very promising at all."

"What other way should I put it?"

"That even without the exploration of intelligence, Rushmere has the chance to get credit for the truly groundbreaking discovery that a previously unknown species of elephant ancestor lived more than five million years ago in a place never before known to have elephants." Claire dropped her voice to a near whisper. "And the dig comes fully funded."

There was a moment of silence. "Did I hear that right? With fifty percent overhead for the department?"

"Just a sec . . ." Claire turned to Hayden, who had been watching the interchange with an amused smile. She turned back to the screen. "There's someone I'd like you to meet."

After Hayden and Friedl had talked for a few minutes, Hayden motioned for Claire to come back to the computer. "He's got a few more questions for you."

Once she was settled, Friedl got right to the point. "What about Benoit?"

"In an ideal world, he would cooperate for the good of science. In *this* world, he'll cooperate because he's got one bone, and our team has the rest, plus the 'cranium'"—Claire made air quotes—"and who knows what else."

Friedl either didn't notice or didn't care about her vagueness about the "what else." "OK, I'm on board—but be very careful about the ancient intelligence stuff."

After she ended the Skype conversation, she turned to Hayden. "Thanks."

They sat for a moment in silence.

"OK if I vent a little bit?"

"Can I stop you?"

Claire stood up and started pacing. She mimicked Friedl's voice. "Be very careful about the ancient intelligence stuff?" Claire shook her fists. "Are you kidding me? Why does he think I put my career on the line?"

Hayden said nothing, and Claire sat in silence for a few seconds. Then she stood up and walked to a window. "Twenty minutes on the phone with Bill . . . and I'm thinking Kazakhstan's too close to New England."

She turned to face Hayden. "That," she said, pointing to the now blank screen, "is why any scientific progress is a miracle."

Hayden got up and poured a scotch for her. This time it was a thirty-five-year-old Macallan. After he poured himself a shot, they clinked glasses. "Go on."

"Friedl is a behaviorist, which means that he tends to dismiss consciousness and explain all complex behaviors as the result of stimulus and response."

"And?"

Claire downed a slug of scotch. "Well, is it such a big step from that to acknowledge that the pressures that produced intelligence in humans might occur in other animals? Yet, he dismisses it out of hand. Worst of all, I've got to kiss his ring—that's a euphemism, by the way."

Hayden snorted. "Behaviorism! Even if your man reduces everything to mechanical monkeys, I'll bet you a large amount of money that he still thinks he himself is something special.

"Look, it's never fun to suffer fools, but you did the right thing," said Hayden more seriously. "With Rushmere behind this, you'll get a hearing." He paused. "And, you may not want to hear this, but he also described a prudent path forward: first establish what the bones are, then explore why they were arranged and who or what arranged them. If you lay it out right, it will be obvious that an intelligence of some sort was involved. How long would it take to uncover the objects?"

Claire guessed about a week, since the sedimentary rock was easy to pick off. Hayden said that he had to get back to his other life, but to call if there was a crisis. He promised to return once the bones were uncovered. "If you need anything in the short term, Sergei can get it from Ripley."

After she finished her drink, Claire said, "One thing you should know. I've talked it over with Sergei and Rob, and we all agree that if the bones are from a new species, we're going to name it after you."

She watched Hayden's reaction and discovered that the man could actually blush!

"Claire, I'm deeply honored, but there'd be no discovery without you."

"Actually, there'd be no discovery if you hadn't stepped up."

"I don't believe that. Make no mistake—I'm deeply touched by your offer. But I'm going to decline." Seeing the look on her face, he hurried on. "Remember when I said that if I bought ten tables I could be man of the year for organizations that hated mining? Well, the same is true about funding a dig. All I've provided is cover and money; you and your team have done the work . . ." A thought occurred to Hayden. "Actually, when you think about the situation, it might be more politic to name the species after the Kazakh president."

33

BEZANOV HAD JUST PUT DOWN THE PHONE WHEN THERE WAS A knock on his office door and his wife poked her head in. "Is this a good time to talk?"

Irritation flashed across his face before he turned around. It was never a good time to talk these days when it came to Ludmilla. It wasn't that she was high maintenance—quite the contrary. All she wanted to do was work with rescue animals. She refused to go out on his yacht, saying the conversation was excruciating, no matter how celebrated the guests. They were always so guarded, she complained that they only talked about where they had been, where they were going, and which jet or yacht they took to get from place to place. Dinner conversation consisted of gossip rather than ideas, and wit was nowhere to be found. In fact, Bezanov largely agreed with that assessment, but he also expected Ludmilla to appreciate that in his position he had to keep up appearances.

"Keep it short," he said curtly.

"OK, how about this for short?" She gave him a level, affectless look. "We're finished. Is that short enough?"

Bezanov's expression did not change. This was not unwelcome, but he had planned on being the one to deliver the news. His voice was icy cold. "You can leave any time, but know this: if you walk out now, you get nothing."

Ludmilla barked a bitter laugh. "If you knew anything about me, you'd realize that I want nothing. There is nothing you could give me that would mean anything to me. My biggest mistake in life was choosing money over the chance of a real life. So you can be happy and cackle about all the rubles you won't need to give me!"

Bezanov looked at her appraisingly. She was no longer the Ludmilla who had so captivated him and whom he'd so cleverly campaigned to win. Stress had etched lines around her eyes. But, though worn down, she was not defeated. He'd won her, but he didn't own her. Worse, it wasn't that she didn't know the rules, but rather that she knew the rules but didn't care about abiding by them. And she still knew how to get his goat.

"You mean Sergei Anachev? Yes, think about the future you might have had with him. Do you want to know where he is? He's in Kazakhstan, doing my bidding."

Hearing this, Ludmilla went pale. "What have you done . . ." She fled the room without finishing the thought.

Bezanov felt some satisfaction at his wife's reaction but kicked himself mildly for being provoked into saying something about the geologist. He did not want her wondering whether he had any role in the documents that poisoned Anachev's relations with her family. He'd never mentioned Anachev in all the years he and Ludmilla had been married, and his policy was never to say anything unless it served some purpose.

34

TWO DAYS PASSED AS THE TEAM CONTINUED THE DELICATE work of exposing the objects revealed by the scan. Dr. Tabiliev came out with two young paleontologists with expertise in geology. Claire appreciated this, as it supported Sergei's point that the finds predated anything that might remotely be considered cultural.

The third day, Claire awoke to find a surprise email from Adam Constantine, the *Times* correspondent. He began by noting that he had been to see Byron Gwynne about his new, much anticipated book on the evolutionary history of elephants and that he had asked whether he was aware of Claire's new find in Kazakhstan. Gwynne had said yes, but that the image he saw seemed like a juvenile form of *Deinotherium*.

Apparently, Gwynne had said much more, because in parenthesis, Constantine had added, "By the way, Gwynne is not your friend." His interest piqued by Gwynne's hostility, Constantine had contacted William Friedl at Rushmere. Claire grimaced when she read that Friedl had made some dismissive remark about her fixation on animal intelligence, but he'd then let Constantine know that she had found several more objects and that she would be continuing the dig under the distinguished aegis of Rushmere. Constantine ended by saying that in the light of these new developments, he would like to arrange a visit. He went on to suggest that if things went well, they might talk about an exclusive for the *Times*. What Constantine didn't tell Claire was that the prospect of a big controversy with a big name involved was almost a sure thing for the front page—with the controversy, not the find, front and center.

Claire considered what Constantine did tell her with both exhilaration and trepidation. An exclusive in the *Times* was exactly what the dig needed in some sense: it would lift the profile of the project, but even as it made her bulletproof from the type of pressure Tamerlan and other corrupt officials might bring, it would also put a target on her back in some parts of academia. On the other hand, given Constantine's warning about Gwynne, that target was already firmly in place. He could come out, she reasoned, but the story would have to be embargoed until a credible scientific journal was given the opportunity to publish a letter announcing the discovery.

These ruminations were cut short by a phone call from Tegev Aliyev, Sauat's father.

"Mr. Aliyev, thanks for calling me back."

"My pleasure, Dr. Knowland. How is Sauat doing?"

"He's been a real pleasure to work with, but that's why I'm calling."

"Is something wrong?"

"Not that I know of, but I've left the dig, and I wanted to say goodbye to him before I left, but I did not see him. I'm wondering whether you've heard from him?"

There was silence on the other end of the line. Then, "No, I haven't. You are no longer in charge?"

"No, the foundation that sponsored the dig has installed someone else. I will be continuing my work at Transteppe, where there has been a significant find. I was hoping that Sauat could continue to work with me. I asked about him before I left, but the staff hadn't seen him that afternoon—no one seemed concerned," she added somewhat lamely.

"I will call Tamerlan and then call you back."

"Good. While you're doing that, I'll call the camp."

She managed to reach Benoit, who hadn't seen Sauat. New to the dig, he assumed that Sauat had gone off to see his family. She told Benoit that Sauat was the nephew of his liaison to the Kazakh authorities, which got his attention, and that he should immediately interview all in the encampment to determine when Sauat disappeared. "Oh, and Benoit," she said just before hanging up, "keep this low-key. Remember where we are."

Tegev rang back twenty minutes later. "Tamerlan said that Sauat was your responsibility and that he holds you accountable for his well-being."

What was going on? Hostage taking for use as a bargaining chip was standard operating procedure in this part of the world, whether it was grabbing an American journalist in Iran or the CEO of a fertilizer company in Ukraine. But would Tamerlan endanger his own nephew to extract leverage over Claire? She doubted it, but then, she thought that if someone else had grabbed Sauat, Tamerlan would have no compunctions about turning suspicion toward her.

"Mr. Aliyev, we will find your son. There are people here who I think can help. I will call when I have any news. And please call me if you hear from him."

After speaking with Tegev, Claire called Rob and asked whether she and Sergei could meet at his office. Rob knew better than to ask what it was about over the phone. Then she called Sergei and asked if he could break away and meet with Rob before heading over to headquarters. It was her first time in Rob's office, and she felt as if she had entered the situation room at the White House. The utilitarian space was filled with banks of video monitors with feeds from all over the concession buildings and gates. A technician manned a computer screen and communicated by walkie-talkie with various security staff as they checked in. Sergei was already there, and Rob waved Claire into a separate room. As soon as they sat down, Claire filled them in on what she knew. Sergei stared at the floor grimly. "I know this game—too well." Rob looked at Sergei curiously, but the Russian did not elaborate.

Rob turned to Claire. From the look on his face, she could tell that she was losing him. Once again, she felt a contraction in the pit of her stomach.

"You gave us fair warning back on the bluff," he said to Claire, "but I thought we were facing an academic dustup, not kidnappings and God knows what else."

"I never should have brought Sauat into this . . ."

"Let me finish!" Rob interrupted. "As you know, I've been worried that this would blow back on Transteppe, and this is one of those moments where we—I—have to be very careful. We cannot pay ransom, for instance, or it puts a target on every single employee. Also, we don't know that whoever took the kid—if someone did take him—is looking for leverage over you"—nodding at Claire—"the dig, or Transteppe. We're the deep pockets and so I know where I'd put my odds."

Claire felt miserable. "I understand, Rob; Sauat's not your problem, he's mine."

Rob waved her off. "I'm not saying I won't help; I'm just saying we've got to be extremely careful, and I'm going to have to spend some rainy-day money from the favor bank . . ." Rob thought a second. "I'll make a couple of calls—see if anyone knows anything. I'll ping you after I hear . . . and let's keep this tight: if he's been snatched, we'll need all the wiggle room we can get."

35

CLAIRE WENT FOR A WALK TO CLEAR HER HEAD. SHE FELT LIKE she was burning more bridges than a retreating army. She stopped by the commissary. Lawrence was sitting outside, possibly on mouse patrol, she hoped. It was blazing hot, but she decided to walk out toward the garden, where the staff was making a valiant effort to grow some tomatoes, squash, and lettuce—long odds given the heat. Lawrence trotted after her, making several digressions to chase bugs or investigate whatever smells cats liked to investigate. Looking at the wilting and dust-covered vegetables, her mind wandered back to the elephants.

What was it like here, five and a half million years ago? What did they eat? It was an interesting question, and it prompted her to return to her room to finish that email to Keerbrock.

She looked at her earlier draft, the body of which mentioned the discovery of a mysterious elephant bone in a place elephants had never been known to inhabit at a time of extremely rapid evolutionary change. That part was fine. What she couldn't decide was whether to mention that they had crossed paths before, a decade earlier.

Claire had been in her third year at Berkeley studying comparative psychology, which fell under both anthropology and psychology. She met with her thesis committee to launch the study that would be the basis of her doctorate. Claire's idea was to formally demonstrate the notion that great apes know that when another ape points, the reference is to some object in the distance and not the end of the ape's finger.

After Claire had finished presenting her own formal design to test her hypothesis, there were initial murmurs of approval from the committee. Claire was something of a star in the department, and the chair had invited Keerbrock (who was spending a semester at Berkeley) to sit in. He was silent during her presentation, and after the committee had asked a few perfunctory questions, the chair had turned to Keerbrock and said that while they knew this was not an area of expertise, all of them wanted to hear his reaction.

Keerbrock was a lanky man with tousled hair and a penetrating stare. Back then, he was about sixty-five and already a legend for developing a series of precise proxies for dating events in climate history, as well as for overturning the conventional wisdom on the speed at which climate changes. Having refined the dating of several abrupt climate changes in prehistory, he then ventured into evolutionary biology and provided rigorous data to back up the then novel argument that surviving climate change made you smarter, which set the stage for Benoit's work in recent years. But then he'd abandoned this work, famously saying that if crises like climate change made you smarter, why didn't we find evidence for a lot of other smart animals? This was why Claire figured he would be interested in this find.

Keerbrock had no particular expertise in animal cognition, but that did not stop him when the department chair invited his comments. At first it wasn't clear that he had even heard the invitation. Then he knocked the table with his knuckles and turned his stare on Claire.

"Here's what's going to happen if you go ahead with this study you just described. You will spend a couple of years getting everything just so; you'll enlist some students to help you implement the experiment, you will gather your data, and then you will come back to this committee." He paused. It was as though no one was breathing in the room. "There will be some appreciation for your diligence, but then someone, probably one of the more quantitative types, will ask, 'How do you know that in every case you describe that the ape is not merely remembering a previous scene in which pointing was involved?' You will not be able to answer that question given the design you have laid out. Then someone else will ask why it is necessary to impute a mental state to this action when it might be the simple result of association or memory." Keerbrock paused again. One of the committee members, a junior faculty member, had a look of sadistic glee as he watched Keerbrock dismantle the reputation of the department's star.

"You will not have an answer for that, either," Keerbrock continued in his level tone, "given the study's design. And even if no one asked those questions during your thesis defense, I can guarantee you that someone will bring it up later, and, well, you know what will happen. Suffice it to say that after the expenditure of so much time and energy in this futile quest, you will find your future prospects to be very dim indeed."

Claire's stricken look must have reached some vestige of humanity in Keerbrock that he had not yet extirpated, because he softened his tone. "I'm telling you this now because I think the topic is well worth investigating, but only if done properly. Now is the time to fix it, not later. Take it from someone who knows—when you push the boundaries of conventional wisdom in any scientific field, you'd better be bulletproof."

With that, Keerbrock thanked the chairman for inviting him and took his leave. There was an awkward silence. To the chairman's relief, Claire managed to say, "I guess it's back to the drawing board." There was a squeaking of chairs as people got up and left. The chairman asked Claire to come see him. Claire sat alone in that room for a long time and then quietly sobbed for some time more.

In the days following, Claire had come close to a nervous breakdown. She went through every stage of dealing with a deep emotional wound—despair, rationalization, rage—but the worst part was that she knew that Keerbrock was right.

Big integrative ideas sometimes attract the best and brightest, but more often dreamers, kooks, mystics, and the undisciplined. As one of the world's most celebrated big thinkers, Keerbrock knew how easy it was to marginalize a new idea because all new ideas threaten the established order. He knew that in order to push the boundaries of science in new directions, a scientist had to have impeccable credentials in the old order. Keerbrock must have hated it every time a daring new hypothesis went down in flames because of laziness or oversight or unjustifiable assumptions, because each case made it easier for the scientific establishment to dismiss his theories as well.

Keerbrock had survived many attempts to dismiss his ideas, and he was now—to use his term—bulletproof. Her find was his missing piece, and he was the missing piece in the letter she envisioned announcing the find. But should she avoid mentioning that previous encounter? Would he dismiss a collaboration out of hand if she was associated with the find? Or was Claire just one of scores of grad students whose lives he had ruined?

Claire stared at the screen. "Fuck it," she said and began typing.

36

AFTER SENDING THE EMAIL, CLAIRE WALKED OVER TO THE warehouse to see how the team was progressing. They were through the taphonomy stage, in which they documented as best they could how the objects were buried. Sergei had supervised cutting the objects out of the lip, along with a cushion of surrounding rock. Now they were using rock hammers and picks to remove the remaining rock. Katie was working on the mysterious circular find.

With the surrounding rock reduced to manageable size, Sergei had been able to do a much more finely resolved 3-D image. Katie was staring at it when Claire came in. "Well," she said, "one mystery solved: our ancient buddies were big into curling!"

On the screen, the object did look like a curling stone. It was circular and concave on the top, with a slight nub in the center. Claire peered at the image. "What the hell?"

"No idea. Once we know what it's made of, we can narrow the search."

Claire nodded. She was heading over to Francisco when Rob called. She listened, hung up, and turned to the group.

"I need Sergei for a few minutes." Sergei got up, and they both left.

Once they were outside, she said, "Sauat." He nodded but seemed distracted, almost bitter.

"You OK?"

Sergei immediately snapped back to the present. "Uh-huh."

They continued in silence, with Claire stealing occasional glances at Sergei until they got to Rob's office. Once they were seated, he wasted no time. "The president's got him—as a 'guest.'"

"What does that mean?" asked Claire. "How's he being treated?"

Rob spread his hands. "I really don't know. It sounded like he was OK, but I'm sure he's scared shitless."

"Why take Sauat?"

"Apparently, word of your find got to the president. He wants the bones. My guess is that he figured he couldn't snatch any of your staff or mine, so he took a Kazakh as a hostage."

Sergei seemingly had returned to his usual, problem-solving self. "Does *he* want the bones, or does he want them to be given to a museum or ministry?"

Rob's eyes widened. He'd missed something. "You're right, Sergei. My contact said that he wanted the bones. He already knew that they would be coming to the museum through Tabiliev."

Claire watched this exchange, confused. "Why does this make a difference?"

Sergei turned to her. "It makes all the difference, and it could be very good news!"

Claire was even more mystified.

"I don't get it."

"It's simple—we give him the bones!"

By now, Claire knew not to rise to Sergei's provocative remarks. "Great idea, Sergei! Why didn't I think of that?" she said.

"I'm saying give him some of the remaining bones from the original discovery, not all the bones. By taking Sauat—an expendable Kazakh—he's telling us that he doesn't want this all over the Western press. If he wants them for himself, he's less likely to throw a lot of red tape to keep your research from going forward. Moreover, those bones are fully documented, and we have the new bones from the lip—plus whatever else there might be in the bluff."

Claire realized Sergei wasn't done. "There's more, right?"

"Of course. Given what Rob said about setting a precedent on ransom, I think the approach should be that Transteppe has decided to

make a direct gift of the great discovery to the president—with the hope
that the bones don't show up the next week on eBay!" Sergei looked at
both of them expectantly, but neither laughed. Disappointed, he continued, "And at the same time, Transteppe should solicit the president's
office's help in locating an intern who has been a valuable intermediary
between the paleontological team and their Kazakh counterparts."

Claire shook her head. Machiavelli had nothing on the young Russian geologist. Again she wondered why she always was attracted to
men with baggage. "Makes sense to me—although we seem to be handing out priceless bones like party favors." She had another thought.
"How do you know so much about this?"

Sergei's bitter look returned. "Such scenarios are an unfortunate
fact of life if you are Russian."

Rob looked uneasy. "Could work—but it's anything but simple." He
paused. "Who hands the bones to the president? Usually that would
involve the CEO or chairman of the board, and if he wanted them for
himself rather than the national museum, it could leave Transteppe
open to being charged with racketeering under RICO, or a violation of
the Foreign Corrupt Practices Act."

That brought Claire up short. "I hadn't thought of that."

"Coming from Russia, I *never* would have thought of that," said Sergei. "But now that you mention it, I think it best that bones be turned
over informally, rather than in a big ceremony. If the president wants
the bones, he'd probably prefer that it be done quietly."

Claire nodded. "And I wouldn't worry about the bribery issue. If
we give him the bones now, before any analysis has been peer reviewed
and published, they really have no value that can be determined . . ."

Sergei looked at Claire admiringly. "Are you sure you don't have
some Russian blood?"

Rob had heard enough. "OK, OK, I'm not sure I'd want to argue
that in court, but you're right, we are a mining company, not an archaeological expedition, and if the president asks for the bones, we can't

very well refuse him. I'll get the wheels turning—we want to do this real quiet and real quick."

As Sergei and Claire walked back to the warehouse, he turned to her and said, "I'm sure we'll get Sauat back, but there's one more thing, Claire."

Claire, lost in thought, barely heard him. "What's that?"

"If the president wants the bones for himself, that means that you did the right thing when we moved the bones in the first place. Think about that and feel good. You were right."

Warmth flooded through her, and she put a hand on Sergei's strong shoulder, something she'd wanted to do for a long time, and hugged him before they both realized it was a bad idea.

After they broke off the hug, Claire smiled and asked him, "By the way, Sergei, how'd you get those strong shoulders?"

Sergei actually blushed, then shrugged. "Geologists do a lot of scrambling and climbing."

"Not windsurfing, then?"

"What's windsurfing?"

37

TWO DAYS LATER, CLAIRE WAS WORKING ON UNCOVERING THE last of the objects when she got a call from security. A man named Tegev Aliyev was at the gatehouse asking for her. He was accompanied by his son. Claire almost dropped her tools in excitement. She turned to Sergei, who was already tossing her the keys to her van.

After signing them in, she brought Tegev and Sauat back to the warehouse. Tegev marveled at the scale of the buildings. Sauat, who looked none the worse for wear, wanted to see the bones and equipment, but

Claire first wanted to hear about his ordeal. She led them to a small office where they could talk in private.

The young man said that two men had come for him, both wearing the uniform of the presidential guard. They came in silently, quickly bound his hands, gagged him, and took his phone. One of the men was rough, but he heard the other tell him to back off—that Sauat was just a boy. They had told Sauat that they were taking him somewhere where he would be safe, though they never said from what. He was kept in a house in a remote area that he did not recognize. There were books and he was allowed to walk around outdoors, but there were eyes on him all the time. After a few days, he was driven back, given back his phone, and let off just outside the camp. He said his uncle Tamerlan had taken credit for his being released.

Tegev snorted. "If Tamerlan had such power, why was Sauat taken in the first place?" He turned to Claire and asked, not in an unfriendly way, "Why do *you* think he was taken?"

"I don't know. I'm just so glad this ended happily."

Tegev looked at Claire just long enough to convey that he knew that she was holding back. Then Sauat interrupted. "Is it all right if I see what you are doing here?" His eyes were glowing in anticipation.

"You bet, Sauat! I've got just the guide for you."

Claire asked Katie to show Sauat around. Sauat grinned when he saw her. *Not cool, this one*, Claire thought with affection as she noticed Sauat's reaction to Katie.

Claire asked Tegev to stay behind so that the two of them could talk. They walked outside into the baking heat and found some shade under the overhanging roof of the warehouse.

"Tegev, first of all, I'm so sorry if my work had anything to do with why Sauat was taken. Second, I really don't have the full picture of why he was taken, but I can say that these bones are important and that it's probably not safe for Sauat to be connected to them."

Tegev sighed and gave her a long look. "That is what I told Sauat when I picked him up at your old camp. I also know that you were involved in getting him released . . .

"No, no, no . . ." Tegev said as Claire shook her head. "You don't have to say anything. Sauat is very bright young man, yes?" This time Claire nodded. "And he told me that this is the most exciting thing he has ever done—Kazakhstan offers plenty of excitement, but it's usually the kind you would be wise to run away from. So he begs to continue to work with you—here." Tegev gestured toward the high fence, topped with concertina wire and festooned with security cameras. "He will be safe here, yes."

"What about Tamerlan?"

Tegev was stone-faced. "Tamerlan is my brother and *my* problem. I will deal with him."

Claire sighed. "OK, so long as you recognize the risks . . . I could use help coordinating with the Kazakh scientists and Dr. Tabiliev."

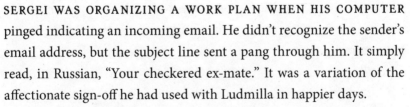

SERGEI WAS ORGANIZING A WORK PLAN WHEN HIS COMPUTER pinged indicating an incoming email. He didn't recognize the sender's email address, but the subject line sent a pang through him. It simply read, in Russian, "Your checkered ex-mate." It was a variation of the affectionate sign-off he had used with Ludmilla in happier days.

He considered deleting it without reading it, but curious as to why Ludmilla would write after all these years, he opened it, scarcely breathing, and began reading.

If you are reading this, it means you did not immediately throw this email in the trash, which I'm grateful for, even though that is what I deserve. I can never apologize sufficiently for the cowardice, stupidity, and narcissism that characterized my leaving you, but know that I have paid for my sins every day since in ways no amount of luxury or security could balance.

I only found out about how to reach you because Andrei (yes, Andrei is my husband, though that is one mistake I'm now correcting) let slip that you were at Transteppe. I'm not arrogant enough to ask for forgiveness, nor do I deserve it, but I want you to know that I will never forgive myself for turning away from the one chance at true fulfillment I have had in my life.

I also want to warn you. Nothing good comes of any association with Andrei, more often awful things, and I would hate to have you suffer any more pain because of Andrei's cruel and vengeful nature. He must have some leverage on you, but please be on guard!

Lastly, I hope you have found someone worthy of you. If it means anything, the two years we had were the happiest of my life.

Sergei closed the email and spent long minutes thinking. Several times he reopened the email and hit reply only to close it again. The tide of mixed feelings that swept over him almost had a palpable physical presence, as though the air was being squeezed out of his chest. He thought he had successfully put Ludmilla out of his thoughts, but deep down he knew that he could never completely suppress memories of the one time in his life he had enjoyed something approaching domestic bliss. Then he reopened the email one more time, hit reply, and began typing.

Ludmilla,

Clearly you are hurting deeply, and I will not pile on more hurt. To some degree I brought Andrei's revenge on myself because of my own cockiness and blindness to the rules of the world beyond chess. I was also blind to danger because of my infatuation with you, an infatuation

that turned into love and then despair when you left me. I appreciate the
warning, but know that I'm as interested in protecting myself as anyone.

Sergei stopped there. He meant to say much more, but he simply couldn't. The wash of emotion was too powerful, and he couldn't reduce it to mere words.

He hit send. For a moment he felt deep sadness for all the pointless hurt of life and the knowledge that the brief flirtations with infinity that we grasped for when we were young can never be recaptured.

39

BY THIS POINT, THE TEAM THAT CLAIRE HAD PUT TOGETHER consisted of herself, Sergei—when he was available—Katie, Francisco, a Kazakh paleobotanist named Kiril Usenov, a fetching young technician, Kamila Valikhinova, who was an expert in tomography and other imaging technologies, and, of course, Sauat. Kiril hit it off with Sergei, and the two would often argue about chess. Sauat eavesdropped and told Claire that Sergei knew an enormous amount about the game.

The team had very little interaction with the Transteppe staff. Ripley, the site manager, had put out the word that the paleontological workspace was off-limits—an injunction put out to protect Katie and Kamila, both of whom caused heads to swivel in their comings and goings. Some of Sergei's geological staff peered in from time to time but were politely but firmly rebuffed. Claire's concerns were twofold. First there was the integrity of the process, which they meticulously documented, and then there was the worry about treasure hunters. Claire was convinced that the longer they could keep up the impression that what they were doing was vague and boring, the easier life was going to be.

With Sauat safe and sound, Claire felt she could breathe again. And with the president presumably preoccupied with his newly expropriated bones, Claire even started humming as she worked. After bidding goodbye to Tegev and installing Sauat in his new room, she went back to her own quarters. She went over to her phone, which she had rigged to a couple of tiny speakers, and found what she wanted, an R&B mix she had put together years ago when she would unwind by dancing by herself. She had discovered R&B from the sixties at a professor's wedding and loved it. This mix was a bunch of classics recorded long before she was born: "Hully Gully" by the Olympics, "Please Mr. Postman" from the Marvelettes, "Tossin' and Turnin'," "Twist and Shout," "I Need Your Lovin'," "Locomotion," and "In the Midnight Hour." With the music on loud, Claire stripped off her dusty work shirt and shorts, went to the refrigerator and poured a generous portion of vodka into a water glass, dropped in a couple of ice cubes, and topped it with orange juice. She took a long swig and let herself go. She was far too young to know the actual steps to any of the songs, but the rhythms were primordial.

She had gotten a good buzz when she heard a knock at the door. She dashed to the peephole. It was Katie, who had a mischievous look on her face. "I love that music! Can I come in?"

"I was just unwinding . . ." Claire didn't think it was a good idea to let Katie in, but she had no choice.

"Well, that's *just* what *I* need," Katie said. Twirling to the music as she stripped off her own T-shirt and shorts, she began to dance. Before Claire could say anything, Katie joined her. "Let's try a line dance." She gave Claire a faux meaningful look. "We can look at it as a team-building exercise."

Katie radiated confidence and artless sensuality. Had she ever tried the wanton moves she was doing now in public, a riot would have ensued.

OK, thought Claire, *team building it is*, and she went with the flow while trying to keep up with Katie as the twenty-something led the two of them through various moves, each one more provocative than the last.

After the song ended, Katie pointed toward the vodka bottle and raised her eyebrows in a question. Claire poured a drink for her and another for herself. Katie toasted Claire and took a sip. "I was just wondering," Katie laughed, "how much Sergei would have paid to have a video of that."

Claire turned that thought over in her head. Sergei was a complicated guy, but he was still a guy, and at one level all men were one-celled organisms.

"OK, I'm going to ask," said Claire. "Any of the crew have any appeal? And I'm including Rob and Hayden—even Tamerlan."

Hearing this last name, Katie laughed. "All of them, 'cept poor Tamerlan. But it's not going to happen."

That was the right answer, but Claire wondered why. Everyone knew that romances among colleagues on digs could be terribly destructive—she thought of Tony and Abigail, though that one was more comical than distracting—but every research project Claire had been involved in had been rife with romance. Indeed, some of those, including a good number she would like to forget, had involved Claire.

"Oh, is there a Mr. Katie waiting in the States?"

Katie laughed again. "Not that I remember . . . it's what I said before. I'm trying to reorient my life . . . and my reputation. I haven't even kissed a guy in a year! Try to have a little innocent fun, next thing you know, you're persona au gratin!"

Claire laughed. With Katie out of the equation, she couldn't imagine any other possible combinations among the crew. "So no births, deaths, or marriages. That's good to hear."

"Nope, pure as a Vatican conclave—maybe that's not such a good analogy these days." Katie took another sip of her drink. She looked at Claire conspiratorially. The girl was sex incarnate, Claire thought, and then she wondered whether that phrase was redundant. Her chain of thought was interrupted when Katie continued, "Sergei certainly seems to snap to attention when you come into the room."

Claire blushed deeply and changed the subject. "What do you think of Rob?"

"Dreamboat! He's someone I'd want in my foxhole—in the military sense of the phrase. He seems total WYSIWYG—but nobody's that straight-arrow."

Claire figured that Katie had a solid database to draw on in making that opinion. "Hayden?"

"All we can do is hope that he's what he seems to be."

Katie stood up and started putting her clothes back on. "Thanks for this," she said. "I needed it, or maybe I would have done something stupid." As she headed out the door, she turned around. "Kiril—very cute guy, by the way—thinks that the curling stone looks just like a root vegetable—an elephant yam."

Claire was stunned. "A yam?"

"Yup. Is that important?"

"I'll say. For one thing, it's impossible. When will you have it uncovered?"

"Couple of days at most."

Claire looked at Katie. "I don't want to get ahead of ourselves, but I'd suggest you give yourself a crash course on elephant yams. If that's what your object turns out to be, everybody's going to want a piece of it."

40

AFTER KATIE LEFT, CLAIRE POURED HERSELF ANOTHER VODKA and went to take a shower. She was pleasantly flooded with endorphins. After dressing in shorts and a T-shirt, she took another sip of her drink. Perhaps it was relief over the safe recovery of Sauat, or the odd sensuality of her dance with Katie, but for the first time in many months,

Claire felt physically moved. These musings were interrupted by a knock on her door. Her quarters seemed to be turning into a happening place. Before answering, she cued up Rimsky-Korsakov's "Polovtsian Dances" on her machine.

She opened the door a crack and saw Sergei. He looked troubled and unsure of himself. He saw her bathrobe and looked down, saying, "We need to talk, but maybe now's not the time?"

Claire hid her alarm. "No, come in. You look like you need a drink—I seem to remember that you'd asked to have a drink with me not too long ago." She moved to the counter. "I'm not profiling you, but is vodka OK? Hope so, because it's all I've got."

Stepping in, Sergei regained a little of his poise. "Yes, my people like very much the vodka."

Claire fetched him a glass filled with a generous portion. She handed it to Sergei and plunked herself down on the couch. Sergei looked around for a place to sit. It was clear that he was still trying to make sense of the situation. Moving as though he was picking his way through a minefield, he started walking toward the desk chair.

Claire patted the spot beside her on the couch.

Sergei sat down, took a sip of vodka, briefly glanced at Claire, and then looked off in the distance.

After sitting in silence for a few minutes, Claire finally spoke. "Sergei, what's wrong?"

Sergei sighed and took another sip of vodka. He looked really uncomfortable. Then he muttered, "I'm being stupid," and put down his glass. He got up to leave.

He hadn't advanced a step before Claire leaped up and grabbed him. "You're not going anywhere, mister, until you tell me what's going on."

Sergei looked miserable but collapsed back into the couch. "Claire, I'm uncomfortable because we have a professional relationship and what I came to tell you presumes we have something more than a professional relationship." He fidgeted.

Unsure of whether she should be elated or devastated, Claire drew Sergei to her and kissed him softly on the lips. She offered a shy smile. "Does that answer that question?"

Sergei sighed. "Yes, I think so."

Claire gave him a direct look. "So?"

Sergei shrugged. "This is difficult for me, but here goes. A woman from my past reached out to me."

Claire held her breath, or rather, didn't breathe, because she couldn't.

Sergei continued, "I had been deeply involved with this woman, and when I read her email, it brought back so many memories of that part of my life."

Claire had been dumped a number of times, but never before a relationship had started. But, if this was going to be it, she wanted to get it out right then. "Do you want to go back to this woman?"

"That's why I'm here," Sergei said, causing Claire's heart to freeze. "What all those feelings made me realize," he ploughed on, apparently unaware of the impact of his phrasing, "was that in my heart, I really want to be with you."

Claire could breathe again.

But Sergei wasn't done. "But then I wondered whether I am being a complete fool since we work together and have never even gone on a date."

Claire felt tears of joy well up. "Oh, Sergei. We can have that date right now!"

Sergei smiled. "You mean like American prom?"

"Yes!" Claire clinked his glass and thought about her own high school prom, where, despite heroic—borderline wanton—efforts on her part, she had failed to detach Anthony Marberry from his friends. She looked Sergei right in the eyes. "Very much like prom." She gently put a hand on his shoulder and pulled him toward her as she half closed her eyes. After first touching his lips, she pulled back a tiny bit. "Only better." She kissed him again. "Much, much better," she said softly.

After that long kiss, Claire said, "I was just thinking that I should drink vodka more often." She got up, dimmed the lights, and reached for Sergei's hand. "No more talking," she said as they moved toward her bed.

Later, actually much later, they lay languorously intertwined. Claire ran her fingers over his shoulder and back. "So, not a windsurfer," she murmured.

Sergei kissed her lightly. "I'd probably better be getting back to my room."

Claire didn't want to break the spell but knew that he was right. She nodded, and Sergei rolled over to start getting dressed. Once he was walking to the door, Claire roused herself. Still naked, she walked over to him and put her arms around his neck. After a minute she pulled back to look him in the eye. "I knew this was going to happen, but I don't know if it will ever happen again—and we have to act as though it never happened—but I want you to know that I loved tonight."

Sergei smiled sadly. "I did, too." He gave her one more long kiss. He opened the door, looked around to make sure the coast was clear, and was gone.

Claire went back to her bed and lay down. It wasn't the first time she had had a fling with a coworker, but she didn't feel the usual pangs of remorse that, in the past, had usually set in within minutes of an exit. What was so remarkable about their lovemaking, she thought, was how normal it felt. How did that happen? It was just good, she decided, and vowed that she wasn't going to do her usual molecular-level deconstruction of the evening.

So, she decided to think about what she knew about him. Not much, she realized. She imagined her mother's first question. That was a no-brainer: "So, have you met anyone?"

"Actually, yes."

"That's wonderful! Another scientist?"

"Yes."

"What state does he come from?"

"I'm not sure, but it's in Russia?"

"Russia!"

There would follow a disapproving silence.

"What do you know about him?"

"Not much. He came to Kazakhstan under mysterious circumstances."

"How do you know he's not a spy?"

"It's possible that he is."

"Claire, what have you gotten yourself into?"

"I don't know."

"Well, why are you attracted to him?"

"He might be the most intelligent man I've ever met, and he's also got a wonderful sense of humor. He doesn't take life too seriously, but he always seems to know what to do in tricky situations. He also saved my career. He's beautiful, too. Oh, and he *knows* me, and that's all I've ever really wanted from anyone."

"OK, OK, I'm sorry I asked. How serious is this?"

"I'm not even sure there will be a second date."

"Really." Her mother would sound hopeful.

"But I hope there will."

41

HAYDEN WAS GOING OVER PLANS FOR THE NEXT STAGE OF development of the concession at the headquarters when Rob poked his head in the door. He looked concerned.

"What's up?"

"One of your Russian partners just showed up and asked for you." Rob arched an eyebrow. "It's Andrei Bezanov, the head of Primorskichem."

Hayden leaped to his feet. "Bezanov! Here?"

Rob nodded, waiting for instructions.

Hayden's mind raced. *Why would Bezanov show up unannounced?* He knew the rules. Yet Hayden couldn't stonewall him. He turned to Rob. "Show him in, and while he's here, see who he came with. Text me when you know. And be fast—this is going to be a short meeting."

Rob left and a minute later reappeared, silently ushering Bezanov into the room.

Hayden rose, offering a casual handshake. "Andrei, what a pleasant surprise. What brings you all the way from Vladivostok?" He pointed to a chair and the two men sat down. "Tea? Drink?"

"Thank you, no, Fletcher. It seems that I'm not the only interested party showing up unscheduled at Transteppe. You, for instance—why is it that our major partner shows up suddenly? I can only think—make that hope—that there has been some major discovery."

Aha, thought Hayden. It stood to reason that word would get out that he was at Transteppe. He thought a minute.

His phone pinged, and Hayden glanced at the text—"He came alone—just security." Hayden thought furiously. Clearly something was up. The best way to stall, he decided, was to tell Bezanov the truth.

"Things are going well, Andrei, but that's not what brought me here." Hayden briefly described the discovery of the bones and his interest in archaeology, stressing that he was paying all associated costs personally and that the company was cooperating with the relevant authorities in Kazakhstan. When he finished there was a brief pause.

Bezanov listened intently. "I see. That does sound interesting," said the oligarch in a voice that suggested that he didn't find it interesting, or, thought Hayden with a start, surprising. Bezanov somehow knew about the bones. There was another pause.

"Ah, I see. Perhaps I can meet this archaeologist." Hayden nodded noncommittally.

"And I hope," Bezanov continued, "that they turn out to be sufficiently significant to justify your extraordinary visit."

Hayden nodded again—he didn't like the slight sarcasm in the word *extraordinary*. He waited for Bezanov to get to the real point of his visit.

"And while I'm disappointed that you don't have a breakthrough to announce, I've been hoping for a chance for us to talk face-to-face."

Hayden tensed. "If this involves Transteppe business, you know there are well-established channels for communications among the partners."

"I know, I know, but this is informal chat, and it's not about Transteppe business, but Transteppe *ownership*. You were put on the board by two Canadian groups that together control 31 percent of Transteppe. You're *exactly* the man I want to talk to."

Hayden was on high alert. "Andrei, as you well know, the concession falls under investments of strategic significance, and the ownership structure was set at the treaty level."

"Again, I know, but if the external investors agreed to buy or sell their interest among each other, I'm sure the Kazakh authorities would be accommodative."

"I don't want to sound stiff, Andrei, but this kind of conversation is only appropriate in a formal setting."

"Bah, you know as well as I do, formal meetings only ratify arrangements made earlier through personal relationships."

"Andrei, my hands are tied. The ownership structure that took years to work out delicately balances a lot of competing interests, and I'm not going to enter into any conversation that might upset that balance. I'm sorry you came down here for nothing."

"I'm sorry, too, but before I head back, I'd like to look around for a bit. Do you have someone who might show me around—a Russian speaker, perhaps?"

Hayden knew he meant Sergei. Why would he want Sergei to show him around? On the other hand, he could hardly deny a major partner a chance to inspect the operations. He buzzed Rob. "Mr. Bezanov would like a Russian speaker to show him around for a bit before he leaves. Could you see if Sergei's available?" He turned to Bezanov. "He'll be here in a minute."

At this, Bezanov seemed to start. He got up. "Thank you, I'll wait for him outside." He pulled out a pack of cigarettes. "I've been wanting a cigarette, and even oligarchs don't want to deal with antismoking Nazis."

After a perfunctory handshake, Bezanov left, leaving a puzzled Hayden to wonder what the oligarch didn't want him to see.

He rang Rob. "Don't hover, but keep an eye on them."

Hayden was deeply worried. Bezanov was an oligarch with close ties to the Russian leader, which meant that Primorskichem's interest in expanding their stake had the government's blessing. Moreover, Bezanov had to know that Hayden wouldn't talk informally about something as sensitive as ownership. That meant, reasoned Hayden, that Bezanov was either going through the motions or he was feeling out where Hayden stood. But why?

42

ROB WAS WORRIED, TOO. WHEN HE HAD CALLED SERGEI AND told him that Primorskichem's owner specifically wanted Sergei to show him around, he could almost feel the instant tension on the other end of the phone. Rob kicked himself for not telling Sergei in person so that he could gauge his reaction.

Sergei was unusually quiet when Rob picked him up. "Do you know this guy?" asked Rob, casual as can be.

"I don't travel in his circles," Sergei snorted, with a dark look that shut down that conversation. Then, quickly, he lightened his tone. "Life is too short as it is," he said, sounding like the old Sergei, "and the closer you get to people like Bezanov, the shorter it gets."

"Want me to come along?"

Sergei shook his head. "Thanks, but not necessary." He thought a second, and then said, "But it might be a good idea to get everyone out of the workspace and back to their rooms. Like right now." He looked at Rob to see whether he got the message.

"Got it," said Rob, reaching for his phone.

They found the oligarch smoking in the shade outside the headquarters building. Rob was easygoing as he made the introductions, but he watched the handshake intently. Bezanov seemed amused and casual, and Sergei also tried to maintain a polite front. Rob could tell, however, that Sergei was struggling mightily to contain some powerful emotion.

Rob had provided Bezanov with an immaculate luxury SUV for his visit and also had acceded to the oligarch's wish that his security detail do the driving. Bezanov got in the passenger seat in the front, and Sergei and a bodyguard took the back.

After they were in the vehicle, Rob sent Hayden a terse text. "They know each other and hate each other."

In the car, Sergei sat silently. He had only one ambition in this meeting: to keep Bezanov away from Claire and the area where she was working. They sat in silence while the car idled for a minute. Finally, Bezanov turned slowly to look at Sergei.

He stared for a long time before saying, "Let's go see the lab where you do your work."

So much for the game plan. He gave the driver instructions for the short trip, and as they were driving over, he desperately tried to think of a diversion. He couldn't.

As they entered the giant warehouse, Sergei was pleased to see that it looked deserted. *Good job, Rob!* He didn't ask what Andrei wanted to see but launched into a flat description of the workspace when Bezanov interrupted him.

"Hayden told me that some ancient bones were found on the concession. Show me."

Sergei looked at him levelly. "I'm not sure I would even if you asked politely, but no."

The oligarch flared with disbelief. "You won't!"

"They're not here. One set is with the archaeological dig, and Kazakhstan's great leader has the other."

Andrei waved the air in exasperation. "Then let me meet this sorceress who gets everyone to jump at her beck and call."

Sergei didn't dare look up, but he was absolutely sure that Bezanov was looking in the rearview mirror to see his reaction. "You would have to go through Mr. Hayden to arrange that—he is sponsoring her work here."

"Oh, you don't have her number?"

Bezanov was clearly enjoying this. *He knows!* thought Sergei. *But how?*

Sergei was so intent on maintaining his cool that he didn't notice that Bezanov's attention had shifted to the far end of the building.

"Ah," said the oligarch, "it looks as though I won't have to deal with some tiresome bureaucratic procedure."

Bezanov immediately started walking toward Claire, who was walking toward them.

"Sergei, what's going on?" said Claire. "I just . . ."

"Dr. Knowland," said Sergei sharply, interrupting her midsentence, "this is Andrei Bezanov, owner of Transteppe's Russian partner, Primorskichem. He's interested in your discovery. I was just telling him that Mr. Hayden could set up a meeting, but here you are." He offered a weak smile and hoped she got the warning in his words.

Bezanov ignored Sergei and offered his hand to Claire, who shifted her gaze in some confusion between the two men as she returned the handshake.

Not letting go, Bezanov looked her directly in the eyes. "A great pleasure, Dr. Knowland. Hayden only just mentioned your discovery. I'm told the bones are very old. Have you dated them?"

Claire carefully extracted her hand. She didn't see Sergei subtly shake his head. "Yes, we're narrowing the time frame, but Sergei's initial estimate of over five million years is very close."

"Ah, so Dr. Anachev has been helping." He looked at Sergei in mock reproval. "Why didn't you mention that you were involved in Dr. Knowland's study?" Turning back to Claire, he said, "And it's all going on here at Transteppe. Perhaps you could brief me on your project?"

By now Claire had gotten Sergei's message. "Forgive me, Mr. Bezanov, but I've got a team meeting. And it's very early on in my research. I'd be delighted to show you what we're doing once we've got more to tell."

"I'll hold you to that," Bezanov said with an awkward smile. If it was meant to be playful, it came off as menacing. "Perhaps when you're further along, you can brief me? We could make this very pleasant and have the meeting on my yacht. I will send a plane. It would make for a nice break, yes?"

"Sounds very enticing," said Claire, keeping her tone level but not brusque, "but let's hope we get something to report that's worth all that trouble."

She started to turn, but Bezanov was not done. "You know, I've always been fascinated by the past. Not the deep past like you, but the near past. One reason we can't escape the past is that the decisions we make every moment become the DNA of both the past and our future. Isn't that right, Dr. Anachev?" Sergei, trembling, didn't say anything.

"As a chess player," Bezanov continued breezily, "I've always been amused by how players can see every move they make in a mere game as life or death, but then they return to real life and give very little thought to decisions that turn out to be life or death." He looked at Claire. "Even simple decisions, like coming through that door. Human nature, I guess."

With that he turned and walked away, signaling with a finger for his security to follow.

Claire waited a few minutes after the oligarch exited before saying anything. She could see that Sergei was still trembling but couldn't decide whether it was rage or fear. Maybe both. She knew it wasn't the time to ask but couldn't help herself. "What was *that* about?"

Sergei shook his head. "Nothing good will come out of your meeting him. Let's make sure you never see him again."

Sergei's intensity scared her. Questions swirled, but she was certain that if she pursued them, it would lead to a fight—their first fight. "When you're ready, I'll listen."

Sergei looked up, grateful. "Thank you."

43

ANOTHER TWO DAYS PASSED, AND THE SUMMER HEAT CONTINUED to build. Then, on an intolerably hot day, Claire got a call from Benoit. Usually prone to banter, the scientist seemed subdued. Claire asked how it was going.

"That's the thing," said Benoit. "It's not."

"Not going?"

"Nope. Not going as in stopped, kaput, ended. Total shit show, to be frank."

"Hold on, let me get somewhere where I can talk." As she moved toward Sergei's office, Claire waved to the crew. Katie was signaling for her to come over. Claire held up one finger and pointed to her phone. Katie gave a thumbs-up as Claire closed the door and sat down. "OK, continue."

"Delamain freaked when they heard an intern had disappeared, and then your pal Tamerlan took possession of that bone you left us. In short, there's no project. Delamain's pulled the plug, citing security concerns. Everybody else is gone, and I'm just handing the camp to the Kazakhs—who'll probably just distribute the spoils."

"I'm sorry."

There was a long pause. Claire was in no hurry to fill the silence. Finally, Benoit spoke.

"Claire, I know we got off on the wrong foot, but I actually think you're on to something big, and I'd like to help. You know I can—that's why you emailed me in the first place."

Claire reviewed the events of the past weeks, which included Benoit using the substance of her email to make his own deal with Delamain, usurping her position, and then undermining the significance of the find, and decided that yes, all that could be described as getting off on the wrong foot, in the same way that mass murder might also be described as youthful hijinks. On the other hand, he was right: there were very good reasons why she had contacted him in the first place.

Benoit continued, "And I might even be able to bring the remainder of the Delamain grant with me."

Claire did a double take; Benoit really had no idea what had transpired at Transteppe since Claire had left the dig. "Let's be clear," Claire said crisply, "I'll think about it. I'll give you an answer within a day. But in no case is Delamain going to be involved. I don't need their money; I will not accept their money. They made their decision when they threw me under the bus."

"OK, OK, let me know. I just thought, you know, that research always needs more money . . ." He trailed off.

Claire was sitting in Sergei's office in the warehouse. Benoit was an amoral opportunist, but he was smart. She thought about Lyndon Johnson's remark about it being better to have a potential enemy on the inside of the tent pissing out than one outside pissing in. And she knew from Constantine's latest email that the immune reaction of the evolutionary biology establishment was already well underway. She also thought about the cranium they were uncovering. She could use Benoit's help. First she called Sergei, who said he had to check with Ripley on quartering, but the answer was yes.

Then she called Rob.

"Hi, quick heads-up: we're going to have one"—she thought of Constantine—"maybe two more staying with us for a bit. Sergei's given the OK. Is it OK with you?" She thought she heard a harrumph but took it as a positive that he didn't hang up immediately.

She then called Benoit. "OK, we're on, but there are going to be some house rules . . . " And she laid out exactly how things were going to go.

44

CLAIRE SAW KATIE WAVING EXCITEDLY FROM HER WORKSTATION. Clustered around her was the entire team. She was using a tool that combined high-pressure air and a rapidly moving stylus to remove the final millimeters of sedimentary rock from the object. Up on the screen was the latest, extremely high-resolution image of the round object. Alongside the image was one Katie had found of an elephant yam. They were an exact match.

Katie had exposed a tiny area of the surface. She was now using the stylus and airbrush to widen the exposed area. It was clear that this was not a petrified yam. Under Katie's spotlight the lovely, pale-green material appeared translucent.

Wearing gloves, Sergei picked up a magnifying glass and peered closely at the small patch. "My guess would be jadeite, but this is smooth." He looked up at the image on the screen. "Looks like the whole surface is smooth."

Claire put on a pair of gloves and touched the surface with her finger. Although she already knew the answer, she asked, "What does that mean? Smooth?"

Sergei looked up. It was the first time Claire had ever seen him awestruck. "Well, we know it's not a petrified elephant yam. And here's what a typical jadeite boulder looks like." Sergei bent over Katie's keyboard and with a few strokes called up some images on the screen. Some were relatively smooth, many jagged, but all were irregular in shape. "So it's not an elephant yam, but it looks exactly like an elephant yam except that it's perfectly shaped and smooth. And jadeite is found in metamorphic, not sedimentary rock. It's not impossible, but again, very low odds. Multiply the odds to find the compound probability, and it's about the lowest odds you can get."

Claire spoke to Sergei but turned to Katie. "And that's not the whole story, is it? Tell them, Katie."

Katie looked flustered. "No, it's not. The elephant yam has been used for its medicinal properties, particularly in Ayurvedic medicine. More importantly, yams are famine food—at least for people. When climate cools and dries, yams tend to move deeper into the soil, away from the harsh conditions, and so, when other food disappears, people turn to yams, which may be the only thing that still grows."

"Which are precisely the conditions that prevailed five point five million years ago," Claire interrupted, "so you get the picture: a perfect replica of an elephant yam found in substrate that dates back five point five million years—not impossible. But this yam is found next to an array of bones that are exactly the same age. If the yams were a lifesaver for primitive tribes in human prehistory, then they might well have had significance for whatever ate them five million years ago."

"Like elephants," said Katie. "They need phosphorous in their diet, and yams are a good source."

"There's one more thing," said Claire, completing her train of thought. "There's a relationship between harsh climates, plants burying carbohydrates in response, and intelligence. Go through any vertebrate order, and the most intelligent species turns out to be the one that has to dig to find food. Pigs are the most intelligent ungulate, bears the most intelligent carnivore, and then there's us."

Francisco was shaking his head. "I want to see the look on the faces of the editors of *Nature* or *Science* when we submit a letter introducing the world to five-point-five-million-year-old Ayurvedic yam farmers who happen to be elephants and dabble in the arts."

They all laughed. Claire thought about what he'd said. It wasn't only the editors of *Nature* and *Science* she was worried about. William Friedl had specifically warned her off pushing too hard on animal intelligence. And what would Keerbrock think if the minute he signed on he was told that not only were these ancient beings smart, but that they were into stone carving?

From this perspective, the new find made it more difficult, not less to get a fair hearing in the scientific establishment. "He's right," she said. "If these finds were ten thousand years old, there'd be no problem—it would make perfect sense that someone would carve a totem honoring a life-saving food in bad times. Five point five million years old? There weren't even hominids in Asia that long ago. We'd be pigeonholed with the Piltdown Man."

Katie looked up, cool as a cucumber. "I've no interest in publishing anything that undermines the credibility of the project or opens us up to ridicule."

This brought Claire up short. It was Katie's subtle way of reminding Claire that she had given Katie the lead on this object. She was grateful in a way—Samantha probably would have said, "What's this 'we,' white bitch?" Claire was chagrined. She'd participated in all too many research projects where the lead investigator had bigfooted the best work done by the graduate students.

She put a hand on Katie's shoulder. "Of course not! And, as the lead on this particular object, you have to figure how best to present the find. You're going to do more than one paper off this, right?"

"Sure hope so."

"So think about this. First publish a simple description of the object, its dating, its context, its physical orientation relative to the other finds. Then subsequently, there can be more collaborative explorations of what it might mean. Better to be pushed to where you wanted to go in the first place than to try and drag everyone where they've never been."

Katie thought about that a second. "That could work."

She turned to Sergei. "We're absolutely sure on the dating of the surrounding rock?" Sergei nodded. "And we've documented every step of the way?" Sergei gave a thumbs-up.

Claire was about to let everyone get back to work when something occurred to her. "Francisco, you said elephants. Why are you assuming that whatever did this was an elephant?"

"Everything about the find says elephant. Our ancestors back then were tiny, and pretty clueless to boot. Oh, and they didn't make it to Asia for another four point five million years."

"Makes sense."

Claire turned back to Katie when Francisco said, "And then there's this."

He walked over to his workstation and called up a high-resolution image of the object he'd been working on. "Just got this image this morning," he said apologetically once Claire and the others had come over.

He punched another few strokes, and the 3-D image on the screen started rotating slowly.

"If the editors see this, maybe they'll be more open-minded about that," he said, pointing over to Katie's workstation.

Claire stared dumbly. "What should I be looking for?"

On the screen was an image of the eye sockets and forehead of a skull. She could imagine it was some kind of elephant skull, though the forehead was higher and less sloped than she remembered from her work on elephant anatomy.

Francisco pointed toward the forehead. "Back then, elephants were more primitive in every way than they are today, particularly in brain size. This is the kind of forehead you'd expect to see in a smarter elephant from the future, not a specimen from millions of years ago. Also, look at this in comparison to its contemporaries." Francisco pulled up some other images of ancient elephant skulls. "They were all more bony and thick. Bart looks more delicate, gracile."

"Bart?"

Francisco laughed. "Sorry, we've been calling it Bart—you know Bart Simpson, the cartoon character who's sorta got a jar head? Well, so does our guy."

"Bart it is," said Claire. "Could it be an adolescent—like the cartoon Bart?"

"Possible, but doubtful for reasons I can go into later. It could also be paedomorphism—like you see with bonobos today. We'll know more once it's uncovered. But then"—Francisco hit a few more keystrokes, pulling up images of the ulnae—"there's more. If we assume that the skull and the ulnae came from the same species—big assumption, I know—we come to the conclusion that this guy had a very big head relative to his body size—both compared with elephants back then, and even today."

Francisco turned away from the screen. "So, if it turns out that something made Katie's yam, and if I was looking for the maker, my logical suspect would be this guy." He jerked his thumb toward the screen. "The perfect Ganesh."

The group digested this for a few moments. Then Claire said, "Hayden's going to want to see this, so hold off the final uncovering until I see whether he can get back here for it." She then pointed toward Katie and Francisco. "You two. Let's leave that new 'array'"—she made air quotes—"in its block for the time being. I want people to see exactly what these things were like when we found them. We've got some bone chips for further chemical analysis, anyway."

She handed out a few more assignments and then begged off. She had some thinking to do.

45

CLAIRE WANDERED OUT TO THE GARDENS. SHE'D WORKED WITH elephants for years and she knew all the stories, including studies that showed that elephants used some of the same medicinal plants as did tribes in Africa and for the same purposes—to ease labor pains and reduce inflammation. So why would it open them to ridicule to publish the logical implications of what they had found—if it turned out that this is what they found?

She thought about Keerbrock. If she was going to get him on board, she was going to have to meet his austere demands. She thought about the array, the cranium, and the "yam." One: they had no proof that some yet unidentified third party hadn't arranged the bones, deposited the cranium, and carved the yam. Two: it was not impossible that the yam was just a random piece of jadeite, polished by some long-vanished water source. Three: the cranium might come from an adolescent elephant suffering from some deformity—hydrocephalus?—although Claire had to admit it was doubtful that an elephant with that kind of malady would live long enough to reach adolescence. Four: the two arrays of bones were the result of Benoit's random deposition, and the jadeite just happened to be in the same place.

Then she thought about answering these critiques. The first one only worked if the bones and yam had been arranged much more recently. If it was 5.5 million years ago, the third-party explanation was even more sensationalistic than the smart-elephant hypothesis. Dating of the material and the bones could probably settle that one. The second was more difficult because it really was possible that the jadeite was formed by accident rather than design. Nature could produce anything given enough time. The cranium being a deformity was another tough one to reject, but presumably Francisco could settle whether or not it was an adolescent through a more thorough examination. Someone could always throw reason number four at them, but as the number of finds mounted, it became more stretched.

Paleontologists regularly built whole theories about the size, intelligence, social organization, and diet of human ancestors based on a single tooth or small bone. Why weren't they held up to ridicule? She knew the answer: because we know how that story continued, the most recent chapter being *us*.

What she was dealing with was evidence of an ancient animal intelligence—at a time when intelligence was in short supply in any creature—from a line that either died out or got dumber. Put that way, it was perfectly natural that anything Claire's team tried to publish would be greeted with skepticism.

Depressed by this thought, Claire went back to her room to check her email. Her eyes alit on two that had come in, one from Constantine and one from Keerbrock. She took a deep breath and opened Keerbrock's. It read, "Let's talk," and gave a phone number.

Then she turned to Constantine's message. He wanted to come out, and soon. This posed a dilemma. He could be valuable. In documenting the find, his story would lend the credibility of the *Times* to the seriousness of the discovery. But would he and the *Times* respect an embargo?

She was aware of the so-called Ingelfinger rule, which for decades had been the ironclad policy of leading journals and held that a scientific journal would reject any submission that had been previously published in the media. She also knew that some respected journalists would occasionally leak an embargoed story to an online outlet and then publish their own story claiming that the embargo had been broken.

While trying to decide what to do, she opened an email from her mother. It was the usual mélange of gossip—her sister had been in a screaming fight with her husband that brought a cocktail party to a halt—and mixed metaphors, writing that it was time for Madison's husband to "lay his cards on the table and step up to the plate." Rarely did global events penetrate her mom's country club world, so Claire paused when her mom went on to say that a third year of intense drought in Kansas City had led to the closing of the country club's golf course—can you imagine!—which was causing her to think again about this global warming stuff. She also said that Fran Woodleigh, whose family owned a large farming operation in Missouri, was complaining that fertilizer prices were through the roof. Part of it was the drought, but Fran also said that the Russian invasion of Ukraine had shut down a huge fertilizer factory.

46

THAT SAME MORNING SERGEI WENT OUT TO THE RAIL DEPOT. A shipment of building materials and heavy equipment was arriving. Sergei was taking delivery of a new mass spectrometer, and he wanted to ensure that it was handled carefully.

The unloading was well underway when he arrived, and the landing was a jumble of crates, spanking-new pieces of moving equipment and machinery, and stacks of girders, braces, and other prefabricated building materials, all being checked in by teams of foremen and technicians. Roughly fifty uniformed Transteppe employees were involved in feeding all this into the insatiable maw of the giant concession. One of the foremen saw Sergei and waved to him, pointing to the crate he had separated from the rest of the shipment for special handling as per Sergei's instructions.

Sergei started walking over and passed a group of men taking a cigarette break. Most were Transteppe, but a few of the train crew were also smoking and chatting. One of the men looked familiar. He was in a jumpsuit, signaling that he was the lowest-level Transteppe employee, and he was talking with another man who must have been one of the train crew. They were standing in front of a stack of rectangular crates, each about five feet long and two feet high.

Between the buzz of forklifts and other moving equipment it was hard to hear any voice, but as he passed the two men, he thought he heard one speaking Russian, specifically the word *mir*, or peace. He turned around, but the group had already broken up, and he couldn't make out who had spoken.

Sergei made his way to the foreman and, after checking the crate, gave the man further instructions for delivery. Then he headed back to his pickup. Once he got in his car, it came to him why the Kazakh's face had seemed familiar. It was the meek janitor he had come upon several weeks earlier in his workspace.

47

CLAIRE AWOKE THE NEXT MORNING TO AN INSISTENT KNOCKing on her door. It was Rob, and he looked grim. "My office ASAP."

After throwing on some clothes, she headed right over. The grounds were alive with activity. It looked like offices were being packed and trucks were ferrying high-tech equipment and files. Diesel fumes made it difficult to breathe. Moving among the workers were tough-looking security types in black uniforms. They were carrying sidearms. One of them was wrestling a worker to the ground. Once he'd subdued the man, the guard pulled out a laptop the man had stowed under his shirt.

She was already thoroughly alarmed when she got to Rob's office. Sergei was already seated, as was Hayden. No one was smiling. Sergei looked utterly deflated. Remembering their evening together, Claire couldn't help smiling at him and was upset that he didn't smile back.

Something big had happened. She gestured out the window. "What's going on?"

Rob spoke. "Remember how the Ukraine civil war started? Ethnic Russian uprising in Crimea? Well, it looks like that was a trial run. Tell her, Sergei."

Sergei turned wearily. "Here's a crash course in Kazakh history. It's been dominated by Russia for two hundred years. In 1959, there were more Russians than Kazakhs here, then a bunch left after independence in 1991. Now the population is about sixty-three percent Kazakh and twenty-four percent Russian." He paused a bit. "Except here."

"What do you mean here?"

"This district, North Kazakhstan, is nearly half Russian, and only a bit more than a third Kazakh. The capitol, Petropavl, is on the Russian border, and . . ." Sergei looked ashamed.

". . . and what, Sergei?" prompted Rob, coldly.

"And, I guess, this morning, North Kazakhstan decided that it missed the good old days of being part of Russia. The entire regional government declared the district's independence from Kazakhstan and its allegiance to Russia. They arrested the ethnic Kazakh federal officials and replaced the Kazakh leadership in the military with Russians. So far, it's been largely bloodless—so far . . ."

Rob looked sharply at Sergei. "That was just a guess, Sergei?"

Hayden stepped in. "Easy, Rob. Sergei tried to warn us."

"When?"

Claire knew *exactly* when and how. "The phospherite?" As she said this, she thought of the oligarch's visit. All of this was connected.

Hayden nodded.

Rob softened his tone. "What did you know, Sergei?"

"I didn't know anything. I just put two and two together when Primorskichem asked me to let them know of any major phosphorous deposits in the area."

"So why didn't you just tell us?"

Sergei looked miserable. "I couldn't."

"What do they have on you?"

Claire listened intently. She had been hoping that Sergei would tell her more about that bizarre visit from the oligarch, but Sergei clearly did not want to talk about it.

Sergei shook his head. "I have to fix this on my own."

Hayden took charge. "We'll discuss that later. Rob's got to get back to his men. Here's what I think will happen. The president is sure to respond to the Russians, and this is the prize of the region." Hayden thought back to his conversation with Bezanov. "I think the uprising is all about this concession. Ripley's gotten the OK to evacuate all but a skeleton staff until things get sorted out." He turned to Claire. "Pack the objects and the documentation, and have your team ready in an hour. Your guys are getting on that transport plane sitting on the runway—my plane's in Astana and can't land on this runway."

"What about Rob and Sergei?"

"I've got to stay to keep an eye on things."

Sergei added, "Since it's Russians, I can be helpful."

"What about Sauat?"

Sergei spoke up. "I'll protect him until it's safe for his father to get him."

Looking toward Sergei, Claire felt torn. "I should stay, too. Sauat's my responsibility."

Hayden cut her off. "Don't even think about it. You need to be with your team and those objects. Understood? And I can't leave foreigners here who both sides might want to use as bargaining chips."

Rob could see that Claire was getting ready to argue. "Claire," he said quietly, "at Transteppe, Mr. Hayden's word is final. Besides"—he looked somewhat sharply at Sergei—"Sauat will be in good hands—Sergei speaks Russian."

Claire held up her palms in surrender. "OK."

She and Sergei started for the door, when she remembered. "Mr. Hayden."

"Fletch. I'm only Mr. Hayden when I'm giving orders."

"Fletch then. There's a scientist from my old dig, Benoit Richard, who was going to join the team. Is there room for him on the plane?"

Hayden nodded toward Rob, who got on the radio to Ripley. "One more for the plane?" He gave Claire a thumbs-up.

48

SERGEI'S MEN WERE ALREADY PUTTING FOAM IN THE CARRYING cases by the time Claire had weaved her way through the trucks, dust, and diesel fumes to the warehouse.

She held up her hand before anyone could speak. "Things are going kablooey in Kazakhstan and we're getting out of Dodge," said Claire, thinking that her mother couldn't have done better in the mixed-metaphor department. "I'll explain when we're on the plane. Sergei's men will help you pack laptops and backup drives. You two," she said, pointing to Francisco and Katie, "pack the bones and the jadeite. Just you, no one else, and try to do it out of sight, or, if that's impossible, look casual, like you're just packing rock samples." Claire looked at the jadeite and was delighted that they had not progressed in cleaning the rock. Covered with sedimentary crust, it looked like an ordinary sample. "Once packed," she continued, "the stuff has to be in sight of one of us every second until they are on the plane—chain of custody is absolutely critical. Once this is done, race to your rooms and grab what you can in five minutes. We're either coming back, or the stuff will be sent on. We've got"—she looked at her watch—"fifty minutes."

Operating amid chaos was familiar territory for Katie, and she jumped into action. She suggested to Claire that they keep thumb drives with critical data on them in case the laptops got damaged or lost. Francisco didn't do hurrying, but he seemed to recognize that speed was of the essence, and he divided his time between securing files and supervising the packing.

He yelled over to Claire, "How should these cases be marked?"

Here we go again, thought Claire. Yet again they were moving priceless objects with a cavalier disregard for paperwork and protocol. This time, however, she had no compunctions. Leaving them in what might become a war zone was impossible. She thought for just a second. "Mark them 'Samples for Further Analysis' along with the legend for the sector they came from. And put 'one' for the yam, 'two' for the cranium, and 'three' for the new array."

Claire still felt uneasy. She remembered that when American presidents traveled by helicopter, two identical marine helicopters would fly so that potential attackers wouldn't know which one carried the president. "Just to be safe, in case someone comes snooping around, let's also prepare three identical boxes, packed with equal care, but carrying rocks. Just make sure the real samples get on the plane."

Katie wandered by and packed a bunch of laptops and printouts. As she walked by, she looked over her shoulder. "So! Where are we going?"

Claire had to laugh. She didn't know. She shrugged. "I think we'll both find out on the plane."

Claire saw the two Kazakhs sitting at their workstations, watching the frenzy of activity with a mixture of wonderment and anxiety. Sauat was hovering nearby. She went over to him.

"You stick with Sergei. OK?"

"Yes, I will. Are you coming back?"

"Of course! I'll be back as soon as I can." She gave Sauat a big hug. "Oh, and Sauat? I'm putting you in charge of Lawrence, OK?"

Sauat smiled weakly. "I will make sure he is fed and safe."

"When your father comes to get you, can you take Lawrence with you?"

Sauat nodded.

She turned to Karil and Kamila. "Rob can get you both to Astana. Have you talked with Dr. Tabiliev?"

Karil looked at Kamila and then said, "Yes, we spoke with him. If it's OK, we'd like to stay. Dr. Tabiliev says that soldiers are moving everywhere in the cities, and people are . . ." He looked confused for a second. "Settling scores, attacking each other?" Claire nodded. "And it might be safer to stay here. He says that both sides want these mines in working condition."

Claire felt a pang of guilt. If they could stay, shouldn't she be there with them? But she knew that she had to get the objects somewhere safe. She could envision thugs walking through the warehouse, taking what looked interesting and smashing everything else. Or, worse, she could picture a more disciplined force, doing a systematic inventory of the warehouse. Either way, the finds would get destroyed or disappear.

⌐

A thoroughly alarmed Benoit showed up just as they were preparing to move the boxes to the transport plane. He'd made the trip in under an hour—quite possibly a new speed record given the roads. He said the road was absolutely empty coming in this direction, though he'd had to dodge a number of vehicles racing in the other way as furloughed workers left the concession.

49

CLAIRE WAS IN HER ROOM, THROWING CLOTHES AND NOTE-books into a rolling duffel, when she got a call from Rob. "Get packed, but then stand by—transport plane's not going anywhere until we figure a safe path out of here."

They had gotten reports that the insurgents had surface-to-air missiles, and no one wanted to risk a repeat of Malaysian Airlines Flight 17, which was downed during the civil war in Ukraine. Rob turned away from the phone for a second and then said to come over to his office.

There was less chaos now, but somehow the mood was more ominous. The black-uniformed guards were everywhere, and many now kept one hand on their holstered sidearms. She passed a few workers huddled in conversation who looked at her with hostility as she passed. A couple of men nudged each other and pointed at her. She quickened her pace.

The civil war was outside the fence, how far away she did not know, but it had cracked the veneer of normalcy, and the evil ether of war flowed through, creeping over the concession like swamp gas. The comforting sense that tomorrow would be like today was gone. The future was now an abyss for Kazakhs.

She could see a cluster of men in the distance. One was delivering a speech. He wore a white cap, headwear that had recently come into vogue among Islamic extremists. Claire wondered whether the Russians who thought up the current action had considered whether radicals might also see the chaos as an opportunity. Then she thought of Sergei, who always seemed to be two steps ahead. Russia was populated with Sergeis—chess players, mathematicians, conspiracy theorists, men and women who saw machinations everywhere, probably because in their lives, machinations *were* everywhere. She remembered that Russians—Christians—dominated Petropavl, while Muslims were dominant in the rest of the country. Of course, the rebels knew that Islamic extremists might see an opportunity in the civil unrest. They were probably counting on it. The sound of the angry harangue resolved any doubts about whether she and the team should stay. They had to get out—and fast.

Something else caught her attention. Behind the man in the white hat stood another man, calmly surveying the crowd and surroundings. It was the janitor that they had encountered in the off-limits workspace, but now he looked anything but meek.

Claire called Sergei. "Make sure the team stays in the warehouse. No wandering around outside—especially Katie."

Sergei understood. "Got it."

They paused for a moment, both realizing that this might well be the last time they speak to each other.

A convoy of buses and trucks gunned its motors and began moving toward the gate, presumably destined for Astana. She wondered how long it would be before border posts popped up as the breakaway republic and the regime grappled with territorial claims.

After walking past the commissary and checking to see whether anyone was following her, she abruptly stopped. All clear. She turned around and went to the side door. Everyone had cleared out. Lawrence was curled up in a corner. He clearly didn't like the hubbub. Claire remembered reading something George Orwell had written about the Spanish Civil War. When the bombing started, the cats got as far away from humans—and their bombs and guns—as possible, while the dogs, wanting reassurance, followed their owners everywhere.

Lawrence got up and came over to be petted. "Might be time for you to try your hand at being a desert cat," she said as she lightly scratched his head. Lawrence clearly missed the point Claire was making, as he started purring mightily. "For God's sake, Lawrence," she said, "now's not a good time to start acting like a dog."

She was almost at Rob's office when she got a call from Katie, who said one word—"Trouble." Claire raced back to the warehouse. On her way, she noticed that some of the workers were chanting and the crowd was even more agitated. Things were rapidly deteriorating.

She texted Rob, telling him that something was up at the warehouse. When she got there, Katie intercepted her and shot her eyes over to Claire's left. There she saw Azamat Suleimenov, the liaison to the mining ministry, in animated conversation with Karil. To her alarm, they were standing next to the six sample cases, three of which carried the artifacts, the other three mere rocks. They were about to be loaded onto a motorized trolley, but Azamat was blocking the path. Kiril looked both angry and apprehensive.

"What seems to be the problem?" said Claire more calmly than she felt, as she knew exactly why Suleimenov had showed up.

"I am here to make sure that nothing relating to Kazakhstan's great heritage leaves the country. Moreover, I will take possession of any such artifacts and deliver them for safekeeping to Astana."

Claire smiled. "Oh, you're talking about the array? I can assure you those bones already are in a very safe place."

This brought him up short. He kept looking suspiciously at the packing crates.

"How can you be sure?"

"Because we delivered our priceless find to your president as a gift over a week ago. Didn't the presidency inform you?" Claire pretended to think a second. "No? My guess is that they didn't think the issue was material for the *mining* liaison." She hated having to use this bit of synecdoche and felt unclean because she was getting so good at this stuff.

Still, it worked. The mention of the president had the desired effect on Suleimenov, but he still didn't want to let go. "So if our beloved president has everything, you won't mind opening up a crate?"

She noticed that Sergei was walking toward her with something in his hand.

"Actually, *I* mind," Sergei said as he stepped in. "I'm sure your president wants us to continue our analysis while work is suspended here, and we need those samples at our research lab in Canada to do that. The transport plane is leaving any minute."

Claire noticed that Rob had entered the back of the warehouse, accompanied by one of the black-uniformed security team. He was wearing a holster and had his hand on the butt of a pistol. Suleimenov hadn't noticed his presence.

Maybe it was because Claire and Sergei seemed to think the crates significant, or maybe because Suleimenov had some sixth sense for opportunity, but he wasn't going to let go. "So, in that case, maybe you should open a crate quickly."

The crates were numbered one through six. "OK," said Sergei, and Claire watched in horror as Sergei moved toward the crate with the cranium, holding a claw hammer. What the fuck was he doing?

Just as he was about to wedge it under the top of the crate, Suleimenov grabbed his arm. "No, open this one," he said, pointing to one of the three containing ordinary rocks.

She hadn't told Rob about her ruse with the dummy crates. She noticed that his grip tightened on the pistol, but she couldn't warn him.

Sergei pried up the top. Suleimenov poked around the rocks, and then sighed with exasperation. "OK, go," he said, and wheeled and strode toward the door of the warehouse where his driver and vehicle were waiting outside.

She noticed that her hands were trembling—was that what Suleimenov saw? She looked over at Rob, who cocked a finger at her and then headed out the door. She turned to Sergei.

"What if he hadn't grabbed your arm?"

"Big mess! But you saw Rob? Suleimenov wasn't going to get those crates."

As things turned out, it didn't matter.

50

AFTER MAKING SURE THAT THE CRATES WERE EN ROUTE TO THE transport plane, Claire headed back over to Rob's office. Hayden was on the phone, and Rob was talking rapid-fire on the radio. As soon as Hayden hung up, he invited Claire to sit. He looked remarkably untroubled.

"This must be my tenth coup . . . uprising . . . civil war . . . expropriation," he began without preamble. "Unfortunately, minerals and precious metals can't anticipate future political stability when they decide where to deposit themselves underground."

"Well, as you might imagine, this uprising is of particular interest to me."

Hayden gave a short laugh. "Understood. I've been on the phone with our intelligence guys, and there's good news and bad news on that score. The good news is that the rebels look disciplined, and they are clearly taking orders from Moscow."

"Which means?"

"Which means that they want to at least have some appearance of legitimacy—minimal violence, no revenge killings, respect for foreign property . . ." Hayden waved around the room. "I think their druthers would be to simply have us shift the direct deposit from Astana to their bank account in Petropavl. Then the Russians can try to take control the way they usually do—de facto expropriation through trumped-up tax evasion, etcetera but that brings me to the bad news . . ."

"OK, I'm ready." Though Claire wasn't at all.

"Astana can't let this go. Apart from the insult to an ego the size of Jupiter, the president simply can't keep this country together if he loses the jobs and potential income this place represents."

"So he'll fight to keep it."

"Yep, and this breakaway regime can't make it without Transteppe, either. So this is going to be the center of the battle."

Claire had never been in a war zone, and despite her brave words earlier, she didn't want to find out. She remembered the white-capped man and told Hayden about him. She also mentioned the janitor who had morphed into a menacing bodyguard.

Listening, Rob got on the radio. After a hurried conversation, he turned to Hayden. "There's a mob gathering, and they seem to be heading toward the runway. You've got to take off—now! Islamic radicals don't give a hoot about what either side wants."

Hayden looked at Rob levelly. "I'll take off as soon as Claire and the others are in the air."

Rob clenched his fists in frustration.

Claire was alarmed but kept her voice even. "Heading where?"

"That's the question, isn't it? You look at a map, and Kazakhstan is surrounded by a bunch of Stans. Rob?"

Rob picked up his radio. "Any progress?"

"Think so. If the transport heads due south—right now—there's no credible way either side could shoot down the plane under false flag."

"Are we sure they care whether their footprints are covered?"

Claire was alarmed. "What's this false flag?"

"Oh," said Rob calmly, "it's when one side perpetrates some heinous crime, like shooting down a civilian plane, and then plants evidence blaming the other side. It's all the rage for dirt bag regimes."

Hayden was looking at Claire. "I'm going to take the helicopter to Astana to get to my plane. Maybe you should come with me."

Claire stood frozen for a moment. Then she turned to Hayden. "I can't leave my team . . ." She paused as an idea formed. "But can you take the array with you? It doesn't weigh much more than I do with a bag. We should split up the objects . . . in case something happens . . ."

"I understand." Hayden turned to Rob. "Have them take the array from the transport and move it to my helicopter—"

Claire interrupted, "It's marked 'Samples for Further Analysis,' box number three."

Rob nodded and picked up his radio. After giving instructions, he called another of his team. He listened and then signed off. "OK, confirmed. Best they can come up with is head south, refuel in Tashkent and then head for Abu Dhabi. Our law firm there will expedite transfers of cargo and passengers."

"What about all this?" Claire waved a hand at the concession.

"Our hope is that both sides realize that damaging the infrastructure would be self-defeating. So we think the fight will be outside the concession, though the rebels are probably going to try to use it as a garrison. We're trying to get word to the Russians through Primorskichem that this would be a bad idea."

They were interrupted by one of Rob's men wearing desert fatigues. He pointed to the phone. Rob picked up the receiver, listened for a bit, and then said, "Hold on." He pointed to the phone next to Hayden. "You'd better hear this." When Hayden picked up, Rob said, "OK, Mr. Hayden is on. Repeat what you just told me."

Claire was growing increasingly alarmed as Rob and Hayden exchanged glances as they listened. Finally, Rob spoke. "OK, who's the contact?" He listened a few seconds more and jotted some notes on a pad.

Hayden turned to Claire. "Looks like things are ratcheting up. I don't have time to go into all the details, but the headline is that the US will not allow Russia to extend control over a major mine—somehow they knew it was a phosphate source—and they've gotten the Kazakh president to ask for logistical help. The US is sending two teams, accompanied by Special Forces, up from Uzbekistan . . . and God knows how the Russians are going to react to that . . ." Hayden looked uncharacteristically distracted. "The teams won't get here until tomorrow. If the separatists get wind of this, they're going to try and grab this place—like right now!" He looked her directly in the eye. "You've got to get cracking," he said, signaling that the meeting was over.

51

THERE WAS NO TIME FOR EXTENDED GOODBYES AS CLAIRE'S team joined a ragtag group of expatriates filing on to the Boeing Globemaster transport sitting on the runway. Rob's security forces had flanked the group on either side as they made their way to the plane. Claire craned her neck but could not see the agitated crowd that had gathered earlier. Once they got to the plane, the crew grabbed their bags as they shuffled up the ramp in the back. Claire broke away to give Rob and Sergei a hug. Sergei seemed calm, but he hugged her a little longer than necessary, and when she pulled away, she was startled to see that there were tears in his eyes.

"Are you going to be OK?" she asked, reluctant to move away.

"I'll be fine," said Sergei. "This is my job . . ."

"I'll be back," she said with an intensity that surprised her.

Hayden's pilot beckoned him to his helicopter, which was beginning to rev up. Claire looked back and saw a vehicle was accelerating toward the runway. It was headed off by a truck. The crew frantically warned the group to hurry up. As Claire reached the top of the ramp, she saw Hayden boarding the chopper.

Adjusting to the dimmer light, Claire looked toward the front of the vast fuselage. The center was reserved for cargo. Rudimentary seats were arrayed along both sides of the fuselage. Claire, Katie, and Francisco were guided toward the front, where there were two rows of more traditional airline seats. They passed an assortment of expatriate engineers, managers, technicians, and heavy-equipment operators already strapped into seats. All stared curiously as they passed. Katie elicited particular attention. A burly, heavily tattooed roughneck wearing a T-shirt patted the seat next to him. Katie nixed this with a quick "naughty boy" wag of her finger, a judiciously softened rejection given the words on the front of his T-shirt: "Guns Don't Kill People" on one line, and then, "I Do," on the line below.

They passed Karil, who was standing sentry next to the two boxes holding the yam-like stone and the cranium. He gave Claire a thumbs-up, indicating that the boxes had been continuously in his sight and then ran toward the rear to exit the plane before the ramp was pulled up.

Benoit was already strapped in when the team got to their seats. The big plane started accelerating even before they had fastened their belts. There were no windows, but there were pop-up screens that came with each seat, tuned to an exterior camera. Claire looked and on the far edge of the screen, she saw Hayden's helicopter taking off. As it gained altitude, she saw a man—it was the janitor!—pointing something balanced on his shoulder at the aircraft. There was a glint as something flashed toward the helicopter. A huge fireball erupted, and an instant later the transport plane was rocked by turbulence. Claire screamed, "No!" and started to move from her seat. Katie grabbed her arm to hold her back and then reached around her shoulders and gave her a fierce hug, feeling the shudders of Claire's uncontrollable sobs.

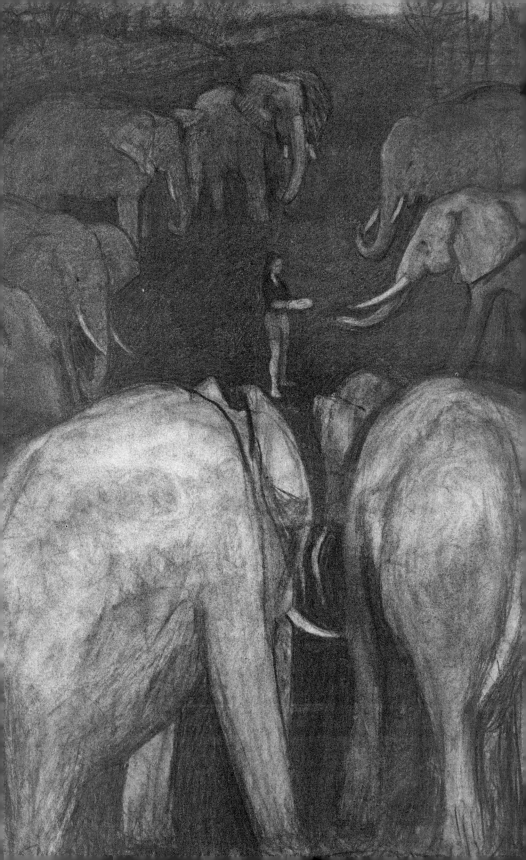

RUSHMERE

52

CLAIRE STOOD AT THE BACK OF THE HUGE CROWD THAT HAD assembled at Hayden's graceful, Pacific Lodge–style mansion on Vancouver Island. That she was there was something of a miracle, as she'd been sleep-walking since the escape from Transteppe. Katie had assumed the role of aide-de-camp and nurse, dealing with logistics and trying to get Claire to eat. Earlier, Helen, one of Hayden's two grown daughters (he also had a son), had come up to Claire and said that her father had been truly energized by her discovery. She said that the children had asked a number of people from various parts of his life to say a few words at the service. Claire looked anguished. "I don't think I could get words out," she said, and then seeing the daughter's disappointed expression, she added, "Your father was the most truly good man I ever met."

Now it was Helen's turn to break down. She embraced Claire in a silent hug.

Don't hug me, Claire thought, *I'm the reason your father's dead.*

Since the escape, the scene where Hayden had said he wouldn't board his helicopter until Claire and the team were on the plane had replayed in Claire's mind in an endless loop. For this reason alone, the funeral was torture, even though the setting was benign. His family plot was at the top of a broad lawn running down to the water, backed by towering Douglas firs. His grave was set beside a stone commemorating Alicia Tellstrom Hayden, who, from the dates, Claire assumed had been his wife.

Were it not for the circumstances of his death, Claire would have appreciated the testimonials, which documented a lifetime of generosity, courage, and gracious gestures. The last speaker was Helen, who spoke movingly of Hayden as a father. At the end of her remarks, she looked at Claire at the back of the crowd. "One thing I know is that Dad died happy. In the past few months, he had gotten involved in an archaeological venture. He never told us what it was, but his excitement was palpable. It gave him a new lease on life after the death of our mother. Speaking for the family, we hope that work will see the light of day."

A number of people turned to see where Helen was looking. This brought a whole new level of agony for Claire. Given that her last array had gone down with the helicopter and the other bones were in the hands of dictators and a petty bureaucrat, it was very much open to question whether the discovery would ever be published.

Claire couldn't face the reception and left for the hotel, asking Katie to fend off any questions about what they were working on. The next day, on the flight back to Boston, Katie decided it was time to shift her role from nursemaid to drill sergeant. She turned to Claire. "You heard Helen at the funeral. If we're going to honor Hayden's memory, you've got to pull yourself together."

Claire bridled. "Honor his memory? Do you know who you're talking to? I'm the woman who got him killed."

Katie was having none of it. "That talk stops right here—you were just one of dozens of passengers. It's not as though Hayden would have done anything different if you weren't on that plane."

Katie's reference brought back the memory of Hayden's death. In the fog of shame and grief into which she descended afterward, she'd forgotten something important about that moment. The janitor! Someone who worked at Transteppe had deliberately killed Hayden. The why was important, but more urgent was the fact that he might still be there. Rob needed to know that; Sergei needed to know that.

53

THE FIRST THING SHE DID UPON LANDING WAS CALL ROB. SHE told him about the janitor who'd pointed the thing on his shoulder at Hayden's helicopter.

"Others reported the same thing."

"Have you found him?"

"No, he's disappeared, but we've got the rocket launcher. It's a Stinger, American made, but popular in the Chechen war, which explains how it got in the hands of extremists, but not how it got here."

"Why did they kill him?" Claire choked up at the memory, and the words came out haltingly.

Rob had a developing theory on this, but he did not want to alarm Claire. The obvious answer was that the helicopter was a target of opportunity for crazed extremists, but Hayden had told Rob about his conversation with Bezanov, and Rob realized that eliminating Hayden might smooth the way for a distressed sale to Primorskichem by one of the external partners, particularly since Transteppe was now in a war zone. It was awfully convenient that the extremists rose up at that exact moment and that the one notable act of violence was to take out Hayden's helicopter.

"That's what we're trying to piece together. We don't know if Mr. Hayden was targeted or just a target of opportunity," said Rob. "It's chaos here."

"Is Sergei involved in figuring this out? He's so smart, and he may have seen something."

"No, and I don't want him to be. Sergei's got his hands full between shifting sensitive docs off-site and intermediating with the Russians." What Rob didn't mention was that he feared that if he shared his suspicions with Sergei, it might change Sergei's demeanor during negotiations in ways that might put him in mortal danger. He had not told Sergei about the role of the janitor.

Hearing this, Claire said, "Still, I'm worried that Sergei's in danger... and you, too, Rob," she added.

Rob laughed. "Don't worry about us. Almost all the local staff have been evacuated, and we've got American Special Forces guarding the concession. We're probably safer here than in the States."

54

IN THE ENSUING WEEKS, CLAIRE, CHEERED ON BY KATIE, BEGAN to think about finishing the letter formally announcing the discovery. When she asked Katie how they could present the find without the array, Katie gave her a buck-up speech. "You've still got the cranium and the jadeite. We play it as it lies. That's what fighters do."

"OK, I'll try."

Katie gave Claire's hand a squeeze. "I'll be right there, too!"

Back at Rushmere, Claire discovered that William Friedl, expansively generous with Hayden's money, had set her up on the first floor of the spanking-new behavioral science complex, the gift of an alumnus who had made obscene billions shorting derivatives in 2008. Claire had no particular instinct for making her office homey. She had a functional wooden desk, now covered with papers and notes, a rolling chair, a couple of other chairs for visitors, and a bookshelf against the far wall.

The campus itself basked in the full glory of a New England summer. Most of the undergraduates were on vacation, though high school students were trooping through for college visits, and there was a constant stream of scholars arriving for conferences. She could see the perpetual Frisbee game on the common as well as students reading in the shade of a row of sycamores against the quiet, reassuring hum of the June heat.

The charm of Rushmere, however, could only be enjoyed if one turned a deaf ear to events beyond the campus. Claire had only been gone from the States for a few months, but, as she came out of her daze following Hayden's death, she was struck by the degree to which the country was becoming disheveled. In the faculty dining hall, she over-heard colleagues speculating about which departments might be shut down next as grant money dried up and students dropped out, often citing financial stress in an economy that perpetually seemed on the brink of recession. That morning, listening to NPR, she heard a long report on the fires, floods, and droughts accompanying the extreme weather that gripped much of the country. It was almost biblical.

Still, Rushmere was a world away from Kazakhstan. Claire had been receiving carefully worded updates from Sergei and Rob. Though thousands of miles apart, they were, in a sense, huddling the way fam-ilies do after the death of a loved one. With the arrival of the American advisers, the breakaway putsch had devolved into a simmering stale-mate that so far had spared the concession. The Kazakh military had bivouacked between Petropavl and Transteppe. Evidently, the presi-dent had decided that he could live with the defection of the city so long as the seized territory did not include the concession, and so far the rebels had not tested his resolve on that issue, though that might happen at any moment. Work at Transteppe was paralyzed and every-one remained on high alert. As the news filtered in, Claire was relieved that she and the team had gotten out when they did, though she still hated leaving Sergei behind.

She had terrors of a different kind facing her in the US. Keerbrock was coming to see the cranium and talk. She had gone over this meet-ing countless times in her head but still dreaded his arrival.

And now, here he was. Claire watched him walk up to the entrance of the building accompanied by Friedl and the head of the geophysics lab, who was clearly excited to have the great man's ear. Trailing along were a couple of star-struck grad students. She couldn't tell from Keerbrock's expression whether he was interested or completely bored. He had to be seventy-five, but the years had not diminished his intimidating aura—at least in Claire's eyes. The group stopped at the door to her building. Keerbrock said something to Friedl, shook the geophysicist's hand in a perfunctory brush-off, and then walked in alone. A moment later the intercom on her phone buzzed, and a few seconds later there was a knock on her door.

When she opened it, Keerbrock just stood there for a few seconds. He looked at Claire. He wasn't hostile, more noncommittal. Still, Claire had the feeling she had failed some test. "Well, you've been busy since we last met," he finally said. *He remembered!* In no hurry at all, the tall scientist looked around her office. He walked over to her bookshelf and picked up an article lying on top of a pile, "Evolution and Environmental Change in Early Human Prehistory" by Richard Potts, tapped it a couple of times and then put it down. Without turning around, he said, "Why don't you fill me in, and then let's take a look at what you've found."

Nervous as she was, Claire knew that the only chance she had was for Keerbrock to see the cranium and her virtual presentation of the array before they talked. "Actually, why don't we take a look before we talk."

Keerbrock appeared amused. Apparently, he was not used to his suggestions being countermanded. "As you wish," he said, almost graciously.

Claire led the way to a locked, windowless storage room. Opening the door, she turned on the lights. On a worktable in the center of the room were the cranium and the yam, as well as chunks of the sedimentary rock in which they had been embedded. The array was conspicuously absent, but represented by photos on a whiteboard behind the table that depicted objects as they appeared in the scans as well as how they looked after the surrounding rock had been picked away. Another had photos of the lip as it was in the badlands, complete with photos of the recumbent fold, which had brought the objects toward the surface, while a third board displayed some of Sergei's work dating the various strata and objects.

Keerbrock first went to the whiteboard showing the lip in its natural context, then the other two boards. Only after studying the photos and data did he turn to the objects on the table. Neither had spoken a word since they left Claire's office. Keerbrock spent a good deal of time looking at the cranium. He then picked up a chunk of the sedimentary rock, felt its texture, and studied it closely. Next he peered at the jadeite and sighed. The stone was still encrusted with rock, but its shape was clear, as was the small patch of surface that looked smooth and polished. Claire clenched her fists. She knew what was coming.

"You realize that this"—he pointed at the rock—"is radioactive?"

"I think I know what you mean . . ."

"It would have been far better had you never uncovered it." Again Keerbrock shook his head. He sat down in a chair next to the worktable.

Claire didn't know what to say.

He looked up and down the table, slowly tapping his fingers. "OK, we'll get back to this. What's your plan?"

Claire took him through the suite of studies and papers she had sketched out, starting with a description of the find, its geological context, and dating techniques. It was a conservative approach that explored the possible origins of the bones, whether the cranium and the ulnae came from the same animal or species, what was the age of the creature or creatures at death, whether there was any evidence of disease or malnutrition, and, finally, how the bones fit in the taxonomy of the Elephas line. She then described other parallel tracks the team would pursue, trying to fit the elephants into a climatic and ecological context.

Keerbrock slightly arched an eyebrow, as much a show of approval as he was ever likely to give. "So far so good, but there's more, isn't there?"

This was the moment she dreaded. "Yes, there's more."

"So I feared."

Claire drew a deep breath. "Yes, there's another track. If, as we suspect, the features of the cranium point to an explosive growth in the frontal lobe—rather than random deformity—then we'd like to try to fit this into the biogeophysical template—the one that Potts and you pioneered that at times of rapid climate change, specialists tended to die out while generalists survived. What other animals underwent rapid evolutionary change at that time; what were the environmental stresses driving adaptation; what ability was that explosion of brain size enhancing or enabling?"

"With just one cranium, you'd be constructing a pretty large building on a very small foundation . . ."

"You know better than me that some grand evolutionary stories have been built on far less," said Claire.

"That's right, you've got *pictures* of bones in an array—but not the bones themselves—and a rock that looks very much like the type of food that a smart animal would survive on—and subsequently worship—in a time of extreme dearth. I'll bet that you even have a working hypothesis about the ecological drivers, yes?" He looked right at Claire. "Something about the need for communication and cooperation driving social complexity, producing a positive feedback, and an ecological surplus ability in the form of consciousness and a capacity for symbolic expression?"

Claire was miserable. Keerbrock was heading down the path to the same cavalier dismissal he'd given ten years earlier.

"And," Keerbrock continued in a reasonable tone, "when you publish this hypothesis, I think you know what happens next—all the solid work you and your confederates have done on the noncognitive aspects of this find get buried under the avalanche of ridicule that will greet the announcement of five-and-a-half-million-year-old elephant Picassos."

Keerbrock stood up. "I know why you contacted me—your find might be the missing piece I talked about in years past. But one reason I gave up that chase was that finding it was one thing; proving it an impossible problem."

Keerbrock got up to leave. Claire took a couple of deep breaths. "Ten years ago you were right." Keerbrock stopped but didn't turn around. "But now you're wrong."

Keerbrock slowly turned. "I'm wrong?"

Claire met his gaze. "Yes, you're wrong. You're wrong because the world has had four decades to see that the scientific method fails when it comes to things like consciousness, and you're wrong because people like me have learned from past mistakes. We've learned how to frame the issue in terms of drivers and noncognitive abilities rather than getting mired in improvable assertions and unanswerable questions."

Keerbrock came back and stood by the worktable. "Say that last part again—and, by the way, I don't accept that first part."

"I'm saying that I recognize the limitations of the empirical method for dealing with matters of the mind. I don't need to jump to the obvious conclusion; all I need to do is lay out a plausible scenario for the dramatic physical changes in the size and, so far as it can be inferred, the structure of the brain, and what functions—stress functions—these changes enabled." She took a breath. "It's going to take some time even to get to that point. I can leave questions of culture and cognition for later—though I'll tell you straight out: that's why I'm doing this!"

Pointing to the jadeite stone, Keerbrock asked mildly, "And what about this?"

Claire ran out of steam. "I don't know. When the scans showed it in the rock, I gave it to Katie Segal, one of the graduate students, to study..." Claire's eyes widened as she realized what she had done.

There was a silence. Keerbrock shook his head sadly. "So let's frame the situation: you're starting several hard-science parallel tracks that will involve several different teams of scientists, and you've outsourced the most delicate thing of all—the part that you've got to be scrupulously careful to avoid overinterpreting, which would undermine the credibility of everything else; in other words you have given the part that could blow the whole thing up—to an untested graduate student?"

"I trust Katie," Claire offered lamely, wondering to herself what Katie might do. She owed Katie her sanity, and the young woman had been extraordinary after Hayden's death. But she had brought Katie on board in part because she was a rebel. Now that rebellious streak could undo everything. Still, she had to trust her. "Katie took a big leap when she abandoned the dig to come with me. I can't toss her aside. And besides, I'll be vetting any submissions for publication."

"No doubt, but it's not the scientific journals I'm worried about."

Claire knew exactly what he meant, and she thought of Constantine at the *New York Times* and the slew of emails he had sent her that she had yet to answer. She couldn't put him off much longer, and he was smart enough to start contacting the rest of her team if she continued to stonewall him.

Claire saw her chances to enlist Keerbrock's involvement slipping away. She had no idea what to say at this point, but she had to make her pitch. The scientist, seeing that Claire was about to speak, held up a finger.

"Before you ask something to which you won't like my answer, let me say a couple of things. What you've found *could* turn out to be *very* important. Or—by now you know what the 'or' is . . . Let's keep in touch, and let's see how things go . . ." Once again, he started to leave and then stopped. "Oh, and I don't need to tell you this, but I'd keep things very close to the vest until you're ready to publish."

"Let's keep in touch" was a far cry from what she'd hoped Keerbrock's response would be. But she noticed that in leaving he had left the door open. She thought about that. It was true; he *had* left the door open. And he wouldn't have cautioned her about keeping things quiet unless he thought what she was doing was worth protecting.

55

IT WAS A DAY FOR TELEPHONE CALLS. FRIEDL RANG NOT LONG after Keerbrock had departed to ask how it went. Claire didn't want the department chair to get nervous or, worse, smell blood, so she decided a low-key response might be best, as though Nobel Prize winners dropped in on a regular basis. "It was fine. He had some useful suggestions. We're going to keep in touch." *That* should buy her some time. "I'm *very* happy." This last sentence was about as far from the truth as was possible.

After she got off the phone, she thought about Keerbrock's warning about word getting out. In Kazakhstan, she hadn't really worried about the press or the blogosphere. But since she had returned, a couple of reporters had contacted her and some of her team about the events in Kazakhstan, but, fortunately, they had focused on the upheaval. Kazakhstan barely registered with the self-absorbed American public.

Back home, the stakes were much higher, and she realized that word already was out—Constantine had warned her about Gwynne, after all. Who knew what he was saying? And while she had warned her team about casually discussing the find, who knew whether they took her seriously? She didn't worry about Katie or Francisco, but Benoit was a proven quantity when it came to treachery, and then there were Waylon, Tony, Abigail, not to mention Samantha who knew juicy stuff about the find and had no stake whatsoever in keeping it to herself.

Claire had told Katie, Francisco, and Benoit to take some much needed R&R once they got to Germany (via Dubai), and the team had scattered. Now, she knew she needed them back at work, and she sent out emails asking them to get in contact ASAP and reminding them not to discuss the find. She sent a separate email to Sergei and the two Kazakhs helping at Transteppe laying out what she had in mind.

Even before Keerbrock's visit, Claire had formulated a plan for rolling out the discovery. She'd hoped to have Keerbrock's imprimatur on it, but now she was going to have to go ahead without it. And she had a good plan, though it only worked so long as the world was populated with honorable people who played by the rules.

Her train of thought was interrupted when her phone rang again. Her heart leaped when she saw it was Transteppe.

"Sergei?"

"Yes, it's me."

"Thank God! Is everything OK?"

Sergei laughed. "Sure, we now have a karaoke hour at five every night. You should hear Rob's version of 'Stayin' Alive.'"

"Seriously!"

Sergei dropped the bantering tone. "Seriously, I miss you, and, by the way, I can't remember the last time I said those words to anyone— in any language."

"Oh, Sergei . . ." Claire said wistfully. "Wish you were here."

"As do I."

This reminded her that Sergei had other, so far unnamed, problems besides the uprising. "About your situation—"

Sergei cut her off smoothly. "Don't worry, I'm a very good juggler," he said and quickly ended the call.

She barely had time to reflect on Sergei's call when her cell phone rang again. She looked to see who it was, but the ID was unavailable. She debated a second before answering. "Hello?"

It was Constantine. "Hi, Claire," he said cheerily.

"Hi, Adam," she said, wondering where he had gotten her cell number, and whether his pride would let him complain about her unresponsiveness.

"Heard you had a hairy escape from Kazakhstan."

"No big deal. Could have been far worse."

"Glad to hear that." Constantine paused, apparently done with the small talk. "Are you near your computer?"

Uh-oh. "Should I be?"

She could hear a chuckle. "*Old Bones*, the paleontological gossip site, just put out a tweet about your ancient elephant bones saying that they fell off a truck."

"Fuck's sake!" A few clicks and there it was, full frontal snark:

Word is that there is no "there" there regarding the "discovery" of a five-million-year-old elephant culture. So clumsy, those Silk Road camel jockeys! Madame Blavatsky on hold on Line 1.

"Thanks for the good news, Adam."

"Just sayin'," he said, keeping up the breezy tone, "it might be good to get *your* story out before someone else—for instance the slime bucket who fed the item to *Old Bones*—takes over the narrative."

Claire wondered for an instant whether Constantine had fed the story to *Old Bones*, but she quickly put the thought out of her head. He was persistent but not slimy. She made an instant decision. "OK, Adam, here's how we're proceeding: we're submitting something soon for fast-track scientific publication. You'll be my first call once we know it'll be published."

"Thank you, Claire, that's very kind, but how about letting me in the tent under embargo so I can be ready to go?"

Claire thought about this. Even if she trusted Constantine, what about his editors? What if another blog put something out? The *Times* could say that the embargo had been broken . . . "Sorry, Adam, but I do mean it about being my first call."

There was a silence on the other end for a few seconds. "OK, how about an exclusive?"

Claire felt a frisson of panic. These were dangerous waters, as she had no idea how these things worked.

"Meaning what?"

"Meaning that the *Times* will commit to prominently featured coverage of your find in return for exclusive access up until publication, which will occur immediately after your work is published in a leading—meaning peer-reviewed—scientific journal."

Claire didn't know the ins and outs of the newspaper business, but common sense told her that Constantine would not have made that offer without prior approval from his editors.

"Can I get that in writing?"

"Sure, so long as we're clear: no peer-reviewed publication, no article."

"Sure, if there's no publication, I've got other problems . . ."

"And no leaks from your team to other publications—that's another deal breaker."

Claire thought about Keerbrock's warning, and about Benoit, the only one she was really worried about.

"Again, if this gets out before journal publication, I've got bigger problems." She thought a bit. "We can start talking after the letter is accepted—that'll give you a couple of weeks."

"Not now?"

"Sorry, we need to focus without any distractions."

56

FRANCISCO LOOKED AGAIN AT THE THREE-DIMENSIONAL MODELS slowly rotating on two computer screens in his temporary office in a drab administration building at the National Zoo in Washington, DC. With Benoit's help (an important positive on the Benoit ledger, which had heretofore been laden with nothing but negative checkmarks), he had secured visiting scholar status at the Smithsonian. Claire had insisted that Francisco's real work be kept under wraps until they were ready to publish, and so Benoit had described his project as computer modeling of the evolutionary history of the elephant brain. To further insulate Francisco from other scientists, he'd been installed in the administration building rather than the sleek new glass-walled genetics lab the zoo had recently built.

Though naturally sociable, Francisco understood the need for secrecy, and he was happy to listen to Rhonda, the sunny middle-aged lifer zoo administrator in the adjoining office, talk about her babysitter problems. During work hours he kept to himself. He'd bought a trail bike and would take long, sweltering rides through Rock Creek Park during lunch hours and after work. After months in Kazakhstan, he simply loved Washington's buffet of restaurants and bars. He'd taken the phone numbers of several young women but hadn't yet followed up.

Mostly, he worked, taking advantage of the Smithsonian's vast database on mammalian anatomy. After fine-tuning the quick and dirty computer model of the likely shape of Bart's brain that he had done at Transteppe, Francisco had continued to work on the comparison with the brains of modern African elephants.

One distinctive aspect of the modern elephant brain is that there are a huge number of neurons in the cerebellum in relation to the cerebral cortex, which is where most thinking takes place. This disproportion—ten times the ratio in other mammals—had led to a lot of speculation about what these neurons were doing. The consensus was that the explosive growth had something to do with sound processing. Elephants used extremely low-frequency vocalizations for long-distance communication, and their reliance on sound might have spurred the growth of neurons to process the information. There was similar growth in the cerebellum of toothed whales and bats, animals that relied on extremely sophisticated echolocation abilities.

The other candidate to spur such growth were the demands entailed in controlling the elephant trunk's one hundred fifty thousand muscles, which give the elephant the ability to both pick up a paintbrush and pull down a tree. The need to process the extraordinary amount of sensory and motor information involved in the animal's trunk could alone explain the huge number of cerebellar neurons.

The demands of the trunk and vocalization might also explain why the elephant had a disproportionate ratio of cerebellar neurons to cerebral cortex neurons. In physical terms, a brain is an expensive piece of equipment, at least for land animals that have to deal with gravity. The more a brain grows in size, the more blood is diverted from the muscles—there's a trade-off between brains and brawn—and also, the bigger the brain, the better the diet required to supply its energy. And in this expensive piece of equipment, perhaps the most expensive part is the cerebral cortex, where we think and make purposeful decisions. So, an animal doesn't have more brainpower than it needs, and particularly an animal doesn't have more cerebral cortex than it needs. And that seems to be the case for modern African elephants.

But not Bart. As Francisco stared at the rotating simulations, his mind flooded with the implications. He sat back and did nothing for a few minutes. Then he grabbed his phone and typed out a brief message. *I've got something.*

57

KATIE PLUNKED HERSELF INTO THE ONE SPARE CHAIR AND dropped her bag. She was wearing jeans and a T-shirt and could have passed for an undergraduate.

"So, what's the plan?

Claire had scheduled a teleconference call for the evening so that Sergei and the Transteppe crew could join. Francisco would be calling from his office at the National Zoo in Washington. Benoit would be working from his office at the University of Montana. So Claire had a few hours to brief Katie.

"I never really enjoyed college, but for whatever reason, it's nice to be back on a campus," said Claire. "How about you; how was home?" Katie had taken a few days to go back to San Francisco.

Katie cocked her head. She didn't miss much. Katie laughed. "You're right, it's good to be back on campus."

Claire took a deep breath and plunged right in.

"Keerbrock came by."

Katie's eyes widened.

"Jesus! Is he on board?"

"He's not the kind of guy to go all the way on the first date, but there will be a second date."

"Totally cool!"

Claire looked down. She hated what she was about to do. "And he warned me about you."

Katie looked like she had taken a bullet in the gut. It was the first time Claire had seen her lose her cool. She put a hand on Katie's shoulder.

"Not you specifically."

She saw relief flood over Katie's features. What *had* she done in the past? Claire remembered a line, "Nobody goes through life undefeated." She quickly filled in Katie on the substance of Keerbrock's reservations. She told it straight, including the part of trusting the potentially most explosive part of the study to a graduate student.

After discussing how far they could push the boundaries without being dismissed, Claire asked, "So I need to know. Can you live with publishing far less than you are certain is true? If it's any consolation, I had to make a similar compromise to get this affiliation with Rush-mere."

"I am who I am," Katie said soberly, "but I am loyal." She fixed Claire with a direct look. "You, of all people, should know that."

Claire felt like a combination of an ingrate a war criminal. "You're right, I do know that."

Katie left shortly afterward to explore the campus. They planned to meet just before the conference call. Claire looked at her phone and saw that there were a few unread messages. One was from Benoit, confirming that he would be on the teleconference. Another was from Francisco: *I've got something.* Given Francisco's laconic nature, he really must have something big. Claire responded, apologizing for not getting back to him sooner and saying that she would call on Francisco first when they got to the progress report.

At nine o'clock, Katie and Claire reconvened in her office for the conference call with Benoit, Francisco, Sergei, and the Kazakhs (including Sauat) at Transteppe. Claire had invited Rob to participate in the call, but he begged off, explaining that the situation in Kazakhstan was very fluid, and that the board, the US State Department, intelligence agencies, and the management team were in almost constant contact. He also said that Sergei was doing double duty as an intermediary with the breakaway group as well as chief geologist, and that he might need him to be called away. He suggested that the Transteppe group make the call from his office so that if Sergei was called, he'd be right where he was needed.

The Transteppe tech people had set up a video connection to Claire's computer, but the Kazakh crew were the only people she could see. As she watched, Rob came into the frame and waved. He smiled, but his face was drawn.

"Just wanted to say hi. By the way, Sergei's"—he clapped a hand on Sergei's shoulder—"been a stand-up guy."

"You mean like comedian?" said Sergei, using his thick Russian movie-villain accent.

Everybody laughed but the Kazakhs, who looked at each other, confused. "Yeah, like comedian," said Rob. He sounded wan. "I've got to get back . . ."

"I miss you guys," said Claire, hoping that Sergei realized that she particularly meant him. She also wanted to ask about the investigation into Hayden's death, but now was not the time.

She noticed that Karil was staring at her with a moonstruck look. What was that about? Then she realized that Karil was not staring at her, but at Katie. With a mixture of curiosity and amusement, she thought, *Aha!* She stole a quick look at Kamila, and her suspicions were confirmed: Kamila was looking at Karil with somewhat narrowed eyes.

Claire got down to business. She laid out the plan to submit a letter to *Nature* or *Science* as a way of rapidly getting the word out, and stressed the need for utter secrecy until it was published.

"Who's going to be the corresponding author?"

Benoit, of course, just asked the one question for which she did not have an answer. Typically, the etiquette of publishing in a peer-reviewed journal would be for the scientist who made the discovery and did the lion's share of the work to be first author, with other scientists listed who contributed to the analysis. The last author listed would be the corresponding author, which typically was an eminent scientist whose blessing lent some gravitas to the submission. Claire had prayed that Keerbrock might lend his name, but that did not seem to be in the cards—yet.

"I'm working on it—there are a lot of moving parts."

"What about Gwynne?"

Claire stiffened. It could have been an innocent question—Gwynne was the preeminent expert on elephant evolution—or it could be Benoit twisting the knife. Claire thought of Constantine and his warning, *Gwynne is not your friend.*

"Good idea. I'll keep that in mind." Claire quickly moved on to soliciting a quick progress report.

As planned, Claire asked Francisco to go first. He first offered some ideas. Based on tooth development, he said that the elephant was most likely a mature animal, and also that the shape of the cranium was not consistent with the thesis that the enlarged cranium was the result of a deformity such as hydrocephalus, Francisco explained, because an animal suffering from hydrocephalus almost certainly would not live beyond infancy. He also said that tooth decay suggested that the animal was suffering from malnutrition, a hypothesis supported by an examination of the ulnae, which were bent in ways that suggested vitamin D deficiency. Francisco had made no further progress on whether the cranium and ulnae came from the same species, although he could claim with some confidence that they did not come from the same individual, unless there were twelve-legged elephants roaming around five million years ago. Francisco was enjoying his star turn. Claire knew that he had something big, so he was setting the stage.

Francisco paused a minute. "So," he said, "what about Bart's brain?"

Francisco quickly went through the basics of the cerebellum to cerebral cortex ratio, the likely reason for the disproportionate ratio in elephants, and the ecological calculus that made growth of the cerebral cortex very unlikely in land mammals.

"In the case of Bart," said Francisco, "nature threw out the rule book. Unless his forehead was filled with sand, he's got an enormous cerebral cortex. We had some sense of that when we first looked at the cranium at Transteppe, but it's even larger than we thought."

Francisco went on a bit about its comparison with modern African elephants, noting that Bart's cerebral cortex was proportionately outsized compared to modern mammals, even humans, but that it was off the charts compared with the brains of the contemporary mammals 5.5 million years prior.

"So think about it," he concluded. "If modern elephants can run a trunk and vocalizations largely through the cerebellum and without an outsized cerebral cortex, something must have happened to initiate fantastic positive feedback that favored a bigger forebrain. Bart's ancestors somehow found it useful to process the flood of information that most elephants can react to without thinking. Why did they need to do this, and what were they thinking about?"

Listening to Francisco, Claire felt her pulse beginning to race. She had some hunches about what he was driving at, but she kept quiet. She stole a glance at Katie, whose eyes were wide as she listened intently.

Sergei spoke next. He had done additional testing and had slightly changed the dates of the bones from 5.5 Ma (the notation for millions of years ago) to 5.4 Ma. He also confirmed that both the bones and the surrounding sedimentary rock were contemporaneous. He gave a confidence level of 95 percent that this new date was correct with an error range of plus or minus fifty thousand years. He then excused himself to resume his role as intermediary between Transteppe and the rebels.

Claire asked that he call later so that he could fill in the gaps. Katie elbowed her in the side and winked. Claire hoped nobody saw that she was blushing.

Benoit was up next. "First off, I want to say how grateful I am to be included on this team." He paused, apparently struggling to find the right words. "Thank you, Claire. You were right and I was wrong. I want everyone to hear that."

Claire was embarrassed. "Don't give it a thought, Benoit. What matters now is how we put this picture together."

Benoit cleared his throat again. "OK, here goes. First off, Sergei's new date is a big deal. I'll get to that in a moment. As you know, these bones are dated just before the beginning of the Pliocene, which has been the epoch I've focused on, trying to see the correlations between speciation, climate change, and brain size. Turns out that had I looked back just a little farther, I'd have found one of the most dramatic and violent events in the world's oceans since the end of the Cretaceous. And if I'd studied what was happening around the world at that time,

I would see that species were dying off and new species emerging in a whole host of animals . . ."

The upheaval Benoit was talking about was the Messinian salinity crisis, which began 5.96 million years ago and lasted 640,000 years before abruptly ending about 5.33 million years ago. The trigger for this event was the isolation of the Mediterranean from the world's oceans, either by tectonic shifts or changes in sea level. Though sea level in the basin fell on a jagged curve over several hundred thousand years, there were a number of violent shifts, culminating 5.4 million years ago when the bottom of the Mediterranean was exposed to the sun, creating a death valley over fifteen thousand feet deep. Scientists estimated that in summer, temperatures on the desiccated sea floor reached as high as 176 degrees Fahrenheit, and the interruption of global ocean currents played havoc with the great ocean conveyor that distributed heat around the world, as well as the jet stream and associated storm tracks. When sea level rose enough to breach the Strait of Gibraltar and refill the Mediterranean, it did so in a flood of water that was the equivalent of a thousand Amazon rivers. Sea level in the giant basin rose thirty feet a day, and the Mediterranean was a sea again in a matter of a few months.

"So," Benoit concluded, "our friend lived and died when the drying and cooling in the steppes resulting from the Messinian was at its most intense. If I was looking for an elephant that could survive in these conditions, I would look for an animal specialized for digging up tubers, because that's where plants hide their biomass in tough times. You see where I'm going with this—an elephant specialized in digging up yams, for instance . . . By the way, what's the story with the rock, anyway?"

Claire jumped in before anyone could say anything. "Katie's working on that and needs more time. It's too important to do quickly, and it would be too much of a distraction to include in this first letter, so we will hold that for another meeting." There was silence as the group digested this. Claire looked at Katie and raised her eyebrows in an "OK?" gesture. Katie nodded, but slowly.

Claire continued, shifting her glance between Katie and the monitor, "And another thing—until Katie is ready to go public, no one outside of those on this call is to know that the rock even exists. Speculation in the popular press could kill any chances she has for publication. Is that clear?" There were murmured assents, but Claire could feel that there were a lot of unspoken questions. She needed to move on.

"Karil? Can you give us an update on pollens and vegetation?"

Karil positioned himself in front of the monitor. "Yes, I can," he said. "There's a puzzle here."

Claire hadn't expected this. "A puzzle?"

"Well, I looked for polymorphs"—organic microfossils—"focusing on pollens and other proxies, and they say that vegetation in that area five point four million years ago was characteristic of desert."

"That makes sense, doesn't it?"

"Of course, it is what you would expect." Karil looked uncomfortable.

"So what is the puzzle?"

"OK, I did study of vertical slice of rock—going back in time, yes? I find evidence of lush vegetation—in that immediate area."

"How far back in time?"

"Just before the time of the bones. It's a really thin layer. Very easy to miss. We only found it by accident."

Benoit jumped in. "But the dry period lasted hundreds of thousands of years?"

"I know, and I checked records for loess plateau and other neighboring areas for same period, and vegetation was dry there, too." Karil paused. "But not here. Here lush."

Claire spoke very slowly. "How long does the lush period last?"

"Hard to tell—very, very thin layer in the sediment. Not sure I'll be able to tell exactly, because the resolution is not so good, but I'm guessing ten thousand years."

Benoit spoke slowly. "So at the same time the Messinian drying was at its most intense, that area had a lush period?"

"Yes."

"Jesus."

Claire was stunned. "Karil, as you might imagine, we need to check this seven ways from Sunday . . ."

Karil interrupted, "What is this seven ways from Sunday?"

Claire laughed, realizing that Karil's confusion was real, unlike Sergei's. "Sorry, Karil, I mean we have to check this from every conceivable angle—it's too important not to. I'm going to try to find some help for you to see if there were some special circumstances creating a microclimate or some such."

"I agree."

"OK," said Claire wrapping it up, "clearly we need to do some digging. And please remember, not a word."

After she ended the call, Claire and Katie sat in silence for a few minutes.

Finally, Katie turned to Claire. "Are you thinking what I'm thinking?"

Claire buried her face in her hands. "I don't even want to say it out loud."

"I know we've got to eliminate every other possibility, and of course it's a long shot."

"Don't go there."

Katie, who was just the type to go there when warned not to, went there anyway: "Farming."

Claire tensed. The mere mention of the word brought visions of Keerbrock's possible reactions, none of them good. She didn't want to think about that now, so she changed the subject.

She looked Katie in the eye. "Karil?"

Katie blushed.

Claire continued, "I thought you said, and I'm quoting verbatim here, 'not going to happen.'"

Katie looked sheepish. "I *meant* it when I said it," she said lamely, "but then it did happen." She fidgeted. "It seemed pretty uncomplicated—he's not leaving Kazakhstan, after all."

Claire laughed. "Kamila was watching him like a hawk."

Katie put her hands out. "Well, I'm not stopping her, at least not anymore."

Claire smiled warmly. "Don't worry. To quote Pope Francis, 'who am I to judge?'"

Not long after the conference call ended, her cell phone rang. The call identification read "unknown." After a moment's hesitation, she answered. It was Sergei, calling from Rob's encrypted phone.

"Sergei! I'm so glad you called!"

"Me, too. It's difficult to maintain the formality . . ."

"Yes!" Sergei was saying just the right thing.

"And please don't read anything into any coolness in a professional situation," he continued. "I come from a country where it's a survival skill to hide your feelings . . . there's a lot more going on in my head than I might say."

"Thank you, Sergei, it's good to hear that."

There was a momentary silence. "I've got to get back to things. I'm still juggling, but now it's chain saws."

Claire was alarmed. "Tell me!"

"I can't, but don't worry about me, Claire. You've got enough to worry about."

He rang off, leaving Claire deeply worried.

58

THE DAY AFTER CLAIRE'S TEAM HAD THEIR CONFERENCE CALL, Byron Gwynne took the stage at a special symposium entitled "All Things Elephant," which was being held at the Wildlife Conservation Society's gleaming, LEED platinum–certified global headquarters building at the Bronx Zoo. The event brought together elephant experts and handlers from around the globe. It was an impressively varied group, including the behavioral scientists who had shown that elephants recognize themselves in a mirror, animal trainers, zookeepers, explorers, ecologists, conservation biologists, evolutionary biologists, and paleontologists. Francisco had begged Claire to permit him to attend, but she had told him not to get within two hundred miles of the meeting. She knew that this would be the perfect conference to introduce Bart to the world, but it was just too soon. There was no way she was going to jeopardize the chances of publication by some inadvertent comment leaking out. What would Francisco say if someone innocently asked what he was working on? Francisco grudgingly accepted the reasoning.

Because the publication of Gwynne's book was imminent, he had been asked to lead a panel discussion entitled "The Next Frontier: Unanswered Questions on the Elephant's Past, Present, and Future." It was the marquee event of the afternoon, and the auditorium was packed. As the discussion proceeded, Gwynne couldn't have been more pleased. The panelists were prepared, with the conversation efficiently ticking off the many vexing questions facing elephants in the wild, how to treat the giant animals in captivity, and the unanswered questions about elephant communication and cognitive abilities. As the moderator, Gwynne had the last word, and he noted that, having just completed an omnibus survey of the fossil record, the evolutionary history of the elephant was, at last, coming in to sharp focus. There weren't many people in the room who did not know that Gwynne had spent years on his upcoming book, and so there was some appreciative applause when he made this modest allusion to his own work.

With that, he opened the discussion for questions. The first few came from eminent conservationists and focused on issues like poaching and conflicts between farmers and elephants in Africa and Indonesia. Gwynne didn't want the discussion to be hijacked by the greens, and so peered out, looking for a zoologist. He recognized a face in the back of the room and pointed, nodding when the young man pointed to his own chest and said, "Me?" Gwynne gestured yes, and the scientist stood up, waiting while an attendant hustled over with a microphone.

"Professor Gwynne," the young man began, "in your closing remarks, you implied that we are close to having a complete evolutionary history of the elephant. Lately, I've heard rumors of a find of some new elephant ancestor in Kazakhstan—of all places—and dating to Messinian. Any thoughts on what such a discovery might do to that picture—if it turns out to be real?" There were chuckles throughout the room as the man sat back down.

Gwynne thought furiously. It was the perfect group, and here was the opportunity he'd been waiting for, but the stakes gave him pause. On the other hand, he'd already embarked on this path and there was no turning back. He took a deep breath.

"Well," Gwynne began, "I can tell you that these are more than rumors." He paused as a hush fell over the audience.

"The bones exist. I've seen photographs." The room buzzed. Gwynne chose his words carefully. "But what they are and where they came from remain very much open to question. It's a long road from finding bones in Kazakhstan to proving that five point five million years ago some form of elephant was indigenous to Kazakhstan. Until we know more, the more likely hypothesis is that the bones fell off a caravan coming through in the recent past."

The buzz in the audience became a hubbub. Gwynne held up a hand. "Please, let me finish. There is also a long road between finding an ulna and positing that it comes from a new species. As many of you know, there have been many assertions of new species found in all sorts of mammals, only to later discover that the perceived anatomical differences were the product of disease, malnutrition or developmental anomalies. While no scientist worth his or her salt would rule out the possibility that a new elephant ancestor might be discovered, I'm not holding my breath. The odds are just too long, and there are just too many unprecedented assumptions we have to accept."

The room erupted again. Gwynne thanked the crowd, but his words were drowned out.

59

CLAIRE WAS JUST GETTING OUT OF THE SHOWER AFTER HER run when she heard her cell phone buzz. It was 7:30 a.m., a strange hour to be getting texts. It was Constantine, and the message was just one word, "Urgent." She looked at the phone; she'd missed six calls. She was just about to scroll through to see who had called when the phone rang. It was Constantine. She decided to answer. Fatalistically, she thought she knew what this was about.

"Let me guess—the whisper campaign continues."

Constantine chuckled, "Well, yes—if you can call the most eminent expert on elephant phylogeny trashing your supposed discovery at a major conference a whisper campaign."

Claire was stunned silent.

"You still there?"

Claire had known pushback was coming; hell, she'd predicted it. "Tell me."

"It was Gwynne. We had a stringer there . . ."

Constantine had warned Claire, who tried to remember why she had ever thought Gwynne would take up her cause. She was seriously questioning her judgment. Two of the people she had sent pictures of the bones had turned on her—though Benoit was well on the path to rehabilitation.

Constantine took Claire through what had happened and then innocently asked whether she had any comment.

"C'mon, Adam, I'm supposed to comment on a secondhand remark concerning something we haven't even announced? You can't be serious."

"Just askin' . . ."

Claire thought a second. "We're getting close . . ." She glanced at the emails on her laptop. There were eighty new messages, of which thirty weren't spam. One was from the news section of *Nature*. Now that was something.

"Adam, I may be able to advance the schedule, but let me make this absolutely clear: I'm not commenting on anything until we put out the initial description in a journal. Got that?"

"I guess. Worth a shot. I'll hold off on doing anything on this until you hear whether or not your paper is accepted. And remember, we have a deal."

"Yes, you've got the exclusive for the first nonscientific publication. Now I've got to go."

After hanging up, Claire wrote an urgent email to her team, warning them about loose lips.

Claire got up from her desk, realizing that she hadn't even finished drying off, much less gotten dressed. She was headed for her closet when her cell phone rang again. She was tempted to ignore it but grabbed the phone when she saw who was calling.

It was Keerbrock, part of whose genius seemed to be an instinct for appearing when Claire was most vulnerable. He was going to hear about Byron's black ops at some point, so Claire decided that he might as well hear it from her.

Keerbrock listened as Claire took him through her conversation with Constantine. Then he chuckled. "So Byron's gotten out over his skis on this. Don't worry about him."

"If I were Willem Keerbrock, I wouldn't worry about him, either. But I'm not."

There was silence on the other end of the phone.

"At this point," Keerbrock said, "I'd suggest that you get out something fast on the details of the find."

Claire told Keerbrock about being contacted by *Nature* and her plan to hustle out a bare-bones letter.

Keerbrock took this in. "Look, Claire, I understand what's going on. I know that you'd like me to join the letter as corresponding author. It's not in any sense your fault, but the lack of the actual bones makes that very difficult for me. The array supports the interpretation of the cranium—as does the jadeite, which cannot be mentioned. I actually believe that this is an extraordinary find, but science doesn't proceed on belief." Keerbrock paused and took a breath. "Let's use the analogy of a murder—no body, no murder charge; it's the same in science. Unfortunately, the fact that the only accessible evidence for the array is digital won't work for the most respected journals, who are paranoid about being suckered . . . Byron's assault doesn't help, either."

Claire, crushed, remained silent.

"That said," Keerbrock said, surprisingly gently, "keep going. Maybe something will turn up."

60

IN A PERFECTLY TIMED PASS, SAMANTHA TOOK THE BATON from Gwynne—at least that's how it seemed to Claire. A day after hearing about Gwynne, Claire learned that Samantha had written a blog for a feminist forum sponsored by Oberlin. The thread was "When Women Are Bad Bosses," and in Samantha's contribution (helpfully forwarded by Waylon—"not that I agree, just thought you should see this"—to whom Samantha had sent a link and a request to like the post on Facebook), Claire, given the pseudonym "Hortense" (Claire got the juvenile inversion immediately—"tense whore") was worse than any man. Blinded by ambition to be accepted by "the patriarchy that dominates archaeology and paleontology," Hortense had capriciously abandoned the mission of the dig, jeopardized the local standing of her funding organization, insulted her noble Kazakh counterparts, and ignored every carefully thought-through protocol of how to conduct a dig, which led to the destruction of a priceless discovery (or worthless, because, at a different point in the post, Samantha questioned the provenance of the find). Hortense then abandoned her team altogether, leaving them at the mercy of the Kazakhs (who apparently weren't so noble). Aside from the many internal contradictions, Claire admitted that there was a kernel of truth in each of the other accusations.

If Gwynne had deftly planted a seed of doubt about the significance of the bones, Samantha had performed a clumsy but nevertheless effective job of character assassination. Claire knew that it would be useless to respond, which would only confirm that Hortense was Claire, not that anyone in the scientific community wouldn't already know that. Even though most interested parties would recognize that Samantha was motivated by some personal animus, the combination of the two seeds of doubt would dampen the ardor of those in the scientific community who might otherwise be eager to hear more about the discovery.

It was at times like this when Claire most wished that Hayden was still alive. She imagined the conversation that might follow. "Well, there's some good news, some truly weird news, and some very bad news. Which would you like to hear first?"

"Might as well get the bad news out of the way."

"OK, you might as well hear it from me first. Congratulations! You've put your money behind a naïve nut ball who's an excellent candidate for boss from hell."

Hayden would digest the series of unfortunate events before replying. "You knew going in that you were going to have to have a thick skin. Don't worry about it. I'm in mining and have heard worse said about me. Put everything into getting out that letter."

61

THE NEXT WEEK WAS A NIGHTMARE. THE REVERBERATIONS OF Gwynne's betrayal and Samantha's frontal assault ricocheted around the web. Claire felt that the bones—and her career—were rapidly being relegated to fringe science before she had even had a chance to speak. She had replied to the reporter from the news section of *Nature*, and clearly their ardor had faded. After several days she got a perfunctory email saying that the editors had decided to wait for peer-reviewed validation before going ahead with a news item.

Claire knew the stress was getting to her. She had stopped running. She had a sense that she was failing in every aspect of life, a feeling she hadn't experienced since grad school. At least the letter was coming together and rapidly, but any warm vibes from this good news were tempered by her dread of the inevitable conversation with Katie about how to proceed in the investigation of the jadeite.

She wasn't sleeping well, and she wasn't eating much, either. Parts of the day she had a metallic taste in her mouth. During a video chat with Sergei at Transteppe, Sauat showed up with Lawrence in his arms, and this cheered her up a bit, but as soon as the call ended, her anxiety returned. One day she woke up with some lines from "Take Me Out to the Ball Game" running through her head. Ordinarily, it would have signaled an upbeat mood, but then she realized the line "and it's one, two, three strikes you're out . . ." was in a continuous loop.

There had been an avalanche of emails after Gwynne's talk, but she had only responded to the few that she just couldn't ignore. Her mother had called several times, but she wasn't up to talking with her, either. Her mother had taken to leaving helpful messages: "I know you're busy with this paper, honey. Call me when you can, and keep in mind: If you're going to shoot for the king, make sure that all your ducks are in a row."

Friedl got wind of the rumors as well. He called her in to his office and asked her directly whether anything had gone on in Kazakhstan that he should be worried about, noting that he had to protect the reputation of the department and the university. Claire simply said that she was solely focused on producing a publishable description of the find and that she wasn't going to respond to baseless rumors, as neither she nor any of her team had spoken to anyone about the find.

Claire could see he wasn't reassured, so she used her last card. "Keerbrock's been offering a lot of moral support, which helps."

Friedl sighed. "Moral support is one thing, but I'd feel better about all this if Keerbrock formally endorsed your discovery."

Claire wanted to say, "I would, too," but kept her mouth shut.

Two weeks after the team's first conference call, Claire had a draft of the letter they would submit. It was highly disciplined, even minimalist. It laid out the discovery of the bones and the arguments for why the bones were of a previously unknown species of proboscidean mammal that was indigenous to the area and survived at least until the peak of the Messinian. Benoit had contributed the climate backdrop as well as evolutionary context; Francisco made a powerful case that the bones and cranium were not representative of a known species at a different developmental stage or suffering from some disease (though he did stipulate that they did show the effects of malnutrition); Sergei provided the geological context; and Karil described the changes in vegetation. At every turn, Claire restrained interpretation, liberally using the phrase "This is a matter that bears further investigation." So it was with the intriguing lush period, which the paper referred to but did not explain. And so it was with the jadeite, which was only referred to as "a contiguous object."

Dr. Tabiliev had written a paragraph on previous explorations of the area and generously agreed to add his name. Claire should have been elated but, except for Benoit, there was no one with any standing in any of the pertinent sciences affiliated with the paper. Worse, Claire realized with chagrin, the lead author was best known to the scientific community as the object of slanderous rumors in the blogosphere. She was loath to push the send button.

As she soon discovered, she should have heeded her instinct.

The answer from *Nature* was short and to the point. They could not publish on a find as potentially explosive as this when a significant part of the physical evidence that was crucial to the argument was unavailable. The one ray of hope was a concluding sentence, encouraging resubmission if such evidence could be provided.

Then things got worse. Claire had felt duty bound to tell Constantine that there would be no letter to *Nature*, but she couldn't bring herself to make the call. Nor did she answer his calls or emails. Members of the team emailed her, saying that Constantine was calling them for comment. Claire had simply said, "I'm not saying anything that might prejudice future prospects for publication, but follow your conscience."

The following Tuesday, she opened the *New York Times* to see the following headline in the lead article of the Science section: "Discovery of Relic Elephant Species in Kazakhstan Shrouded in Controversy and Ambiguity." The article then went through the history of the find, with quotes from Gwynne. There was some small consolation in the sentence "Multiple efforts to reach Dr. Knowland and her team members were unsuccessful," but then, anonymously, one source, described as "a scientist who had seen the submission to *Nature*," noted that the bizarre goings-on in Kazakhstan and the disappearance of the bones created a barrier of skepticism that the submission simply could not overcome. "They found something" was the source's most devastating quote. "But who knows what?" Finishing the article, Claire realized that she was well on her way to junk science. Worse, with a sob of anguish, she imagined the reaction of Helen and other members of Hayden's family, who were being told that their revered father was a fool.

Good job, Claire, she thought, *First I get him killed. Then I ruin his memory. This is what you get when you put your trust in me.*

Through her despair, Claire realized that she still had responsibilities. She emailed the members of the team, telling them that she was not sure of the next steps, but that she needed to take a break. She ended these emails with the sentence "Do what you think is right."

She emailed Katie, telling her the same but that Claire was giving her responsibility for the jadeite and she was welcome to continue her work. She got an immediate reply: "Wait! I'm coming over."

Claire responded, "Thank you Katie, but I won't be here." Then she headed for Friedl's office.

He was looking at the *Times* article when she entered.

"I'm taking time off."

Friedl almost looked relieved. "Take as much as you want—the project's funded for five years."

"In my absence Katie's going to continue work. She can use my office."

Friedl thought about this for a second. "I guess that's OK," he said slowly. Clearly, he would rather this project disappeared entirely—leaving the money behind, of course.

"That's it then," said Claire and left. *So*, she thought to herself, *this is what rock bottom feels like.*

62

CLAIRE LEFT FRIEDL'S OFFICE WITH THE FIRM CONVICTION THAT she had to disappear, but without any idea of where she was going. So she started driving west. She ended up on Interstate 88 in New York, and it was getting dark. She turned off at the exit for Schoharie, New York, a tiny town just north of the Catskills. She looked around the town. Population under one thousand and a sign saying "Schoharie" was a Mohawk word for floating driftwood. She smiled grimly—perfect! She found a derelict group of cabins and made a deal to rent one for $250 a week in cash.

She had left her computer in her office and hesitated before tossing her phone in the lake. She knew that doing so would eliminate any chance of talking to Sergei, but she shuddered at the damage a conversation in her present state might do to their relationship. She was not the woman she was a month ago, or even a week ago.

She bought some groceries. She also bought a big bottle of gin. She didn't really have any appetite, and two doubles on an empty stomach knocked her out. She woke up the next morning at five a.m. She made herself a peanut butter and jelly sandwich with a plastic knife. That filled her stomach, but she doubted that she could ever fill the emptiness that engulfed her.

Emptiness periodically gave way to anger. She was sure that if Keerbrock had put his name on the paper, *Nature* would have published their letter. She thought of Gwynne, who had betrayed her because of petty jealousy and because he didn't want to reopen discussion of elephant phylogeny. She couldn't sustain the anger, though. Hayden, Sergei, Rob, Katie, even Keerbrock had all backed her in their own way, and she'd let all of them down.

She spent the first day in her room, wallowing in self-loathing and guilt. Day two, she picked up a pad and pencil, but phrases and thoughts were a jumble and seemed just out of reach anyway. She stared at the blank pad. After a moment, she drew three lines, then two more. That looked like a musical stanza. She tried to remember the first notes of Beethoven's *Variations on a Swiss Song*. She couldn't remember the notes, but she hummed the melody. The simple notes, pure as high mountain air, breached some dam inside her, and for several minutes she just sobbed.

When she stopped, the emptiness had vanished, at least for the moment. She didn't feel good, but she felt as though life was a possibility. She looked around the room. There was a guidebook for local points of interest. Idly flipping through the pages, she came to a section describing a spot for fossil hunting. *Why not*, she thought.

She jotted down the directions—the site was open to the public and consisted of a bunch of boulders at the base of a cliff. She blinked as she exited the cabin, blinded by the sunlight after two days indoors. It was a brilliant day in May, and the air was sweet with pollens. She found the spot easily enough and spent the afternoon looking for trilobites and other Devonian marine fossils.

The next day she returned. The previous day, she'd had the place to herself, but today it looked like a professor had brought his class on a field trip. The kids, who looked college age, were examining and chipping some of the boulders and scree while he wandered among them. The professor looked over at Claire, and Claire instinctively turned away and moved farther from the group.

She didn't return the next day, but that evening Claire encountered the group again at a local tavern. The professor waved to her and signaled that she should join them. Claire forced a smile and shook her head. Returning to her drink, she didn't notice that the man continued to stare at her.

63

THE MAN SERGEI KNEW ONLY AS THE JANITOR SAT IN A CAFÉ IN Astana and weighed his options. He wasn't worried about being caught, because he no longer looked like a Kazakh. Now he looked like a forgettable midlevel accountant. He had assumed so many aliases over the years that he sometimes forgot his real name. More recently, he had opted for complete anonymity when taking on an assignment.

He knew that Bezanov would have him taken out in a heartbeat now that he had completed his assignment, but he was also comfortable that Bezanov would have no more success than dozens of other prior employers who had entertained similar thoughts . . . though there was just one loose end, the result of a brief chance encounter at the Transteppe train depot. He couldn't be sure that the Russian geologist had heard anything, but he'd seen him look around. Leave a loose end unfixed, he thought, and, next thing you know, an entire sweater has unraveled.

64

CLAIRE ONLY STAYED A WEEK, BECAUSE SHE HAD PAID FOR A week and didn't know where she would go next. She tried to get some exercise every day and usually ended up at the tavern. She found it soothing to watch the baseball games that were perpetually on the TV above the bar. The idle chatter of the color commentators and torpor-inducing progress of the game matched the lazy pace of summer, and then moments of extreme drama would emerge like a thunderstorm. Yankees fans predominated, but she didn't like the barfly regulars, most of whose IQs were ten points short of a root vegetable, so she decided to become a Mets fan. Being a fan wasn't the same as revolutionizing paradigms of the origins of intelligence, but it seemed to give meaning to life for many of the patrons, and if it was good enough for them, it ought to be good enough for Claire, she reasoned. She had nothing else.

The night before she was due to check out, Claire decided to go to the tavern one last time. She entered the bar and froze. Sitting at their customary round table were the geology students and their professor. This time, however, they were looking awestruck at the older man and the beautiful woman standing next to them. Claire wheeled to make a getaway when Katie yelled, "Claire!"

The students turned goggle-eyed to stare at her. Claire's shoulders slumped in defeat as Keerbrock and Katie came over and guided her to the bar. She sat down, looked at them both in silence for a moment, and then said, "Do you think they should fire Mickey Callaway?"

"They should have done it years ago!" announced Keerbrock, adding, "Who is Mickey Callaway?"

The three nodded at each other. Katie ordered three drafts. Keerbrock took a sip and said, "We need to talk." The shock had knocked all fight out of Claire. Anyway, the last thing she wanted was a scene. Claire led Keerbrock and Katie over to a far booth.

Katie had yet to say a word, but before they sat down, she smiled and gave Claire a huge hug. Claire couldn't help herself—her eyes welled up, as did Katie's. Keerbrock, who, apparently, had reached late middle age unaware that humans had emotions, looked extremely uncomfortable.

Claire felt miserable. "I'm not the person you thought I was."

Keerbrock waved that remark off.

"How did you find me?"

Keerbrock shifted uncomfortably. "We"—he nodded at Katie—"set up a string on one of the paleontological sites asking for clues as to your whereabouts, making it sort of a 'Where's Waldo' contest. People had you everywhere from Tibet to Timbuktu. Then, that guy"—Keerbrock nodded toward the professor—"put up a note simply saying, 'Found her!'"

Katie interrupted. "Sergei's been going nuts. He was vastly relieved when we told him you were alive."

Claire felt a deep pang of guilt for the pain she had inflicted on Sergei. She hoped he would understand that, in an odd way, her lack of contact was her way of preserving the hope of saving, not ending, their relationship.

"Anyway," Keerbrock continued, "we're here—we tracked you down—because something has happened, a discovery of something wonderful, something that validates everything you've been arguing, and by rights this should be yours. We want you to come back."

Claire was not ready for this. She had no idea what to say, so she didn't say anything. Katie stepped in. "Remember how we left the jadeite encrusted with the surrounding rock when we brought it here?"

Claire nodded.

"Well," Katie continued, "after you left, I didn't have much else to work on, so I cleaned the rock."

Claire nodded again.

"And you were right, it's a perfect polished representation of an elephant yam."

Now Claire spoke, confused. "But we knew that."

"That's right, but then I picked it up."

Keerbrock was watching this byplay with a look of anticipation, almost excitement.

"So you picked it up," said Claire. "It's not that heavy."

"But I couldn't hold it for long," said Katie, turning to Keerbrock. "Neither could Dr. Keerbrock."

"You couldn't hold it? Why not?"

"The jadeite has properties."

"Properties," said Keerbrock. "It looks for all the world as though these ancient elephants of yours purposefully imbued the rock with some very powerful field for what purpose we have no idea, but it does seem purposeful."

"What happens when you pick up the rock?"

"You're going to have to experience this for yourself, but if you hold it with your hand underneath, you start to feel something like an electrical current that builds until you can't stand it."

"Why would they do this?"

"I've been thinking about that. If you were an elephant, your whole sensory system is built on sound, right?"

"Right." This was familiar ground for Claire as she had done basic research on elephant use of sound.

"So," continued Keerbrock, "as you know from your work in Florida"—Claire felt a jolt of pleasure—Keerbrock had followed her work!—"an elephant with its highly sophisticated auditory processing system might express itself through sound waves, yes?"

"Yes."

"But sound waves are transient, yes?"

"Yes . . ."

"Assuming that your elephant had a big enough brain to be conscious and was smart enough to want to leave a record, how do you do that with something as transient as sound?"

Claire had no idea where he was going and decided to keep silent.

Keerbrock wasn't waiting for an answer anyway. "You might create some sort of standing wave. Sound is waves. At some level, everything has a wave property. Think interference patterns. If you doped the appropriate medium the right way, you could create a complicated—perpetual—record with standing waves."

"Of course!"

"I thought you'd get it," said Keerbrock. "Think about paintings in the caves at Lascaux; think about what our Neanderthal friends might have done if they'd only had sound waves to work with."

"Right."

"And think about the type of skills you'll need to get to the bottom of this—familiarity with quantum mechanics, solid state physics, cymatics, acoustics . . . a world-class code breaker . . ."

Claire felt the thrill of intellectual adventure begin to course through her, and it was only as this warm flood returned that she realized how truly empty she had felt. Then she came back to earth. "Dr. Keerbrock. I couldn't even get a paper published establishing Bart as a new species. How on earth could we convince the journals to accept the idea that these animals were acoustic wizards?"

"Oh, you're right, this can't be published." This last statement drew a sharp look from Katie.

Claire laughed bitterly. "So, you came all the way out here to tell me to come back so that I could fail again at getting anything related to Bart published?"

Keerbrock waved a mollifying hand. "One step at a time. I wanted to tell you about the jadeite, yes, but I also can say that you can now get your original letter published."

Claire couldn't suppress a surge of pure elation. "How? They wanted the bones."

Keerbrock turned to Katie. "Why don't you show her?"

Katie fiddled with her phone and then turned it so Claire could see the screen. On it was a picture of Sergei holding an ulna.

Seeing Sergei sent a different kind of pang through Claire. "How?"

"You know Sergei," said Katie with a meaningful look, "he finds a way. Apparently, the civil war and the president being on the defensive left Tamerlan feeling exposed, and Sergei convinced him that Sergei would use his influence with the Russians to protect him should the little weasel find himself on the losing side. As insurance he brought Tegev, who said that if Tamerlan didn't return the bone, he was dead to the family—a very big deal in Kazakhstan."

"But it's just one bone, and *Nature* wanted to see the array."

"You can thank Rob for that part. The president won't return the bones, but he will let qualified scientists examine them."

"One more thing," said Keerbrock. He leaned back and paused before speaking. "If you think it would help, I'd be honored to join the letter as corresponding author."

Claire was overwhelmed. She waved one hand and covered her eyes with the other. "Give me a minute, please." She got up. She took a few deep breaths and sat down again in the booth.

She looked at Keerbrock. "I've been trying to forget my failed career."

Keerbrock interrupted her. "Your career was never a failure."

"It was in every way that mattered to the people who put their trust in me."

"All the better then," said Keerbrock, and with characteristic insensitivity. "It will make vindication—redemption—that much sweeter."

"And if I fail again?" asked Claire, having learned the bitter lesson that no matter how deep the abyss, there is always one deeper.

Keerbrock nodded, realizing the stakes for Claire. "Then science doesn't deserve you."

"Let me think for the evening. Where are you staying?" After they named a motel just off the interstate, Claire said she would either meet them at seven in the morning or disappear once again.

65

KATIE RODE WITH CLAIRE ON THE WAY BACK (BOTH SHE AND Keerbrock had positively beamed when Claire showed up the next morning). Katie filled her in on the news. Gwynne, riding a wave of admiration for his monograph, had been named a fellow at All Souls College, Oxford. Samantha had become a very high-profile consultant on organizational ethics and morale and had made an appearance on CNBC.

Claire also learned that her disappearance had caused quite a stir. The blogosphere had turned sympathetic and assigned some of the blame to Constantine, who found himself on the defensive. He'd tried to reassure the other members of her team that he was just doing his job, but they were having none of it. Katie told her that the team had held together. While many had suspended work on the bones, none, not even Benoit, had given interviews to the press, with all of them saying that they could not comment prior to publication in a scientific journal. This, in turn, had led to a number of contacts from *Nature* and *Science*, asking for a timetable for resubmission.

Toward the end of the drive, Katie asked, "You don't have to answer, but it wasn't just the rejection by *Nature* that caused you to disappear, was it?"

Claire took a deep breath. She still didn't know how things would turn out, but her depression had lifted. "No, it wasn't rejection, it was shame. Hayden had put his trust in me, and his family had put their trust in me as guardian of his reputation and legacy." She almost couldn't get the words out. "And for all this trust and money, my response was to leave them exposed to ridicule."

Katie looked at her with a dazzling smile. "That is going to change!"

JADEITE

66

CLAIRE'S FIRST CALL AFTER *NATURE* PUBLISHED THE LETTER IN late September was to Helen. "I have some happy news," she said.

"I already saw the *Times*. Congratulations! You should feel very proud, and I'm sure Dad is clapping up in heaven. Thank you for honoring his memory." Claire had insisted that the article mention Hayden's funding.

With the perspective of vindication, Claire had realized that Constantine, while doing her no favors, had only been doing his job given the demonstrable facts he had to work with at the time. She also felt that, this time, he would be motivated to give her the benefit of the doubt. Anyway, the *Times* was still the *Times*. So she had offered him the same exclusive they had negotiated a year earlier.

Nature published on Thursdays, and that same day the *Times* ran a straight news story on the find. Then on the following Tuesday, a much longer article by Constantine appeared as the lead article in the weekly science section. This piece described the drama that surrounded the discovery and included extensive quotes from Claire and Keerbrock, as well as comments on its significance from a number of eminences in paleontology and mammalian evolution (notably absent were any quotes from Gwynne). Against the context of the ongoing chaos in Kazakhstan, Claire's unconventional actions seemed justified. *Nature* had also produced a news article about the circumstances of the discovery, which noted that two Kazakh scientists—Karil and Tabiliev—shared the credit for the description of the discovery, and which also detailed the many unanswered questions entailed in the find that would be subject for further exploration. At a press conference at Rushmere where journalists were permitted to photograph the ulna and cranium (but not the jadeite, which Claire had removed for the occasion), Keerbrock stressed that this first paper only scratched the surface of the significance of the bones. When pressed, however, he refused to speculate on what he expected further studies to uncover.

She expected the next call.

"This is Byron Gwynne."

Claire knew what was coming.

Claire kept her voice neutral. "Hi, Byron."

There was an awkward pause. Claire felt no need to help Gwynne out.

Gwynne cleared his throat. "I'm calling to say that some remarks I made at a conference were taken out of context, and I want you to know that the last thing I intended was to undermine your discovery." He paused again. "And I want to apologize if some misinterpretation of my remarks caused you any hurt."

Claire had to suppress a laugh, since the context was completely unambiguous. Clearly Byron had been waiting for an opportunity to undermine the legitimacy of the find, and the only possible misinterpretation would have been if the audience had somehow thought that Byron was endorsing the bones.

"Thanks, Byron, I appreciate that."

She thought she heard a sigh of relief.

"I want you to know that I've called my publisher and insisted on rewriting the pertinent chapters. They're screaming and it's going to cost me a pretty penny, but I cannot put out a phylogeny of Elephantidae without fitting your extraordinary discovery into its rightful place. Anything new I should add?"

Claire now knew that Gwynne never did anything without calculation and guessed that his standing at All Souls was coming under review. Clearly, he wanted to come and see the bones for himself. She wasn't going to help him out there.

"Well, the *Nature* letter gives a pretty complete picture of what we can say right now that will pass muster with peer review."

"Absolutely, but to properly place it, it would help if I could see for myself. At this point we don't even know what line this animal came from. Did it derive from *Primelephas*, or perhaps from some earlier split?"

Claire knew that he was right, and he would be better than anyone in trying to figure where the animal fit. But then she thought about the last time she had trusted him, and God knew she didn't want him anywhere near the jadeite. She leaned back in her chair.

"Those are good questions, Byron, let me think about it."

"OK, please do. Thanks. By the way, why did you name it *Simpsoniensis*?"

"Long story, Byron. That's for another conversation."

After she hung up, she thought fondly about the discussion that had led to the name. Hayden had earlier and definitively ruled himself out, and following his death, they felt uneasy about going against his wishes. The group had grown used to talking about Bart, and ultimately they decided to go with that. Even Keerbrock seemed amused.

But Claire's sense of satisfaction faded almost as soon as she hung up. While evolutionary scholars were justifiably excited about the rewriting of the proboscid family tree, the bones opened up whole new worlds of possibilities that would be greeted with increasing suspicion.

There was the question of the link between increased speciation and climate change, which Benoit adroitly introduced but left hanging. This was not a new area, but the relationship was not yet the consensus. In consultation with Keerbrock, Claire had decided that this should be the next paper submitted, largely because this was an area of active discussion in the scientific community and she gave high odds that the team could make a meaningful contribution. Then there was the question of the connection between climate stress and brain size, an area in which

Benoit had some credibility. There were unknowns to be dealt with here—Benoit and Francisco had a great deal of work to do to get a better understanding of what kind of brain that cranium implied—but, again, it was an area where there was prior work to build upon, and Claire had confidence that the team could produce a paper that would get serious consideration.

Beyond this were the truly revolutionary issues such as questions about the connection between Bart's outsized brain, the array, and the jadeite. Why had Bart developed a brain so out of proportion to any animal peer of that time, what was he using it for, and was he endowed with intelligence and language abilities analogous to those of modern humans? Even more preposterous for the mainstream scientific community were the issues raised by the green patch in a generally desiccated region, and the otherworldly power of the stone. Finally, Claire wondered: If their intelligence had enhanced the elephant's chances of survival during a period of extreme environmental stress, why then did they become extinct?

She had talked about this with Benoit, and asked if these elephants were so smart and adaptable, why didn't they migrate to someplace more hospitable? Benoit scoffed, "Look at us—we're pretty smart, and we're being done in by climate change as we speak. Why don't we migrate?"

For Claire the answer seemed obvious. "With seven billion people on the planet, where can anyone go?" Having said that out loud, she wondered whether something similar had happened millions of years earlier. Inconceivable, she decided.

During their last conversation, Keerbrock had said that Claire had to accept that they might never be able to publish the most interesting aspects of the find. Claire had asked him, once again, to clarify why.

"Because, usually for the better, but occasionally for the worse, the empirical method, driven by data, just can't handle ambiguous, subjective concepts like language and intelligence, even in humans, much less in animals. So scientists try and fail to reduce questions to issues that can be rigorously examined, and thereby eliminate discussion of the very thing you want to investigate."

"Doesn't that bother you?"

"Not in the least," Keerbrock had answered. "I'd much rather understand what's going on than get another paper published. If the world isn't ready for something, them's the breaks. One reason I signed on was because discovering the mystery properties of the jadeite—even if it had to remain secret—gave me confidence in the more prosaic assertions the letter made."

Claire thought long about that. Having read extensively about the so-called chimp wars over the meaning of the ape language experiments, she knew he was right. While apes happily used sign language to communicate with humans and each other—sometimes for decades—the behavioral science community only grudgingly acknowledged that the animals even knew the meaning of the words they were using. And papers in *Science* or *Nature* on animal understanding or use of language were few and far between.

"As I've said, what you've stumbled on," Keerbrock continued, once again failing to notice his lack of tact, "may be a missing piece that connects evolution, intelligence, and climate. Think about it: every species dies out, and climate is often holding the gun that kills them off." Keerbrock went off on a tangent. "It's going to happen to us someday, maybe soon . . . That's going to be richly ironic since us humans—the smartest guys on the planet—are blindly creating the climate that's going to kill us off. Anyway, scientists are always asking why a species died out. For me that's backward. I'm looking at your elephants and wondering how they lasted so long. They were in the wrong place at the wrong time, and they must have lasted for hundreds of thousands of years—it takes a long time to build a brain case like that cranium."

Keerbrock paused. "So, I'll be content if we solve that puzzle. I'm not on some crusade to bring science someplace where it may not be willing to go. Do you understand?"

"Oh yes, Dr. Keerbrock," Claire had replied, but even as she said it, she wondered whether Katie would accept this boundary.

"Good. We're getting ahead of ourselves in any event. As I said before, one step at a time. Let's see what we find, then we can decide what to do with it. By the way, now that we're coauthors, perhaps you should call me Will."

Later, thinking about what Keerbrock had said, Claire realized that he'd gotten one thing wrong. Earlier he had felt that Katie shouldn't lead this aspect of the investigation because of the wide-ranging skills required as well as her lack of stature in the community. He didn't know whether Katie's discovery of the properties had changed his mind, but Claire now realized that if the most interesting part of the investigation was off-limits for publication, Katie, with her stubborn streak, might be the only person willing to take it on.

67

IT WAS A CRISP, CLEAR DAY IN EARLY OCTOBER WHEN CLAIRE walked over to the behavioral science building for the meeting. It was approaching peak fall color, and the campus was aflame with various hues of red, brown, and green. It was a morning to enjoy, but Claire was concerned. She understood Keerbrock's qualms about having Katie lead a study that was inevitably going to involve solid state physics, bioacoustics, and quantum mechanics, but she had not been able to bring herself to tell Katie that she was going to have to relinquish the lead. Claire just couldn't get past the fact that a promise was a promise, even though the stakes had changed. Her hope was that after a meeting with the formidable Keerbrock, Katie would accept that she was out of her depth.

They arrived nearly at the same time. Katie was dressed in jeans and a gray sweater and looked cool as a cucumber. Claire appreciated that the girl was trying to look asexual and professional. Claire deemed the effort to be a complete and utter failure.

Claire and Katie chatted a bit about nothing, and then Katie offered to go down the hall to the coffee machine to get a couple of Americanos. She was just handing Claire her cup when Keerbrock arrived. They all sat at the worktable, which held the jadeite. The three of them looked at the stone. None of them moved to pick it up.

Claire cleared her throat. "OK, Katie, this is your show. Why don't you take us through what you're thinking."

"Sure, boss." Katie stood up and took a second composing her thoughts. "I've got a hypothesis and a proposed plan of action . . ."

Claire stole a glance at Keerbrock, who, while composed and silent, looked like an adder getting ready to strike. His quasi-human side, which had brought him to find her, was nowhere in sight.

"But let me quickly put things in context before I lay it out." Katie then ticked off how their thinking changed about the significance of the jadeite—the recognition that it was shaped exactly like a yam, the significance of the yam, the mystery of the jadeite's special properties, and Karil's discovery of a lush area in the middle of a desert. "So by itself," she continued, "the jadeite is interesting, but there is a very strong likelihood, as Dr. Keerbrock has noted, that it was purposefully shaped by Bart or his peers, and has some special significance for that species at that time. Obviously, there's a great deal of work to be done trying to eliminate the possibility that it wasn't shaped at all, but, clearly the prize will be analyzing the meaning of the stone's ability to cause a physical response when held. So let's talk about that. OK?"

Katie looked at Claire and Claire looked at Keerbrock, who seemed about to say something. Before he could, Katie continued. "Look, I know and agree that there's a well-defined way to study the properties of the rock." She paused. "But that's not why you're here, right?" she asked, looking directly at Keerbrock.

If Keerbrock was offended by what bordered on impudence, he didn't show it. Claire was beginning to enjoy the show.

Katie smiled. "Right! OK, I did a small stint with Katy Payne's infrasound project studying low-frequency communication in elephants in Kenya. What we know is that below twenty hertz, humans cannot hear sounds, but they can feel them." She looked apologetically at Claire. "I know you're aware of all this from your work. I'm just setting the context."

Keerbrock was getting impatient. "Yes, we talked about this when we first tracked Claire down."

"So, after touching the rock and feeling that response, I began to think about how simple movement on a spectrum can shift between the senses, from hearing to feeling. Think about stoners listening to a heavy-metal band. They get close to the speakers to feel the sound."

Keerbrock still looked impatient, so Katie moved on.

"Was it within the repertoire of an elephant to create a wave that could cause a feeling? Then, the question becomes how do you capture and preserve that feeling. Waves are transient—they don't hang around for five million years."

Now Keerbrock was truly interested. "Exactly!"

"We all know that any mineral has a vibratory signature—hence the New Age stuff on healing crystals."

Keerbrock winced.

"And we know that waves can be manipulated to create interference patterns that are stable—e.g., a hologram. So if it's possible to create a hologram with photons at one end of the frequency spectrum, shouldn't it be possible to create complicated standing waves with phonons at the other end?"

Keerbrock gave the slightest of nods; he'd earlier said much the same thing.

Instead of continuing, Katie went over to the table and picked up the jadeite. Claire started. "What are you doing?"

Katie held up a finger. "Stay with me."

Katie slowly ran her hand over the stone while she kept her gaze on Keerbrock. After several seconds, she shuddered. She still kept moving her hand slowly over the rock. The shudders almost became a seizure. She lurched forward, almost dropping the rock, which she just managed to put down. She sat in her chair, and it seemed an eternity before she could talk. Keerbrock looked at her with a combination of curiosity, alarm—and admiration.

"I don't know what would have happened if I hadn't had to put down the rock, but that little experiment tells me one thing."

"Which is?" asked Keerbrock.

"Which is that whoever endowed this rock with these properties expected that it would be picked up by some creature weighing ten thousand pounds, not a hundred twenty—give or take . . ."

"Tell us more about what happened when you held it that long?" asked Claire. Almost immediately on returning, she had insisted on picking up the stone, but could only hold it for a few seconds.

"First I felt the power, and then some kind of rumbling sound or wave began to intensify. It was a little like whale song."

Katie paused and shook her head. "But that brings me to my second point. If I'm right that the jadeite was intended for elephants, if there's a message in there, we will never get it just by touching it as I did. We simply don't have the auditory processing capacity. I'm probably just getting a fragment of what's being conveyed. And the nature of the message could be an image, not just sound. Experiments in cymatics show that sound waves can sort matter into stable patterns. Maybe the rock conjures a diorama for an animal the size of an elephant? How could we determine that?"

"We *do* have computers," offered Keerbrock mildly.

"Of course, and we could spend months of computer time trying to analyze the patterns, but think about what we'd be doing."

Keerbrock clearly wasn't used to graduate students putting him on the spot.

"And what would we be doing?"

"We'd be building a virtual elephant."

"And?"

"So why do that when next week we could bring the rock to a *real* elephant and see how it reacts?"

Claire almost gasped. This was pure Katie, bold and, Claire had to admit, brilliant, but so far outside the boundaries of formal scientific investigation that she shuddered in anticipation of a magnitude-eight earthquake that would be coming from Keerbrock. In fact, the professor did jerk his head, but he only looked at Katie and said mildly, "Gee, wish I'd thought of that. But what would we learn?"

"OK, we wouldn't learn much about the internal structure of that energy field, but we might learn a lot about its function—and that could point us toward its structure."

"Keep going."

"Think about what it would be like to live in a world of low-frequency waves." Katie directly addressed Keerbrock. "I know I'm not qualified to talk about quantum mechanics, but I want to describe something with broad strokes, OK?"

Again, the slightest of nods.

"Our—human, that is—thinking is dominated by particles. Think about pixels, think about the pointillist movement in art." She turned to Keerbrock. "Forgive me for encroaching on your territory, but think about how hard a time Einstein had accepting quantum mechanics, which derived from his own work. We tend to think in terms of localized events—that's why science can't countenance things like ESP—even though there's actually an aspect of quantum mechanics that can explain how an action in one place might simultaneously trigger an action very far away . . ."

This elicited another wince from Keerbrock.

"But imagine if your worldview was oriented to waves. Instead of seeing things localized and discretely, you would be comfortable with and tuned to the distributed and connected. And, assuming you had the mental capacity to do so, and you wanted to leave a record of some important event for posterity, you might create some stable portrait through the interaction of sound waves by using the vibratory properties of the minerals around you.

"The key is understanding the difference between being naturally biased to thinking about the world as the interaction of particles, as we do, and thinking about the world from the point of view of waves. The easiest analogy I can think of is to compare the jadeite to a solar cell. Imagine if the tables were reversed: that we were the smart creatures five million years ago and the smart elephants were alive today. The smart elephants of today uncover a solar cell and a lightbulb and when they bring this piece of metal and silicon into the sunlight, the lightbulb goes on. All very mystifying, because there are no moving parts. The solar cell operates because photons knock electrons out of the semiconductor, which are then gathered by an electrical circuit. The elephants, oriented to thinking about waves, might be intrigued by the magnetic waves generated by the solar cell, but might be mystified by the interaction of sun and the silicon because it requires an understanding of the interaction of sunlight and material in a particle mode."

Keerbrock interrupted. "This is what I was talking about when we found you, Claire. Everybody knows what an ultrasound machine is, right? It's just a way of turning sound into an image. So, it's not such a big step to imagine that an animal with a big brain and huge auditory processing capacity might be able to make an interference pattern to convey a static acoustic image. People have been doing that for decades, exploring the wave properties of various minerals and using them to make acoustic images." He turned back to Katie. "Go on."

"So, if an elephant did respond to the stone, it would certainly save us a lot of time in terms of not chasing down blind alleys."

There was silence when she finished.

Claire looked at Keerbrock. He looked at Claire. "She's a pistol, this one," he said as though Katie were not right there in front of him. "There's a quote I remember from my undergraduate days. I think it's attributable to George Bernard Shaw, and it goes, 'Art is the arduous victory of the imagination over reason.' I think that applies here. We're in the realm where science becomes art."

Then he turned to Katie. "So, keeping in mind that there's not a chance in hell of publishing what we find, where do we find this elephant?"

"Oh," said Katie, cool as cool can be, "I've got elephants up the wazoo."

68

CLAIRE, KATIE, KEERBROCK, AND HELEN HAYDEN LOOKED AT the herd of elephants. Zoe Taylor, a dark-haired woman in her early forties with an unnerving stare, turned to Claire. "There's someone here who knows you and wants to say hello." As they approached the herd, one female's ears perked up.

She swung around, putting her trunk in the air as though trying to find an elusive scent. Then she came toward the group. Helen and Keerbrock started to retreat, but Claire stepped forward and with tears in her eyes yelled, "Flo!" The elephant stopped in her tracks and trumpeted before moving up to Claire and nuzzling her with her trunk. Claire was laughing and crying at the same time and kept saying, "Flo." Flo rumbled with unambiguous contentment.

Claire looked with mock reproach at Zoe. "You could have told me."

Zoe explained to the group that after Claire had left for Kazakhstan, Flo had taken up her old habit of throwing stones. The elephant park administration had decided that there were too many opportunities for unfortunate encounters with the public, and Flo had been shipped to Zoe's sanctuary, Boisbeaux, which was more secluded in southern Louisiana. Indeed, she was content in the two-thousand-acre stretch of bayou and bottomland forest. There was a chorus of frogs from the swamp, and they could hear warblers in the still air. Flo and thirty other elephants had freedom, plenty of mud to loll in, cypresses, hickory, oak, ash, and pine trees to rub against—pretty much everything an elephant that found itself marooned in America might want.

Claire had invited Helen Hayden to come as a courtesy and was surprised when Helen not only agreed but also offered to take them on her plane. She said that the jadeite was so precious that she did not want to risk anything happening. This was common sense, since there was no telling how TSA would react if they picked up the stone, or, worse, insisted that it go through the X-ray.

Watching Flo, Keerbrock said, "Give that girl a contract. She hit that tree eight out of the last ten throws. She's got to be sixty feet away."

It was four in the afternoon in late October, but it was intolerably hot. Everybody was drenched in sweat. Noticing the discomfort of her visitors, Zoe didn't offer much consolation. "The heat? Get used to it. We're getting it from all sides. Drought's killing the forests to the north, and sea level rise and the Army Corps of Engineers are killing the bayous from the south. Hate the thought of moving, but we might have to pick up stakes if things continue the way they're going."

Every now and then Flo would pick up a ball instead of a rock and hurl it. Rufus, Flo's rottweiler new best friend, would then take off like a rocket to retrieve it and drop it in front of her.

Keerbrock turned to Claire. "Let's make sure that she can't grab the jadeite when we do this thing . . . and also that there's nothing around that she might throw at us!"

Claire gave a tight smile; she was nervous as hell about what they were doing. "Don't worry about Flo. She's an old soul."

Zoe added, "Also, she's the best of the lot when it comes to medical checkups, so she won't mind the monitoring patches."

Claire nodded. "Sergei's been working on that."

Claire had used some of her funds to bring Sergei from Transteppe (with American troops installed at the invitation of the president, Transteppe had become a de facto DMZ, as neither side wanted to start World War III). Sergei had flown in the night before, and Claire had given him a big hug when he greeted the group upon landing that morning. Sergei had held her shoulders in his hands and said, "Don't ever disappear on me again."

"Yes . . . *sir!*" she'd said, snapping off a salute.

Sergei had brought in lightweight field equipment ranging from ultrasound to monitors for vital functions and even brain-scanning devices.

Zoe's radio squawked, and she picked it up. "OK, they're set up. Just so we're on the same page—any sign of stress and I'm shutting this down. Clear?" She made sure that she got a nod from each of them, including the Nobel Prize–winning scientist.

"OK, you all head back in. I'll be along with Flo in a bit."

Claire started to go with the group and then stopped. Almost shyly, she asked Zoe, "OK, if I hang here with you and Flo a bit more?"

"Sure," Zoe said with no hesitation. "The more time she spends with people she trusts, the better."

As Claire stroked Flo's rough skin, she marveled at how her work had come full circle. From abandoning direct research on animal intelligence for the safer ground of studying ultrasonic communication, now she was back trying to investigate something at the bleeding edge of the study of the evolution of intelligence. Claire found it comforting that Flo, who'd been a stalwart in Claire's earlier work, would be involved in this far more daring effort. And she took comfort that now she had a revered pillar of the scientific establishment watching her back.

Even with Keerbrock's involvement, however, it was actually a small miracle that they had gotten to this point.

Like many seemingly simple ideas, Katie's plan to gauge an elephant's reaction to the jadeite was loaded with pitfalls. It wasn't just a matter of finding the right elephant; they also needed to find a keeper who wouldn't blab what they were doing. Claire had an easy time imagining a *National Enquirer* headline—"Romancing the Stone: Whack Job Scientists and the Elephant Fortune-Teller"—if someone mentioned what they were doing to the wrong person. Then there were the dangers inherent in transporting this unique, irreplaceable artifact as well as the elephant's reaction. What if a five-ton animal freaked out and stomped it?

They did not dare cut any piece off the jadeite, as they had no idea which parts of the stone were vital to producing its bizarre energy. What they could do, and did, was measure and record the stone's various fields with every conceivable measuring device—"only passive devices," per Keerbrock's stern warning—in order to develop as complete a record as they could at what was happening within and around the rock that was invisible and inaudible to humans.

Figuring out whether there was a pattern in the intricate waves was a matter of finding a world-class code breaker with access to an array of supercomputers. What was easy to see, however, was that the energy of phonons—the quantum units of vibrational energy—spiked enormously when someone's hand touched the top of the rock. This did not happen when they raised the overall temperature by putting the jadeite in a hot box, so they speculated that the contrast between the warmth of a hand and the ambient temperature had something to do with triggering the reaction.

Katie had sorted through her vast network of contacts in the animal rights movement before settling on Zoe, who had started Boisbeaux as a sanctuary for rescued elephants. Zoe and Katie had worked together on a number of ops in the old days. Zoe was hard-core. Katie knew that if she reassured Zoe that this would advance the welfare of elephants, Zoe would take what they were doing to the grave. Trouble was, Katie knew there was always the possibility that she was wrong—that the energy of the stone might be amplified rather than diluted by the bulk of an elephant, and produce awful consequences. Knowing Zoe, Katie didn't want to think of what the woman might do if things went wrong.

Then there was the question of how to interpret Flo's feelings. They could set up equipment and put some noninvasive sensors on the animal, but how would they interpret her reactions? Over the next few days, they thought of abandoning the plan several times, but either Claire or Katie or Keerbrock would always come back to the same thought: if the stone was meant to be touched by an elephant, the first step in settling that question would be to see what an elephant did after touching it, even if a modern elephant did not have a frontal lobe the size of Bart's.

Keerbrock was not particularly concerned as they entered the big barn situated away from the main Boisbeaux complex. Claire and Katie, however, were both visibly nervous. Zoe had put Rufus in the house so that he wouldn't distract Flo, and she had ensured that the other elephants and staff were doing things well away from the barn.

Zoe led Flo into the back part of the barn, which was separated from Claire's group by solid iron bars. The barn was used for medical exams, and it had a so-called squeezebox, which could be used to immobilize a large animal. They saw no need for this; indeed, they wanted to make this experiment as natural as possible. In the back of the enclosure were some boards and a couple of pieces of PVC pipe, leftovers from some repairs. On the human side of the barrier, Zoe had left a basket filled with Flo's favorite treats—apples, tomatoes, ears of corn. Flo saw the basket immediately and made a small rumble. "That's her apple sound," said Zoe and held her hand through the bar so that Katie could hand her an apple. Flo happily munched while Zoe set up a ladder and began attaching various sensors with tape to Flo's rough hide.

"So who's going to hold this stone while Flo touches it?" Zoe asked while she worked.

"Who does she like better, women or men?" asked Katie.

"Definitely women—she's a die-hard feminist."

Claire turned to Helen. "Would you like to do the honors?"

Helen laughed and held up her hands. "The only thing I know about elephants comes from Dr. Seuss." She looked at Claire. "This is your work, and you seem to know Flo. Shouldn't you?"

Now it was Claire's turn to hold up a hand. "Katie's discovered the stone"—Claire gave Keerbrock a direct look—"and this is her idea."

Katie looked gratefully at Claire. "And I read Betty Friedan in college. Maybe Flo's a fan, too."

Claire laughed. "OK then."

"The rest of you, stand back and stay quiet," said Zoe, stepping down from the ladder. "Wait till I'm with you, and then we can start."

She passed the leads from the sensors through the bars to Sergei, who immediately began plugging them into the monitoring equipment, which he'd set up on a table near the front door to the barn. Once done, he nodded to Claire. "Ready."

Zoe entered the barn, grabbed a tomato, and gave it to Flo. "OK, it's your show."

They'd packed the jadeite in a foam-lined briefcase. Claire opened the case and handed the stone to Katie, and then retreated to the rest of the group.

Katie, Claire, and Zoe had discussed at length how to approach Flo with the stone. "Don't worry, Flo understands the principle of private property," Zoe had said. "Offer it to her with your hand underneath, and I'll bring her trunk over to touch it. She understands a good deal of English, and I'll tell her what I'm doing."

Holding the stone, Katie slowly walked up to the bars and stood about three feet back holding the jadeite in front of her. Zoe gently took the tip of Flo's trunk and pulled it through the bars. "This nice woman wants to see what you make of this stone," she said as she brought the tip close to the stone and moved it slowly over the surface.

At first Flo did nothing, and Zoe kept gently moving her trunk over the jadeite.

Then Flo took control of her trunk. She held it still over the center of the stone, the tip just in contact with the stone. Her eyes grew big, and she started trembling. Then she spread her ears wide.

"That's a threat!" said Zoe, roughly pushing Katie backward.

Flo let out a roar that shook the building. She reared up on her hind legs, tearing off all the sensors attached to her head and body.

"That's it! You're outta here," screamed Zoe, and she started shooing the group from the building. Katie darted back and handed the jadeite to Claire, who quickly stuffed it back in the briefcase. Sergei started closing the laptops and moving them out of the barn.

Zoe turned on Katie, white with fury. "What the fuck was that about? I trusted you!" She turned to the rest of the group. "Get out! All of you!"

"Not yet," said Keerbrock calmly, standing in the doorway and refusing to budge.

"*What?*" Zoe was beyond irate.

"Look!" the scientist commanded, and pointed to Flo.

Despite her anger, Zoe turned to look. The others gathered in the doorway.

In the back of the enclosure, Flo had picked up the piece of PVC. She wrapped her trunk around it, held it perpendicular to the ground and used all her weight to push one end into the ground.

Once she had driven the pipe into the earth, Flo made a soft rumble.

"What's that sound mean?" Asked Katie.

Forgetting her earlier anger, Zoe looked bewildered. "That's her 'thank-you' sound . . . What's she doing?" Zoe was confused.

Keerbrock directed his answer to Claire and Katie. "I don't know . . . following instructions? I think we should take another look at that ulna."

Claire thought she knew the answer but still asked, "Why?"

"To see if it's hollow."

69

THEY WERE SITTING AT A PICNIC TABLE ON ZOE'S VERANDA. She was deeply apologetic for getting upset at the barn and had insisted that they stay for dinner. Zoe had gone back and offered Flo an apple, but Flo had ignored it and pointed with her trunk at Claire, who was carrying the briefcase with the jadeite. She clearly wanted to touch it again, though neither Claire nor Zoe thought that was a good idea—at least right then. When Flo was let out of the barn to join the other elephants, they had all clustered around her, and there was a good deal of rumbling among them. Zoe did not have a clue what was being said, but she said she had never seen anything like it before.

Zoe had laid out a simple vegetarian meal on her veranda. She did not eat meat. The main dish was something Zoe called "rice and sauce," saying it was a recipe she had cooked up in Sierra Leone when she had gone there some years back to try to save the country's last surviving wild elephant (she failed). Zoe had brought out some rosé wine to accompany the meal. Keerbrock looked dubiously at the label— who knew they grew wine grapes in Arkansas?—but, after tasting it, he announced graciously that it was light and refreshing. After they sat down, Zoe stood up to welcome them with a toast.

"Katie told me that what you are doing is under wraps, but that it would be good for elephants. Watching Flo's reactions, I now believe that. I agree that it's probably for the best not to know the full story until you're ready to go public. Again, I want to apologize for freaking out. It's tough to be an elephant today, and sometimes I overreact."

They all clinked their plastic glasses. Keerbrock was seated next to Katie (not an accidental positioning, noted Claire, who filed this as a confirming detail in the mental ledger she now maintained on the question of Katie's irresistibility). Across the table, Claire sat next to Sergei. She had been so happy to have Sergei back she was content to say nothing. Sergei turned to her and said, "She's right, but I'll bet it was tougher being an elephant in Bart's day."

Claire smiled and squeezed his hand. Now that he was here, she was glad that she had resisted the urge to talk to him when she had hit bottom. Now, she felt like herself again.

They all were hungry, and there were a few moments of silence as they dug in, a silence punctuated by tree frog croaks and crickets, and by brief expressions of appreciation for the spicy dishes Zoe had prepared.

Keerbrock was the first to speak. He turned to Zoe, who was at the head of the table. "You said earlier that you use English when dealing with Flo. What do you think is going on when she hears it?"

"You mean does she understand? I've no idea. But anyone who works with elephants uses language. It makes life easier. For instance, if I say, 'Bring me the log,' she'll bring me a log, and if I say, 'Bring me the medicine ball,' she'll bring me a medicine ball."

"Have you tried saying, 'Bring me the log and then bring me the medicine ball?'" asked Helen, picking up on the thread.

"Nope," said Zoe crisply, "and I'm not gonna. I'm trying to give these animals a life on their terms." Zoe thought a minute and her tone softened. "But I'm pretty sure she would do it in the right order."

After dinner, Sergei announced that he was going to help with the cleanup, and the rest of the group repaired to Adirondack chairs to plan their next steps. Scientifically, the logical next step would have been to have a number of other elephants touch the jadeite and monitor their reactions, but Claire ruled that out, saying that they were lucky to get out of the barn with the jadeite intact, and it wasn't like they had another stone if this one got damaged or shattered. Keerbrock noted that they had come here to answer one question: whether there was some acoustic message in the jadeite intended for another elephant, and the answer was almost certainly yes. So, in one sense they got what they needed—and possibly much more.

"This turned out to be crucial"—he nodded toward Katie—"and now we know that there is one obvious path forward, right?" He continued, looking at Katie. His face had an almost predatory look.

Claire realized that Keerbrock may have fallen under Katie's spell, but this was not a scientist who could totally suppress his critical facilities. Claire held her breath. Keerbrock seemed to have forgotten his earlier misgivings about Katie, but if the young graduate student was going to lose control of this project, now was the moment. Claire thought furiously; clearly his idea had something to do with the ulnae, but she wasn't even sure whether Katie had heard that remark amid the chaos.

Claire's phone buzzed with a text from Sergei, who was still in the kitchen. *And I thought we Russians were tough . . .* Claire suppressed a smile and texted back, *Keerbrock's being much easier on Katie than he ever was on me! Wonder why?*

Katie tapped her finger on the arm of her chair and then turned to Keerbrock with a cool, unblinking gaze. "I'm sure the doctor will correct me if I'm wrong, but I think what we saw today connects the ulnae to the jadeite." She paused. Everybody was listening intently. "And to the lush period Kiril uncovered in the fossil record. We can no longer analyze these three things in isolation."

Keerbrock absolutely beamed and clapped his hands. "That's it!" He turned to Claire. "I'll say it again! This girl's a pistol!"

He turned back to Katie, who, Claire noticed, had turned bright red. She clearly had not been as confident as she had sounded.

"So what next?"

"Here's what I suggest. We drag Sergei back up to Rushmere to see what's inside those ulnae."

Claire had to stop herself from cheering. She glanced up at the window to the kitchen. Zoe and Sergei seemed to be having a grand time. She was laughing and putting her hand on his shoulder.

Katie continued with her new plan. "If it's fossilized mud, we'd know they were once hollowed out. Means we'd have to sacrifice the bone, though."

"Even if we don't possess them, we know there's more bones out there," said Keerbrock.

Claire had not yet caught up. "Why is it so important to find out if they're hollow that we need to sacrifice our one bone?"

"When we first saw the ulnae, we thought they were weapons, or something ritualistic. Then Karil tells us that there was a thin layer of fossilized vegetation suggesting that the immediate area had been green in the years leading up to Bart's demise. Then we discover this stone, which is shaped like a type of yam, and we know that yams are foods that people turn to during times of drought—when plants bury their carbohydrates underground. Then we find that the yam-like jadeite also has this bizarro energy field. Is it some freak of the stone, or was it somehow created by Bart and his buddies—and for what purpose? Religious? Nope, Flo answered the question when she drove the PVC into the ground. It looks like it was an instruction manual . . ." She paused. "On how to irrigate."

Keerbrock interrupted. "I wouldn't get too wedded to that instruction-manual idea, though I think the connection with irrigation is spot-on."

Everyone was curious. "What are you saying?" asked Katie.

"Just that Flo might have been imitating something she saw rather than following instructions. It's a subtle but meaningful distinction. Maybe Bart's peers knew that they were approaching the end and wanted to leave a record, a phonon diorama—to use your word—of who they were and how they survived. That's also possible."

The penny dropped for Claire. "I get it! What Flo did with the PVC answered one big question for me. When I first saw the bones and how freakishly out of place these elephants were, I wondered whether we were looking at an example of the island rule." She quickly reviewed how isolated populations tended to get smaller or bigger and why. "But the steppe is as far from being an island as anything that can be imagined." She paused for effect. "Except . . . maybe not."

She had Keerbrock's total attention. "That green patch Kiril uncovered emerged at the point at which the rest of the steppe was an uninhabitable hell. Once Bart's ancestors started growing food, they couldn't leave, as the drying intensified over tens of thousands of years they became addicted to farming. Obviously I'm guessing here, but given their biogeographic isolation, they could—or evolution could—divert blood from the muscles to the brain without cost. If they couldn't get out, predators couldn't get in. That's how you get runaway evolutionary change."

Keerbrock looked truly excited. He turned to Claire, "The missing piece! This will never be published in a million years! But wouldn't it be good to know for sure?"

He turned to Katie. "Who's the vegetation guy, Karil? I'd suggest having him look for evidence of bamboo in that green period, pollens."

Helen was fascinated. "Farming? Do other animals farm?"

Claire jumped in. "Ants bring back leaves and use them as fertilizer to grow mushrooms; wasps turn other insects into livestock; I could go on. Oh, and tribes have been driving hollow sticks into the ground to bring up water for thousands of years."

Keerbrock turned to Helen and summed it up. "You see? We have a story. Somehow, an elephant ancestor has the bad luck to get isolated in the Kazakh steppes, and then the Messinian salinity crisis hits, starting several hundred thousand years of whipsawing climate, always trending toward the drier. Each violent shift in climate produces a crisis for

the elephants, with the more adaptable ones surviving and the specialists dying out. Over time, the survivors find they need to cooperate to
find food—who knows, maybe also to distribute it—and these social
pressures also favor the smarter ones. If you were to look for a candidate to prove that intelligence is an ecologically surplus ability, you
couldn't find a better candidate than an elephant, with its extraordinary auditory processing facility and the exquisite control of its trunk.

"So, on the one hand, as food dries up, they start looking for yams
and other underground plants. Maybe it's not enough to find them, so
they figure out how to grow them. But still things get drier. They figure
out how to use bamboo or some other hollow plant to bring up and
collect water, but then the bamboo disappears, and they find they have
to use hollow bones. But irrigation gets more difficult and complicated
as the drought deepens and they have to communicate how to connect
the bones as they need to go deeper. Ultimately, right around the time
Bart lived, they run out of tricks—the climate is just too harsh. And . . ."
Keerbrock snapped his fingers.

A slot machine's worth of pennies dropped for Claire. "Will, you
had this figured out all along, didn't you?"

"I suspected it," he admitted, "and much as I knew it was a lost
cause proving anything, you just can't shut down your mind—at least
I can't."

He pursed his lips. "And I'm happy I didn't. What you've uncovered
is so much richer than what I imagined. You know my history—first I
worked on climate cycles, then I integrated evolutionary change, then
I noticed correlations between climate crisis and jumps in brain size in
the hominin record. As you remember, my question was: Why only us?
If rapid environmental change is a driver of intelligence, why don't we
find a bunch of other smart animals? Now we know; they've come and
gone. And—even better—we glimpse an entirely different intelligence.
Bart is the missing piece"—Keerbrock smiled mischievously—"make
that *link*, in a whole lot of developments."

Keerbrock was just getting warmed up. "And there's a lot more that we haven't even mentioned. When I first felt the jadeite, it occurred to me that maybe there was some extremely powerful interference pattern associated with the stone. But the ancient elephants could have made that discovery by chance. Now, thanks to Flo, we know that Bart or one of his pals somehow imbued that stone with an explicit message." He turned to Katie. "What does that mean?"

Katie thought a minute. "It means that they understood the wave properties of various materials?"

"I'd put it more broadly. It means that they had an ability to model the world—even if the thrust of their intelligence was very different than ours."

There was no stopping Keerbrock now. "Think about the nature of Bart's intelligence, assuming that his fellows 'programmed' that stone. He would have possessed an extraordinary facility with the wave properties of any number of materials. Bart would have understood quantum mechanics in a heartbeat. When I grew up, quantum mechanics was assumed only to apply to the invisible world and not reality in general. Now the conventional wisdom is that the wave function applies to everything, which would have made perfect sense to Bart. Today, everybody's trying to figure out how to make a quantum computer—a machine that would use peculiar characteristics of the quantum world to compute all possibilities simultaneously. Bart could have helped us there." Keerbrock broke off for a moment, then added, "Maybe the jadeite *is* some form of solid state computer . . . So it is a very good story, but it's unfinished. And I have to say it again, it will never be published . . ." He looked at Claire and Katie. "At least not in our lifetime."

"Tell us again why not?" There was a challenge in Katie's voice, which Claire caught even if Keerbrock didn't.

"I would have thought that would be obvious," Keerbrock replied with a bit of edge. "The scientific community can handle the stuff on climate change because it's data driven, but it cannot handle the assertions of intelligence, language sophistication, and agriculture abilities because they are not data driven and contain a mess of subjective inferences." Keerbrock smiled. "Oddly, the public is ready to embrace animal intelligence, but not the notion that climate change is a killer. I suspect that by the time the public realizes that climate change is a killer, it will be too late, since it already is too late . . . so maybe whoever survives us will publish this posthumously."

Nobody laughed at the melancholy Dane's attempt at gallows humor.

Claire was particularly unhappy. "So what do you envision in terms of future publications from this discovery?"

"I think there's a great deal to be published—a fuller description of Bart and his big brain, the biogeography and climate context. There's a lot of straight science to be done. But the narrative that fits these pieces together? That's a bridge too far."

This was the moment of truth for Claire. She turned to Helen. "As you might guess, one of my principal reasons for coming back was to honor my commitment to Fletcher Hayden's memory. For better or worse, he backed me, and I'm going to decide what lines of inquiry we pursue going forward, and what gets published going forward. Moreover, the very things he says we can't publish are the reason I got into this work. So, my plan is to pursue the science as well as the narrative. And I *will* write the narrative, even if you and Dr. Keerbrock and the team are the only ones who ever see it."

Helen, who had been listening intently, took a deep breath and spoke directly to Keerbrock. "My father chose to back Claire in this research, and while it goes without saying that we are honored that you have shown an interest, I have to say that my father would have insisted that Claire have the final say on how the research should proceed going forward."

Claire had trouble catching her breath. "If that's unacceptable, all I can say is that we have done so much more than I could have ever hoped for. And Dr. Keerbrock, you turned my life around and I'm truly grateful." Claire hoped that no one could see that she was crying.

Katie came over and gave Claire a hug.

Keerbrock was slow to respond. He was still trying to figure out this strange new world in which an ever-growing mob seemed to feel that they had the right to challenge him. After a moment he said, "I completely agree that Claire should make all decisions about lines of inquiry going forward. It is her discovery and her project. But, if asked, I will strongly advise against publishing inferences that go beyond the data, and which might jeopardize the credibility of all the work you've done." He looked in turn at Helen and Claire. "I'm a scientist, and the integrity of science is built on rigor. I cannot put that aside after a lifetime of commitment to its principles and methods."

Only Sergei noticed that Katie had become extremely quiet, and an upbringing in a country where the wrong word could bring on a world of hurt had endowed him with an exquisite sense for dangerous moments.

He stared hard at Claire to get her attention, and when she glanced his way, ever so slightly he shook his head—this was not a battle to fight that day. Claire exhaled, and Sergei quickly changed the subject. "You said it was too late to do anything on climate, why?"

Keerbrock seemed happy to change the subject. "When you look at climate cycles, which is what I do, you see that the last ten-thousand-year span has been a rare span of good warm and relatively stable weather in a record of upheavals and ice ages that extends back to the dawn of our species. This blip has been an extraordinarily good climate for humans. So, the entire sweep of modern civilization has taken place within a blink of the eye in geological terms. People think the present weather is the norm. But it's not. Who knows how long the good times would have lasted, but, thanks to fossil fuels, we're not going to find out. Since the 1980s, the climate has become more and more unstable, and it's only going to get worse. Imagine what Bart would have thought of us. He and his peers found out that climate was an 'angry beast,' as one of my colleagues described it, but they didn't create the climate that killed them. Us? We're poking it with sticks." Now there was real fire in his eyes and his voice. "Can you imagine *anything* more *stupid*?"

Nobody said anything.

The conversation petered out. Katie said she was heading back to the motel.

"I'll come," said Claire, "perhaps Sergei will come, too." She noticed that Katie was chortling. "We have a lot of loose ends to go over," she finished somewhat defensively.

70

IT SHOULD HAVE BEEN AN EBULLIENT FLIGHT BACK TO NEW England the next day, but it was not. Keerbrock's memento mori for the planet and his downer about publishing had cast a pall over the group. What he had said was hard to digest but harder to dismiss.

Helen surveyed the mood of the group and decided they needed a distraction. She broke out some cards and chips and a bottle of single malt and proposed a game of poker, seven-card high low. She set a limit on betting so that nobody could be wiped out on one hand. Everybody had some experience with cards, but they played a couple of hands for practice.

Helen was clearly a practiced player. Sergei watched her for a few minutes and whispered to Claire, "What is the saying? The apple doesn't fall far from the tree?" He himself was impossible to read, slow playing strong hands and pouncing when he sensed weakness. Claire held her own, but in the end it was Katie who had the most chips. When asked how she pulled that off, she said, "Dumb luck—I didn't have a clue what I was doing."

Claire snorted, "I don't believe that for a second."

Busted, Katie smiled. "OK, Dr. Keerbrock only looked at other people's cards when he had a good hand; Sergei always looked first at the other cards showing to see if there was a play regardless of whether he had a good hand. If Sergei bet aggressively early with good cards showing, he didn't yet have a hand; if Ms. Hayden stayed in when Sergei was betting, the best strategy was to figure out which way she was going and take the other side; Claire folded more than anyone else. If she stayed in, watch out! Claire was the most difficult to read because she never drove the betting, making it hard to figure her confidence level."

Keerbrock shook his head. "I'm *that* easy to read?"

Claire thought back to Transteppe and her discussion of poker with Helen's father. Katie was so much more than a pretty face.

By the time they had landed at a private airport near the campus, the group had cheered up. Helen was going back to Vancouver Island, and so she stayed with the plane. Keerbrock told Claire that he would be in touch and then headed for his car. Claire told Katie that she would get Sergei sorted out and that they all would meet tomorrow. Katie suppressed a smile and said brightly, "Tomorrow it is."

Claire looked at Sergei. It was seven o'clock. "Let's talk over dinner. Toss your bag in the trunk." Claire popped the trunk and opened the doors of a used Honda that had seen better days. After Sergei dropped off his luggage, Claire took him to a bistro in town that supposedly had a terrific cassoulet.

They didn't talk much until they were seated. Sergei looked over the drinks list. "So, our first date! Maybe we should have champagne?"

Claire blushed but said, "Go for it!"

As they chatted about Transteppe and what it was like living amid the current eerie stalemate that had taken hold, Claire made a decision.

Before she committed to it, however, she had to know something. "Sergei?"

He sensed her change in tone. "Yes?"

"I know you don't like to talk about it, but I need to know more about what that creepy oligarch has on you."

Sergei was silent.

"I promise you, nothing leaves this table . . . I'm serious, Sergei."

"Why?"

One of Claire's mother's admonitions popped out. "Because it's time to lay your cards on the table and step up to the plate!"

This time Sergei looked genuinely confused. "What?"

Claire was delighted. Score one for Mom!

"Because I need to know that you are safe and that I can trust you."

Sergei looked at Claire sadly.

"'Trust me' is the most dangerous phrase in Russia."

"But I'm not Russian, and we're not in Russia."

Sergei looked at the table for a long time before speaking. And then it all came out. He told her of his fit of arrogance in the chess match and the oligarch's sadistic program of revenge. At first he'd used the laws to harass Sergei.

"The laws?" Claire was confused.

"Yes, remember I told you that nobody can be in perfect compliance with the law in Russia. Bezanov has deep ties in the Kremlin, and I don't know at what level he organized the harassment, but I started getting threats of prosecution on various fronts, from tax evasion to fomenting dissent.

"Then it stopped, and I thought he'd finally moved on." Sergei leaned back and gave a short, bitter laugh. "I should have known better. He'd decided that I'd be more useful out of jail."

"I don't get it."

"Let me give you a little background. What I should have realized when I played Bezanov in chess was that he knew that he could lose—he was a master, not a grandmaster, so he knew there were many players who could beat him—but I didn't just beat him. I humiliated him in front of his girlfriend. Then—in his eyes—I stole his girlfriend."

Claire nodded, encouraging him to go on.

"The worst thing that can happen to an up-and-coming oligarch, especially a beast of prey like Bezanov, would be to be made to look like a pathetic patsy. So, as I later came to realize, he didn't just need to get revenge and get back Ludmilla, he also needed to break me."

Claire was missing something. "How does putting you here constitute breaking you?"

"He made me his pawn. He liked the idea of making me take a job I had no interest in—this was before I met you, remember." Sergei smiled. "And a game player and strategist like Andrei never does anything for just one purpose.

"Bezanov knew of my skills in geology and decided that rather than continue to ruin my life, he might turn me to his purposes in Kazakhstan—we now know why. Clearly, he was one of the key plotters in the uprising. But, that's another story . . . If I was to be his pawn here, he needed some lever to control me even though I was outside Russia, so he arranged that the state invite my younger brother, who was studying psychology, for special training at a facility outside Moscow. It's all very subtle. Mikhail was a 'guest,' but he couldn't leave."

"What did Bezanov want from you?"

"Initially, information, mostly about what was underground."

"The phospherite."

"Yes, the phospherite. What seems obvious to me now is that the phospherite made Transteppe a strategic asset from Russia's point of view, and it gave Andrei the opportunity to enlist the government in his own private plans to take control of Transteppe. It's exactly the kind of gambit a chess player like Bezanov would concoct. I haven't figured out by what means he plans to take control, but he will try. He's driven, and he doesn't stop halfway."

"Did Hayden know?"

"Probably, and remember? He wasn't surprised by the uprising."

Claire pulled the conversation back to Sergei. "You said your brother was a guest."

"After the uprising, I realized that my position as a Russian at Transteppe had changed. Bezanov no longer needed me as a geologist. Moreover, even my limited knowledge of their interest in the phospherite might prove embarrassing, as it would suggest that taking over Transteppe was the point of the uprising. Obviously, he could kill me . . ."

Sergei said this casually, and Claire paled.

"But that was not a sure thing, and he didn't know whether I had taken out some 'insurance.' So I let him know that I would continue to play ball and keep quiet, but only once I knew for certain that my brother was with my cousins in Finland. What I figured out was that after the uprising, my brother shifted from being an asset to a liability from Andrei's point of view. Once he was released, *my* leverage was gone, too. Since the pretense was that he was a guest, it was easy for Andrei to get him freed without involving the judiciary. I'm not even sure Mikhail ever knew he was a prisoner."

As he said this, a cloud came over Sergei's expression. He looked at Claire and thought about how easy it had been to gain the release of his brother—almost too easy.

Claire noticed his changed mood. "What are you thinking?"

Sergei snapped back into the present. He tried a joke. "I was wondering whether he would take Mikhail back."

Claire gave him a look that let him know she didn't buy his joke, but she moved on to another thought. "Did you know that there would be an uprising in Petropavl?"

"No, Bezanov would never trust me with information like that. But, given their interest in the phospherite, it was easy to figure out Primorskichem was planning something. That's why I left the bread crumbs for you and Mr. Hayden. Rob felt betrayed at first, but I think he forgave me once Mr. Hayden filled him in. I hope so, anyway. Rob is a stand-up guy."

"You mean a comedian?"

Sergei gave a wan smile. "OK, so not all my jokes are funny."

"Thank you for trusting me." Claire looked into his eyes. She held his gaze and smiled.

Sergei hesitated a moment and then said, "There's one more thing."

Claire noticed the change in tone.

"Remember when I told you that I got an email from Ludmilla?"

Claire tried not to show her panic. "Yes?"

"What I didn't tell you was what I left out in my reply to her email."

"Un-huh?" Again, Claire kept her voice level, even though her pulse was going wild.

"What I didn't say in my reply was that I'd met someone worth living for, and dying for."

Claire launched herself across the table and gave Sergei a fierce hug. "You better not be doing any dying, buster! I want you alive!"

Claire had planned to ask Sergei about the investigation. She didn't know whether Rob had told Sergei about the janitor. She thought about the janitor and Bezanov's intricate schemes and wondered whether the oligarch had anything to do with Hayden's death. It seemed too far-fetched to put as a question to Sergei. Anyway, she wanted nothing to spoil this moment.

71

WITH TRANSTEPPE AT A STANDSTILL, SERGEI FELT NO COM-punction in extending his stay for one week more in order to work on the analysis of the petrified material inside the ulna they had set aside from the array. Sergei had taken the bone over to the geology laboratory so that he could use their sophisticated equipment for scans and assays.

Claire couldn't believe how happy she was. The only cloud was his coming return to Transteppe and the unknowns of his entanglement with the faceless men Sergei referred to as "they." The couple tried to keep up a professional face for the outside world, and Katie, particularly, seemed to relish the dance of feigned ignorance, saying to Claire things like, "If you *happen* to run into Sergei, could you ask him about . . ."

Meanwhile, the other investigations pursued by Benoit and Francisco were proceeding on schedule. The publicity surrounding the *Nature* letter and the *Times* articles opened the funding spigot, and Claire started the process of shifting some of the research budget to more traditional sources.

Claire and Sergei were up all night the day before he left. He'd tried hard to reassure her that he would be safe—that Andrei had nothing to gain and everything to lose by attacking him now—but, try as she might, it was hard for her to believe him. The body count surrounding Russian business deals had been headline news for years, and Bezanov sounded worse, not better, than the oligarchs she had read about.

The next morning, Claire entered the workroom early. She was still feeling the glow of the intimacy left in the wake of Sergei's decision to open up to her. His candor demolished any remaining defenses protecting her heart, and she felt herself opening up to him in a way that had never before happened with the previous men in her life. Claire smiled at the thought that the one man she felt she could truly trust was a Russian whose Machiavellian skills would have served him well in the time of the Borgias.

She turned on the lights. At this point Claire was focused on the badlands where they had first uncovered the bones, and she spent a good deal of time looking at the photos they had pinned to the walls. It was more than fifteen minutes before she looked down at the worktable. At first she didn't notice anything, but then when she returned her attention to the walls and whiteboard, she had a sense that she had overlooked something. The array was in the center of the table where it had always been.

The Lucite box containing the jadeite was also there, but inside the box, instead of the stone there was a folded piece of paper. With trembling hands Claire unfolded the note. She knew exactly what had happened before she read the first words. It said, "I'll bring it back in one piece. I promise!!! But please don't come after me—and please don't hate me."

Through the pounding in her ears she remembered Hayden's subtle warning as well as her own questions about how Katie would react to the restrictions on publishing—questions she should have asked about Katie's earlier life. Claire realized in an instant how perfectly Katie had executed this caper. She knew Claire couldn't bring in the authorities without alerting them and the world to the significance of the jadeite, and they were nowhere near ready to go public. Even worse was the realization that what Katie was doing was not so very different than what Claire had done when she first took the bones.

Claire pulled out her phone but was not surprised when the call went to voice mail. Katie was not taking the call. Claire thought a minute and then sent a text: *I know where you're going and what you're doing. Call me or I'll stop you.*

Twenty minutes later, the phone rang. Claire took a deep breath, trying to control her anger and her hurt. She clicked answer and said nothing.

"Hi, Claire."

Katie sounded subdued.

There was a lot Claire could have said, but she also knew that she had no right to berate anyone. "You know, you could have asked me."

A pause. "You know I couldn't. If you think about it, you'll see I'm actually protecting you by not asking—you never could have agreed."

Claire thought about that.

"I mean it when I say I'll bring it back."

Claire softened a bit. "Why did you do it?"

"You heard Keerbrock. If we're not going to publish, maybe this is the best way to really know what it means."

"You realize you've blown it with regard to your degree."

"I just hope that what comes next makes it worth it."

Claire thought a bit. "If you care about integrity, if you care about our friendship, you'll bring it back. I'll give you ten days."

"Thank you. I won't let you down," said Katie through sobs.

Claire thought about how Katie had helped her function after Hayden was killed and checked herself again from saying the obvious retort: "You already have."

72

ZOE GAVE KATIE A BIG HUG WHEN SHE DROVE INTO BOISBEAUX at seven the next morning. Katie looked exhausted in a sweat-stained T-shirt and dusty jeans.

"You OK?"

"Not even a little bit. But I'm here."

They walked toward the veranda.

Katie almost stumbled. "I've been driving twenty-four hours. I need to sleep. I need a shower, but first fill me in."

"OK, as I said in the emails, it's been very strange since you all left. Flo is really out of sorts. She keeps calling out. The others are unsettled. It's quite clear that stone set off something."

"You're sure you're OK with Flo touching it again?"

"No, but it's what she wants. She can always pull away, right?"

"Right."

"I hope you didn't burn too many bridges to do this."

Katie's eyes filled with tears. "Probably all of them. Hope it's worth it."

"Where's your monitoring equipment? In the car?"

Katie wiped her eyes and pointed to her head. "Right here." She looked around. "Where can I crash? We'll start this afternoon."

Six hours later Katie emerged from Zoe's guest room looking refreshed. Zoe had given the staff the rest of the day off, saying that she would take care of the evening feeding. Zoe wanted to have this session in the barn, but Katie insisted that they do it in open air.

"It's a risk, Katie. These are elephants, not bunny rabbits."

Katie rolled her eyes. "Please—after some of the stuff we've done? I'll sign any release you want. Nobody's going to sue anyway if I get stomped—more likely you'll get a medal and a parade."

"Why is it so important to do this outside?"

"So I can see how other elephants react. Also, I want Flo to know it's her show."

Katie had changed clothes and was wearing a borrowed pair of khaki shorts and top—the uniform for the sanctuary. Zoe wanted Flo to know that Katie was official. Katie had thick gloves on her hands. They were hot, but the insulation prevented her hand from transmitting heat to the stone. Zoe let them in, locking the gate behind them. Zoe was carrying a basket of treats. Katie was carrying the foam-lined briefcase. "Let me go ahead." Zoe started to shake her head. "Really, I'm OK."

"I'll keep ten feet back, no more."

"OK, here goes."

Walking slowly, Katie approached a clearing. They'd chosen it because it was on high ground and well away from the feeding area. In the distance, she could see Flo and farther off some other elephants. Katie turned toward Flo and held up the briefcase. Flo lifted her trunk and then started walking toward her, quite fast. Watching, Zoe tensed. There was no turning back now.

Flo slowed down as she got closer to Katie. Slowly and deliberately Katie opened the briefcase and took out the jadeite. Facing Flo, she held the stone in her hand. Flo flared her ears with excitement, but she approached Katie slowly. Almost politely, she held her trunk just away from the jadeite. With one hand, Katie took the tip of her trunk and slowly moved it over the stone. Then she let go. Flo trembled and started making rumbling sounds. Flo kept the tip of her trunk on the stone. Katie felt the combination of trembling and rumbling in the ground. The rumbling grew louder.

Watching from ten feet away, Zoe tensed further. "The others are coming. Might be a good idea to fold our tents and skedaddle."

Speaking softly and keeping her eyes on Flo, Katie said, "This is why I came. I'm staying."

"Then I'm getting closer. They'll listen to me—maybe."

Answering Flo's rumbles, the other elephants slowly assembled in a circle, much like the defensive circle elephants in the wild might form around a wounded comrade, only in this circle they were all facing in. The group included two gigantic males. Katie looked as vulnerable as a mouse inside this circle of huge forms.

Once the circle was formed, the rumbling increased. Then Flo took her trunk off the stone and stepped back. Another female elephant came forward and offered its trunk to Katie, who did as she had with Flo and ran the tip slowly over the stone. "That's Gertrude," whispered Zoe. After a few seconds, Gertrude gave a small start but kept her trunk on the jadeite. She too began trembling and rumbling. Then she retreated. Katie took the opportunity to shift the stone to her other hand, while another elephant came forward.

After all the females had touched the stone, one of the two giant males advanced. "Leave it to the guys to let the girls check out whether it's safe," Zoe remarked. "But be ready to run."

"Where to?" asked Katie, offering the stone to the male, who slowly moved his trunk toward the jadeite but held it an inch or two away from the stone.

"Smart, best to let him decide," said Zoe approvingly.

The giant animal touched the stone hesitantly. After a few seconds, he pulled his trunk away and let out a giant trumpeting roar that shook the ground. Katie started but held her ground, steadily holding the jadeite in front of her. The big male quieted down and then approached again. This time he didn't pull away, and Katie could feel his excitement. After a few moments of touching the stone, the big male slowly backed up into the circle, and the other male came forward.

Once all the elephants had touched the stone, Flo advanced. She touched the stone and started rumbling. The other elephants joined in, and the rumbling became organized. It was like the loudest and lowest didgeridoo ever imagined, or Tibetan throat singing played at half speed. The waves traveled through the air, down into the earth, up into the heavens, and perhaps through dimensions inaccessible to humans. It gave Katie goose bumps.

"Can you feel it?" Katie asked, her voice choked with emotion.

Zoe could only nod.

The elephants had been swaying, but now the swaying became synchronized, passing from one elephant to another as though they were doing the wave.

Katie started swaying, too, moving rhythmically and slowly from one foot to the other, gradually falling into step with the elephants.

Still swaying, Katie looked over at Zoe. "Do you feel what I feel?"

"I think so. What is it?"

"A connection to the cosmos. Peace. I want it to go on and on and on." Katie slowly put the stone in the briefcase. Then she raised her arms to the sky and slowly turned in a circle, letting the waves completely wash over her. Despite the overwhelming presence of these most chthonic of creatures, Katie felt as though she was transcendently light, barely tethered to the earth.

After several more minutes, the rumblings began to fade. The elephants fell silent, though they still swayed. Then Flo made the same rumble she had after the first time she had touched the stone.

"She's saying thank you again."

Katie reached forward and gently stroked Flo's trunk. "I wish I could say thank you in elephant."

One by one, the elephants slowly broke off from the circle. The vibrations seemed to linger.

Speaking to no one, Katie said softly, "That was worth *any* price."

Neither Zoe nor Katie spoke again until dinner. Zoe went to put out greens for the giant animals. Katie started preparations for the meal. Once again it was to be rice and sauce.

73

THE NEXT MORNING, KATIE HELPED ZOE WITH SOME CHORES around the sanctuary. They returned to Zoe's house for a break from the heat. Zoe was sitting on the veranda when Katie emerged with her rolling bag.

"What are you doing?"

"I've got to set things right."

"What about Flo?"

"I don't know. At some point the staff is going to start wondering why they're getting all this time off. Claire wants this kept quiet. I'm not going to be the one that screws the secrecy. Look what I've done already."

She'd started lugging her suitcase to her car when they both saw a car coming up the driveway. Katie stopped to look as a Toyota pulled up to the house. Claire got out, and Keerbrock creakily exited from the passenger side. Katie dropped her bag and ran up to Claire, throwing her arms around her, sobbing, "I'm so sorry." Keerbrock looked thoroughly uncomfortable—what was it with these women and all the hugging and crying?

Claire patted Katie's back until the sobs quieted. "While not endorsing your method of cutting through red tape, Will convinced me that we had to be on hand to see what happened this next time."

Katie jumped up and down like a teenager. "All I can say is prepare yourself."

Zoe looked really uncomfortable. "Katie! It's one thing for you to put yourself at risk, but I don't think it would be too good for Boisbeaux's future if a Nobel Prize winner got stomped."

Keerbrock perked up. "What's this about getting stomped?"

"No one's getting stomped," said Katie. She turned to Zoe. "We can take them into the circle one at a time, and only if they want to."

"Want to what? And what's this circle?"

Katie laughed. "I can't even begin to describe it." She thought a second. "But you should be happy, Dr. Keerbrock. If it can't be described, there won't be a paper."

Zoe looked resigned. "OK, OK." She thought a second. "There's a vet in Baton Rouge looking to volunteer here. I'll send Bob and Carrie Mae up to interview him. That should give us some peace for a couple of hours."

Katie clapped her hands. "I can't tell you how happy I am that you're here," she said to Claire.

Claire shook her head and smiled, this time with real warmth.

Zoe gave Claire and Keerbrock khakis, explaining why they were necessary. At 3:30 they went inside the fence. Flo was already waiting for Katie at the spot where they had formed a circle the day before. "Whatever happens, just be cool," said Zoe. "You two stay close to me," she said and positioned the three of them behind Katie. Even as Katie opened the case, elephants were coming up the hill, and by the time

Katie had held out the jadeite for Flo, the elephants had already formed a circle. Keerbrock looked concerned, and even Claire wasn't at ease.

There were two new elephant recruits who had not been present the day before. Somehow they knew the rules, because they waited patiently for their turn to come forward and touch the stone. This time there was no drama from the males. In fact, a big male led the rumbling. Both the rumbling and the synchronized swaying became organized much more quickly than the day before, and the sounds much more coherent.

Katie joined in with the swaying almost immediately. "If you close your eyes and just hear and feel it, it's easier to join the rhythm," said Katie.

Claire did so and fell right into sync. Keerbrock first looked self-conscious, but then closed his eyes. "If anyone takes a picture of this, I'm finished," he said.

As the waves became more enveloping, Claire asked in an awed voice, "What's happening?"

"Bart is coming back to life," said Keerbrock quietly.

Then, for the next several minutes, there was nothing but the elephant plainsong.

⌐

Later, back on Zoe's veranda, sampling Arkansas' finest claret, they reflected on the day.

"I didn't feel like driving a pipe into the ground, did you?" asked Claire.

"Nope, but we learned a couple of things," said Keerbrock.

"Such as?"

"Clearly, elephants are getting a more vivid picture out of the stone than we humans with our puny auditory processing capacities, and, also, their reaction points more to idea that the stone is more diorama than instruction manual."

Claire turned to Katie. She cleared her throat. "I think you should stay here . . ." Katie started to protest, but Claire plowed on. "I insist—with the jadeite. I'll make it right with everyone. I don't know what will come of this, but clearly it's the most productive thing for you to be doing right now . . . But it's important to keep this secret. Can you do that?"

Zoe answered for her. "That stone is important to the elephants. I think we can find her a half hour here and there where she can be alone with the elephants."

Claire looked at Zoe. "Maybe you can answer this question: I've always heard that swaying in captive elephants is a type of stereotypical behavior, indicating stress. But what we saw was the opposite?"

Zoe smiled. "I was thinking about that, too. You're right—swaying can mean stress, but elephants also do it to get comfortable." Zoe was a tough customer, but she hesitated a bit in the presence of this high-octane brainpower. "I did have a thought, though."

Keerbrock seemed to sense the reason for her reticence. "I'd like to hear it—you've spent more time with elephants than any of us."

Relieved, Zoe nodded. "Well, I was thinking that elephants can't run, but they can move pretty fast by walking. Similarly, it's hard for a ten-thousand-pound animal to dance, but that synchronized swaying could have rocked the house at any club I've been to."

Katie clapped with delight. "*Saturday Night Fever*, elephant style!"

Claire was deep in thought. "Think about how they fell into synchrony so that the pulse traveled around the circle."

"Like a wave," offered Keerbrock.

They were all silent for a moment, then Keerbrock said, "Why don't they just take the jadeite from you? You couldn't stop them."

They all thought about that for a second. Zoe spoke first. "Maybe they understand and respect the notion of property?"

Claire shook her head, "Maybe, but not in Africa, or there wouldn't be such problems with farmers."

Keerbrock clearly had an idea. "Just speculating here—and if anyone quotes me I'll deny it!—but maybe possession of the stone confers on the bearer the status of an avatar." He sighed. "Anyway, the more I know about Bart, the more I like him—and envy him—except for the part about becoming extinct." He turned to Zoe. "You have the luckiest elephants on the planet."

Zoe nodded. "I think they know that."

Claire was thinking about what Keerbrock had said about liking Bart. "More and more I like Will's idea of a diorama. Maybe what we found is a time capsule, something that would tell future elephants what they were like, and what they did."

Claire knew she was going way beyond the evidence, but she wasn't finished. "So, what do we find in most tombs and monuments from past civilizations: images of battles and triumphs, weapons and the like. Instead, Bart's kin chose to leave for future elephants what amounts to a lifesaving technology, as well as a path to religious ecstasy."

Claire was getting excited. "I know there's more to be found at the site." She fixed Keerbrock with a look. "I'm saying right now that I'll bet that whatever we find, even if it's many more things, we won't find a weapon. I like Bart, too."

Keerbrock actually smiled. "I hope you do get to go back. But let's think a bit about what can be done here."

He turned to Katie. "I'm just going to toss this out: Wouldn't it be interesting to see what Flo communicates to other elephants without the stone?"

Katie nodded, and Keerbrock turned to Zoe. "How do you feel about Flo becoming an elephant missionary?"

Zoe didn't look particularly enthusiastic. "Flo's happy here. I don't know. It would be awfully expensive . . ."

Keerbrock nodded. "I understand, but think about it. I've been using my Nobel money to support offbeat, worthwhile projects, and I can't think of anything more compelling than this. I'd also be proud to make a donation to your refuge." He put a hand on Zoe's shoulder. "No need to decide now."

Zoe nodded. Claire looked at the great scientist in silent wonderment. Who was this new Keerbrock?

A LAND OF
EXTREMES

74

ANDREI BEZANOV SAT AT HIS GLEAMING EUROPEAN WALNUT DESK in his office in Vladivostok and looked with satisfaction at the two emails from his lawyers. Apparently the two Canadian mining giants, Groupe Riviere and Yellowknife Ore, had rethought the wisdom of their investment in Transteppe after the death of their representative on the board and the uprising in Petropavl. They were willing to sell their stakes to Primorskichem for the offered ten cents on the dollar. For chump change, he thought, he not only had a controlling interest in Transteppe—he wasn't worried about too much resistance from the Kazakh government since Transteppe would not likely be in Kazakhstan for too much longer—but once a new puppet government was in charge of the region, Primorskichem could begin to reap the enormous benefits of that minor investment.

The only thing that could screw things up would be if it got out that Russia had engineered the uprising and that he, Bezanov, was connected to Hayden's death. He wasn't worried so much about going to jail; his fellow oligarchs had been bumping off pests for years with impunity, and the Russian government would ignore extradition requests and indictments. Rather it was the fraudulent conveyance provisions that could unwind the sale, and the bother of having foreign holdings seized or frozen as the World Bank's ICSID or the Permanent Court of Arbitration issued damages judgments.

Worse, he would no longer be able to leave Russia, and he loved his home in Mustique, his property on the beach in Malibu, his apartments in New York, London, and Rome, not to mention his hundred-meter-long yacht, *Iridium*. Just the thought of a future of shuttling between Moscow, Vladivostok, and the Black Sea caused an involuntary shudder.

His advisers had reassured him that Moscow's involvement in the uprising could never be proven. As for Hayden, no one at Primorskichem, and certainly not Bezanov's Russian partners, knew that Hayden's death was something more than a random act by homegrown extremists.

As for Anachev, he didn't know anything. Change that—Andrei was fairly certain he didn't know anything. Killing him was always an option, but now, because his anger had gotten the better of him, Ludmilla knew of his manipulation of Sergei. Sergei disappearing right now would bring unwanted attention that he didn't need. Still, Bezanov thought, he needed to plan in case that became necessary.

He thought a moment. Maybe he shouldn't have released the brother, he mused, now that the woman scientist was back in the US and harder to get at. Clearly, she represented a new and better insurance policy, but only if she came back to Transteppe.

His thoughts turned back to covering his tracks. Only one other living person knew exactly what had transpired. That was the man who had organized the operation, the man who brilliantly impersonated a fanatic and then equipped, even better, sold the group he'd attached to the means to bring down the helicopter.

Bezanov had to admit that the man who had contacted him, the man with no name, was something of a genius. But, Bezanov reminded himself, this man had somehow contacted him directly, breaching all the firewalls and security measures the oligarch had erected to prevent precisely that contingency.

This was a loose end, and the more Bezanov thought about it, the more intolerable it became. But how do you tie up that loose end when you don't know the man's name or how to contact him? And, even if you can eliminate him, how do you do that without creating another loose end? That required some thought.

75

BEFORE HE LEFT RUSHMERE FOR TRANSTEPPE, SERGEI CALLED Rob. His friend answered sounding uncharacteristically subdued.

"Something's up? What's wrong?"

"Well, our job security is now about the same as a North Korean general's."

Rob filled in Sergei on the Primorskichem takeover of Transteppe by purchasing the Canadian miners' stakes.

"I should tell Claire."

"Don't! She'll want to come immediately, and the situation is completely combustible with US Special Forces here on the ground. Let's you and I figure it out first."

During the long plane trips Sergei did figure it out, at least some of it. His conversation with Claire had restarted his speculations on whether there was a tie between Andrei and Hayden's death. Now, with the news of the sale to Primorskichem, all the pieces fell into place.

The Transteppe helicopter ferried him from Astana to the concession in the early afternoon, two days after he left Rushmere. He showered, donned work clothes, and strode purposefully to Rob's office. His days as a pawn were over.

Before Rob could say hello, Sergei said, "The Russians killed Mr. Hayden, and we can use that knowledge to stop the takeover."

Sergei then told Rob about the mystery of a janitor speaking Russian to a train crew member while standing beside crates exactly the size that might hold a Stinger rocket launcher.

Rob drummed his fingers on the table. "Did you say a janitor?" he said a bit ruefully.

"I said dressed as a janitor. I don't think he was a janitor."

"You're right, he wasn't a janitor. Claire saw him fire the rocket. So did others."

Sergei looked confused. "Why didn't you tell me?"

"Clearly, I should have, but at the time, we needed you focused on dealing with the Russians and not chasing leads on Hayden's death." Rob thought a minute. "Actually, I'm glad I didn't tell you. Knowing what you now know, you probably would have given away your suspicions and gotten yourself killed."

Sergei gave a short, bitter laugh. "We Russians had seventy years' practice hiding our feelings. I could have carried it off."

Sergei returned to the murder of Hayden. "There's something odd about that murder given the extremely well-planned game the Russians and the company orchestrated."

"I agree," said Rob. "They didn't have to kill Hayden to get control of the company."

Sergei nodded, "It's almost as if there was more than one person calling the shots, and one of the players went rogue. I'd put my money on the greedy oligarch who controls Primorskichem."

Rob gave Sergei a sharp glance. "I thought you didn't know him. What did you say? 'We travel in different circles.'"

Sergei sighed. He'd already told Claire about his long history with the oligarch and couldn't hold back from Rob. So he told him the whole story. When he finished, he added, "You can be certain that I never told Bezanov anything other than what I was finding in mineral surveys, and I did my best to disguise the significance of the find."

Rob took all this in and then gave a rueful laugh. "I'm a rotten security head—way too trusting of my gut."

Sergei looked wan. "Maybe your gut was right—if it came to that, I think I would have sacrificed my brother to save you and Claire. He was always kind of a pain in the ass."

Rob laughed again.

Sergei picked up his train of thought. "By the way, I'm now convinced that when Bezanov came to Transteppe, it was to see whether Hayden would stand in the way of his plan. He has no soul, but for practical reasons, I think he wanted to get control of Transteppe without killing Hayden."

Rob looked wistful. "That means that if we hadn't found those bones, Hayden would still be alive."

"I hate that thought, and I hope Claire doesn't follow that chain of logic," said Sergei, knowing that this was exactly what she would do.

They sat in silence for a moment, then Sergei perked up. "There's always been a battle in the character of the Russian leadership between the bullies and the chess players in our dealings with the rest of the world. The bully part almost always undercuts the best efforts of the chess player. Bezanov is both a bully and a chess player. That can work to our advantage."

Their conversation was interrupted by a phone call from Ripley's office.

"Well, they didn't waste much time," Rob said, getting up and signaling Sergei to follow.

"What do you mean?"

"They're here."

The concession had all but shut down, and the only people Rob and Sergei passed were a few of Rob's black-clad security detail as well as what looked to be American Special Forces troops.

When they got to the site manager's office, Ripley greeted them at the door and gave Sergei a look that put him on his guard. "Thanks for coming," said Ripley carefully. "We've got visitors from Primorskichem who've asked that you give them an update."

Ripley stepped aside to reveal two men dressed in business suits. They were wearing visitor badges. Both were lean and intense. Neither smiled. "OK, let's see," said Ripley, sounding nervous. "If I've got this right, this is Dimitri Lerchov," he said indicating the taller of the two, who gave Sergei a perfunctory handshake while looking him directly in the eye, "and this is Pietr Popov."

Rob looked at the two men but made no move to introduce himself. He turned to Ripley. "How is it that two visitors show up when the concession's locked down, and I'm not even aware of it?"

"They just showed up," said Ripley, "and gate security brought them to me."

Before Ripley could continue, the man named Dimitri spoke in Russian. Sergei translated. "He says that Primorskichem now owns a majority interest in this mine, and its representatives don't have to ask permission to check on the company's investment—particularly in these times." Sergei let that last phrase linger.

Sergei then continued in a neutral voice, "They want to talk to me at the warehouse."

"That's all?"

"That's what they said."

With times so fraught, Rob didn't want to risk an incident. "OK, you know where to find me," he said and left.

Sergei and the two Russians walked in silence to the warehouse.

Once there, Dimitri pointed to a table and said, "Let's talk."

Sergei shrugged and they sat down. Sergei waited.

"Show us the images you have on the phospherite."

Sergei noted the command. Not "We'd like to see..." or "Please...," just "Show us ..." Without a word, he got up and led them to his office and turned on his computer.

He typed in a series of commands, and an image appeared showing the same section of the lip where the bones and the jadeite had been found. Only the phospherite showed up in color. Sergei had assumed his report to his Russian contact would prompt a visit and had prepared.

"This is one rock—phospherite deposits come in thick layers?"

Sergei sighed. "This is taken from a section of a recumbent fold, so the bottom is on the top. I'm assuming that the phosphate rock layer is somewhat below this, but because of the fold I would have to take a much longer vertical sample, and I haven't had the chance to do that yet."

"Why not?"

Sergei made a sweeping gesture with his hand. "You might have heard that the mine has shut down."

"Don't play with us. We're telling you to do more exploratory drilling."

Sergei kept his voice even. "That's not my decision. Management has said there will be no activity that could be perceived to be commercial until we're sure who our partner is."

Dimitri stared at Sergei with a look full of menace. "We now have control, and I think you know very well who your future government partner will be."

Even if they had the authority, Sergei was not going to take orders from these thugs. Rob was right—had he known after the uprising what he was convinced of now about Russian involvement in Hayden's death, he never would have served as an intermediary. Ordinarily Sergei preferred to work from the shadows, but a white-hot anger overtook him. As calmly as he could, he picked up a walkie-talkie. "Hey, Rob, would you send a security detail over to the warehouse? These assholes are leaving."

Then he picked up his phone and photographed the two men. "Get the fuck out of my warehouse," he said in Russian, "and don't come back without an army. These photos will be posted at the gatehouse."

Dimitri turned beet red and started to get up just as Rob and a security detail had burst into the warehouse, flanked by a team of US troops in camo.

Sergei was still shaking from adrenaline when he and Rob returned to Rob's office.

"Well, you clearly need some brushing up on how to suck up to your new bosses," said Rob, trying to lighten the mood.

Sergei took a few deep breaths and sighed. "That was probably the most spontaneous thing I've done in twenty-five years, and probably the dumbest." Rob offered him a bottle of water, and Sergei took a sip. "It wasn't just because of Hayden or stealing Transteppe. It's because of a lifetime of taking orders from Dimitris and Pietrs—and Bezanovs!"

The two sat in silence for a few minutes. Finally, Rob spoke. "You've put a big fat bull's-eye on your chest. I know you just got here, but I can't protect you. You've got to go, old friend."

Rob started to pick up the phone, but Sergei put a hand on his arm.

"I'll go, but not yet. Claire only has a little time to further investigate the mesa, and I'm the only one who can help her."

Rob nodded. "That's a fair point."

"And we might yet stop the Primorskichem takeover. I'm sure there were cameras on the rail landing. Have you looked at the footage?"

Rob shook his head. "You just told me about the janitor and the guy speaking Russian being there."

"Let me look at the footage from the unloading. All we need is a picture of the faces."

Rob didn't waste time weighing the pros and cons. "OK, let's get cracking. I'll get going on arrangements for Claire while you start looking at the video."

76

DECISION NUMBER TWO HAD BEEN EASY FOR CLAIRE. IN FACT, in the end, it was not even her decision, and it happened the day after she returned from Boisbeaux. During the previous weeks on campus, she had come to realize that in her soul she was a field researcher. She had just started planning her arguments to return to Transteppe when

Rob preempted her timetable. He called and said there was pressure to resume exploratory drilling in the mesa and that it was unclear how long that could be stalled. Was she prepared to return to Transteppe and resume probing the mesa on an urgent basis? "Absolutely, give me a week."

"You don't have a week," said Rob quietly. "We've made arrangements for the Transteppe plane to bring you tomorrow."

Claire thought that odd but didn't argue. She couldn't wait to see Sergei.

She also wanted to see Rob, though for different reasons. As much as she had blamed herself for Hayden's death, she imagined Rob would have been much more devastated. He had involved Hayden in the first place, and he was head of security. He had seemed subdued on the phone.

When she stepped off the helicopter at Transteppe, Sergei was there to give her a fierce Russian hug that left her gasping for breath.

It was a very different Transteppe than the one she had left. Where there had been heavy equipment and workmen bustling about, now there were only security patrols. The offices were down to a skeleton crew, and there was a melancholy feel to the near-empty cafeteria.

Over the next few days, Claire caught up with the Kazakhs as well as Sauat—and Lawrence, who seemed to be working on his hunting skills. She would bend down to tie her shoelaces in the warehouse and a paw would shoot out from under the bench. Claire didn't think it was that big a step from hunting shoelaces to catching mice.

Claire was alarmed to learn that Primorskichem now had majority control of Transteppe (the reason they had given her for the urgency of the exploration), but they did not tell her of their conviction about Russian involvement in Hayden's death. They did say that Primorskichem had overplayed its hand in demanding renewed exploratory drilling. The attempted subversion had alarmed Transteppe's remaining independent directors, because resumed activity would be seen as choosing sides in the uprising, and Transteppe had everything to lose and nothing to gain by trying to pick the winner in this stalemate, even if Primorskichem now had a controlling stake. And with the concession guarded by American Special Forces, Primorskichem management had to tread carefully in establishing control.

Transteppe's reaction to the Russians' visit bought Claire time to plan a dig on the mesa, though how much time remained an open question. The conflict might flare up at any moment, or the Russian politicians, who seemed to control Primorskichem, might decide that they didn't care what the rest of the world thought, and simply restart operations. Claire vowed to make the best of it, however, as she was convinced that the ill-starred, ancient beings that had taken the trouble to leave behind traces of their gentle civilization would have left more than just a few bones, a cranium, and that remarkable stone.

77

IT DIDN'T TAKE LONG TO FIND THE IMAGE HE WAS LOOKING FOR. Sergei remembered the exact time and date of the encounter, and so it was easy to find the relevant tapes. Surveillance cameras covered the entire landing area—theft being an omnipresent threat in Kazakhstan—and as soon as he had printed up a few stills of the men talking, Sergei brought the images to Rob.

Rob already had a plan. "First, we'll show the footage to a lip reader to see if they can make out what's being said. Then, let me give these to my contacts in intelligence to see what they've got on these men."

Sergei shook his head. "My experience is that intelligence agencies take but don't give. Why would they share what they find? They might have other fish to fry and prefer to use what they find for leverage."

"That's always a risk, but we'll dole it out piece by piece, and if they don't give, they won't get. Besides, we've got parallel interests."

Sergei shrugged. "So did your CIA and FBI before 9/11, but that didn't stop the CIA from hoarding intelligence that could have stopped the attacks."

Rob looked at him strangely. "How do you know so much about 9/11?"

"I watch *60 Minutes*. OK, do it your way, but if they don't respond in a week, I've got an idea to stir the pot."

Rob raised an eyebrow and faked a Russian accent. "What means this 'stir the pot'?"

Sergei laughed. "The Kazakhs would love to find evidence that the uprising was all about taking over Transteppe, yes? So we let them leak the photo of the 'janitor,' along with the story about Russian involvement to the Astana press, and see which rats start scurrying. And I'll bet we'd then start getting more cooperation from your intelligence guys."

"Why just the janitor?"

"Because it will give the Russians a sense that they are free at home"—a confused look passed over Sergei's face—"sorry, home free, and with that, maybe they'll go after the janitor."

Rob liked the idea but for one thing. "Or, go after you. Look, whoever this is in the picture had the brains to set up an immaculate hit on Hayden. That took meticulous planning. Such a person would assume that we had surveillance on the platform—and for that reason, my guess is that the conversation is innocuous, or even misleading. If the janitor truly is an operative, he would recognize you just as you recognized him, and the Russian probably already knew about you. Which means that once the photo is leaked, the Russian will instantly connect it to you."

"One more bull's-eye won't show," said Sergei, his Russian fatalism surfacing. "Do you have a better idea?"

78

THE MAN WAS KNOWN TO HIS LOVING FAMILY AS TOM FRECHETTE, though even that was not his real name. His wife thought his job was as a troubleshooter for high-tech nuclear-powered turbines, an occupation that explained his abrupt disappearances and unwillingness to talk about what he did. He had once used the name Proteus but had long ago given that up—the nickname was too memorable, and he realized only complete anonymity satisfied his need to be completely unmemorable. Now, in his office, he read the story in *Kazakhskaya Pravda* for the fifth time. There was a picture of the alleged killer of Hayden, and a story saying that there was evidence that he had acquired the weapon used to destroy Hayden's helicopter from Russian sources. As journalism, the story was wildly irresponsible, but what alarmed Frechette was that it was completely accurate. *Bezanov must be shitting bricks,* he thought.

Frechette always assumed that there was no such thing as a guarantee when setting up a hit. He always thought in terms of odds rather than certainties, and he was always ready to trade some degree of certainty of outcome for insulation from blowback should things go wrong, as they often did given the type of people drawn to work in the shadows. The trade-off lengthened the time it took to finish an assignment, but Frechette credited it with keeping him alive and in the game far longer than most in his field.

Despite all his precautions, the man realized that he was now as close to exposure as he had ever come in over two decades of off-the-books black ops. He looked again at the article. Why was there just a picture of the "janitor" and not the Chechen who had made the transfer? They'd been standing quite close, and he doubted that Transteppe had only partial coverage of the platform. That made it likely that whoever had delivered the photo to the paper had purposefully cropped the other man from the photo. Why? Two possibilities presented themselves immediately: whoever planted this story already knew who he was and an operation was already underway to eliminate him, or they wanted him to believe that they thought it was a local operation, tempting him to go after the Chechen.

Frechette opted for door number two. And, he admitted, they were half-right—he was going to go after someone, only it was not the Chechen delivery boy, but the clever man who Frechette assumed had planted that story. He would kill the geologist Sergei who had so casually walked past Frechette and the Chechen on the train platform.

Several thousand miles away in Vladivostok, Andrei Bezanov was brought the same article and instantly realized his whole plan was in mortal danger. He was certain Sergei was behind the planted story. The man certainly had motive. Why couldn't the idiot just walk away as he promised when he freed his brother? Either Bezanov had to get him back under control, or he had to go.

Bezanov then realized, while Anachev was a threat to the Primorskichem takeover, the anonymous black ops man, the now-exposed "janitor," was a threat to Bezanov. He had to go, too.

Bezanov started thinking about a plan. If he got his operative to take the woman scientist hostage, then, he was certain, Sergei would stop at nothing to get her back, or to get back at her killer if she somehow died in the process. He could even drop some clues pointing Sergei toward the assassin. The simplicity and efficiency of the plan appealed to his chess player's mind.

Time was of the essence. He was thinking about how to set things in motion when his phone buzzed with a text message. He looked at the screen and read the words *Dead man's switch*. Attached to the text was a very brief and innocuous snippet of the conversation in which Bezanov had given the assignment to take out Hayden. Bezanov slammed the table with impotent, bitter fury. He now had to root for the survival and success of a man who just a few seconds earlier he was plotting to kill.

He again slammed the table in frustration. This was getting out of hand.

79

ROB AND SERGEI SAT DOWN WITH CLAIRE IN SERGEI'S WORK area. Sergei knew it was going to be a hard sell, which was why he had enlisted Rob to join the conversation. Sergei was pushing a mug of coffee back and forth between his hands. Claire sensed the tension and was on her guard.

"What's wrong?"

"You mean beyond the concession being taken over by thugs and living on borrowed time?" said Sergei, softening the words with a smile. "Nope, not a thing."

Claire looked at Sergei sharply. "What do you mean, living on borrowed time?"

"What Sergei's saying," said Rob quickly, "is that the likelihood is that this stalemate won't last forever, and once it ends, the Russians will likely fire us, take over the concession, and either stop the fossil exploration or take it over." He looked at Sergei. "That about right?"

Claire took this in. "And?"

"And that means we've got to start breaking off pieces of the lip, bring chunks back here for quick analysis, and ship off the promising pieces," said Sergei. Claire started to say something, but Sergei held up a finger. "I know that's not how it's done, but we're in a war zone. We can't bring big equipment out to the area—we don't even have the operators—but we can do a quick survey and I'll use the results to position the cuts. I can split off some chunks and we can collect them at the bottom." He was talking fast. "If you remember looking down from the lip, there were big chunks on top of the scree. That means the rock doesn't disintegrate when it falls."

Claire sighed. "I think that someday there will be an entire textbook devoted to my career as a field scientist entitled *How Not to Do a Dig*." She furrowed her brow and thought a second. "Or maybe I'll be part of a miniseries, *Scientists from Hell*."

"So we agree."

Claire laughed bitterly. "Yes, with one condition. Rob shoots a video of me walking toward the lip with my hands up and Sergei pointing a gun at me—something I can show to my accusers when I'm drummed out of the American Anthropological Society."

Rob deadpanned. "I can do that."

Claire laughed a little nervously. "You know I'm joking."

80

THE NEXT DAY BEFORE DAWN, CLAIRE AND SERGEI BEGAN IN earnest. Instead of horses, they took ATVs that Rob had pre-positioned for them at the dry river crossing. It was mid-November and it was cold, but the real frigid temperatures were still a month away. They followed the tracks created by the giant Bucyrus earthmover that had brought the lip back to the warehouse. Rob had wanted to send a security detail, but Claire and Sergei had been adamant that any large group would attract unwanted attention and the possibility of freelancers plundering the site. No one ever went to the mesa section of the concession, and they wanted to keep it that way.

Sergei's ATV had a small cargo area, and they drove the vehicles right up the sloped mesa and started unloading. He'd brought with them small explosive charges and detonators, a small remote trigger to launch the explosions, a small gasoline-powered boring tool to set the charges, and a lawn mower–size remote-sensing device on wheels.

He had suggested the ground-penetrating radar because the dry, sedimentary rock was well suited to electromagnetic profiling. Claire spent the next hour and a half slowly moving the equipment over the edge of the mesa, working from the edge backward. The radar beamed waves downward, and the recording equipment would show where those waves had been deflected. She was using a thousand-megahertz antenna, which limited penetration to six feet but allowed them to see objects with a resolution to three-sixteenths of an inch. Sergei's logic was that since they had found the other objects close to the surface, it was likely that any future finds would be in the same strata and so sacrificing penetration for resolution was an obvious choice.

The problem was that sedimentary rock contained a lot of ordinary stones. Ordinarily it would be a long and arduous job to sort through the jumble of images once they had completed the survey, but they did not have the time for a thorough job. Claire tried to sort promising images from the background noise so that Sergei could place the charges in such a way that these objects had as much protective rock surrounding them as possible.

She knew this was an awful way to do field science, but still Claire was excited. If Bart's peers were smart enough to send one message to the future, they were smart enough to send more. Even with the high noise level, she could see several objects that looked to be more regularly shaped.

By the end of the day, Sergei had completed the boreholes on what remained of the lip and placed the charges. Claire wanted to videotape the explosion from down below so that they could track where particular chunks fell.

"Here's how we're going to do it," he said. "I'm going to say, 'One, two, three,' and then hit the trigger. We'll be well back from the explosion, so don't worry."

Since it was late afternoon and the light was fading fast, they decided to delay until the following morning. Sergei would take his ATV up onto the mesa, while Claire would position herself a safe distance from the mesa on the desert floor and film the operation.

81

CLAIRE WAS STARTING TO TURN, HAVING SENSED THAT SOME-one was behind her, when she felt the cold barrel of the pistol against her neck.

"You must be the anthropologist. Sorry to interrupt your work."

Sergei was getting organized on top of the mesa and hadn't yet looked down.

"Don't worry," said the man in a reassuring voice. "I just need to ask your friend some questions. Once I get the answers, I'll be on my way and you can resume whatever it is you're doing here. OK?" Frechette always offered his victims hope because he knew the desperate would cling to that hope, no matter how impossible, and it always made them easier to handle.

The man stepped back and Claire turned to look at him. What she saw was at first glance the least intimidating man she could imagine. Slight of build, with mild eyes and a receding hairline, the man looked like a desk clerk at a storage unit. But then Claire saw the veins popping on his neck and realized that he was strung taut as a bow. She didn't believe his story for a second. She knew the three of them would not be going their separate ways after a friendly conversation.

"OK, now give me your walkie-talkie." As he asked, he kept an eye on Sergei on top of the mesa, who still had not noticed what was going on down below.

"I don't have one." She tried not to give away the tension she felt.

"OK," he said as he patted her down with one hand, "so we're going to ask your friend to toss his down to you, OK?"

"He doesn't have one, either."

"Yes, he does. They'd never let you go out here without one."

Claire had never thought faster in her life and realized that there might be an opening. But that depended on Sergei being as smart as she thought he was. She nodded. "OK, but if we don't check in regularly, security will be out here in a helicopter in three minutes."

The man didn't think she was telling the truth but couldn't be entirely sure.

"When are you next scheduled to check in?"

Claire did a lightning-fast calculation. "Right about now, maybe five minutes."

The man chuckled but then shrugged. "OK, so we're going to call up to your friend to toss his down, but to me, not you."

Sergei had now realized what was going on down below and was reaching for the walkie-talkie when Claire shouted up to him, "Stop, Sergei, he's got a gun."

Sergei knew instantly that this was intended to be his appointment in Samara and turned his thoughts to how he might save Claire. "What does he want?"

Claire spoke very slowly. "Right now he wants you to toss him the walkie-talkie . . . very carefully so he can catch it and it doesn't break. Understand?"

Sergei didn't at first, but then he did. "OK, OK, don't shoot," he said plaintively. "Come closer, and I'll drop it on three. OK."

Claire tried not to show her relief. Sergei had understood.

The man looked from Sergei to Claire. Something was off, but he figured that after he had the walkie-talkie and made Claire check in, he could thwart whatever these amateurs had cooked up.

"OK. You"—pointing the gun at Claire—"stay here."

Frechette walked up the apron of scree as close as he could get to the face of the mesa. He briefly turned to Claire. "I'm going to put down the gun to catch, but don't think of running. I will drop you like a rabbit."

He put the gun on a shoulder-height boulder next to him. "OK."

Sergei held the walkie-talkie in one hand out over the ledge. Claire braced herself. She was near hysterical with panic. He was not well back from the coming explosion. Then she noticed that Sergei had one leg braced. She couldn't remember whether there was a delay on the trigger.

"Here goes," said Sergei, his voice very calm. "One, two . . . three!"

As he dropped the walkie-talkie, he simultaneously triggered the charges and launched himself backward, screaming, "Run!" as he did so.

He only had to make it four feet but nearly didn't as the well-placed explosives caused a near-instantaneous collapse of the section of lip. The ground fell away from under him as he landed, but his stomach hit the rim and with frantic scrambling he was able to stay on top. He got up immediately and began running down the mesa toward Claire.

For all his ineffectual look, Frechette had preternatural reactions and a psychotic's strength, but the shock of the explosion and rock fall delayed his response a fateful millisecond. A small boulder hit him in the back, breaking a few ribs and knocking the wind out of him. He turned his head just in time to see a two-ton section of rock hurtling toward him like a vengeful god.

82

SHAKING, CLAIRE AND SERGEI LOOKED AT THE MANGLED MESS that was all that remained of their would-be assassin. She felt sick.

"Why was he after you?" she got out between gasps.

"Because I could link him with the man who killed Mr. Hayden. He looks different than what I remember, but I'm sure this is the man."

Sergei shook his head and kicked the dirt in frustration.

"What's wrong?"

"He may have been our one chance to link the killing to Primor-skichem."

They both let this sink in.

"Partial justice anyway."

Sergei started looking around. "You didn't get to film."

Claire managed a weak laugh. "Damn, I should have asked him, but wait, then he would have killed us." She looked around. "Anyway, we can tell the rocks that just fell from the weathering . . ."

"Claire," said Sergei gently, "this is now a crime scene. I don't think there's going to be much investigation for quite some time."

Claire's eyes widened. She couldn't believe what she had just said. She recognized that she was still in shock. What had happened was too big for her to process.

Sergei continued. "Let's go back. Rob's going to want to get a team out here before the animals get to that," he said, pointing to the mangled, bloody remains. Then he had another thought. "One sec, I'm going to look for the gun," he said as he started to clamber up the rock fall to where he'd last seen the assassin. He disappeared from view, and Claire could hear him moving around. Then he stopped and was silent.

"Sergei? Did you find it?"

More silence.

"Sergei?"

After a few more moments of silence, Sergei finally said, "Come."

83

ANDREI BEZANOV STARED NUMBLY AT HIS COMPUTER SCREEN and watched his world come apart. Canada had launched an investigation into the death of Fletcher Hayden based on new evidence that had come to light; the two Canadian mining giants were preparing to file suit for many billions of damages and also initiating action on the fraudulent conveyance articles of the sales and agreement in order to unwind the sale of their interests in Transteppe. The US, Canada, and the EU had frozen his personal assets as well as those owned by Primorskichem pending the resolution of the suits and criminal cases, and there were warrants for his arrest in multiple jurisdictions. At the invitation of the Kazakh government, the US had sent additional troops to Transteppe.

But that was not the worst.

A call from a source inside the Kremlin had informed him that the Russian president, already feeling the bite of numerous embargos and sanctions, couldn't afford to have the Primorskichem takeover linked to the uprising. His advisers were recommending that he allow extradition to go forward, thereby isolating Bezanov's "rogue" actions from Russian policy. Bezanov knew that if this turned out to be the decision, he would never make it to the airport for extradition.

The now former oligarch never had time to finish that thought. Two unsmiling men entered his office uninvited. He could see several more outside, and his secretary being led away in tears.

84

IT WAS NOW MIDWINTER, TWO MONTHS SINCE THE STRUGGLE at the mesa. Preoccupied with the uprising and the ongoing great power stalemate, the Kazakh authorities had been content to let Transteppe and the US military lead the investigation, and Rob allowed his colleagues to decide that the death was an accident, a conclusion that was made easy because no one could figure out who this man was. The CIA took possession of the body, but neither fingerprints, dental records, nor DNA produced any leads that might offer a clue to his identity or his past. The agency also ran the damning recording that had led to Bezanov's downfall through the most sophisticated voice recognition software on the planet and got nowhere. He apparently altered his voice when he spoke on the phone. They knew the man freelanced black ops and private espionage, and their sources had many stories of the exploits of this man with no name, but no one could remember meeting him in person. "He's like Proteus," remarked one investigator admiringly, "he seemed to be able to change his shape at will without changing his substance."

Claire was interested in the investigation into the man's identity—naturally she wanted to know more about the man who had tried to kill them both—but she was more fully engaged in trying to puzzle over the mysterious round stones that were protruding from the boulder that killed the assassin. As Sergei reconstructed it, a large piece of the boulder had split when it hit the piled rock below, and it sheared along the plane that held these rocks, which, like the ulnae, looked to be arranged. Once they were allowed back to investigate the fallen rocks, they had used a backpack remote-sensing unit to assay other large pieces that had fallen, and discovered that there were likely many more stones. They seemed to be arrayed in conical piles.

Claire noticed one more odd rock that had been liberated when the boulder crashed down on the rock pile. It was crystalline and about the size of a softball. She picked it up and looked at it. She was about to toss it aside, but then she hesitated. She put it in a canvas satchel to bring back to the lab.

She returned to the curious arrays. Once she had cleaned the surface of the boulder and removed the bloodstains from the other side of the rock, she took some pictures of the array and sent them to Keerbrock and Katie. The next day Keerbrock called.

With his customary abruptness, he began, "Most likely, it is just a random pile of stones."

Claire smiled. "Will, you wouldn't have called if you really thought it was just a pile of stones." She could envision the great man squirming.

"OK, ground rules. First and most important: publication is only a description of the new find. You and I, however, can talk about what these really mean."

Claire was dying. "Which is?"

"It's the last chapter of the story—at least, that's my educated guess."

"A tomb?"

"No, think of the narrative we put together down at Boisbeaux. What killed them off?"

"Lack of water."

"Right, and they resorted to desperate measures, but they weren't enough."

"And . . ."

"Think about it, these were extraordinarily intelligent desperate creatures, capable of doing applied science on par with some of the best minds alive today." He paused. "And they are looking for water anywhere they might find it, with the water table dropping below their ability to reach it. So where would they look for it next?"

"The ice caps, but that makes no sense."

"Agreed, that makes no sense."

Claire was getting annoyed. Clearly Keerbrock was pleased with himself. "Will, tell me!"

"One more try: Where is there as much water as there is in all the rivers and lakes on land?"

"Clouds?"

"There were no clouds, remember, but you're on the right track. The air. Clouds hold 2 percent of the air's water, while the rest is just floating around as vapor. It's there, even in the desert, and our elephants would have observed that water comes out of the air and condenses on some rocks as temperatures drop in the evening. The ancient Jews figured out how to capture water from the air; so did the Byzantines and lots of other cultures. So, I'm thinking that as a last gasp, Bart and company built what's called an air well. One form of air well is to pile up stones in conical piles so that the air can flow through them, just like the piles in that image you sent me, only bigger. In the evening, droplets form and can be collected."

Claire absorbed this. "That's brilliant, Will." She thought a bit more. "Then why did they die out?"

Keerbrock was ready for this. "Volume. They could have collected enough water to keep themselves hydrated, but not the amount needed to grow crops. I'm sure you've heard the phrase 'an appetite like an elephant.'"

"Poor Bart."

"Poor Bart, indeed. Regardless of how much of this we can publish, it's clear that Bart and his friends wanted to tell their story. It's coming out in bits and pieces, but keep digging. I'm sure there's more to the story."

"Thanks, Will, thanks for everything. I will keep digging."

After she hung up the phone, she had an idea. She went in search of Rob and Sergei.

They met in Rob's office. Claire dived right in. "Remember Mr. Hayden insisted that he didn't want Bart to be named after him?" Curious, they both nodded. "Well, not to be like a lawyer, but he didn't say he did not want *anything* named after him, yes?"

"Yes . . ." Sergei and Rob said in unison, still confused about where this was going.

"So, how big is the mesa where the lip is located—maybe half a hectare?"

Sergei nodded enthusiastically. He now knew where this was going.

"So, let's ask Transteppe to agree to gift it to the Kazakh government. Maybe call it the Fletcher Hayden Paleontology Site for the Study of the Deep Past."

"Just rolls off the tongue," said Rob, "but I like it." He was perking up.

"I'll bet we could even get it designated a World Heritage Site, which would give it more protection."

"We can get this done," said Rob. "We owe it to him." He opened his desk drawer and pulled out a bottle. I think this calls for a toast. He filled three shot glasses with single malt and lifted his glass. "To the memory of Fletcher Hayden."

"To the memory of Fletcher Hayden," said both Sergei and Claire. No one noticed that Claire took only the tiniest sip.

⌐

Sergei and Claire headed back to the warehouse. She was energized and pleased. Life seemed to be returning to normal. They were greeted by Sauat, who had been getting instruction from Kamila on the tomography equipment. There seemed to be no shortage of women who wanted to take Sauat under their wing.

"Big news!" he said, getting up. He was clearly excited.

Yet another new discovery? Instead of leading them to his work area, Sauat brought them over to Lawrence's food bowls. In Claire's absence, the cat had relocated from the food storage area. Claire wasn't entirely sure whether Lawrence had been fired by food services or promoted by Sauat. Lying in front of the bowls was half a lemming.

Lawrence seemed to be making the transition from shoelaces to prey. "I wanted to show you this before I cleaned up," Sauat beamed, obviously proud of his feline protégé.

Claire smiled. "Where's the other half?"

"It will make its presence known, eventually," said Sergei drily.

Claire stopped by Karil's work area to get an update. He said he was working on identifying the individual plant life with a particular emphasis of evidence of ancient bamboo, but it was slow work. As Claire started to move off, he shyly asked whether Katie would be coming back to Kazakhstan. Claire said that Katie was going to be tied up for some time analyzing the jadeite. She wasn't sure, but she thought she heard Kamila mutter something that sounded like, "Good!"

Claire sat down at her desk. Since coming back, any number of emotions had flooded her. Just a few months in the past, she had experienced both the lowest and highest points of her life. The omnipresent reminders that they were at the center of a flash point of tensions as Russia fought to grab critical resources in order to maintain its position among the great powers summoned anew everything she had felt when she first saw the petrified bones protruding from the harsh surface of the mesa.

꓿

She realized that what had been started might ultimately change science itself. Bart offered the possibility of understanding a world described in waves, a world that the brightest minds had been trying to understand since the ancients tied the movements of the stars, the sun, and the moon to the seasons. But it was a world that looked utterly different from Bart's perspective. The ancient elephants understood connections where Western science saw isolated individual actions.

Physicists glimpsed this perspective through quantum mechanics in the subatomic universe but shied from making the connection to daily life. Claire had experienced firsthand the ferocity with which science holds on to its paradigms, but she now felt she had an answer to the question she had posed herself after Hayden had told her of the great game for control of Transteppe. While the potential for great power conflict overshadowed the dig for the moment, she now believed that the changes unleashed by the discovery of the simple array of bones would prove more consequential than the grinding of the tectonic plates of geopolitics at whose juncture Transteppe now sat.

Claire felt a wave of nausea. She had been experiencing them for the past few weeks. She sat on a bench and resumed her train of thought, ticking off all the forces that might have marginalized this discovery at any point. She marveled—it was something of a miracle that Bart's message had reached an audience across the vast sweep of time.

There was another miracle she was thinking about, one that had a lot more to do with her nausea. She decided it was time to tell Sergei.

She tracked him down and found him studying the conically arranged stones. "Sergei," she said, smiling into his eyes. "Does that ultrasound equipment you've got work on humans?"

It took the geologist a second to realize what she was saying. He put an arm around her shoulder and pulled her to his side. He kissed Claire's cheek ever so softly. To his surprise, tears welled up in his eyes.

"If that one doesn't," he said, "we'll find one that does." Sergei paused. "Besides, I hear they have very good ones in the US."

Claire's eyes lit up. Through her joy, she realized that she now faced a new, unyielding timetable for the dig. But this deadline beckoned joyfully and shined bright.

EPILOGUE

THE MORNING SICKNESS CONTINUED TO DOG CLAIRE, AND SHE found it difficult to work. At Sergei's urging, she had returned to Rushmere. One morning she wandered over to her office to begin unpacking the few things she had brought back with her. Opening one box marked miscellaneous, she saw the satchel that she had brought with her on her last visit to the mesa. Amid all the drama of the past few months, she had entirely forgotten about the satchel. Opening the canvas cover, she saw the dust-covered salt-crystal softball she had absently collected.

Claire pulled it out of the satchel and walked to her desk. As she walked, a wave of nausea hit her and she felt faint. She grabbed for a chair, which promptly rolled away, and as she lurched to regain her balance, she stumbled and dropped the salt crystal rock.

The crystal shattered on the hard floor. Half of it was reduced to shards, but half the crystal remained intact. Claire sighed with a grim smile. For the second time, she had dropped an object collected in Kazakhstan, though in this case, she felt no pangs of guilt. She'd only picked up the large salt crystal because of its unusual shape.

She looked down at the scatter on the floor. In the center of the intact half was a dark-tan object. Claire picked it up. She recognized instantly that she was looking at part of an array of elephant molars. She looked more closely, her mind racing, and then she gasped.

Claire donned surgical gloves and picked up the intact crystal. Forgetting her nausea, she quickly went to the clean room in the lab, where she found a sterilized container. She gently placed the crystal in the container and then placed the container in a freezer that she had acquired in case they needed to preserve biological specimens. It was empty, and now she vowed to ensure that it remained empty save for that container.

She smiled with satisfaction and reached for the phone. She was going to enjoy giving Keerbrock a dose of his own medicine.

With luck, he picked up the phone.

"It's Claire."

"Ah, Claire. Are you a mom?"

"Will, I'm not a hippo—though I'm about the same size—I'm human. With humans it takes nine months."

Keerbrock chuckled. "So, news then."

"Yep, news. "Claire paused for effect. "Will, if you were going to look for really ancient DNA, what might preserve it best?"

Claire heard a sharp intake of breath.

"Are you saying . . ."

"C'mon Will, you've played this game with me many times."

"Claire, you know as well as I do that you can't get DNA from petrified material."

"Who said anything about petrified material, Will?"

She heard another sharp intake of breath. "Just answer the question," Claire said lightly.

"OK, hydroxyapatite, a calcium compound in bones and teeth. Also, aridity and crystal salt would help."

"So if we found a tooth preserved in salt crystal that came from one of the most arid places on earth, that would be a good candidate?"

There was silence on the other end of the phone. "Hmm, five million years, odds are very long, but there's a chance." He paused again.

"Assuming the tooth was encapsuled at the height of the salinity crisis, when it was broiling hot and dry as a pizza oven, lowers the odds a bit more. Yes, there's a chance. What are you thinking?"

Claire's eyes moistened. "I'm thinking that I'd very much like to meet Bart in person."

AUTHOR'S NOTE

ALTHOUGH THE ANCIENT ELEPHANT SPECIES IN *DEEP PAST* IS fictional, the idea that over the great sweep of geologic time another species with great intelligence might have come and gone without leaving a trace is within the realm of the possible—given our understanding of how evolution works. In constructing the story of Bart and his confreres, I've tried to hew to the scientifically possible.

The selective pressures that produced human intelligence had nothing to do with preparing Michelangelo to paint the ceiling of the Sistine Chapel; they had a lot to do with favoring those of our ancestors adaptable enough to survive in a fast-changing landscape. One assumption underlying the story of *Deep Past* is the connection between past, natural climate upheavals and the evolution of human intelligence, and this is a subject that has been actively investigated as the data on past climates has become more precise.

For instance, using data on past climates collected by Peter de Menocal, a paleoclimatologist, and Richard Potts, a paleoanthropologist who heads the Smithsonian Institution's Human Origins Program, has shown that during periods of climate upheaval over the past few million years, our more specialized forbears died out, while the more adaptable generalists (read: smarter) survived—a process that saw *Australopithecus boisei* fade, while *Homo rudolfensis* and *Homo ergaster* began to flourish some 2.5 million years ago. High climate variability returned about 1.65 million and 1.55 million years ago, coincident with the ascendance of *Homo erectus*, who in turn gave way to the even more generalized *Homo sapiens*.

Even as climate change (natural in this case) was creating a smarter human, it was favoring more generalized animals of other species. In Africa, for instance, more primitive forms of elephant, baboon, and hippo among other creatures disappeared during various ancient climate upheavals. Of course, while some of these animals became more adaptively flexible, we became *really* smart, suggesting that, at least in our case, other factors besides climate were at work.

One thing that seems to have happened is that at some point our expanding intelligence became self-reinforcing. Many have pointed out that expanding brain power comes at the expense of diverting blood from the muscles to the brain. As this happened, our ancestors had to organize for hunting to feed this ever more demanding brain of ours. Cooperative hunting and the complex pressures of maintaining order in large groups favored the more intelligent as well so that the smarter we got, the smarter we needed to be.

Could this have happened in other species? Why not? If so, however, why aren't such species still here? Christopher Langton, a pioneer in the study of artificial life at the Santa Fe Institute has an answer to that. As he describes it, in any system when a group of players face new ecological opportunities, various competing organisms try different strategies to exploit the system. I described what happens next in my book *The Future in Plain Sight*, "Over time, this chaos resolves itself into a stable system as the competing groups sort things out. This persists until someone comes along with a special advantage, or something changes the ecology of the system. The favored competitor prospers, driving out rivals, until the whole system becomes unstable and crashes . . ." The point is that there's such a thing about being too adaptable. Even the most brilliant adaptation can ultimately hustle one off the evolutionary stage.

Apart from raising uncomfortable questions about where our species might fit into this cycle right now, Langton's framework situates our rise to the top into a cycle that has been repeated many times over the eons. Other species have used other strategies to get to be top dog over the great sweep of time, but it's not unreasonable to assume that in the past another occupant of that top spot got there through their wits. The difference in *Deep Past* of course, is that it wasn't the elephants who pushed things too far and destabilized the system, but rather a climate cataclysm the likes of which the world hasn't seen for many millions of years (the Messinian salinity crisis described in the book was a real event). It wasn't Bart's fault that he and his ilk died out. It will be ours, though, if we follow suit. Current climate change is a self-inflicted wound.

In order to speed up the evolutionary process which led to Bart, I isolated his elephant forbears on an island, albeit an island that was surrounded by unpassable terrain rather than water. All the references to the magic of the "Island Rule" and island biogeography in the book are taken from real examples.

Similarly, Claire's background in studies of animal intelligence flows from my own investigations of the field over four decades.

And, while the jadeite and its ability to summon anciently imbued images from the deep past is entirely a product of my imagination, the use of sound waves to construct images is as familiar as a sonogram. The field and wave properties of minerals have long been subjects of investigation in mainstream physics, and the question of whether higher mental abilities can be explained by the actions of quantum mechanics is the subject of active debate in the field. On the receiving end, many scientists have studied the elephant's extremely sophisticated abilities to interpret sound waves.

What I've tried to do in this book is imagine how another intelligence might evolve using a working hypothesis that over time natural selection favors those creatures optimized for the context of their times. Thus, utterly different creatures like the pangolin and the anteater might converge in shape as natural selection subtly conditions these animals to dig out and eat social insects. I suspect something similar might happen in the realm of higher mental abilities, even if those abilities have different roots. Our intelligence involves the integration and exploitation of a number of different senses and abilities—visual processing, sound generation, manual dexterity, among others—that developed for different reasons, while the demands of the harsh and changing environment in which my imagined ancient elephants lived placed a premium on the further and rapid development of their already sophisticated abilities to process sound. Where our and their abilities converge lies in the ability to symbolically represent the features and laws of the world around them and manipulate that world to their advantage.

I took some liberties, of course. One of them was to imagine the lighter impact on the planet of an intelligent vegetarian animal that fed its large brain by foraging rather than hunting—an animal that used its intelligence to survive for a long time against the harshest climate imaginable, while still leaving almost no trace. Were it only so . . .